T0286785

BY SARAH ADAMS

BEG,
BORROW,
OR
STEAL

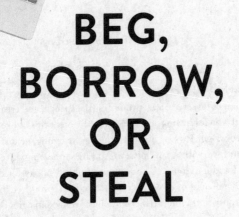

BEG, BORROW, OR STEAL

A NOVEL

SARAH ADAMS

DELL BOOKS
NEW YORK

2025 Dell Trade Paperback Original

Copyright © 2025 by Sarah Adams

Published in the United States by Dell, an imprint of Random House,
a division of Penguin Random House LLC, New York.

DELL and the D colophon are registered trademarks of
Penguin Random House LLC.

ISBN 978-0-593-72369-2
Ebook ISBN 978-0-593-72370-8

Printed in the United States of America on acid-free paper

randomhousebooks.com

2 4 6 8 9 7 5 3 1

Interior art credit: Tatyana Yagudina, zhanna © Adobe Stock Photos

Book design by Sara Bereta

Hello, little honey bees.

You glorious, sharp-edged, perfection seekers.

You've been working so hard, holding everything together; come sit down with me for a while and take a load off.

The best thing to hold onto in life is each other.
—Audrey Hepburn

AUTHOR'S NOTE AND CONTENT WARNING

Dear reader, I am so excited for you to meet Emily and Jackson! If you are the kind of reader who prefers to know the heavier topics and potential triggers before you begin reading, please be advised that there are themes of grief and mild accompanying depression, as well as the portrayal of a narcissistic parent. However, I have written these topics with great care and in such a way that is meant to bring comfort rather than pain. Likewise, if you prefer to read closed-door romances and would like to modify this story so that you are not involved in the details of their intimacy scenes, chapters 25 and 32 should be skipped. Happy reading!

BEG,
BORROW,
OR
STEAL

FROM: Emily Walker ‹E.Walker@MRPS.com›
TO: Jack Bennett ‹J.Bennett@MRPS.com›
DATE: Tue, Dec 19 6:34 PM
SUBJECT: IMPORTANT!

Dear Jack,
I heard through the grapevine that you're moving.
I just wanted to be the first person to tell you . . .
don't forget to take all your crap from the break
room. Specifically: your disgusting dark roast coffee
beans.
All my worst,
Emily

FROM: Jack Bennett ‹J.Bennett@MRPS.com›
TO: Emily Walker ‹E.Walker@MRPS.com›
DATE: Wed, Dec 19 6:38 PM
SUBJECT: IMPORTANT!

Dear Emily,

It's clear my impending departure has left you in a sour mood. But don't worry, you'll find happiness again someday. Don't be afraid to cry when you need to, because just like the poster you have hanging in your classroom claims, *all feelings are important.* Wishing you better taste,

Jack

CHAPTER ONE

Emily

I don't care who you are, when you live in a town the size of your thumb, if you don't like the way your hair turns out at the salon, you stuff it deep down and never acknowledge it.

And that's exactly why I prefer to take matters into my own hands and not allow circumstances to ever reach that point. I tend to speak my mind, and have it bite me in the ass too often, so I know if I tell Virginia that I hate my hair after this appointment, she'll never forget it. By noon, she'll have told everyone in our zero-stoplight town that I'm her pickiest, most unappeasable client. The roasting and poking will start immediately, and by five-thirty when I go to The Diner, someone will pop up out of nowhere and say, *Are you sure that booth is good enough for you or would you like the one we reserve for the queen?*

And it won't stop there. From that day on, they'll put a plaque on the table that reads TABLE RESERVED FOR QUEEN EMILY, and nothing I do or say will get them to remove it.

And if it seems like I'm overreacting, please know this is the very same town that started a petition last year, complete with smear campaign, to encourage my youngest sister (who was twenty-six years old at the time, mind you) to stop dating Will Griffin because they thought she was too good for him. He won them over in the end (*Annie + Will forever*), but the petition with the final tallies is framed and hanging in The Diner alongside the picture of Dolly Parton posing with the town. And I do mean the majority of the town. They heard she had stopped in for lunch while passing through, and one person called another who called their cousin who called their best friend who called their aunt's boyfriend, and they all showed up for one huge group photo.

Moral of the story: *Never underestimate what the town of Rome, Kentucky, is capable of.*

The smell of bleach singes the insides of my nostrils as Virginia—one of only three stylists in the area—combines the powder lightener with the creamy developer right beside my face. She's mixing that stuff so slowly a baby could do it faster, but I keep this thought to myself by picturing the terrifying treasure chest I've created in my mind where I lock up all my most antagonistic thoughts. It's made of black steel and has sharp metal prongs all over it. The thing is deadly and made for keeping the peace in my day-to-day life.

"Well—I don't like to gossip," Virginia begins, weighing in on the conversation beside us that Hannah (the other stylist) and her client, Shirley, are having about the reason our packages have all been delivered late this week. Shirley has been the receptionist at the elementary school where I teach for over twenty-five years. She eats gossip like multivitamins.

Virginia continues, "But I did happen to see a certain someone leaving Brad's house the other morning."

Brad is our mailman, if it wasn't obvious.

Everyone other than me in the salon gasps. I'm too busy staring at the bowl of lightener that's not going to mix itself as Virginia lazily sways it in front of my face. The sassy grin aimed at the other ladies tells me she has no intention of putting any sort of hustle into my highlighting process.

"You don't mean . . . ?" Hannah taunts, pausing with scissors in one hand, and in the other, a thin section of Shirley's white hair, held at a ninety-degree angle—pre-snip.

"*Yes*," Virginia states meaningfully with a vicious small-town twinkle in her eye. Take a picture right now and this would serve as the perfect image to describe Rome, Kentucky.

"But she's *married.*"

"Not for long. When Hayes gets wind of what his wife has been doing with the sexy mailman, I expect we'll see Evelyn's clothes flung all over the yard and the neon boxers Brad is always giving us a peek of strung up the flagpole." She pauses and frowns. "Truthfully, though, I don't think Brad and Evelyn would make such a bad match."

As fun as this is (and I don't mean that sarcastically because I can get down with some juicy gossip along with the best of them), I happen to know that the lightener already painted on the back of my head and tucked into foils is getting dangerously close to frying the hair right off my scalp. I need Virginia to get this second bowl applied ASAP so she can start rinsing out the back while the front processes. I'm naturally a dark-blonde and prefer my highlights to blend seamlessly—not shine so bright they signal extraterrestrials.

The bowl weaves in front of my face again, but I intercept it this time and balance it in my lap to whisk the hell out of this cream. As all good and unbearable perfectionists know, if you want something done right, you mostly have to do it yourself.

Virginia doesn't even spare me a glance. She's used to me by now. The whole town is. When they see Emily Walker coming, they hand whatever it is they're doing over to me and dive out of the way. Usually with a smile because they know I'll do it in half the time and with the precision of a military special ops agent.

I finish mixing and hand the bowl over my shoulder to Virginia, who is knee-deep in speculation about what could have caused Evelyn to stray in her marriage. My next victim: the stack of messy foils on the workstation. I pre-fold each piece, handing them up one by one as Virginia paints the last of the lightener onto the front of my hair. There wasn't much left, so thankfully she finishes quickly, and while the front processes, she spritzes water into the back foils and towels them off.

I tune out as the salon talk show moves through the lives of various town citizens, airing everyone's dirty laundry with a bit of *but it's not my place to judge* sprinkled on top just in case the good Lord is listening.

Madison, my sister just below me in age who is currently living in New York working on her culinary degree, will be angry that I'm not paying enough attention to relay all of the tasty on-dits to her later, but I'm too lost in my head, thinking of all the tasks I can get done now that I'm officially out of school for the summer and no longer have a class full of spunky—yet delightful—second-graders to teach every day. I don't like to leave loose ends, so I cleaned out my classroom on the last day of school even though most of the other teachers will clean theirs out over the next few days. In the past I would go and help them, but I'm not allowed to anymore. They banned me after last year, saying they didn't need a drill sergeant with a clipboard telling them how to efficiently pack up their rooms. *Fair enough.*

So with the school year officially behind me, I can focus on tasks closer to home:

- Help Mabel repaint the porch railing on her inn
- Finish writing the last chapter in my romance novel

- Contact the city about the pothole on Main Street
- Call Annie's Internet provider and haggle for a lower price

The last one is more fun than chore for me. Annie, the most tenderhearted out of us four Walker siblings, mentioned the other day that she was dreading making that call, so I gleefully offered myself up as tribute. There's nothing I love more than going head-to-head with a salesperson.

And believe it or not, I'm not the oldest sibling of our bunch. That title belongs to Noah—but part of me wonders if my parents were too sleep-deprived somewhere along the way and forgot that I was actually born first based on how laid back he is in comparison to me. Too bad my parents are dead, so I can't ask them. Actually there's no one I can ask about my family history now because as of November, my grandma—the woman who raised us after my parents kicked the bucket—died too. Everyone is dead. *Dead, dead, dead.*

And yes, I do like to throw startling little facts like those into conversation whenever I can because shock is always preferable to pity.

The last guy I dated seemed really freaked out when I delivered the dead-parents line with a smile on my face. But these days, I'm happily single by choice. (There's also a chance that I'm single because I'm an unlovable porcupine and got tired of the constant rejection . . . but that thought is terrifying, so I slip it inside my Metal Treasure Chest of Doom and leave it there right next to the memory of my first and only love shattering my heart.)

Virginia tips my head back into the million-year-old plastic salon sink to rinse and shampoo my hair. Rather than relaxing, I spend the entire time convincing myself my neck isn't going to snap. And it's not until I'm back in the salon chair and Virginia is plugging in her blow-dryer that I hear the name that has me doing a mental spit take.

"Well, I've got my own bit of news to share. Did y'all hear about Jack Bennett?" I doubt Shirley realizes that with that one name she has successfully stopped my heart.

"The sexy teacher from the elementary school where you both work?" asks Virginia, her eyes a little too bright. They're downright zesty.

Jack Bennett, aka my archnemesis since college who moved away four months ago, is supposed to be getting married today to a woman who I happen to think is completely wrong for him. But that's beside any sort of relevant point.

"Yes. Well, turns out, he's not getting married today after all. The entire wedding was canceled a few weeks after he moved away with her! How strange is that?"

My stopped heart resuscitates only so it can dramatically flat-line once again.

Jack isn't getting married today?

This can't be true . . .

A rumor. It's just a rumor.

But why am I hoping it's true?

Hannah perks up and abandons all pretense of styling at this point when she angles her body toward us. "What do you think happened? It had to be something big to call off a wedding after moving away together."

Jack. Isn't. Married.

"I'm not sure exactly, but rumor has it that they're not even together anymore," says Shirley, so proud to have delivered this fresh slice of meat directly into salivating mouths. "But I know that Jack is the nicest guy, so it's hard to believe he would have cheated or anything like that."

And that's the thing, isn't it? Everyone feels this way about Jack. He used to swoop in each day draped with kindness, charming smiles, perfect hair, and eclectic outfits that somehow always worked on him. He was excellent at playing the part of a Mr. Rogers wannabe. *Maybe if Mr. Rogers had tattoos and was secretly a devil.*

Jack truly was great to everyone. Everyone besides *me*. I'm the only one who's seen Jack's true colors—who knows that under his cozy cardigans, he's a conniving jerk.

Like any good hostile relationship, our animosity wasn't built on one single moment but rather a collection of many, many little ones that have snowballed into something greater. And now, after a decade of interacting, we have collected so many we could open a museum full of hatred memorabilia.

Hannah cuts her eyes to me, and I realize I'm not breathing. It must have something to do with the fact that despite how much I hate, hate, triple-hate him . . . I've sort of missed him too. I know, it makes zero sense, and I don't even like to consider it.

"Do you know anything about what happened, Emily?" asks Hannah. "He teaches in the same grade as you, right?"

He *did* teach in the same grade as me, but he had his last day at Rome Elementary just before winter break, after which he moved to Nebraska with his fiancée. A substitute teacher took over for him the rest of the school year. The day he left, he made his rounds and said goodbye to everyone in the school. *Except for me.* A thought that still needles me for unknown reasons. Of course he didn't say goodbye, why would he? We weren't friends. We were enemies. Enemies don't pal around with a heartfelt goodbye.

All eyes are on me now, and listen, I truly do hate Jack with all my heart, but . . . for whatever reason, I also don't want to talk shit about him when he's not present. Not because I'm protecting him, but because I'd rather do it to his face where he can react. It's more fun that way.

I shrug and carry a tone of someone who's convinced there's nothing to see here. "This is the first I'm hearing about it. But then again, I try to avoid interacting with Jack as much as possible."

Virginia laughs. "You and only you, hon. I've only seen him a handful of times, but that man is *fiiine,* and if I shared a classroom wall with him, I'd be the first one lining up to get a shot with that bachelor."

"You're welcome to him as far as I'm concerned," I say, standing up from the salon chair even though Virginia hasn't dried or styled my hair yet. "But you'll have a long drive ahead of you. He lives in Nebraska now." Even if he were still here, though, I doubt he would have gone out with her. The teachers tried plenty of times to get Jack to socialize outside of school, but he always had a perfectly constructed excuse at his fingertips for why he couldn't make it. For a guy who was so kind and friendly, he didn't seem to actually want friends.

It's good he's gone. I'll never have to arrive early to school to beat him to the best parking space again. Or debate over which beans to use in the break room coffeepot. No one will fight me over dress-up days and say that attending school as your favorite literary author is "a buzzkill" and push for Wacky Tacky Day instead. (Yes, parents, we hear that dress-up day is a nightmare, but the kids love it, so they win. Take it up with Principal Bart.)

Honestly, the only thing I regret about the day Jack left is that I went outside thinking I'd . . . I don't know . . . say one last cutting remark to him or something; instead, I had to watch Jack drive off in his stupidly nice SUV, not receiving so much as a glance in my direction. Not even a salute or the bird out his window. But really, it's better he didn't stop to acknowledge me. What do you even say to someone who you've feuded with since college? *It's been nice hating you?*

Thanks to this conversation, an uncomfortable feeling is crawling all over me. I need to get moving.

"Where are you going?" Virginia asks in dismay when I hand

her my cape. "You can't leave yet. You look like a wet goat with your bangs sticking to your forehead like that."

"Flattering—thank you," I say with a forced laugh as I smooth the front of my cream knit tank top and tug down the legs of my Levi's jeans so they are no longer creating the wedgie of the century. I eye my damp hair in the mirror and sigh when I see that she's really not wrong. I have the kind of hair that's not truly curly or straight. It hovers in some strange, lazy middle, and when it's wet, it looks wild. Left to air-dry, it's borderline feral. I usually straighten it or put a few wanded curls throughout, but today, I just want out of here.

"I'm short on time thanks to y'all's juicy gossip," I say with an indulgent smile. "I'm gonna grab some coffee and then get going with my day."

"Busy one?" Virginia asks.

Shirley laughs. "Emily's never not busy."

She isn't wrong, but most important (or less depending on how you look at it), I just want to get moving so I can stop thinking about Jack Bennett and wondering if he's okay after his failed engagement—even though I'll never see him again. Even though I often would have chosen to pluck my eyelashes out one by one instead of interacting with him. Even though he didn't say goodbye to me.

CHAPTER TWO

Emily

And by *grab coffee,* I actually mean sit in the coffee shop at my favorite little corner table and work on my romance manuscript, trying to block out all thoughts of Jack and his canceled wedding that has no bearing on my life. *Absolutely none.*

It's my Saturday tradition to go write for a few hours at the coffee shop, and today will be no different. (Fun fact: The coffee shop has recently been renovated and rebranded in hopes of bringing in more customers, and they have uncomfortably as well as ignorantly renamed it: the Hot Bean. And for those who do not enjoy coffee, they've started selling organic juice. It's been a trial unlike any other to hold a straight face while listening to the older citizens of our town go on and on about how they can't go a single day without that new Hot Bean juice.)

On my way through the town square (which is actually laid out like a lowercase *t*) I walk under the familiar blue-and-white awning of the Pie Shop and can't resist the pull to go in. I know Noah will be there because he always works Saturdays. He's the only other person I've ever known who enjoys patterns and routines as much as I do.

The bell above the door rings as I step inside and I immediately smile at the sight of Phil (of Phil's Hardware Store) running his mouth, monopolizing the coveted window seat per usual. He has a rapt audience today. At least five town members are standing around his table, sipping their coffees and holding a box of pie. However, Phil and Todd (partners in business and life) are sharing their traditional slice of chocolate pie.

"Something really juicy must have happened to hold everyone's attention like that," I tell my brother, Noah, as I approach the counter.

His blond head is bowed, flannel-clad forearms resting on the countertop studying a ledger. His only acknowledgment of me is a grunt as he continues tallying the numbers in his bookkeeping (of course Noah would still use a physical book instead of software) and then finally responds with, "They've been going on about someone new moving to town. I don't know, I've been trying to tune them out so I can focus on these damn numbers that keep coming out wrong."

I've never been very good at letting my siblings work through their distress on their own, which is why I take a minute to study the lines of numbers. "You're off on this one."

His forehead creases as his eyes slide to where my cherry-red fingernail is pinpointing a line. "*Dammit.* How did you see that so quickly? I've been trying to figure out where it's not adding up all morning."

"That's because Mom and Dad gave you all the beard hair and saved the smarts for me." I grin at him, and he rolls his eyes. I gently close his bookkeeping journal and slide it across the weathered, generations-old countertop, and then up under my arm. "I'll finish it for you."

His eyes, almost the exact same shade of green as mine, hold both hesitation and relief. "You don't have to do that, Em. It's your summer break now."

"Which means I have all the time in the world to help out. And I'd hate for you to run my favorite pie shop into the ground with your shitty bookkeeping," I tell him with a tilted smile that he grins at in return. He knows better than to argue with me when my mind is set on something.

Noah stands to his full height—only a few inches taller than me—and leans back to stretch like he's been hunched over staring at this book for hours. "Take a free pie, then," he tells me, nodding toward the case.

"As if I wasn't already planning to. Do you have any Vanilla Bourbon Apple?"

"I do—but those are for people who give me money in exchange for pie. What I meant was, take a *rhubarb pie* because those are reserved for sisters who help with things I never even asked for help with in the first place." His eyes crinkle in the corners just like Annie's do.

Looking at Noah is like looking at the original blueprint for each of us four Walker siblings. We are all a slight variation of him—but I tend to favor him the most. Golden blond hair. Tallish. Generally wary of people until they prove worthy of our trust. The difference surfaces when we open our mouths. Noah is more prone to grunting and silence. I'm all too happy to voice my opinions. In fact, I have to hold back ninety-eight percent of the time, and that two percent can still be too much for people.

"Where's your wife? She'll give me good free pie."

"She's on a videoconference call all morning with her label," he says casually, like that doesn't mean what we both know it means. Amelia is the worldwide pop sensation otherwise known as Rae Rose. She and my brother met by sheer luck when Amelia's car broke down in his front yard three years ago. She stayed with him for a while to hide out from her fame and one thing led to another, and now they're married. She didn't tour her last album because she wanted some time to enjoy her new marriage and focus on putting down roots in Rome. It also gave her time to work on a new album, which she tells me is her favorite one yet. I imagine this call with her label is the one where they are begging her to go on tour for it.

A tour would mean at least a year where she and Noah won't see each other much. They were only dating during her last one, and Noah didn't get to visit a lot because he didn't want to be away too much from our grandma, who had been living with Alzheimer's. We all shared a rotating care schedule for checking in and visiting with her at the nursing home, and Noah rarely wanted to miss a single visit.

Although . . . she's gone now.

There's nothing left here holding him to the town.

My heart does that thing where it hurts, and hurts, and hurts and I can't stop it. The feeling scares me. I've been outrunning it ever since Grandma died and all four of us siblings were standing in the church's gymnasium after the funeral, shoveling various casseroles that none of us would take a single bite of onto our plates. We were all prepared for her death in theory, but when it really comes down to losing your last parental figure, it turns out there's really no such thing as preparation.

I think that was the first day things started changing for us. I've always been able to fix everything for them—a Band-Aid on a skinned knee, a pep talk after a breakup, late-night study sessions before a big test—but now they don't lean on me like they used to. They don't need me. Noah was so broken after losing Grandma, but he had Amelia to turn to. And Annie had Will, and Madison had culinary school and her life in New York to focus on. It was clear that grief was swallowing us all, but whereas we used to all huddle together in hard times, this time everyone turned in different directions.

And that was when I started my romance novel. It was basically a desperate attempt to distract myself from that hurt clawing its way through my heart. Everything was changing, no one needed me, and I needed . . . to just be okay. I've always loved reading, and writing seemed like the most incredible thing in the world. So for the first time, I let myself get lost every night in a completely made-up world. A world set in the Regency era where a kilt-wearing Highlander and a virginal youngest daughter of a duke fall in love and escape the pain of reality in each other's arms.

What started as a silly idea quickly became important to me. Meaningful. It felt like stepping into my skin for the first time. There's this unexplainable buzzing joy in my head while typing and plotting and even just daydreaming about my story. It's the one place I have full, bright, and unwavering control. I had no idea what I had been missing out on all my life. And now I'm nearing the end of this story that no one around me knows exists and I'm not sure what to do with it. Delete it? Print it out and burn it in a fire? Those feel like the only two options since I think I might die before letting anyone else read it.

"Does she want to do the tour?" I bring myself to ask Noah in a level, casual tone even though my urge is to bite out something like *But you won't go with her, right?* Because this is what I've gotten great at these days. Pretending I'm okay with everything.

He shrugs a shoulder. "She hasn't made up her mind yet. I told her I'll support her no matter her decision."

"And we'll support you." I use my hands to smooth a stack of paper napkins into a perfect square beside the register. "You know that, right? If Amelia wants to go and you want to visit her . . . we'll make sure the pie shop runs smoothly while you're gone. Just like last time."

This technically may be his pie shop after inheriting it from our grandma several years ago when the first signs of Alzheimer's started presenting themselves, but it also belongs to all of us in the sense that we all grew up in here. Grandma always had a soft spot for Noah, though, and he had one for her. They shared a bond that the rest of us didn't feel as strongly. Not for any real reason other than it's just how some people gravitate more to certain people in this life than others. After my parents passed, Noah needed my grandma, and the girls needed me.

Needed being the key word.

A few minutes later, with the pie shop's ledger in my tote bag and a great idea in mind for how to finish the last chapter of my novel, I'm in front of the coffee shop. It'll be so good to focus on—

Wait. Is that . . . ?

My stomach bottoms out. Because right there in the town's communal parking lot beside the coffee shop is an all too familiar blacked-out Land Rover. It's parked directly beside my red-and-white '85 Ford pickup truck in a move that couldn't be anything besides intentional. The sleek SUV stands out like a sore thumb among the other rust buckets. Or like a snooty thumb—reigning supreme over all the other trucks and trying to assert dominance. *This* is the SUV of my nemesis. My nemesis who apparently isn't married.

What the hell is Jack Bennett doing back in Rome, Kentucky?

Ignoring the weird flock of butterflies storming my stomach, I fling open the doors of the coffee shop like Aragorn entering the great hall in that one *Lord of the Rings* movie. I don't have to even look around to find Jack. There he is, sitting at my favorite corner table with a streak of sunlight slashing over his chiseled face as if he's the hero instead of the villain.

He's wearing a vintage-looking shirt. Notice I said vintage-*looking*. Because it isn't actually vintage. Jack would never thrift a piece of clothing. Everything he owns is new and expensive—and most likely custom made. (Which is wild to me considering his teacher salary matches mine.)

Take for instance the shirt he's wearing. I'm sure if I were to look it up online, I'd find that it easily retails for over a hundred dollars. It's a camp collar button-up with thick sage-and-cream stripes that run vertically down what looks like butter-soft material. On his lower half is an impeccable pair of mustard-colored trousers, rolled once, maybe twice at the hem, and casual brown boots. The only contradiction to his luxury style is the tacky, colorful, plastic-candy beaded necklace he's wearing. He owns a handful of them in different forms. Oh, and he has several tattoos. But they're all cute sticker-style designs of things like a smiley face, a cartoony Polaroid of an adorable worm with glasses popping out of an apple, a swirly ice cream cone, a tiger in a cardigan with a thought bubble that says *rawr* . . . you name an adorable design, and he has it.

This is Jack's hook. His style is whimsical yet so charming, and dapper, and well done. It's part of his tactic to win people over immediately with colors and textures and designs that the average man wouldn't normally be caught dead in. Not me, though. I don't fall for his fashion façade. Or his nice hair that is neither blond nor brown but lives in an undefinable middle that changes without rhyme or reason. It is, however, classically, and predictably mussed. His bone structure is one that most people would consider *exceptionally nice* and sometimes he has scruff on his face and sometimes he doesn't. I don't keep close enough tabs to know for certain if there's a pattern to it or not. But today, he's clean-shaven.

Across from him sits not his fiancée but his leather laptop bag. One light brown, rustic boot is propped up on the foot of the table leg and his attention is focused on his laptop open in front of him like he's someone important. *He's not.* He's a seat stealer, that's what he is.

As if Jack can feel the cold wind blowing off my heart, his eyes rise to where I'm fuming in the doorway. It's now I remember I look like a . . . *what did she call me?* . . . a wet goat. I can see my bangs curling up oddly around my brows, and the rest of my hair is a damp mass pressing down like a muggy bog on my shoulders.

He lifts a taunting eyebrow as if to say *Do you need something?*

Oh, that damn expression. I've had to see it since Jackson and I attended the same private college just outside Rome, Kentucky. We got off on the wrong foot immediately. As the story goes, it was our first day, and I was already running late after waking up to a flat tire. I was hurrying to English Composition 101, and when I turned the corner, I was barreled into by Jack, who had been looking down at his phone while practically jogging with a coffee. The lid popped off and the drink drenched my shirt.

Jack had the audacity to try and spin the moment into some kind of meet-cute, flashing his charming smile and offering to take me out for a coffee after class to make up for it. But (A) I was fresh out of a breakup that had destroyed me and left me with zero desire to interact with anyone in possession of a penis, and (B) showing up late to class and with a huge coffee stain was what my night-mares were made of. I remember saying something to him along the lines of *You think hitting on me is an appropriate apology for dumping coffee all over me?*

As it turned out, we were headed to the same class. We stumbled inside and both made a beeline for the last available seat near the front, and we fought over it. The bickering match started in a heated whisper (where he said he would offer the seat to me but wouldn't want to risk me thinking he was hitting on me) and esca-lated to a crescendo that disrupted the entire class, earning us both a glare from the professor and a sharp retort about how this was college, and if we were going to act like children, we should return to high school. I was humiliated.

The absolute worst of it, though, is that Jack immediately smiled at the professor, apologized, and then cracked a joke about how we had heard that the lectures were so incredible we were willing to fight to get a good seat. The professor ate it up hook, line, and sinker. He waved us off, then told Jack to take the seat and pointed to one in the back for me.

The rest is history.

Jack and I competed our way through college, and since we were after the same degree, we had frustratingly similar course schedules. Everywhere I turned, Jack seemed to be there with a smile and self-deprecating jokes that earned him the love of everyone in the room. Even when I got a job at the smoothie shop by campus, I walked in on my first day only to find Jack already behind the counter wearing the *Go Bananas* hat. He got the manager job a few weeks later because the customers loved him, whereas I got complaints for *being too rude* when they'd ask me to remake a smoothie (that was made perfectly the first time but really they were just gaming the system for a free smoothie).

Everything became an opportunity to beat the other person, from jobs, to grades, to friend groups—everything all the way down to parking spaces. Anyone unlucky enough to share the same air as us had to endure our constant bickering and power grabs. The last straw for me was when Jack managed to get placed at Rome Elementary for his student teaching. I had been begging to be placed in my hometown public school but was instead sent to a private school a few towns over. I know he somehow managed to snag it just to spite me. Because admittedly Jack is better at one thing than me: getting people to like him.

And after graduation, I thought I was finally free of Jackson when he took a teaching job in his hometown of Evansville, Indiana, while I got my dream job at Rome Elementary like I had always planned. That is, until three years ago when Bart apparently remembered him from his student teaching days and reached out to him because he was in desperate need of another second-grade teacher. Jack transferred from the private school in Evansville where he had been working to Rome Elementary—accepting the position in the *same* grade as me without realizing I ended up teaching here. It's like we're cursed to walk adjacent in this life no matter how much we despise each other.

And today, he's in my damn seat.

The worst part, though? I seem to be the slightest bit . . . relieved to see him.

His smirk edges up as I walk with sure strides to *my* table.

"Good morning, Emily," says Jackson with an extra special glint in his eerie, golden-brown eyes that tells me he does not, in fact, wish a good morning for me. He wishes a stain on my favorite jeans. A letter informing me of jury duty. A downpour when I don't have an umbrella.

His fiancée must have stayed with him for so long because he's attractive, right? Because yes, the man is admittedly very, *very* good-looking. I'm not even going to say the predictable thing and claim it's annoying. Frankly, giving me something nice to look at while he frustrates the snot out of me is the least he can do.

But there's something new about him today: Jack is wearing glasses. Circular brass frames that I wish I could say looked dorky on him. Instead, they're giving Clark Kent a run for his money. His cunning eyes lock with mine from behind those lenses and he dares me to make fun of them. I'd never take such low-hanging fruit. Instead, I cut right to the point.

"Why are you here, Jackson?" I glance over his table, note his open laptop, a hardback journal of some sort, and then of course the supple leather laptop bag taking up space in the otherwise empty seat.

"I'm here for coffee, because that's generally what a person is after when they go to a coffee shop," he says, sinking into that infuriating trademark grin of his. It's nearly impossible to describe it accurately. It's more of a tilt of his mouth than a real smile. It's the look of a man who is full of secrets and mischief but will never let you in on them because he enjoys watching you squirm more. It's the grin he gave me when he won Teacher of the Year over me two years in a row.

"You know what I mean. Why are you back here in Rome? Aren't you supposed to be off gallivanting down the aisle at your wedding right now?"

"I've never gallivanted in my life. And there is no wedding."

I narrow my eyes. "Why?"

His expression never changes. "Because I'm six four. I'd look like a giraffe charging across the plains if I gallivanted."

I breathe in deeply through my nose. "I could murder you right now."

"But then we couldn't keep pretending I don't know that you already know that I called off the wedding." His eyes never stray. "Your hair is about to drip on my laptop."

I'm surprised he so easily confirmed that he called off the wedding. Normally if I want information from him, I have to strategically pry it from him as if I'm a skilled interrogator. The fact that he just laid it out on the table like that is throwing me.

I straighten and cross my arms, deciding to see how much info I can get while he's in a chatty mood. "Are you two rescheduling the ceremony?"

"No."

"Are you and Zoe still together?"

A pause. His eyes dip to the ends of my hair and back up. "No."

No. There it is. Confirmed. Jackson Bennett is no longer in a relationship. I don't know what to do with this information. Not that it has anything to do with me.

"Hm. So you and Zoe are over, and you've come back to Kentucky to steal *my* table?"

He tips his head, eyes sparkling. "I didn't see a sign before I sat down, but it does appear that way."

No, no, no. Aside from all the messy feelings I'm having at the moment, it's completely unacceptable for him to be screwing up my routine like this. But this is what he always does. What he lives for: pulling the rug out from under me and delighting in the chaos.

Still . . . one thing is eating at me more than the rest. One ridiculous thing I can't let go of. One thing staring me right in the face that I need answers to. "Jack . . . why are you wearing glasses?"

He's momentarily caught off guard, then smiles in the right corner of his mouth. "So I can see your jealous scowl more clearly."

It would be so much fun to kick him.

Enough is enough. The lid of my Treasure Chest of Doom rattles. Growls. Begs to be freed.

He can tell and his eyes glitter with anticipation.

Aha! Maybe this is the source of these conflicting feelings over his return . . . maybe I'm not relieved to see him. I'm just relieved to have my sparring partner back. Because, like it or not, Jackson is my equal match in every way. He's the one person in this entire world who doesn't shrink from the sharpest words I could throw. He catches them between his fingers and lobs them right back.

The heavy weight of striving for perfection falls away when he gets near. It's the only reprieve I ever get from it.

"*This* is *my* table, Jackson. Ask anyone in town and they'll tell you. I come here nearly every Saturday to sit at this little table and sip my little coffee and type on my little laptop and enjoy my little day. So if you think I'm going to be sympathetic to the fact that you're recently heartbroken and forgo my favorite table because of it, then you're wrong."

Jackson doesn't so much as flinch. "I don't, and I'm not." When he sees my confusion he expounds, adjusting in his seat to somehow look even more comfortable and unfazed. "I *don't* expect your sympathy and I'm *not* heartbroken." His gaze drops to follow the water droplet from my hair as it splats against the table, an inch from his laptop. He looks at me again, but I feel his attention flitting across my bare face and soggy hair. "Seems like I should be, but I'm not—which tells me calling off the wedding and ending the relationship was the right choice." There's so much more here he's not saying. "So now I have all the time in the world to come sit at the coffee shop you talked up so often at school." He gestures lazily to something behind me. "There's a table over there you can sit at."

He opens his laptop once again, effectively dismissing me.

And there it goes: The hinges on my Treasure Chest of Doom fly off. He twists and burrows under my skin until I have no choice but to let those word-spears fly. Maybe it's because some vicious part of me recognizes the vicious part of him—even if the rest of the world is too enamored with his charm to see it in him too. We've perfected and fine-tuned our hatred into an art form.

I snap the lid of his laptop shut so fast that he barely has time to remove his fingers before they're guillotined. "I won't be banished to the Arctic Circle in my own town." I tip forward and point behind me. "There's a vent directly above that table and the air never stops cranking. To sit at that table is to accept hypothermia. Plus I need an outlet, and this is the only table near one."

He shrugs—that grin nearly giving way to a dimple under his smug satisfaction. "Well then, Emily, I guess you're out of options and have to go home."

"You've been here long enough—*you* go home."

"I only got here a minute before you."

"And that's plenty of time to inflict your presence on the world." It was meant to cut but he's clamping his lips together trying not to laugh. "This would have been my table right now if Shirley and the entire salon hadn't been gossiping about your breakup."

He sits back in his seat, loosely crossing his arms. "Ah—so you did already hear the news."

"Yes, and I'll have you know that I shut down all talk of you since you weren't around to defend yourself, not that you deserve the respect."

His lips curl almost cynically. "You have my undying gratitude."

"So you'll move?"

"No. You have my undying gratitude from this seat here in the corner while you freeze to death over there under the air vent."

I grind my teeth. "Get your obnoxious ass out of my seat, Jackson. I mean it."

There's a moment of silence as he slowly unfolds himself from the table, but it's evident by his smile that he's not getting up to move. No, he takes one easy-breezy single step closer—hands dropping into his mustard pockets. His amber eyes are full of ruthless amusement when they lock with mine, standing closer than we've ever stood in the history of our feud. An unfamiliar tingle runs up my legs and settles somewhere in my thighs. "Emily Walker. You might be able to steamroll everyone else around here into submission. But not me. Never me. If you want something from me, you'll have to ask politely."

What I wouldn't give for a steamroller at this very minute to flatten his ass to the floor. But I'd remove his glasses first, because for reasons beyond my mortal knowledge, I like them.

"Why? So you can bask in my politeness and then turn me down anyway? Forget it."

"It's scary how well you understand me sometimes." His eyes

crinkle. "Your only option now is to leave, sit in the morgue over there, or . . ." *Or? I've never heard an* or *come out of his mouth.* "You can get your little coffee and sit in that little seat across from me."

"Sit . . . with you?" My eyebrows are touching my hairline.

"Yes."

"At the same table?"

"It would be difficult to achieve sitting together from a different table."

I breathe in, staring at him for a beat. I really am out of options. (And that's what I'm going to remind myself tonight when I replay this moment over and over again in my mind.)

"All right," I say, breaking the number one rule of battle and turning my back on my enemy so I can move his bag to the floor beside the chair. My canvas tote bag takes its place. "When I come back, I'm going to sit right here. With you. We will share this table, but we're not going to say a word to each other. I will work on my laptop, and you will work on yours, and as far as we're both concerned the other does not exist. Understand?"

He tilts his head, and I again get the feeling he's examining me. Searching for some private answer. "I didn't think it was possible, but somehow you're even meaner before coffee."

It's this little comment that has me hanging back after we've both ordered and tipping the barista fifteen bucks to make Jack's coffee decaf.

FROM: Jack Bennett ‹J.Bennett@MRPS.com›
TO: Emily Walker ‹E.Walker@MRPS.com›
DATE: Sat, May 25 10:30 AM
SUBJECT: TABLE SHARING

Emily,
You type like an angry gorilla. If you press any harder
on those keys you're going to dent your laptop. Quiet
down before we get kicked out of here for disrupting
the peace.
Jack

FROM: Jack Bennett ‹J.Bennett@MRPS.com›
TO: Emily Walker ‹E.Walker@MRPS.com›
DATE: Sat, May 25 10:33 AM
SUBJECT: TABLE SHARING

Typing even louder. Real nice.

FROM: Emily Walker <E.Walker@MRPS.com>
TO: Jack Bennett <J.Bennett@MRPS.com>
DATE: Sat, May 25 10:34 AM
SUBJECT: TABLE SHARING

Emily

CHAPTER THREE

Jack

Emily and I have only shared a table once before. It was sopho-more year of college and we were paired together for a history presentation because whoever runs the universe apparently needed some entertainment. Reluctantly, we both decided it would be in our best interest to mend our broken bridge and move past our feud. We met at the library, where we attempted to find some common ground before discussing the assignment.

We made it all of thirty minutes before the arguments began about the topic for our presentation. Neither of us would budge an inch. Ultimately, we got kicked out of the library for disturbing those around us, and Emily and I decided it was better to split up and do our presentations separately. We both received an F. As it turns out, the point of a group project is to actually work as a team.

I'll admit, when I first met Emily after running into her on our way to class, I thought she was gorgeous. I couldn't believe my luck that I would crash into such a beautiful woman on my first day of classes. I *did* hit on her—and admittedly it was the wrong moment. But she was so combative, and she had decided within two seconds of talking to me that she hated my guts, and she would not forgive me for spilling my coffee on her. Something happened that day. For the first time in a long time, I gave in to the urge to argue instead of trying to smooth things over.

That fight set the precedent for the rest of our interactions, and not a day has gone by in each other's presence that we haven't bickered, verbally sparred, or picked at each other over something. Usually, I'm unbearably annoyed by her. But today, it's oddly comforting to be sharing a table with her again. My life has been upside down the last few months, and I didn't feel settled again until about twenty minutes ago when I saw her walk through the door. Because as weird as it is, our rivalry has been the one constant in my life the last several years. She's the only person who never needs, wants, or sees me as anything other than her nemesis.

I think that's why she was the first person who popped into my head the day after I moved to Nebraska with Zoe. Coffee was on the table, Zoe was on her phone, and I was on the road to ruin, and I knew it. Clear as day. I hadn't realized until I was sitting at the breakfast table in the wrong state with the wrong person that my life had gotten way off track.

And when my chest caved in at the thought of breaking Zoe's heart by telling her this wasn't right for me and I couldn't go through with it, when I nearly backed out from fear of hurting her, Emily's smirking face popped into my mind and I could perfectly picture her saying: *Do it, Jack. I dare you.*

I needed that. I needed *her* in some weird, twisted way.

The months following the breakup were rough too. I was lonelier than ever. And I've been blaming that loneliness for my constant thoughts of Emily. I haven't been able to get her out of my head. Which is essentially why I'm back in Rome. Not just because I've always liked this town and wondered what it would be like to really be involved in it, but because I need to prove to myself that this weird tug I've been feeling to come back to her is a fluke—like how people lost in the desert will hallucinate and see visions of water when they're dehydrated. I was just lonely and so my creative mind concocted a ridiculous narrative where Emily seems to mean something to me. I'm back here to squash that idea once and for all. To remind myself of just how much I hate Emily and then I can put it behind me.

But it's not lost on me that the people who end up chasing those visions of water in the desert usually follow them all the way to their death.

So on that happy note, I'm fresh out of the realtor's office where I just signed on the dotted line to purchase the shittiest house of all time. *Ah—it'll be good as new after you give it some paint,* said Carol, whose nameplate on the desk claimed she was voted number one realtor in Rome, Kentucky, even though she is apparently the only realtor in Rome. (Her business cards for her party planning company were situated next to the nameplate.)

Well, Carol, it's going to need a lot more than a coat of paint, seeing as how the siding is falling off and the porch looks seconds from collapsing. It'll be a complete renovation, but I really had no choice. There was nothing else for sale within a fifty-mile radius, and after driving an hour into school every morning from Evansville, I'm ready to have less of a commute. Ready to put down official roots in this odd town.

Carol seemed unfazed about the state of the house and said that someone named Darrell had a construction crew who handled all the renovation projects around here and could get it done in no time. One quick call and he confirmed it.

"So . . . what did you do?" Emily asks after ten minutes of sitting in silence drinking weak-tasting coffee and trying not to notice how her hair is apparently some kind of naturally curly. I had no idea.

"Excuse me?"

She tsks. "Feigning ignorance doesn't look authentic on you. Why are you back and unmarried? Signs point to you screwed up."

"Sorry to disappoint you." I take a sip of coffee and set it back down. "But I didn't do anything wrong. We just weren't right for each other." And even though I should stop there, I can't seem to keep myself from saying more. "It wasn't until after I told her this that she informed me it was okay because she already had someone who *was* right for her."

If I didn't know better, I'd say that it's sympathy on Emily's face right now. For a split second, her expression softens to a look I've never seen on her before. It's open and smooth. And of course, I have to exploit it because that's just what we do. Also because it pinches something raw inside me that I wish didn't exist. "Is that concern I see in your poison-ivy eyes, Ms. Walker?"

Those eyes shutter. "Only for your students. I'm worried you're going to get their hopes up and then suddenly bolt when you and Zoe get your shit together and you take her back."

My jaw tics. "Don't worry about that."

Zoe and I are finished. It was something that didn't feel right from the beginning, but I was so lonely and desperate for someone to wake up to in the mornings that I overlooked too much. Loneliness will make a person do scary things. Like convincing myself I'm in love with a woman I never even felt safe enough with to share my biggest secret without making her sign an NDA first.

I do think Zoe and I had something genuine in the beginning. We had fun. She returned my kindness and affection—both things I really needed at the time. But then things started breaking down pretty quickly, and instead of ending it like I should have, I allowed it to drag out. In hindsight I should have been concerned that she would never leave her phone unattended. That I was getting random massive charges on my credit card for lunches and dinners. That she always seemed to encourage me to hide myself away and write because she used those times to disappear for most of the day. I didn't know what she was doing, and most alarming of all, I didn't seem to wonder either.

It took moving with her to Nebraska where she got a new job to realize I felt lonelier with her than I ever felt by myself. It took being stripped of my work and . . . Emily . . . to see the truth. Zoe didn't love me—she loved the lifestyle I could provide because of my writing career, but not me. And I didn't love her either. I loved the companionship she could offer when I needed it. The wedding was going to be a Band-Aid for something that was hemorrhaging from the start. Even the proposal was born from an argument where Zoe said we weren't moving fast enough. I kept thinking she was fighting for us, but now I know she was fighting to keep my money. Embarrassing to realize. Even more embarrassing to remember how comfortable I was remaining distant from her.

It was just a mistake . . . all of it. And I stuck with it for so damn long because I clearly have issues I need to deal with.

"I *do* worry, though. For your students," says Emily, sitting forward. "And you would too if you were in my shoes and anything close to professional."

I balk at that. "I'm always professional."

"Your shirt says you're not." What a very specific and random attack. *I like it.*

"What the hell is wrong with my shirt?"

"Why are the top two buttons undone like that?" She looks disgusted at the sight of my skin. Or maybe my necklace. "Are you trying out for an island love show?"

"Came up with the answer pretty quickly. Either you've been thinking about my clothing for some time now, or it's on your mind because you're currently applying for one of those very shows yourself." I nod toward her laptop. "Let me see if you're innocent."

Her eyes are pancakes and she quickly lowers her laptop screen until it's only cracked open. "No. I mean . . . no, I'm not applying to one of those annoying shows. I don't even want a relationship. And also, I don't have anything to prove to you by showing you my computer."

I scrunch my nose obnoxiously. "You seem pretty guilty."

"I am not. Show me what's on yours."

"No." I inch it shut too.

"I guess I'm not the only guilty one, then. See you on Love Island."

It's a struggle not to laugh. I enjoy our fights more than any emotionally healthy person should. They don't always make sense. They're a little unhinged. They reek of pettiness. But there is also a realness to them I don't tap into easily with other people.

And what would Emily think if she knew I was actually writing a book on this laptop? Too bad I'll probably never get to tell her and see the shock on her face.

My dad is Fredrick Bennett, a world-renowned mystery writer for the last three decades. He has hit number one on the *New York Times* bestseller list with thirty-one out of his forty published books and usually holds one of the top coveted spots for months at a time. He's brilliant and is touted as one of the best mystery writers ever. But what none of his readers know is that most of the time, he's an absolute bastard. Especially to my mom, and especially when he's on a deadline.

The thing is, I understand deadline stress. The occasional blowup or snippy attitude from time to time would be normal. Especially if the man knew how to apologize. But this is different. This bleeds into every corner of his life. He faces each day thinking the man who looks back at him in the mirror is the most important person in the world.

I want my mom to leave him once and for all, but I don't think she ever will, because like me, she has issues. And that's why my dad has no idea that the only other mystery writer the media and readers have ever deemed as his rising equal—is me.

Growing up with Fredrick as a dad really should have made me hate writing, but I had a story in my head I needed to get out. So I wrote it in college, and I loved every second of it. And when it was done, I thought it was maybe okay, so I pitched it to several agents under a pen name so I could know for certain that if I made it, it was by my own merit and not because of who my dad is. I was only hoping to hear back from at least one agent, and was floored when I was offered representation by all of them. I hadn't even told anyone I was writing a book because I wasn't sure I believed in myself—and there I was, on the brink of success.

And then I thought of my dad finding out. I thought of all the ways I would either fade into his shadow as Fredrick's son who also writes, or he'd suck every last drop of joy from my writing process by insisting he was the reason for my success, or he wouldn't be able to handle the competition and it would send him spiraling back to alcohol, which would in turn make my mom's life miserable. Most likely all of the above.

So I signed with my agent and together we got that book plus two more published—but I kept it a secret. My entire identity is hidden, and no one (other than my agent, Zoe, and my core publishing team, who have all signed NDAs) truly knows who the man is behind AJ Ranger, *New York Times* and *Sunday Times* bestselling mystery writer. My writing has become my safe haven. A place where no one can reach me. I've never felt that kind of security in my life before, and it's hard to want to risk giving it up.

Before I can challenge Emily further, Carol, my favorite realtor/

party planner, rushes into the coffee shop and looks around quickly until she spots me. Her shoulders droop with relief and she makes a beeline to my table.

"Good! You're still in town!" she says while walking at such a sharp clip that her bouncy, very fluffy hair bobs with every step.

At the sound of Carol's voice, Emily's head whips in her direction and she snaps her laptop shut. *Guilty indeed.*

"Did I forget something in your office?" I ask when she approaches the table.

Carol does a double take between me and Emily sitting here together and seems to be pleasantly surprised. Actually, hesitantly happy might be a better way to put it. I haven't been in Rome very often outside of school hours, but I've attended enough community events to have made an impression where Emily and I are concerned.

"Emily, hi, hon! Good to see you." And oddly, I know she means it. Everyone around here likes Emily for reasons I've never been privy to. Her gaze swings to me as she sets a piece of paper and a pen in front of me. "Jack, you left this page in your contract unsigned."

"Oh—sorry about that." I pull it to me and click my pen open. It's a struggle sometimes to remember to sign my real name and not my pseudonym. Which sounds like a douchey thing to say, but it is what it is.

Emily is watching me closely—her blond bangs, the same color as melted gold, curling up tighter and tighter on the edges with each passing second. "What contract?"

Carol smiles at her. "For his new house here in Rome. We just closed this morning."

Emily looks like she might be sick, and that thought gives me far too much joy. "Here? In Rome? You're moving . . . to Rome? Permanently?"

"Correct." I hand Carol the paper with a smile that makes her blush. "And Carol, you've been incredible to work with. Thank you for your attention to detail."

Emily butts in again. "Are you sure you didn't mean to move to Rome, Italy? No one would fault you considering your IQ," she says, batting her eyes with over-the-top innocence.

"Why would I move to Italy? My favorite corner table is right here."

Carol's shoulders are growing more rigid by the minute. She would rather be anywhere but here. "I guess this is going to be interesting for you two, isn't it?" Carol asks, gesturing between me and Emily.

"Oh no . . . there's no *you two* where Jack and I are concerned."

"Well, no, I meant with you two being neighbors now and all."

Both my and Emily's eyes zero in on Carol. I lean forward slightly. "Come again?"

The longer she looks between us, the less I like the expression on her face. It's slowly melting—like a realization is dawning that she doesn't want to share. "Wait. You didn't know?"

I shake my head at a loss. "I'm not sure what you're referring to."

"Oh god." Carol grimaces.

Emily seems to reach an understanding first. She sits back heavily in her seat. "Carol . . . don't tell me . . ."

"He bought Old Pete's place."

"*No,*" Emily whispers hauntingly.

"Yes."

I look at Carol and then Emily. "Who's Pete?"

No one acknowledges me.

"Carol! You're joking! That place is half-rotten and falling down." Well, now I know we're all talking about the same place at least.

"Who is Pete?" I ask again, this time getting Carol's attention.

She looks at me with sympathy. "I'm sorry, Jack. I thought you knew."

"Knew *what*?"

"The house you bought . . . it's directly next door to . . ." Her eyes slowly trace a line to the woman who would like to scoop me out of her life with a melon baller.

"*Dammit*. You're my neighbor?"

"Like hell. Just cancel the sale." She gestures toward the paper Carol is holding, which she clutches tightly in her fingers and pulls protectively to her chest looking for all the world like she's already spent the cash offer I used to buy the house. "Just rip up the papers and find a new house."

There she goes again—barking orders at me as if she owns me.

I sip my coffee. "No—that's not how it works, and you know it. Also this was the only place available in town." I've lived on the fringes long enough. I'm ready to *be* here.

"Okay! Well . . . it was nice seeing y'all but I've got to—" Carol is backing away but Emily's hand juts out and stops her, eyeballs still pasted to my face.

"No, no, no. This really can't be happening. I can't live next to him and work next to him every day of my life too." Her eyes finally slide up to Carol. "Surely the house is unsellable anyway! I mean . . . it's practically falling down. There must be a loophole to cancel the deal."

It's not that I would have expected Emily to be happy to live next to me, but I didn't expect her to look like she just stepped out of a haunted house either. Living in Nebraska for the past few months and constantly expecting to see Emily around every corner, simply because life has repeatedly brought us unexpectedly together, must have caused some irreversible damage. Because suddenly, I don't want her face to look like that when she thinks of me as her neighbor.

Carol waves off Emily's words like she did mine. "The house isn't too bad, really. Darrell is going to fix it up. A few weeks of renovation and it'll be gorgeous!"

I don't miss the moment Emily's eyes sharpen on Carol. "Wait. Darrell's company is going to do the reno?"

"Sure is. I talked to him this morning on the phone and he said although he's slammed, he'd be willing to make it work. And since Jack is able to pay out of p—"

"Your house is the white one with the obsessive-looking flower garden?" I know where Carol was going with her sentence, and I don't care to have her finish it in front of Emily. She has *always* been suspicious of my lifestyle. She's made more than one pointed comment about my "nice things." I don't need her sniffing around this too.

Emily narrows her eyes. "You could have just said the house with the *beautiful* flower garden. But yes—that's mine. Jealous?"

Of course it is. *Of course it is.* When I went by to look at the crapshoot that is now my home, I all but drooled over her house. I even asked Carol if the owner would be willing to relocate if I offered them double the estimated value. She said there was no way that particular homeowner would be open to selling. Now I know why. Emily will live in this town until her last breath. I've never known anyone to love a place or its people more.

"Emily . . ." Carol says carefully, her eyes dropping to the hand keeping her from moving. "If you don't mind, I've gotta get going."

With a defeated sigh, Emily lets go and I see the moment she doesn't want Carol to feel bad, because she plasters a soft smile on her mouth and aims it up at her. "Sure thing, Carol. Tell Billy I said hi and I'll see y'all at Hank's next Friday."

"Will do, hon! Bye, Jack! Oh—and you'll get keys for move-in by next weekend." And with those parting words she's off, rushing out of the coffee shop as quickly as she entered.

I expect Emily to immediately pounce on me, suggesting that if I don't cancel the sale of the house, I should lie in front of a moving bus instead. Which is why I'm surprised to find her completely silent and staring off in the distance at nothing in particular. One soft little frown between her brows. *Shit.* I've known her long enough to recognize that the line between her brows is not good. Last time I saw that frown it preceded her going after the same editorial job as me for our college paper junior year after my friend Harris frustratingly asked about my interview while Emily was nearby. I wanted that job so bad, and she knew it. And then she went and interviewed for it too—and beat me. (I got her back, though, when I talked to our professor and snagged the student teaching placement I knew she wanted at Rome Elementary. *Jeez, are we cruel people?*)

Bottom line, *that* is an Emily Walker scheming frown.

And when she suddenly looks back at me and her lips curl into a devious smirk, I know I'm about to have some sort of hell to pay.

"I've gotta go," she says quickly, shoving her laptop back into her tote bag and standing.

"What happened to needing this table so badly?" I don't trust whatever is going on in that head of hers but I'm excited for it all the same.

"Something more important just came up." She smiles another smile that tingles up my spine. "Enjoy your coffee, neighbor," Emily says before walking away and leaving me with an eerie feeling. One that instinctively has me throwing this coffee out and ordering a new one.

FROM: Emily Walker <E.Walker@MRPS.com>
TO: Jack Bennett <J.Bennett@MRPS.com>
DATE: Mon, May 27 9:00 AM
SUBJECT: Word to the wise . . .

I saw you got your keys to the house early. If I were
you . . . I wouldn't unpack yet. You never know when
something might go wrong and you'll have to climb
back up that beanstalk.

FROM: Jack Bennett <J.Bennett@MRPS.com>
TO: Emily Walker <E.Walker@MRPS.com>
DATE: Mon, May 27 9:30 AM
SUBJECT: Word to the wise . . .

Oh god. Was that really a Jack-in-the-beanstalk joke? I
haven't heard that since freshman year of high school
when I shot up a foot overnight and had to wear
high-water pants for a week.

Give me a minute. I'll think of an embarrassing
name to call you.

For now, I know you're obsessed with me, but try to
keep your eyes on your own property.

FROM: Emily Walker <E.Walker@MRPS.com>
TO: Jack Bennett <J.Bennett@MRPS.com>
DATE: Mon, May 27 9:33 AM
SUBJECT: Word to the wise . . .

Good luck. There's nothing embarrassing about me.
I'm perfect.

FROM: Jack Bennett <J.Bennett@MRPS.com>
TO: Emily Walker <E.Walker@MRPS.com>
DATE: Mon, May 27 9:35 AM
SUBJECT: Word to the wise . . .

Oh really??? . . . *Emily Stalker* . . .

FROM: Emily Walker <E.Walker@MRPS.com>
TO: Jack Bennett <J.Bennett@MRPS.com>
DATE: Mon, May 27 9:35 AM
SUBJECT: Word to the wise . . .

Please. That was barely even a zing. You can do better
than that, Jackson *Bonnet*.

CHAPTER FOUR

Emily

"Okay, where is she?" says Annie, practically shoving me out of the way as she barrels through my door to get in my house.

"You know, ever since I got this cat, you never come over just to see me anymore."

"That's the price you pay. Where is the little angel?" Annie, my youngest sister, is a tender soul. But right now, she looks like a gremlin while dropping to her hands and knees in her green overalls to search under the couch for the cat. Her head is whipping in all directions, pretty blue eyes bugging out of her head. I've never felt terrified of her before—but right now . . .

"She's probably back on my bed. That's where she likes to sleep." I end the search just so I don't have to witness her like this anymore.

Annie is little more than a puff of smoke as she races down the short hallway to my room, emerging a few seconds later with a squishy orange bundle of fur in her hands. She holds Ducky up so she can smoosh their noses together. "*I love you I love you I love you,*" she says in the babiest of baby voices.

Honestly, I don't blame her. I love Ducky more than anyone should ever love a cat. I got her a few weeks ago, when I couldn't take the complete isolation in my house anymore. I went down to the animal shelter and spent the afternoon there, sampling kittens like Ben and Jerry's flavors. I played and snuggled with probably twenty different cats before finding Ducky. She was a little underweight after living on the street for too long, and I was told she would need a lot of love and attention. We were an immediate match made in heaven.

Once again, my front door swings open, and my sister-in-law, Amelia, rushes in. Her eyes zero in on Annie and Ducky and she shape-shifts into a missile about to launch. "Give me the child!" she says, racing to Annie's side and snatching the kitten away to the sounds of Annie's protests.

Amelia looks me in the eye and, with the most serious expression I've ever seen, says, "I'll pay you a million dollars for her." I think she might be serious. Her bank account would be good for it.

I smile at Amelia. "No deal. I love Ducky more than anything in this world."

"I would say ouch," says Annie, "but I completely get it. I'm contemplating moving back in just so I can be near her."

I give her an incredulous look. "You're going to leave your super sexy boyfriend's house and move back in with your spinster sister?"

"It's the only way to this cuteness," she says primly, snatching Ducky back and snuggling her up in the crook of her neck. We all three look down at the kitten just simply breathing and gaining all of our admiration for it.

But then Annie and Amelia share a glance before their eyes slide to me. "Umm, but really, have you been okay here by yourself?" Annie asks. "I'll move back if you need me to—cat or no cat."

Suddenly, this impromptu visit is feeling like an intervention. I expect to look over my shoulder and find a banner that reads *ADMIT YOU'RE LONELY, EMILY.*

Never. Because I know if I was honest with her, she would leave her wonderful life with Will behind and hop right back into this house with me. It's not her job to make me happy. She doesn't need me anymore, and that's my problem to come to terms with, not hers.

"Don't you dare. I love having this place to myself. It finally stays clean just as I like it." The coffeepot beeps in the kitchen, giving me something to do to avoid my sisters' searching gazes. I pull down three mugs and fill them nearly to the top. Making a full pot of coffee each time is a habit I haven't been able to break since Annie and Madison moved out.

"So . . . not that I don't love having you two over, but what are you doing here in the middle of the day? Did Will propose again and you accepted this time?" That last question is aimed at Annie.

Annie and Will's relationship has been the funniest, most unexpected thing in the world to watch. Will was Amelia's bodyguard when he and Annie first met, and also a notorious playboy. We all thought Annie craved a sweet traditional life. Boy, were we wrong. Will was so gone for Annie almost immediately. She surprised us all when he proposed to her and she turned him down, saying she wanted to date for a while because she was getting to know herself all over again.

I respect the hell out of her.

Anyway, they moved in together and have been happily coupled for the last year. But Will has proposed to Annie no less than three times now (always lighthearted and never pushy; it's actually become an inside joke between them at this point). The man gets rejected every time with a kiss and a *Not yet but ask me again another time, please.*

"No—no proposals this month. We're both here for the hot goss." She sets a squirming Ducky on the ground and then retrieves her coffee mug, grinning wildly at me over the top of it.

Amelia picks up where Annie left off. "Why didn't you tell us that your work nemesis is back in town, no longer engaged, and apparently moving in next door?"

I'm actually surprised it took them this long to hear about it. Gossip must have been moving slowly through Rome this weekend, given I called Darrell the second I left the coffee shop on Saturday. Two whole days ago.

I shrug and sip my coffee. "I didn't tell you because it's not a big deal. There's nothing to tell."

Annie scoffs. "You're getting a new neighbor who you've done nothing but fight with since freshman year of college, and there's nothing to tell?"

I smile . . . *deviously.* "Nope. Because he's not going to be my neighbor for long." I set my coffee on the counter and walk around to the breakfast nook that overlooks my cute little living room. There's a basket of clean clothes on the table that I've been working on folding this morning.

"Wait!" Annie says, following me and setting down her coffee so hard it sloshes over the edge a little. She's fishing her phone from her back pocket. "Maddie will murder me in cold blood if I don't have her on the screen for this." *Doubt it.*

I fold a dishrag into a neat little square and relocate it to the appropriate pile. "On the phone for what? I'm telling you, there's no story here."

"You're smirking like a devil," says Amelia. "There's absolutely a story here, and Maddie will be so sad if she misses out on it." *Yeah right. She probably won't even answer.* Lately it's been increasingly hard to get Madison on the phone. We plan calls in advance and she texts me and cancels five minutes before, saying something came up. It kills me. We've always been close, but ever since she moved to New York, I feel her slipping away.

I give Annie a face that lets her see just exactly how thrilled I am about being the center of this sister chat, though.

I'm both a little shocked and relieved when a second later, my brown-haired, dark-eyed, spunky middle sister, Maddie, is on the screen. I think because we're so close in age—thirteen months apart—we've always been best friends. We've fought the most. Grown together the most. And trusted each other the most. Just the sight of her is a balm, but I try not to let on just how much I miss her. Because even though I'm pissed at her for rarely calling or coming home, I also don't want to guilt her into doing either of those things.

The ugly truth is, I wish I'd never supported her decision to go after her culinary degree. And deep down, I think I was really hoping she'd go out there, take a look around the city, hate it, and quickly come back. *That* is a horrible thing to wish, though, so I lock up that thought along with the rest in my Treasure Chest of Doom.

"Hello, ladies—let me see the cat," she says in a whisper—the little nub of a bun on the top of her head bobbing as she tips closer to the screen.

"You too? I swear I could disappear completely and none of you would notice as long as Ducky is around." I say it as a joke but then my heart constricts around the words.

Madison grins. "I'm not even sorry."

"Of course you're not." *Dammit.* That came out sharper than I intended. Normally I wouldn't feel bad at all about saying something like that to her. We've had little petty fights like all good sisters. But lately . . . I don't know. Bickering with her doesn't feel safe. I don't want to do anything that will risk her not coming home. And also I know how hard it was for her to decide to go to New York in the first place. I'd pushed her into being a teacher like me.

I'd basically kept her chained to Rome by insisting that we all needed to live close together. And she decided to break through all of that and go after her dreams. It killed me to realize I was truly the one holding her back from living her life. I refuse to do it a second time. I want her to come home when she wants to come home. To call when she wants to call.

I hurry to pick up Ducky and hold her squishy little face toward the camera to distract everyone from my comment. She yawns and it earns her extra oohs from the girls.

"Oh my god, my jaws are hurting from gritting my teeth so hard!" says Madison in a whine.

Amelia voices what's been running through my head. "Come home for a visit so you can meet her! It's been too long, Maddie." Six months to be exact. She came back for Grandma's funeral, but not since.

The whole gang, however, visited her in New York over Christmas when she couldn't make it home. It was Annie's idea that we surprise her, and though I was worried how she would react to finding us there, she did seem genuinely happy we came.

Her apartment was too small for everyone to fit, so the couples stayed in a hotel and I smooshed into Madison's bed with her. Those moments were good. Maddie and I fell right back into the same close groove we had before she left Kentucky, and I was hopeful that whatever the weirdness was between us since she'd been gone was all just a result of the physical distance and maybe we'd stay in touch better moving forward. But in the end, we went right back to missed calls and strained text messages.

Madison smiles now and I find myself dissecting it—wondering if it's real or not. "Well, now it seems I *have* to come home for two reasons. To meet my cat-niece and watch Emily slowly destroy her new neighbor, *Jack Bennett*!"

It's going to be hard to keep the truth of just how bothered I am by Jackson moving in next door hidden from Madison because she's the only one who has seen me interact with him the last few years. She knows firsthand how often we were at each other's throats. But maybe this strangeness between us will come out in my favor for once and allow me to fly under the radar.

"First," I say, dipping my head a little closer to the screen, "can we talk about why you're sitting on the toilet in your bathroom? That's where you are, right?"

"Yes," she says casually. "But I'm not using it."

Annie tilts her head. "And why are you whispering?"

The sly grin that covers Maddie's mouth tells us the answer before the words are out. "There's a guy in my bed. A cute chef from my program." She shimmies her shoulders underneath her baggy T-shirt. Or I'm guessing, *his* baggy T-shirt.

"The same guy from a few nights ago?" Amelia asks.

"Nope." Maddie has never looked more proud or mischievous.

An image of James Huxley, Noah's best friend, staring longingly at Madison during Noah and Amelia's wedding flashes in my mind. We were all raised together since our parents were best friends, and so in a way, James has always felt like my brother. I had never even considered that one of us could have felt differently toward him until I saw the way he looked at Madison.

It doesn't seem like Madison has thought twice about James, though, since she left. Hasn't thought twice about any of us.

"What's this guy's name?" I ask Maddie, trying to hold back from blurting *Be careful! Always use protection!*

Madison waves me off. "Doesn't matter. He won't be around for long."

Maddie is definitely more sexually adventurous than the rest of us. I think my siblings assume I'm just like Maddie in how much I hook up, but they'd be wrong. It's actually a rare occurrence—especially lately. And when I do sleep with anyone, I never linger after. And I never bring men back to my place unless we are exclusively dating. Which hasn't happened since Liam—my high school sweetheart, otherwise known as the person who first proved to me that *forever* is just an empty word that means nothing to some people—so basically I didn't even need to mention the last part.

I really think I can trace most of my trust issues back to him. We had been together since freshman year of high school all the way through senior year. We were the couple that everyone voted Most Likely to Get Married. We were homecoming king and queen. We had plans. We were going to move in together and attend our local college with an aim to get married within two or three years. We were in love—real, honest-to-goodness love—and I believed our happily-ever-after with all my heart.

That is, until May 23 of our senior year—the date is etched into my mind—when Liam came to my house with a letter in his hand. He had applied to a college out of state without telling me and he was accepted. Not only that, he was going. He had a plan B all along that didn't include me and had kept it a secret, even knowing that I was planning for our future. Noah was there; he had been eavesdropping outside my bedroom door for the entire thing. I'm not sure I've ever told him how grateful I am that he never pushed me on it when I told the family that the breakup was mutual.

But I was destroyed. I locked myself in my room for one day and cried it out, and then I made myself pick up the pieces of my heart and move on. (Publicly, at least.) Privately, I ached for so long. Between my parents dying and Liam leaving, my heart couldn't take any more pain, so I boarded it up.

Now, romance is just not something I'm built for. I've grown into the soul of a woman made for getting shit done—something men don't typically enjoy about me. A few years ago, I really put my back into it and set out to date as much as I could as a last-ditch effort to see if maybe my forever partner was out there. Not some great love, just a companionable person to spend my time with. None of them lasted long.

Brian couldn't take it that I liked to stick to my daily routine. At least ten times he told me, *Just go with the flow, Emily.* Jeremy hated that if my order came back wrong, I'd (kindly) ask for it to be corrected instead of just eating it. Zane was offended that after two breakfasts in a row where he cracked shells into our scrambled eggs, I insisted on cooking them from then on out, because who wants to feel like they're eating Pop Rocks while biting into eggs? And Harrison, he hated that I wouldn't snuggle after sex. He was the only one who outright in the breakup speech said, *I'm sorry. You're just too cold for me, Emily.*

Each of those guys were looking for women like Annie and Madison. But me? I'm more akin to a Brillo pad you keep under your sink for when you need to scrub out those really tough grease stains.

"Back to Jackson Bennett," Maddie says, putting her eyeball so comically close to the screen I can see the outline of her contacts. "He's your neighbor *and* he didn't get married! Are you furious? Annie, tell me if that vein on the right side of Emily's head is popping out."

I take a leisurely sip of my coffee and then smile. "All this gossip is pointless. Believe me, Jack is nothing to worry about."

"Why? And where did you hide his body?" asks Madison.

"There are much more creative ways to get rid of Jack. And you can rest assured that they're all being implemented as we speak."

Annie looks at me with a hesitant smile. "Okay, but can I just say this one thing?" She pauses. "Would it really be such a bad thing for him to be your neighbor? I mean . . . maybe y'all could become friends. Maybe if you stop fighting for a minute you'll find something you have in common."

Maddie and I exchange a look that stands as evidence that we were once best friends, and then I turn to my tenderhearted sister. "Oh, Annie, I love you. But there's no way in hell that Jack and I will ever be friends. Or neighbors."

I can't have him here. This is *my* town. *My* safe place. Too much in my life already feels like shifting sand—I can't have him invading the last solid plot of my life as I know it.

"How are you getting rid of him, then?" asks Amelia, pulling out a chair and sitting at the table with her coffee.

"My business is my own."

All three of them groan. I could swear even Ducky makes a sound.

"How is it fair that you can demand that our business be your business and your business is your own too?" Madison is outraged.

"Simple," I say, shrugging a shoulder. "Is your name Emily?"

"That is *not* an answer."

We're suddenly interrupted by a knock on my front door. I smile to myself because everything is working out exactly as I calculated.

I hold Ducky so she doesn't dart out under my feet and leave me forever the second I open the door. On my front porch, I find Mabel, the woman who is like a second grandma to us. She's wearing her favorite yellow sundress that brings out the warm undertones of her dark skin. Matching yellow hoop earrings peek out from under her shortish, curly, silver-and-white hair. And her smile—oh, it's downright mischievous.

She was my grandma's best friend but pretty much her opposite in every way. Grandma was gentle like Annie and Madison, but Mabel . . . Mabel and I are cut from the same utility cloth. We have both been likened to hot sauce more than once in our lives. And she's clutching a casserole dish so famous around this town we've named it the Information Dish.

This is how the best secrets of Rome, Kentucky, get extracted.

Mabel tempts you with brown sugar, marshmallow, and sweet potato goodness, and then snatches it away until you give her the answers she's looking for. It's a good thing the military doesn't know about her or this casserole.

"Morning, sugar," she says in her scratchy southern drawl, laying it on thick today. "Just thought I'd drop by with a little casserole." On the word *casserole* she waves the vintage Pyrex dish under my nose. It's the same color as Jack's mustard trousers.

Normally I wouldn't cave so easily. But since I want this piece of gossip to hit the town like a wildfire, I take one whiff, look her straight in the eyes, and waste zero time. "Yes, Jackson Bennett is single now. And yes, he bought the house next to mine. But no, I don't want him there, and as far as I'm concerned, he's not welcome in our town. Now . . . *gimme.*"

She smiles proudly and hands it over with a soft pat on the back of my forearm. *Mmm, the dish is still warm.* Betrayal has never tasted so sweet.

"Got it." She winks. "And you'll have our solidarity as always. See ya tomorrow, hon."

I close the door and turn around with my spoils in hand. My sisters meet me with a pitiful look (Annie turned the phone so Madison could watch the whole situation unfold). Guilt hunches my shoulders—but I can't give in to it. Where Jackson is concerned, I get a free pass.

"Emily, that's going to be all over town by tomorrow, you know? Everyone is going to shun him." Annie looks distraught. "Are you sure that's what you want?"

"Absolutely." I grab a fork and dive headfirst into this damn good casserole, imagining with every delicious bite the look on Jackson's face when he realizes he's been bested. Hopefully this was enough to keep him from invading my life any more than he already has.

FROM: Emily Walker <E.Walker@MRPS.com>
TO: Jack Bennett <J.Bennett@MRPS.com>
DATE: Tue, May 28 2:00 PM
SUBJECT: E.T. phone home?

Is that giant metal box in your front yard here to take you back to your home planet???

FROM: Jack Bennett <J.Bennett@MRPS.com>
TO: Emily Walker <E.Walker@MRPS.com>
DATE: Tue, May 28 2:05 PM
SUBJECT: E.T. phone home?

This, Emily Stalker, is the accumulation of all the belongings I have left after my split with Zoe—freshly shipped to me from the good state of Nebraska.

FROM: Emily Walker <E.Walker@MRPS.com>
TO: Jack Bennett <J.Bennett@MRPS.com>
DATE: Tue, May 28 2:07 PM
SUBJECT: E.T. phone home?

Jack . . . that's a very small pod. You didn't get to keep more than that???

FROM: Jack Bennett <J.Bennett@MRPS.com>
TO: Emily Walker <E.Walker@MRPS.com>
DATE: Tue, May 28 2:10 PM
SUBJECT: E.T. phone home?

I offered for her to keep most of it—a clean slate sounded pretty nice.

CHAPTER FIVE

Jack

'm not sure why I thought it would be a good idea to live in the house I'm going to renovate while it's happening. It seemed like a no-brainer: I'm a bachelor. No kids. I can easily rough it in an old house for a few weeks during the summer amid some construction.

Except for one problem: I forgot that I'm high maintenance. As in, I like to be comfortable and surrounded by things that make that outcome possible. I'm not twenty anymore—and it shows. I didn't feel like putting up a fight with Zoe to get half of our things in the breakup, so I just took the stuff she didn't want anymore and had it shipped in a pod to the new house, where it will live in the front yard until construction is complete.

So for now, I'm only moving a few basics into my rotten, crusty house and keeping everything to my bedroom while they renovate the living room, bathroom, and kitchen. (The bathroom will still be usable while under construction—it just won't be pretty.) Once they begin work on my room, I'll move my stuff into the living room and sleep there for a while. Shouldn't be difficult since literally all I have right now is a desk and a *very* temporary twin-sized bed that I ordered online with next-day shipping. My clothes will remain in a suitcase.

I might as well be camping for how much I'm roughing it.

Darrell—my contractor—is stopping by later today so I can sign the contract, and then construction is set to start next Monday. I'll have a functioning kitchen and walls that are not rotting around me in no time.

But today, I'm at the local market shopping for groceries that can be prepared without a kitchen. So far I've got crunchy peanut butter and bread. I take my grocery haul to the front of the store and silently unload all of my items onto the countertop. When I finally look up, I'm startled to find two people staring at me. An older woman, maybe in her early seventies, is behind the counter wearing a black dress with her gray hair tied back in a severe bun with skin so translucent I can see her blue veins. She's watching me with an indistinguishable expression. And the other is a white middle-aged man with cargo shorts, rosy red cheeks, polo shirt, tall socks, and sneakers standing on this side of the checkout counter, leaned back against it, and surveying me openly.

"Hello," I say hesitantly, because I am incredibly good at reading people's moods—you can't have a narcissistic father without becoming an expert in the art—but these people are giving out mixed signals. Almost looking like they want to talk to me but are equally concerned I might be about to rob the place. Have they seen the crunchy peanut butter? How threatening can a person be with a jar of peanut butter?

"Hi there." The man's eyes bob all over me, and then a small sad frown puckers between his brows. "I'm Phil—owner of the hardware store across the street. And this here is Harriet. She owns this market."

"Nice to meet you both." I'm still not sure what the weird vibes are about, but if there's anything I'm excellent at, it's winning someone over.

I smile and extend my hand to Phil because he looks like the kind of guy who would appreciate a nice firm handshake. My suspicions are confirmed when our hands meet and his eyes light up. "I'm Jack. I just moved into town, and I teach at the elementary school."

"Oh, we know all about you, Jackson Bennett. Thirty-two years old, grew up in Evansville but just purchased Old Pete's house. You've taught in the second grade alongside our Emily for the last three years, you drive a fancy-schmancy Land Rover, and your dad is the mystery writer Fredrick Bennett," says Phil with startling accuracy.

Harriet is quick to add, "Don't forget recently jilted by your bride. It's really too bad."

I try not to chafe at the (almost) thorough accounting of my life. Especially having my dad's name dropped so casually into conversation. I knew word traveled fast around this town, but damn. I wouldn't be surprised if they somehow also know I'm Ranger. And is it just me or did Harriet definitely smile when she said *it's really too bad*?

Normally, this is where I'd say something polite and flattering (read: distracting) and then I'd get out of here before they have a chance to ask me anything personal. I've always felt uncomfortable being known. It's why writing under a pseudonym has worked so well for me. But part of my great awakening in Nebraska was realizing that I've kept myself hidden too much. It's a harrowing feeling to look around and realize you don't have a single friend to turn to in a hard time. That's when I thought of Rome again.

I was happiest teaching here in this town and had envied the tight-knit community they all seemed to have. Originally I stayed living in Evansville when Bart asked me to come teach at the school because that was where I'd always been and it seemed easier to commute than pick up my life and move it. Also, if I'm being honest it was so I could look out for my mom—be nearby if she needed me.

Diana, my mom, didn't come from a financially stable home, and so when she and my dad got married at a young age, she felt like he'd rescued her. She's never been an adult without him, and I think that's made her feel dependent on him. Which in turn lets him get away with talking down to her, expecting her to be there for his every need, and shutting her out when he doesn't like something she's said. Basically treating her like dirt.

I learned early on that I can't fight with my dad or expect him to learn from his mistakes. He's not a gracious person. I have, however, learned how to manage him. From time to time my mom, who is sweet to her core, calls or texts me to come defuse his mood. I liked to be nearby when situations like that would arise.

And then I met Zoe, who in no way wanted to move to this small a town, so the idea completely fell to the back burner until I found myself at a crossroads. But now that I'm here, I want to really *be* here. I want to make an effort to be part of the community. (I'll still go when my mom needs me, though. I'm used to the hour commute at this point.)

The other reason I'm not rushing to leave this conversation, though, is because there's one part in particular in Phil's speech that snagged my curiosity even more than the rest.

"Thank you for your sympathy," I tell Harriet with a playful smile, letting her know I picked up on her distinct lack of it. "Is Emily related to you all?" I look to them both.

"No," Phil says simply, arms folded and looking disinclined to expound.

"Oh. It's just . . . you said *our* Emily."

Unmistakable affection enters his eyes. "Emily was born and raised in this town. Her and each of her siblings. To those of us who have been here since their birth, those Walker kids are *ours*. Just not by blood."

"Especially after their mama and daddy died when the kids were so little and Silvie raised them," adds Harriet.

That's . . . something I didn't know. Her parents died when she was young? I'm assuming Silvie is Emily's grandma, who died a few weeks before I left Rome. Or maybe not, since I only remember Emily taking one day off from work and then coming back like nothing ever happened. I assumed she wasn't that close with her grandma, but then again, I know as much about Emily as she knows about me. A fact that's oddly starting to bother me.

"And as such," continues Phil, sucking in a deep breath and adjusting the belt around his waist before letting it out in a heavy sigh—and the belt once again disappears beneath his stomach, "I feel the need to inform you that our allegiance lies with Emily, no matter how polite you are."

"I see." Except I don't. Not yet at least, but some sort of realization is definitely tingling on the edge of my awareness. "Well, loyalty is a wonderful character trait, and I could never fault you for that. Especially since you have great taste in socks."

He beams just as expected. "No one ever comments on my socks except to say they're dorky."

I hike up the pant leg of my chocolate trousers to reveal yellow-and-white polka-dot crew socks. "I have an affinity for dorky socks."

"Oh—I like those! I might need a pair."

"I have a couple more just like these. Stop by my house sometime and I'll let you steal a set."

"Really? That would be—"

Harriet clears her throat and takes my peanut butter, scans it, and places it in a paper bag with the logo Harriet's Market printed on the side. She glances meaningfully at Phil. "*Emily*," she says with emphasis, "has always been faithfully loyal to us. And like Phil was trying to say, that loyalty isn't going to be swayed by some big-city boy trying to infiltrate our sweet town like those gushy romance movies I see on TV."

"Well—I wouldn't call Evansville a big city by any means, but it does have a few large grocery stores." And because I want to be part of this town, and want to establish some friendships, I pause and run a quick calculation of what would make Harriet happy to hear. "But none of them are as great as this place."

Her eyes sparkle—I've struck gold. "You think so?"

"Absolutely. You have a much better selection. And so well organized. I had no trouble finding anything." I'm not even lying—that's the trick with getting people to like you. It's not about making up shit, it's having an eye to find the best parts of them to bring up. Paying attention to the small things. Yes, it is pretty exhausting, but in my experience worth it.

Harriet lights up. "It *is* the best market. I think the secret lies in all the little details like—"

Phil clears his throat. "*Emily* has always known it was a good market too, bless her."

At this point . . . I'm getting a kick out of hearing their praises of Emily. It's clear that something specific has inspired this speech and I think I'm almost to the root of it.

"Yes, the dear girl. Even when she and I have butted heads in the past, she still came through for me and played Mary in my church's Christmas play when Hannah-May got sick at the last minute."

"That's high praise. But really, there's no need to worry about me trying to take her place in the Christmas play. I'm not really a churchgoer."

Her eyes widen, and I think I've scandalized her, but instead, her eyes fly to Phil, and she looks oddly pleased. "Doesn't go to church either!" She slaps the counter in an I'll-be-damned sort of way.

He tsks. "I know, Harriet."

I look around briefly, wondering if I'm being pranked somehow. I truly have zero idea what's going on in this little market. "Do I have to go to church to live in the town?"

Phil laughs. "Goodness, no. The Walkers don't go either."

"We can thank Mabel's rebellious influence for that one," she tells Phil with a disapproving look in some sort of private conversation. She turns to me again and smiles, and then seems to remember something and drops to a more subdued look. "But you're of course always welcome in our church. It's the one up on the corner over the hill by the gas station with the logo of the hooker-looking lady in cowboy boots."

"Those are some well-detailed directions."

She nods. "First Church of the Nazarene Hills Beloved Assembly of Christ."

Don't laugh. Don't laugh. Don't laugh.

"No one can decide on the denomination, and we didn't want to leave anyone out. Which is why you're absolutely welcome." She pauses when Phil gives her a look. "But of course, you'll have to sit in the back. Alone."

This conversation has felt like the equivalent of swimming in the darkest part of the ocean and realizing I'm completely turned around with no surface in sight. *Do they like me or do they hate me?*

"I only recommend going to that church if you're looking to be bored out of your damn mind," says a scratchy voice from behind us. We all three startle. I look over my shoulder and find an older Black woman wearing a bright pink dress.

"Mabel . . ." says Harriet with a frightening glare. "What have I told you about cursing in my establishment?"

"That it's strictly forbidden. Which honestly makes it a hell of a lot more fun to do, Harriet, so you have to quit bringing it up if you want me to stop," she says, giving me a little wink. *I like her.*

"When'd you come in here? I never heard you," asks Phil.

Mabel extends her foot between us. "New loafers. They've got those fancy memory foam insoles. Makes me stealthy as a cat so I can sneak up on Harriet and frustrate the shit out of her." She grins. "Good for gathering gossip too." She hitches her thumb in my direction. "It's a shame about this one, huh?"

I open my mouth to ask what she means by that when Phil speaks up with a sad shake of his head. "Really is. I just know he's over six foot too. Would've been perfect for her height."

A new voice enters the mix. "Mabel, I swear to god, you have to quit spiking the tea at poker night," says a dark-haired guy emerging from the aisle just behind us. Probably in his early thirties—he's wearing jeans and a black short-sleeved tee. Flower tattoos wind all the way down his arm to a butterfly that's inked on top of his hand. "I'm tired of waking up with a hangover."

"I thought you were made of stronger stuff than that, William. Sweet tea just isn't the same without a splash of Jack Daniel's."

"I'm pretty sure you mean Jack Daniel's with a splash of sweet tea."

Mabel waves dismissively. "Tomatoes potatoes."

I'm in a conversational hurricane with no end in sight.

The guy turns to me and sticks out his hand. "Hi, I'm Will Griffin. Fellow Rome circus member."

"Jack Bennett. Newest circus member, I guess?"

"Oh—*you're* Jack," he says, as our handshake finishes. "Sorry about the wedding."

Was it printed in the damn paper or something?

But then he looks at the others and lifts his brows, joining their previous conversation like I'm not even standing here. "Pretty eyes and a good sense of fashion? It's a damn shame."

Okay, what the actual hell?

The group continues to size me up very openly, commenting on my features and personality (in a surprisingly complimentary way but almost like I'm . . . dead?). I tune out for a second, though, as I feel my phone buzz again and open it only to find a series of texts from my contractor who I'm supposed to meet with later today. (Note to self: There's a bar of service right in front of the checkout counter.)

> DARRELL: Hi Jack. Sorry to do this so late in the game but the project I'm currently working on is running longer than anticipated.
>
> DARRELL: I'm not going to be able to take on your house next week after all.

I fire back a text.

> JACK: That's unfortunate. How much later are you anticipating the project running? It's not ideal but I'm willing to wait and book you and your crew for when you're finished with your current project.
>
> DARRELL: Well . . . actually . . . I can't help you after this project either.

Huh. That's concerning.

> JACK: Do you mind if I ask why?
>
> DARRELL: Because I'm moving.

DARRELL: To another country.

DARRELL: Have a nice day. Sorry I can't help.

I might have actually thought he was genuinely booked up until those last two texts. I clue back into the conversation around me right as I hear them speculating that I would have been a great resource for the local softball league too.

I shove my phone back in my pocket. "Okay, I'll bite. Someone tell me what's going on. Why are you all talking about me like I'm already one foot out the door when I just moved to town?"

Harriet's lips press into a line. Phil's gaze drops to his sneakers. Mabel elbows Will in the side. He grumbles a little but then looks at me. "We may or may not have been warned to give you the cold shoulder because there's someone here who doesn't want you sticking around . . ."

"*What?* Who would do something so . . ." But then it all clicks into place, and I remember the little furrow between Emily's eyebrows. All the comments about the town's loyalty to her too.

Emily Walker, you sneaky, conniving . . .

My thoughts are interrupted when my gaze snags on the very woman in question as she's passing in front of the market windows. I'm ready to meet her out there and let her have it, until I notice she's wearing cutoff shorts that display her mile-long legs and a thin white tank top. Her golden hair is pulled back in a clip with her bangs wild around her face. She's always so polished and professional at school but . . . this must be summertime Emily.

And before I realize it, I've been walking backward trying to keep sight of her until—

Bam.

I slam my back into a center display full of soup cans. It tumbles to the ground in a long slow slide of horrifically loud crashes. One after another in an onion soup avalanche.

Once the onslaught is complete and an awkward silence finally blankets the room, I look back at Phil, Harriet, Mabel, and Will. Their mouths are hanging open and I can practically see their feet itching to run and tell everyone they know about this.

Especially their ringleader: Emily.

"I'll buy all of this right now if you swear not to tell *anyone* what just happened."

Harriet nods.

TWO YEARS AGO

FROM: Emily Walker <E.Walker@MRPS.com>
TO: Jack Bennett <J.Bennett@MRPS.com>
DATE: Tue, Sep 20 6:25 AM
SUBJECT: Field trip presentation

I'll cut to the chase. I woke up sick today—but I was supposed to present my proposal for the second-grade field trip at the all-teacher meeting after school. If you present it for me, I'll take over your carpool duty for two weeks.

FROM: Jack Bennett <J.Bennett@MRPS.com>
TO: Emily Walker <E.Walker@MRPS.com>
DATE: Tue, Sep 20 6:28 AM
SUBJECT: Field trip presentation

Interesting. Why not ask Jessica?

FROM: Emily Walker ‹E.Walker@MRPS.com›
TO: Jack Bennett ‹J.Bennett@MRPS.com›
DATE: Tue, Sep 20 6:30 AM
SUBJECT: Field trip presentation

And risk her terrible monotone delivery? No thanks.
You may be a jerk, but I'm mature enough to admit
your presentation skills are above average.

FROM: Jack Bennett ‹J.Bennett@MRPS.com›
TO: Emily Walker ‹E.Walker@MRPS.com›
DATE: Tue, Sep 20 6:33 AM
SUBJECT: Field trip presentation

Three weeks and you have a deal. But I'm going to
spice up the presentation.

FROM: Emily Walker ‹E.Walker@MRPS.com›
TO: Jack Bennett ‹J.Bennett@MRPS.com›
DATE: Tue, Sep 20 6:35 AM
SUBJECT: Field trip presentation

Fine. Three weeks. But don't do a damn thing to my
presentation, Jackson!

FROM: Jack Bennett ‹J.Bennett@MRPS.com›
TO: Emily Walker ‹E.Walker@MRPS.com›
DATE: Tue, Sep 20 6:30 PM
SUBJECT: Field trip presentation

Oops—didn't see the email before spicing it up. Your
presentation won thanks to me. You're welcome.

CHAPTER SIX

Emily

This morning started out tough. Without having anywhere to go or any pressing needs, I struggled to get out of bed. It's been happening more and more lately and if I'm being honest, it scares me a little. During those moments I just feel so . . . heavy. Sad. Dark.

I lay there for a while just staring at nothing until I got a text from Madison saying she's coming home next weekend. The news was enough to get me out of bed and power the most productive day of my year. I cleaned my house from top to bottom. I officially put away all of my winter clothes and traded them out for my summer stash. I washed my truck. I went thrifting for new classroom décor and found the cutest little tufted stools that will go perfectly in my reading corner. But most of all, I managed to somehow avoid all contact with Jack.

Unfortunately, I wasn't able to avoid thinking of him every time I glanced at the sad pod out front housing his stuff. In his email, he told me it was so small because he wanted a clean slate. *Why?* What could have happened between him and Zoe that would make him want to give up nearly everything he owned? She told him she already had someone in mind to take his place; does that mean she was cheating? And why does that thought bother me so much?

This is the same guy who joined the Scholastic Book Fair planning committee only after he found out I was the one leading it, just so he could suggest the opposite of everything I'd already suggested—and since Jack is eight times better at getting people to like him than me, he had those teachers eating out of his hand. I was outvoted on every damn suggestion.

So why would I care that Zoe cheated on the world's most annoying man? *I do, though.*

It's the end of the day now, and with each step of my bedtime routine I complete, a knot in my shoulders loosens. I turn on music so the house isn't so quiet, read in the bath (hello, Scottish historical romance), apply skin care products, brush teeth, put on my PJs, and snuggle Ducky eighteen thousand times in between each step, wondering how I got through my days before her. Everything goes back in its exact place when I finish using it, because even if everything around me is swirling into chaos, at least I have this: My house. My routine. My cat.

I linger in the hallway, missing the hell out of my sisters, for only two minutes tonight before that slimy, dark pain starts creeping in and I have to force myself to move on.

"Okay . . . little fluffball, you know the drill," I say to Ducky, who is rubbing against my ankles.

I pat the mattress and she promptly jumps up onto my bed. I cozy up under the covers and pull my laptop in front of me as Ducky curls up next to my legs.

Technically, my book is finished—but it's also a long way from done. I'm not confident enough to call myself a real writer yet, but I've read enough books to know that maybe it has potential? It's just messy as hell. The plot is all over the place. The characters' motivations somehow changed halfway through the book without my consent, and one character disappeared entirely. But I also haven't a clue how to fix any of it. Or if I should even bother.

I suppose I could ask my sisters to read it, but *gah . . . no*. Every time I consider it my stomach knots up. Right now, whenever I open the document and work on it, I'm happy. My fear is if someone reads it and confirms my worst nightmare (that it's actually horrendous garbage), this joy I've needed so badly will pop like a soap bubble. I want to balance it on my finger as long as possible.

I tinker with the first few chapters for a bit and then when my eyes are heavy, I put my laptop away and give in to the part of the night I dread: cutting off my light. When there's nothing but gaping darkness, the word *alone* seems to pulse around me. It's a salivating monster in every corner.

But tonight, I don't get a chance to listen to the darkness because a dense banging sound thunders through the air. I fly up ramrod straight, my bangs impale my eyeballs, and Ducky shoots from the bed—only a ghost of her fur left behind.

What. The. Hell.

I listen for a minute, squinting into the dark, and then realize it's . . . *hammering*. And it's coming from the direction of my new next-door neighbor. My mouth curves in a distinctly villainous smile because I've been waiting for his retaliation to my petty attempts at ostracizing him from the town. To be honest, I was starting to feel disappointed he wouldn't do anything.

But now I go to my window and open it. Yep, that sound floating on the wind at nine P.M. reeks of retribution. *What a soulless goblin,* I think with a hand over my stomach to quiet the excited hum.

I shut my window and pace my room wondering how I'm going to go about this. Do I put on headphones and white noise, so he doesn't get the satisfaction of knowing he's successfully annoyed me? (Not as fun.)

I'm reaching for my oversized jean jacket before I even have a chance to think twice about my decision. And yes, it is a million degrees outside, but I'm too tired to fully change my clothes, and this satin PJ tank and shorts set is too magnificently thin for Jackson's eyes. I pause at the front door just long enough to hop into my worn old red cowboy boots and instruct Ducky to call the sheriff if I'm not back in thirty minutes.

Suitably clothed, flashlight in hand, I'm off to storm across the front yard. We're still a few days away from June and already the humidity is oppressive, licking at my neck and making the baby hairs around my temples curl up.

When I make it to the front of the house, I sail up the three front porch steps (feeling thankful I didn't fall through from how rotted they look) and knock on the door. And when Jack doesn't stop hammering immediately, I knock louder, my knuckles stinging a little against the wood.

I wouldn't be surprised if he was purposely ignoring my knocks.

Sweat gathers on my back as I wait and wait and wait until I reach the conclusion that he's not coming to the door, and he's not stopping the racket anytime soon either.

I leave the porch and walk around to the side of the house and face the window of the room where the construction seems to be loudest. There's a light on, but I can't see Jack. And because of the way the house was built up off the ground, I can't reach the window either. There's got to be a way to get his attention. *Oh . . . hello, water hose.*

A minute later, after unwinding the hose and turning on the water, I aim it at the window, click the nozzle to firehose-level pressure, and let her rip. The sound of water crashing into the window is so loud that even I jump.

The hammering immediately ceases.

Some primal instinct insists I turn tail and run before I'm

caught, but I hold my ground and continue blasting the water, waiting until Jack surfaces at the window so I can properly tell him what I think of his construction after dark. He never shows, though, and my shoulders hunch in disappointment as I cut the water off.

"Are you finished watering my window?"

I squeal, drop the hose, and whirl around, raising my hands in the air at the sound of his voice behind me. And then when I realize it's just him and not the sheriff coming to take my ass to jail—although I would kindly remind Tony that I bought eight boxes of his daughter's Girl Scout cookies this year and it would probably get me off the hook—I drop my hands to my hips.

"What do you think you're—"

He frowns and holds up a finger, cutting me off. I watch him remove an earplug from his ear. *So that's how he can stand the noise.*

Unfortunately, it's at this moment that I take in the full state of him. Jack—the second-grade teacher who has worked across the hall from me for the last three years in trousers and colorful sweaters and button-downs—is wearing nothing but black slim-fitting athletic shorts, a colorful beaded necklace, too many abs to count, glasses, and a cocky smirk. I'm incapable of doing anything but stare. Gawk. Ogle.

Dear lord. Heavens to Betsy. Good gracious.

I am unwell.

And this is completely unacceptable. His skin is so smooth and taut. He can't look like this under his clothes. My greedy eyes are incapable of doing anything besides sliding across his chest, over his sculpted shoulders, and down his tattooed muscular arms to where his right hand is clutching a hammer. He's a salacious film waiting to happen. Someone's pipes have burst and he's here to fix them. I always knew Jack was well-built and attractive—but this . . . this is a new level.

Once again that terrible thought hits me: Jack is single. And there's no amount of memories or moral obligation to look away out of respect for his fiancée that can keep me from feeling a tug of attraction to him. To keep me from noting how his body is ripped but also somehow very natural and genetic. I don't think he had to work too hard to look like this. He probably woke up one sunny morning and looked in the mirror and thought, *Good God, I'm masculine.*

He's . . . *perfect.* And to top it all off, sweat is clinging to the ends of his hair and dripping down the center hollow of his chest.

How can he be so relaxed and casual about being this exposed in front of me right now? It's some sort of HR nightmare I've stepped into. Or fantasy. No . . . ah—nightmare. *Jack is your nemesis.*

Nemesis, nemesis, nemesis.

The look of enjoyment on Jack's face snaps me out of my trance. "What was it you wanted to say to me, *Emily Stalker?*"

CHAPTER SEVEN

Jack

'm not surprised to find Emily Walker outside my house. I am, however, surprised to find her dressed like *this*. A cream-colored silk top and matching tiny shorts, trimmed with lace—neither covered up enough by the jean jacket—and those damn cowboy boots. The same ones that I was staring at when I had to buy hundreds of dollars' worth of soup from the market and then drive an hour to drop them at a food bank.

Red. The boots are red. They match her nails.

"Why are you out here without a shirt?" she asks, sounding like an indignant debutante and making me wonder if her head is in a similar space as mine.

We are standing in front of each other as a man and a woman—not teachers. This is . . . *new.* And the surge of attraction racing through my system is also new.

"Does it bother you?" I ask with a taunt.

"It's impolite." I think she's blushing.

"But coming over to your neighbor's house in absurdly thin satin pajamas is better?" Oh, judging by her narrowed green eyes, she did not like that. Emily loves to dish it out but can't stand to have her own morality confronted.

Apparently I've just awoken the beast. The pink splotches on her cheeks are gone. Her hands move to her hips. Shoulders set. She will strip naked right now just to prove to me that my barb didn't land.

"From the rumors around town about you knocking over an entire display at Harriet's Market just so you could get a good look at my legs, I'd think you'd be excited to find me in an *absurdly thin* PJ set." She tips her brows. "Yeah, I heard."

So much for buying their secrecy.

"I couldn't help but stare." I pause and smile. "They just looked so real for a humanoid. Your person does incredible work."

"He might be able to find you an actual heart if you want me to ask."

"Nah—I prefer mine frozen and cold."

Emily steps a little closer and my bare skin prickles. "Why are you doing construction right now, Jackson?"

I give her a look that implies how obvious it is. "Because this house is so dilapidated that if I don't work every chance I get, it might collapse on my head."

Her eyes widen slightly. "Please tell me you are not doing your own renovation?"

"Who else would do it? A woman who has nothing better to do with her time than annoy the shit out of me called my contractor and asked him not to take the job. And while she was at it, she told the whole damn town to stay away from me too. You wouldn't know anything about that, would you?"

Emily blinks and looks to the side, clearly biting her cheek to hold back a smile. *Vindictive woman.* "I take it you couldn't find a different crew to take it on?"

"Oh, I did—but they're not available anytime in the next six months."

Not a lick of remorse on her face when she looks in my eyes. In fact, she shrugs and her chin dimples. "Oh well, I guess you'll just have to sell the place and move. I hear the North Pole is nice."

I hold up my trusty hammer. "Why? I've always wanted to build a house. Looks like I finally get my chance."

Her smile falls. "You can't do this renovation yourself, Jack."

"And why's that?"

"Because you're a teacher, not a contractor. Have you ever built anything in your life?"

"If you saw my Lego creations as a kid you wouldn't be asking me that question. Now, if you'll excuse me, I have a wall to finish working on." I head back around the house and up the porch stairs, making it to the landing before I hear the click of Emily's boots following behind.

"You're going to do more work *tonight*?" she asks.

"Yep."

"No. You can't. It's too loud for me and Ducky to sleep."

"Who the hell is Ducky?"

She's trying to peek around me to see in my house. "Ducky is my cat."

I find this endlessly amusing. "Why do you have a cat?"

"To cook in my soup for dinner tomorrow." She rolls her eyes dramatically. "She's my pet! Why else would I have a cat?"

Sometimes it's so hard not to fully smile around her. Not to bust out laughing if I'm being perfectly honest. But I don't because that would just go to her head and make her think she's won this round. (*Which . . . maybe she has.*)

Something else I shouldn't do: notice how the hairs at the back of her neck are curling up. Her bangs too. She always wears her hair perfectly styled to school. But right now, and like the day I saw her with wet hair, it's messy and waving in every direction. A little frizzy. And it's so damn charming. Emily orchestrates and micromanages every facet of her life to perfection, but she can't control her bangs against humidity.

I have the strongest urge to wrap one of those curls around my finger.

"I didn't take you for a pet owner."

"And I didn't take you for someone who would present his nipples to anyone on the other side of his front door, but here we are learning new things about each other," she says, gesturing to my shirtless body. And again, I'm having to smother my laughter. Judging by the sparkle in her eyes, I think she is too.

Finally, she sighs and glances over my shoulder to where I left my front door cracked open. "At least let me see what you've done so far."

Emily takes an advancing side step, but I match her, barricading her from going any farther. In no way can Emily Walker go into my house right now.

"You're really not going to let me see?" Her eyes are wide, mouth slightly parted in disbelief.

"Nope."

"That proud of your work?"

The state of the house has nothing to do with it. Okay, well, maybe it has a few things to do with it. But the main reason I can't let her in there is that nothing escapes Emily's notice. She pays ruthless attention to detail and has the memory of a steel trap. Wouldn't be surprised if she told me she has a photographic memory actually. Which is why I have no doubt that Emily will walk into my house and immediately scent her way to my room, currently littered with sticky notes full of scene ideas for the book I'm due to begin writing soon. Not only that, but books one through three of my Echoes in the Dark series are lying on my bed from where I just scoured through each of them trying to find the one line I needed to reference for the scene I'm writing. She would put two and two together in no time. Less than no time, knowing Emily.

I guard the door, hoping my bare nipples are enough to scare her off. "It's not safe for you in there. There are nails sticking up all over the place."

Her suspicion grows. "I would think you'd like nothing more than for me to go inside and accidentally impale myself so you wouldn't have to deal with me anymore."

"Tempting. But if you died there'd be an investigation and all that. It would take too much time away from the renovation."

"Fine." She turns away. "If it's really that dangerous I don't want to go in." Her boots *clip-clop* back toward the porch stairs and I follow like a bouncer escorting her away from the club.

Of course, it's a mistake on my part, because the moment I leave my post, she fakes me out and darts around my body, right through my front door.

"*Dammit,*" I mutter, hurrying in after her—half expecting her to have somehow teleported directly into my bedroom and skipped the living room altogether. But when I get inside, I nearly run straight into her back. She never made it past the living room.

She's standing here, slack-jawed, blinking at the space. "Jack!" She breathes out my name in awe. Not in awe of how incredible this project is. In awe of how terrible it is.

"To be honest," she starts, as if she's not always brutally honest with me, "I was only joking when I thought you were ashamed of your work. You're one of those people who are good at everything they do, so I didn't expect . . . *this.*"

"I think there might actually be a compliment in there somewhere?"

She's eyeing the kitchen area. "You don't have a stove. Or a fridge."

"Overrated appliances. Have you ever had peanut butter?"

I close the front door and take a few slow steps in her direction (aka closer to my bedroom door) so I can slip by her and close it before she notices. At least that's what I mean to do. Except at the sight of her, I can't move. I'm frozen here, watching Emily Walker assess my new-old house and I realize that possibly for the first time ever in the history of our acquaintance, we are completely alone. Not only that, but I'm not wearing a shirt and she's in the flimsiest pajamas I've ever seen. The satin is so thin it's practically sheer. And the bottoms are cut high. Or maybe it's just that her legs are so long they seem skimpier than the average shorts.

God, if it weren't for that jean jacket . . .

No. Never mind.

Because I don't want to be attracted to Emily. I don't want to find her absurdly beautiful. And I don't want to know why during my months in Nebraska after Zoe and I split, I kept finding myself wondering what Emily was doing at random moments in the day. Even feeling uncomfortable with the prospect of never seeing her again. I hoped it was just because I was bored without my sparring partner, but now, having that memory paired with the attraction curling around my spine, I'm not so sure anymore. What if it's because I missed seeing the glint in her poisonous-green eyes and the curve of her cherry-red mouth?

Those eyes slide to the wall where I've sledgehammered away the inner drywall down to the studs. "Well, this explains all the noise," she says, then cocks her head to the side as she inspects the new studs I put in. "I think those are supposed to be standing at a ninety-degree angle."

"They'll be fine."

She whirls around and she's closer than I realized. She smells good—a fact that's going to be difficult to forget after this night. "This is a house you're going to live in, Jackson. It can't just be fine. What if the roof collapses in on you because you haven't properly installed the studs in the walls?"

"Then you'll get your wish."

Something flashes in her expression. Almost like hurt or regret or worry. It's gone before I can decide. She blinks several times. "I don't want . . ." She pauses and takes a breath. "If you can't hire someone to do this, move out and sell it to someone who can."

I smile, feeling that warning hum of incoming confrontation build under my skin. In the early days, I used to hate the way Emily made me feel in moments like this: a little unhinged and unpredictable. I am always levelheaded and able to pull anyone out of even the worst of moods. But Emily—she's always been immune to my kindness. She draws something venomous out of me. And now, I've learned to lean into it. To welcome it. With her, I can always say exactly what I'm thinking. "What have I told you about barking orders at me?"

She steps closer, angling her defiant chin up to me. My heart beats firmly against my chest, ready for the fight. "You are not qualified for this renovation. It's not going to work. And you can't live on peanut butter sandwiches!"

"Well, now I just have to prove you wrong." I look at her mouth, trying to see if her fangs have dropped down yet.

And because I'm too distracted by the shape of her bottom lip, I miss the moment her hunter's nose catches the scent I've been trying to hide. As if she were some sort of mind-reading sorceress, her head snaps in the direction of my bedroom door. And there, perfectly visible twelve feet from where we are standing, are the sticky notes, stuck to a corkboard and leaning against my bed. She makes a move in that direction, and knowing I can't make it around her in time, I do the only thing I can think of. I take her hand.

I don't just take her hand, though. I accidentally take it *gently*. Tenderly. The word *reverent* even crosses my mind. My hand and body are holding on to Emily in a manner that looks and feels worshipful. And an awareness I've never known before snaps into place: I have more respect for Emily than I've ever had for any other person. *What do I do with that?*

She feels it in my touch and freezes completely before swinging her gaze to where my fingers are intertwined with hers.

"Don't go back there," I say quietly. "Please."

For three torturous seconds when I wonder if I've just handed her ammunition on a silver platter, I study her green eyes. The large freckle at the base of her throat. Her collarbones rising and falling with every breath coming as quickly as my own.

And then she swallows, pivots to face me, and pulls her hand free. She raises it and for a brief second, I wonder if she's going to slap me. Her index finger taps the rim of my glasses instead. "Are these real?"

I huff a laugh. "Of course they're real. Why would I wear fake glasses?"

"So when you came back to town you'd look more intelligent than me."

"I don't have to wear glasses for that to be true."

A thrill twists around my ribs as Emily's hand once again rises, but this time to softly pull the glasses off my face. She tries them on—and although my vision is blurry, I still catch her grimace as she verifies that the lenses are prescription.

Emily holds on to my glasses a beat longer. Her face is still angled up at mine and I wonder if she's using this opportunity to study me. The back of her hand grazes my bare chest in a touch like a bolt of electricity. It takes me a second to realize she's signaling for me to take my glasses back from her.

"I've never seen you wear them before," she says, returning to focus as I replace my frames to my face. I see her with 20/20 vision . . . and the question she's tiptoeing around too.

"Contacts are easier."

"Nope. What's the truth?"

I bite my smile. "You're a relentless pain in the ass."

"Thank you."

I draw in a long breath. "Zoe thought I looked dorky in glasses, so I stuck to contacts. It's really not some big thing. Happy?"

Her face is a study in expression. Open and intrigued and then a steep slope into angry and protective. "No. That answer makes me very unhappy actually. A partner should never make you feel insecure about your glasses. Especially since you look so . . ."

The energy in the room is all off. It's taut. It's charged. It's waiting for something.

"Fine. You look fine in them." She passes me and heads for the door—mercifully never looking back at my room. I should let her go so we can get back to normal as quickly as possible. Put this upside-down night behind us.

"Emily," I say, just before she makes it to the front door. "Before you go, I want to give you something."

I once again close the gap between us—though leaving it wider than before—and pull something out of my pocket. I take her hand in mine and she watches hesitantly as I turn her palm face up and then drop my present inside.

"*Ear plugs,*" she scoffs.

I smile and step away to open the front door for her. "You're going to need those, because I'm going to be in here keeping you up every night this summer while I create the best damn house you've ever seen."

Even though a vicious smile curls her lips, I notice her shoulders sag with relief. She's glad to have the status quo restored too.

"Jackson, I hope you get a really big splinter under your nail bed," she says before her cowboy boots carry her back home where she no doubt falls asleep to the thought of running me over with her truck.

May 31

Jack (8:45 AM): I found a breakfast casserole outside my door this morning. You wouldn't know anything about it, would you?

Emily (8:47 AM): I didn't give you permission to text me.

Emily (8:48 AM): And I have no idea what you're talking about. What's a casserole?

Jack (8:49 AM): I saw you running away from the window after dropping it off.

Emily (8:50 AM): That was my twin.

Jack (8:55 AM): Tell her thank you. It was the best casserole I've ever eaten in my life.

June 1

Jack (7:04 AM): I take back all my charitable words from yesterday. Did you flip the breaker to my AC last night and then put a bike lock on my fuse box?

Emily (7:06 AM): That was my twin . . . ?

JACK (7:07 AM): Your twin forgot to Sharpie over PROPERTY OF EMILY WALKER from the back of the lock.

EMILY (7:10 AM): Hm. Maybe you should have stopped construction last night after I asked nicely the first time.

JACK (7:12 AM): My mistake. I didn't realize yelling "knock it off" through my window was you asking nicely.

EMILY (7:15 AM): You know . . . you sound like someone who is very unhappy with his neighbor. Maybe you should consider moving somewhere else with a neighbor you could enjoy living by.

JACK (7:25 AM): Who said I don't enjoy living by you?

JACK (7:30 AM): *Picture of broken bike lock outside Emily's front door*

JACK (7:31 AM): Your move . . .

CHAPTER EIGHT

Emily

"Thanks again for helping, Em," says Annie, as I carry another bucket of flowers to the trailer hitched to the four-wheeler. "I feel bad you're sacrificing your morning to do this for me—but it's a huge help."

And I know she means it. Annie hates taking up any kind of space—especially when she thinks it's at a cost for anyone else.

"Annie," I say, turning to face my overalls-clad sister. "Helping you is literally a fun activity for me." I wish I could say I was joking, but I couldn't get my boots on fast enough when she called this morning. "And getting to do it on a sunny day at the farm, surrounded by flowers instead of asking twenty second-graders if they heard what I said for the tenth time in an hour? That pretty much makes it a vacation."

She smiles fully, looking like some sort of royal flower nymph in her magical garden. The woman is stunning and glows kindness. She and Maddie share that quality. They possess a charm that makes you want to either be them or be their best friend. Annie is tender, and Maddie is wild, but they're two sides of the same coin. But me . . . I don't think anyone would ever accuse me of being soft.

For instance, a few nights ago when Jack told me Zoe didn't like him in glasses, I have never felt so *unsoft* in all my life. How dare she? First, she's wrong. He looks so sexy in glasses it physically hurts. Second, it's clear he prefers to wear them. What kind of partner would make someone they love feel insecure over something they need to wear? I know from watching Madison's experience with glasses that wearing contacts all the time is miserable. And yet one day, he found out Zoe thought he looked dorky in glasses, so he just took them off and put them in a drawer and left them there. Because that's what he does. He's so considerate of everyone else's feelings (except mine) that he just bends over backward for them. And Zoe took advantage of it.

Why didn't he wear them anyway? Why is he always so damn nice to everyone? And why doesn't he treat anyone else like he treats me? I mean, he's had no trouble pissing me off all week by waiting to start construction until right after I turn off my light to go to sleep. Or intentionally taking my corner table again last Saturday.

I've been retaliating in kind, however. The bike lock on his breaker box was my favorite. But sneaking into his house while he was gone the other day to steal all his nails was a close second. And I even managed to talk Phil into moving all of his boxes of nails to the back and claiming they were out of stock when Jack came sniffing around for more.

It's killing my poor town to ostracize Jack, though. I don't know how much longer I can ask them to keep it up. They like him—and of course they do because everyone loves Jack. He's charming like my sisters—which makes him so much harder to compete with when charm doesn't come naturally for me. It makes me wonder how long it will take for him to sweep everyone off their feet entirely—until they like him better than me.

"Where's Will today?" I ask to distract myself.

Usually Will loves to help Annie any chance he gets. It's rare for her to ask me for anything instead of him these days.

Annie sets another bucket of flowers on the trailer and wipes her forehead with the back of her hand. "He's studying for a test tomorrow."

"Ugh—I do not miss those days."

Annie looks at me with a knowing smile. "Yes, you do."

I laugh. "Fine. I do. Actually, does he need any help? I have excellent study techniques that are just going to waste." Back in college, the only other person I found in the library as often as me was Jack. We were usually the ones closing down the place. I remember how sometimes, when it would get exceptionally late, the empty library would pulse around me. I would feel so alone and sometimes even nervous, until I'd look around and find Jackson several tables away, his nose in a textbook. He never left until I did, and sometimes I wonder if—

"He's thriving actually," says Annie, snapping my attention back into the garden. "I knew he was smart, but it's been incredible to see just how intelligent he really is."

Will has recently had a massive life change. Before he was Amelia's bodyguard, he was in the Air Force. But what he's really always wanted to be is a teacher. Apparently he's always been academically gifted and was even accepted into MIT after high school but chose the military instead as a way to get out from under his toxic parents. But with Annie's support, he decided to finally go for those dreams and enrolled in our nearest private college (my alma mater, I might add). I tried to talk him into working with me at the elementary school, but he's pretty set on either junior high or high school.

Annie and I finish up our work and when all the flowers are snipped and buckets are loaded, she grabs two water bottles from the back of the four-wheeler and gives me one. We both take a minute to cool off—and in these still moments, I can't help but feel nostalgic.

"It's wild to think Mom started this, isn't it?" I say, looking out over the rows and rows of budding flowers—a vast aquamarine sky with dabbles of puffy cotton-ball clouds above. Even this little corner of Rome feels like home. My parents not only worked on this farm but were best friends with the owners (James Huxley's parents). Mom talked them into letting her have a little plot of it for a cheap price to use for her roadside flower business. She always intended to grow it into a brick-and-mortar flower shop in town, but she died before she ever got the chance. Which is why Annie did it for her.

"It is." Annie stares out at it like she's trying to see what I see. "Do you have any memories of them here?"

I have to clench my teeth to stave off the tears. "I do—but . . ." It's hard to get out this next part. "They're getting fuzzier and fuzzier with time."

"Tell me one," Annie says with a soft plea in her voice. She was really young when they died, and I know it hurts her not to have had the chance to know our parents like Noah and I did. Maddie remembers more than Annie, but not by much.

"I'll tell you my favorite memory." I clear my throat and point to the left corner of the flower patch. "Right over there, they had the biggest fight."

Annie's head swings to me—a concerned frown etched between her brows. "Not really the memory I was hoping to get."

I laugh. "They bickered because Mom swore she told Dad they were spreading sunflower seeds on that row, and he swore she told him they were spreading dahlia seeds instead . . . which is why they both had planted two different types of flowers in the same row." A small laugh bubbles out of me when I remember how angry my sweetheart mom was at my dad that day. "She was livid because apparently sunflowers and dahlias are incompatible flowers. Neither will grow well if they're planted together because of something sunflowers do to the soil. Anyway, she felt like all their work for the day went to waste and she just dissolved into tears." I remember Mom always being a big feeler. Like Madison. My gut tugs and it's going to be a struggle to get it out. "But Dad pulled her into a hug and reminded her the two of them were incompatible too, but so far they had gotten along okay." I remember her playfully tickling him after that, which led to a sweet kiss. And when she found me watching, she told me to find someone someday who will hug me when I'm sad and then help me look on the bright side of things when all I can see is the dark.

Grief grows fresh claws in my heart, and the pain of losing them is new all over again.

I screw on the cap to my water bottle and make a big show of looking at my watch like there's somewhere incredibly important I've got to get to. I give Annie a quick hug and avoid her gaze as I walk by her so she can't see my heart bleeding out, but she stops me before I get too far away.

"Wait, Em!" I pause and look back at her. "Did the flowers actually grow or was the crop a bust?"

Whoever said time heals all wounds was a damn liar, because sometimes my heart hurts the worst from the memories that time has erased.

"I can't remember."

———————

Driving has always made me feel better. Not just driving in general, though, but driving on my hometown's back roads in my truck.

I enjoy splurging every now and then and buying something nice. Top-of-the-line bed linens. Quality makeup. Luxurious PJs. But when it comes to my truck, I like it old and rusty. There's just something about driving with my arm out the window on a long stretch of country road when the air is warm and the radio is blasting "Take It Easy" by the Eagles. It's a unique kind of drug.

And that's what I'm doing now, savoring the feel of the sun singeing my forearm and the wind tearing through my hair when I see a person on a sleek black motorcycle—a sports bike—come speeding up the road behind me. The loud engine competes with mine and I expect the person to pass me, but he doesn't. Instead, he hangs back a bit. I check my rearview mirror a few times trying to figure out who it is. I know everyone around here, but I do not know this man. And I'm convinced it is a man judging by his body type. No one drives one of these bikes in Rome either. The kind where you have to lean forward and hug the body of the bike with your thighs.

I glance in the mirror one more time and study the rider. He's wearing black leather gear (not the Harley-Davidson riding kind, but the nimble racer–type material), and it would appear black is his favorite color since his outfit matches his bike. Black as ink. The visor of his helmet is pulled down and it's so tinted I can't see through it. Maybe I'm experiencing what's universally known as the Helmet Effect, but a pleasant chill runs down my spine at the sight of him. He could be a troll under that helmet and as long as the visor is shut, he would be the sexiest man alive to me.

He must have noticed me looking at him because next time I peek, he raises his black glove in a relaxed, amused wave, and somehow I just know that he's smiling under that helmet.

Maybe it's because I need to fully escape the lingering pain that visiting the flower patch brought on, but I find myself deciding to play a little. I raise my hand outside the window in my own casual wave. Just a friendly hello.

Next thing I know, his engine is revving and he's curving around me to ride right up beside the window of my truck. I squeal and dart my gaze back and forth between him and the long open road ahead of us.

"Stop!" I yell, but I can't keep a laugh from bubbling through my voice. "That's not safe!"

His helmet looks in my direction and he does a very theatric *me?* gesture, pointing his index finger at his chest.

"Yes, you! Don't be so reckless!"

This time he puts his hand to his helmet, pretending like he's cupping his ear. He then shrugs and opens his engine up, tearing off ahead of me in the oncoming lane and popping a wheelie.

I scream and pray to anyone listening that this man doesn't tip over backward and crash while trying to be a show-off for me. But a few seconds later, he sets the front end back down like it was nothing. An oncoming car is approaching a ways up the road now, so he holds out his right arm, gesturing that he's going to enter my lane. *Suddenly so responsible.* A moment later, he leans to the right and cruises in front of me. I don't want to, but I have to admit, I'm more than enjoying this interaction.

After the car passes by and he sees the road is wide open once again, he drops in beside me. Apparently he's enjoying this as much as I am because the fool points at me and then balances the bike with no hands so he can hold up a heart to his chest before once again pointing his index finger, but this time to himself. I'm laughing so hard I nearly have tears in my eyes. But still, I shake my head and wave him off, so he'll leave before he gets himself hurt.

He's sitting upright on the bike now, left arm holding the handlebar and the rest of his body angled casually in my direction. He cocks his head like he's waiting for me to play again, so I yell, "*I've seen better.*" Even though I absolutely haven't. Maybe it's just the pads in his leather gear, but I can't help but notice how good his body looks. I'll never know for sure, and maybe that's a good thing.

He presses the back of his hand to his head. *A comedian.* I have no idea who this guy is but I'm starting to wish I did. There's no way he's from around here, though. Must be passing through.

Just up ahead is my turn and I feel a tug of disappointment knowing I'll have to say goodbye to this random sexy speed racer. I motion to the approaching turn and wave my goodbye to him. At least I'll always have this memory of the man on the bike flirting with me.

He mimes a tear running down the front of his helmet and then gives me one final wave, dropping back behind my truck once again. My heart sinks as I turn onto my road, and I realize the fun is over.

But then that feeling is replaced with an entirely different one when I notice that he turns with me.

Ohmygod.

Is he following me?

Maybe I shouldn't have flirted so hard with a stranger like that. Oh lord, what if he's a murderer? What's the protocol here? Do I keep driving so he doesn't know my location? But . . . I don't get the feeling he's a creep. Then again maybe I'm once again experiencing the Helmet Effect.

I'm trying to decide what to do as I approach my driveway, but he makes up my mind for me when he suddenly slows way down, dropping back. But then he turns the bike sharply. Right into . . . Jack's driveway.

Oh my god, please no. This can't be what I think it is. Please please please tell me that Jackson is not the man beneath that helmet! Why can't he just be a serial killer? I'd like to go back to that option, please!

I'm still holding out hope that maybe this is simply someone coming to visit Jack as I steer into my driveway too and we ride parallel to each other up the gravel until we're both parked. He turns his head, black visor pointed in my direction, and I watch with a sinking feeling as he lifts that damn visor and reveals Jackson's face.

Son of a bitch.

I'm out of my truck in two seconds flat without even shutting the door. He sees the fury in my eyes and pulls his helmet off while putting down the kickstand and jumping off the bike. I'm around my truck in record time aiming for my house.

"Emily, wait!"

"No!" I yell without looking back at him. I hear him toss his helmet to the ground and rip off his gloves, and then the crunch of gravel as he runs to me. I walk even faster, trying to make it into the house before he can reach me, but I'm out of luck. His long legs eat up the ground, and he's racing behind me on the stairs.

"Go away, you asshole!"

"Emily, please. Let me—"

"No!" I shove my key into the front door lock and frantically jiggle it, willing it to open on the first try for once. I don't like change and this sticky lock has always been like a little decadent morsel of familiarity. This is the first time I've wished it was a properly functioning lock. "You catfished me! I don't want to hear anything you have to say."

Embarrassment is clawing at me from under the surface of my anger. Jack has done some annoying things, but this is maybe the lowest.

"Yes, I did." His voice is firm behind me. I feel him at my back. I see his shadow at my feet, and I want to stomp it.

And the key won't turn in the damn lock! I should have replaced it ages ago. All I want is to get inside my house where I can shut the door in his face. I feel so tricked. So vulnerable.

"Will you turn around, please?" he asks with urgency.

"No. You purposely misled me so you could humiliate me! Congratulations—you accomplished what you wanted." The lock finally gives way and I sigh with relief as I wrench the door open.

I fly inside and try to immediately shut the door, but his hand catches it before I can, holding it open a few inches. "I did *not* set out to humiliate you. I'm sorry if that was the result."

"What a half-assed apology."

His eyes burn. "It *was* half-assed. Because that's the only part I'm sorry for."

I laugh once and without humor. "That's low, Jack, even for you."

"And I would do it all over again."

"Thanks. I've heard enough." I try to force the door closed, but he holds it firm, his face leaning closer to catch my gaze through the opening.

"I'm not sorry you thought I was someone else because for once I got a taste of what it's like to be a person you don't hate, and I . . ." He stops, his chest heaving. He seems to think better of whatever he was going to say, but I've played enough *Jeopardy!* to solve the puzzle. *He liked it.* "I can't bring myself to regret that."

He's breathing heavily but I don't think I'm breathing at all.

"Please don't feel embarrassed." His voice is softening. "There was nothing to be embarrassed about. You were having fun, and . . ." A sad sort of smile tugs at his mouth. "I had fun too. I'm sorry, Emily. I'm so sorry I humiliated you—*that* was never what I meant to happen."

"Then what *was* your intention?"

"When I pulled up behind you, I forgot you didn't know I owned a bike. And then when you smiled at me so openly, I realized you didn't know who I was. And I just wanted to see if . . ." Again he stops, but I'm not sure of how he was going to finish it this time.

But I have a hunch.

My grip loosens on the door. I'm not quite sure where to go from here or what to do with what he just said, but I do know two things for certain:

1. I did have fun with him out there.
2. Jack Bennett just apologized to me.

"Why did you do that?" I ask, looking him right in the eye so he can see that even though I'm humiliated, I'm not a coward.

His head tilts. "Flirt with you?"

That is a question I didn't even consider asking, and even though I desperately want that answer now, I continue with my first. "No—why did you apologize?" It goes against everything we've ever been to each other.

He drops his hand, and when I don't immediately slam the door in his face, his shoulders relax. "Because I may be a lot of things, but I never want to be the kind of person who can't apologize when I'm in the wrong. I grew up around someone who was a real dick and never said he was sorry . . . so, I don't know, I just don't want to repeat his pattern. And I was firmly in the wrong today. So again, I'm very sorry."

Huh. Jack as a child—there's a thought. Jack with a motorcycle. Jack with an entire life outside of school. Jack as a multifaceted human.

My gaze drops from his eyes to his neck where his sweat-dampened hair is clinging to his skin, all the way down his jacket to his hands, where his gloves were a few minutes ago. A memory of those gloved hands raising to me in an amused lazy wave flashes and I should have instinctively known it was him. Effortlessly sexy has always been his thing.

But outside of our first bad encounter on the way to class, he's never used it on me. It was . . . *interesting* to be on this side of it without the usual bad blood flowing between us.

According to Jack, he saw an opportunity and took it. I don't know . . . maybe it's time I do the same.

"When did you get a motorcycle?"

His expression is hesitant of my abrupt change in subject, like he's preconditioned to watch out for any unexpected grenades I might throw at him. "I've had it for a few years."

"How come I've never seen it before?"

A bead of sweat rolls down his temple and he catches it with his forearm. "I only ride during the nice-weather months. And during the school year, my commute was too far, so I pretty much only rode on the weekends."

I don't like the thought of him riding that thing on the interstate. Can't say I like the idea of him riding it at all actually. It was one thing when it was just a stranger I'd never care about but now—wait, no . . . I didn't mean that I care about him. *Take it back, brain!*

"Have you ever ridden?" he asks, unlatching the top of the leather jacket and unzipping it before peeling it off, leaving him in only a sweaty white T-shirt and riding pants. And yep, I can confirm it was not just the pads making his body look so good—damn him.

I take a reflexive step away. "No, I have not."

He smiles and runs his hand through his hair. "Do you want to? I have a spare helmet at my hou—"

"*Absolutely not.* I value my life too much to put it in your hands like that."

His head tilts. "My hands are very competent, Emily."

I bypass Jack's innuendo and the funny thing it does to my stomach, and instead, I advance on him. I go out the door, backing him up until he's forced to go down a step. We're eye level now and

I'm only inches from his face. I've been working through something during our idle chat, and I just made up my mind.

He looks braced for a slap and can only blink in response when I say, "I forgive you."

Understandably Jack is silent for a long moment. This is new terrain for both of us.

"You . . . forgive me?" he repeats, shifting on his feet and looking between my eyes. "Is this a trap? Are you trying to lure me into passivity so you can stab me in the back when I least expect it?"

What a twisted relationship we have.

"Maybe," I say, smiling at him over my shoulder as I go back into my house—leaving the door wide open behind me. "Or maybe I'm already holding too many grudges where you're concerned and don't feel like adding any more to the pile. We'll have to wait and see, I guess."

I don't know what I'm doing leaving that door open. Jack doesn't either, judging by the look on his face as he cautiously steps inside. He watches me slip out of my boots and hang my purse on the hook.

His shoulders suddenly jump, and he looks down—startled by Ducky, who is now wrapping herself around his ankle.

"What is that?" he asks as if his eyes are betraying him.

"A cat."

"You really do have a cat."

"You thought I was lying?" I laugh, scoop her up, and nuzzle my face into her fur. Now he really looks like he's seen a ghost as he watches me snuggle her. Apparently he thought I went home every night and plugged myself into the wall to recharge.

"I'll admit," he says, cautiously, "I've always pictured you as more likely to wear animals than snuggle them."

"First, that's horrendous and I never would. Second . . ." I lift a brow. "Just how often *do* you picture me, Jackson?" I guess a little of that flirtation from the road has lingered.

His smile is a feral thing. "More than either of us is comfortable with."

Oh.

He steps in a little farther and does a complete circle, seemingly taking in the scenery. It makes me nervous. I love my house and my décor, but I live on a teacher's budget. Everything is pretty minimalist because I enjoy a tidy space. Big white couch. Cozy blankets. Pottery vases passed down from my grandma. Golden-toned, wooden breakfast table and chairs acquired from a yard sale. But there are a few choice pieces in my house that I saved and scraped and eventually splurged on, like my couch, my cushy area rug, and my mattress. Those things were nonnegotiable for me.

Having Mr. Top-of-the-Line-Everything in here is making me antsy. "I wasn't expecting company."

"Is that why there's one coaster out of place?" he asks, pointing to the rogue one sitting on the arm of my couch instead of the coffee table.

I hurry across the room and return it to its pile, then realize it was a trap. Jack's motorcycle boots creak on the floor as he moves around slowly to run his eyes over every corner of my space. I half expect him to be taking pictures of anything slightly incriminating. He'll point and laugh at any mess he can find.

"You decorate your house like your classroom," he says, eyeing an end table I picked up at Thrift N' Stuff.

"Well, not all of us are willing to live outside of our means, and—"

He turns to me with a smile. "Let me stop you there. That wasn't in any way a criticism." His smile is so warm right now I could roast a marshmallow in front of it. "You have the best classroom at school. Every year I find myself just trying to keep up. And you thrift a lot of your stuff, right? I think I heard you tell Shirley that once. It's amazing. Your classroom feels like walking into a home every year."

Did Jack just compliment me? Like an outright, blatant *compliment*. And honestly, it was the greatest one he could have ever given me.

Since the classroom is where my students spend the majority of their days during the school year, I want it to feel like a second home for them. Or maybe a first home when I know they don't get the love and attention they deserve from their parents.

Every year at least one of my students goes through something terribly difficult. It's a fact of life. It was a fact of *my* life when my parents died mid-school year. And when it happened to me, I didn't have a teacher who strove to make my days at school comforting and safe. That's why I got my degree and teaching license and decided to become the second-grade teacher I needed back then.

And for me, the first step in creating that comfort is ambiance. I strive to make it look like a cozy living room with nice rugs, standing lamps, cushy chairs in various places, and a peace corner where kids can escape to when they need a minute to themselves full of things like fidgets and cute stuffies to snuggle. (All of which are fire marshal approved.) Most people think I spend a lot of money on my classroom décor, but in reality, like Jack said, almost everything is donated or acquired through yard sales and thrift shops. My siblings like to drop stuff off for me now and then too.

Every teacher in our school tries to make their classrooms special in some way, but Jack is the only other one who has ever gone as overboard as me with his decorating. Where my room is a cozy escape, Jack's classroom is always a sensory explosion. Not in a bad way—but engaging. It's colorful in all the right places. I would have hated him for how amazing his classroom is if I didn't also know how much the children deserve it.

"Thank you," I say, hesitantly. "I just want the kids to feel peaceful when they're with me."

He nods. "I need you to go shopping with me when it's time to furnish my house. You have an eye for decorating that I don't." He pauses and grins. "Though I imagine you'd struggle with the amount of color I'd want. If you haven't noticed I lean toward retro colors. Reds, warm brown. Green."

As he says it, my beige living room automatically repaints itself in my mind. I've never considered it before, but . . . suddenly it seems even cozier.

And then, as if he hasn't just completely blown my mind with apologies and compliments and statements about shopping for home goods together, he casually turns to my bookshelf/record collection and peruses my inventory. Natural as can be.

I've been openly collecting old records for a while, but my romance book collection has been tucked in a box beneath my bed until last year when I found out my sisters shared the same love of delicious bodice-ripping romances, and I moved them proudly to the bookshelf in my living room. Jack isn't looking at the romances, though; his eyes are focused on the top shelf at my small collection of mystery novels. It consists of two series. Both were given to me by Noah because he wanted to be included in our book club but didn't own any romance novels.

Jack's body is unnaturally still. If not for the subtle rise and fall of his broad shoulders, I might have thought he stopped breathing.

"Jack?"

"I've gotta go," he says quickly on the heels of his name. He pauses on his way out the door. "Thank you . . . for accepting my apology."

And then he's gone.

June 4

EMILY (9:45 AM): I googled the stats on motorcycles last night.

JACK (9:48 AM): Needed some light happy reading before bed?

EMILY (9:50 AM): They're very dangerous. Not a little dangerous. Very.

JACK (9:52 AM): I know, isn't it great?

EMILY (9:55 AM): No more wheelies.

JACK (9:58 AM): But you liked the last one I did so much . . .

EMILY (10:00 AM): NO MORE WHEELIES.

JACK (10:01 AM): Careful, it almost seems like you care about my well-being.

EMILY (10:02 AM): . . . No more wheelies.

JACK (10:02 AM): All right. No more wheelies.

CHAPTER NINE

Jack

There's been something odd in the air the last several days. When I walk through town, everyone waves. Normally people in town eye me with sad regret before turning away. Now they're smiling and waving, though? And yesterday, at the market while I was stocking up on my sad peanut butter again, Harriet not only mentioned that softball tryouts would be happening soon and she hoped to see me there, but she also applied a coupon that I didn't even know existed.

If that wasn't strange enough, The Diner wasn't mysteriously out of pancakes this morning. They've been subbing my order with stale bread since day one, but today, Jeanine brought me a huge stack of pancakes with a complimentary side of bacon along with the biggest smile I've ever seen.

And I hate it.

It's all wrong. It feels like the town has chosen my side over Emily's—and in the past, I might have enjoyed that. Strived for it even. But right now, it's oddly eating me up. I have no idea when I started caring what Emily wants. I just know that keeping the town in line to shun me is now my top priority. I refused the coupon. I sent the stack of pancakes back. Phil hand-delivered several boxes of nails to my house earlier, and I told him I didn't want them.

I think this is what officially losing your mind feels like. My actions are the opposite of logical. It's all mayhem.

Currently, I'm leaving the town parking lot on my way to the coffee shop where the teenage baristas don't care if I live or die as long as they get a paycheck. And I'm wearing a hat with my head ducked as I move swiftly down the sidewalk—hoping to fly under the radar so townspeople don't pop out of nowhere and try to gift me nice things.

And that's probably why I slam right into a woman whose arms are full of various shopping bags. I mumble an apology while grabbing her around the waist to steady her, but she probably can't even hear me over the soundtrack of crinkling paper bags. "Sorry! I didn't see—"

"Jackson!" Oh, it's Emily. And she does not look happy.

It's history repeating all over again. I'm back in college, looking down at the prettiest woman I've ever seen, and she looks like she wants to slap me. At least there's no coffee involved this time. And I definitely won't be hitting on her either.

"Emily, sorry! I wasn't looking where I was—"

"Why are you not accepting everyone's kindness?" She's wearing white shorts, a tan button-up tank top blouse, and that same clip in the back of her hair, holding it up off her neck. Her bangs are styled today, though, swooping purposely to her temples to frame her face. Her face that looks mad as a hornet.

"I . . . *what?*"

She adjusts her stance to fold her arms saucily while wearing big paper shopping bags like bracelets. The pop of her red polish against her white and tan clothing draws my eye and then forces me to connect the dots all the way up to the matching color on her lips. I'm having trouble focusing because of it.

Her cherry mouth moves. "I have it on good authority that Mabel brought you a tray of homemade cinnamon rolls yesterday morning and you refused them. Do you not like to eat delicious things?"

"I very much love to eat delicious things."

"Are you gluten intolerant?"

"No."

"Lactose intolerant?"

"Not that I know of."

"Are you kindness intolerant, then?"

"Well . . . I've never been officially tested but I suppose anything is possible." I smile as her scowl only deepens. An angry little fireball. That's what Emily is ninety percent of the time. Why the hell do I enjoy stepping right in her path so much?

There's that tug again. The one that keeps drawing me to her.

"You're supposed to accept their gifts," she responds, like this is a fact.

"I am?"

"If you actually want to live in this town, then you're supposed to accept them. Promise me you'll accept them from now on."

"Okay," I promise even though I'm at somewhat of a loss as to what's happening at this moment. "I thought . . . I thought you hated having me here."

"I do," she says primly while adjusting the bags on her arm an inch to the left.

"And I thought you were trying to get rid of me."

"I am." She looks to her left. "I was."

I cock my head, eyebrow lifting. "*Was?* That's an interesting word."

Emily's green eyes snap to mine. "I've decided to have pity on the town. It's killing them to exclude you, and Harriet is dying to have you on the softball team. No matter how I feel about you . . . I love my town. I'm willing to let you be part of it for their sake." She pauses. "So . . . I told them I wanted you to be included from now on."

"Huh."

Her eyebrows drop. "That's all you're going to say? *Huh?* I thought you'd be happier."

I take a step to the right, out from under the awning, and look up at the sky.

"What are you doing?"

"Looking for flying pigs . . ."

She scoffs and rolls her eyes, but I still catch the curve of her lips before she smothers it.

"No, seriously? Has hell frozen over? Because I never thought I'd see the day that Emily Walker wanted me to be happy."

She holds up a finger. "I never said I *wanted* you to be happy. I said I thought you'd *be* happy. There's a difference."

I'm grinning and she obviously hates it. "This is such an unexpected turn of events." Not an unhappy one, either. Because I've always enjoyed teaching here in Rome, but now actually living in the town and seeing how it operates, I can really see myself living here happily for a long time. I like its quirks. I like the way I feel here.

And . . . I like getting to know Emily in a different way too. I thought that by coming back and seeing her again, I would prove to myself that I really and truly hated her with no room for any other feelings toward her.

So far, only the opposite is proving true.

Her eyes are bobbing everywhere. "Well—I aim to keep you on your toes." She pauses and presses her lips together like she doesn't know what to say next but isn't eager to leave. "Okay, I should . . . go."

"What's with all the bags? Not going to your favorite corner table today?" I ask, not ready to let go of this moment yet.

"Oh." She breathes a smile, and it jolts me back to the one she gave me on the road the other day when she didn't realize it was me. I've been chasing the high of it all week. And the one after where she let me in her house. Where we talked like something damn near friends for the first time. Sort of like how we're talking now.

"Not today. Madison is flying in for a quick trip. It's been a long time since she's been back, so I wanted to stock the house with all of her favorite things." She's got a little something from everywhere. Baguettes peeking out from the top of a Gemma's Breadbasket bag. What looks like several different kinds of Doritos packed into a bag from the market. Even one from the Pie Shop that definitely has more than one pie inside.

"She probably doesn't even miss them all that much, but I just thought—" She pauses and sets down her bags to pull her phone out. "Oh my god, I have service right here? It's a miracle." Her face lights up as she answers. "Hey, Maddie, are you about to board the . . ." She stops, and I watch as her smile slowly fades. She turns and takes three steps away from me. "*Oh*—no, of course you should stay! Oh my gosh, yes. Don't even think twice about it . . . yeah, that's a huge opportunity . . . oh please, I'm totally fine." She forces a laugh. "I'm serious, Maddie, it's all good. You caught me just before I left to get all the stuff." A longer pause this time and with every passing second I see Emily's shoulders sink lower and lower. "Okay. Have so much fun! Take pictures!"

She laughs again, then tells her she loves her before hanging up.

I don't say anything as Emily silently replaces her phone in her back pocket and takes a few seconds, just staring out at nothing.

Her shoulders rise and fall rapidly like she's trying not to cry, and then she takes one final large breath and turns as she lets it out. A fake smile put right back in place.

"Was that Maddie?" I ask even though I already know the answer.

"Sure was," she says in a chipper tone that grates on me.

"Is she on her way?"

Emily blinks several times—obviously trying to keep tears from building. "She had an important opportunity come up in New York and can't make it home after all." She bends to pick up each of her packages, and when I start to help she snaps at me. "I've got them."

"Emily . . . are you okay? I know you were excited—"

"Stop," she barks. "You don't know me. I am perfectly fine. Everything is just *fine.*"

Emily walks away and I don't try to stop her. In the past, I would use this encounter as another reason to keep hating her. To feed this animosity with unrelenting energy. We've had more than ten years of this cycle—so of course it's easy to slip right back into. But the smile she gave me in the truck surfaces in my mind again, and suddenly, chasing this old feud doesn't seem nearly as appealing as chasing that smile.

10 YEARS AGO

FROM: Jack Bennett ‹Bennett.Jack@Greenfield.edu›
TO: Emily Walker ‹Walker.Emily@Greenfield.edu›
DATE: Tue, Dec 9 9:45 PM
SUBJECT: Library

Did you two just break up?

FROM: Emily Walker ‹Walker.Emily@Greenfield.edu›
TO: Jack Bennett ‹Bennett.Jack@Greenfield.edu›
DATE: Tue, Dec 9 9:47 PM
SUBJECT: Library

What? No. He just left to go to bed.

Why the hell are you still here? Don't you need to go home and polish your horns before a fresh day of terrorizing tomorrow?

FROM: Jack Bennett ‹Bennett.Jack@Greenfield.edu›
TO: Emily Walker ‹Walker.Emily@Greenfield.edu›
DATE: Tue, Dec 9 9:49 PM
SUBJECT: Library

I just couldn't think of another reason why he'd leave
you alone in the library fifteen minutes before closing
late at night if not because you broke up. But I guess
it's just because he's an idiot.

I'm still here because I'm studying for the same
test as you—the one I plan to score higher on than you.

(My horns *are* looking dull. What polish do you
usually use for yours?)

FROM: Emily Walker ‹Walker.Emily@Greenfield.edu›
TO: Jack Bennett ‹Bennett.Jack@Greenfield.edu›
DATE: Tue, Dec 9 9:58 PM
SUBJECT: Library

He is not an idiot. He has an early shift at the cafe
before class. And I don't need him to hang around and
babysit me after dark.

FROM: Jack Bennett ‹Bennett.Jack@Greenfield.edu›
TO: Emily Walker ‹Walker.Emily@Greenfield.edu›
DATE: Tue, Dec 9 10:00 PM
SUBJECT: Library

Fine. You may not be scared of the bogeyman, but I am,
which is why I plan to walk right behind you all the way
to our cars and let him get you first. See you outside.

CHAPTER TEN

Emily

I'm on the floor and a little drunk.

I didn't mean to get drunk. I was perfectly sober before I started drinking.

But Madison didn't come home. I got all her favorite things, and I cleaned her room and I felt hopeful and excited for the first time in a while and . . . she canceled. At the last minute she was offered an opportunity to shadow a big-time chef in a famous kitchen. She couldn't pass it up. I don't want her to pass it up. But I also want her to come home. I need her to come home—but she doesn't need me. No one needs me. And when they don't need me, they don't come around anymore either because I am a utility sponge. I am useful. And if I'm no use to someone anymore, they throw me under the sink.

Ugh. I press the bottle of wine straight to my lips but there's not a single drop left. But before anyone is too concerned about me, the bottle wasn't full when I started.

I tried everything to distract myself from the ache. I cleaned my fridge and completely rearranged my closet and then scrubbed my floors with a toothbrush because usually that makes me feel better when nothing else does, but none of those things worked this time. As a last-ditch effort I turned on an audiobook for a little background noise and the next thing I knew, I was sobbing on the floor and clutching a bottle of wine in my pajamas because the hero loved the heroine and I'm never going to be loved! No one wants me! I'm all alone in this life!

Oh, this cat bed is on sale.

I set my empty wine bottle aside so I can click *Buy Now* on the cat bed. Ducky purrs on the floor beside me, curled up against my legs. "You love me right, Ducky? As long as I feed you and snuggle you and shower you with gifts, you're not going to leave me behind for a better life somewhere?" A hiccup jumps out of me. "And it'd be great if you could not die. I hate when people die." I lean my head back against the wall. "Dying sucks because it hurts so bad in here . . ." I slap my hand against my chest. "And there's nothing I can do about it." I close my eyes and then get struck with another thought. "You can't get married either. That's against the girl code. If we're going to live out our lives as thriving spinsters, you can't ditch me for a hot alley cat you meet in the city. And listen . . . I like to crack the eggs, okay? Because I don't like eating shells, so you're going to have to be okay with that."

Ducky is sound asleep. Not listening to a word I say.

"Fine. Get your beauty sleep. I'll just make myself busy until you wake up."

I click around on my laptop some more and then find myself staring at my manuscript. I aimlessly scroll through all eighty thousand words of it and wonder for the millionth time what I should do with it. Is it any good? I have no idea. And that really, really scares me. The idea of sending this out for submission and epically failing scares the shit out of me. What if this little mustard seed dream has sprouted into a giant beanstalk-size dream, but I'll never catch it? *Beanstalk,* of course, has me thinking of Jack, which has me imagining his taunting smile and telling me I'm braver than this.

And then I think of Madison facing a huge city by herself and going after her dreams. I think of Annie opening a flower shop all on her own. I think of Noah taking a chance on love and getting freaking married. To a pop star. And then I zoom out and find me, on the floor, drunk and with no plans for my future. Suddenly this thought is unbearable. The darkness I keep running from opens up in front of me and offers to keep me warm for the next few days.

Instead, I fight.

I don't want to be consumed with loneliness. I don't want that to be my secret defining characteristic. I want to look forward to something. I want to chase my dreams. I wrote a book! I wrote a book that I love and enjoyed every second of creating. I found a balm for my soul, and I want to keep pursuing it. So here we go . . . I'm going to submit it to an agent for representation!

Yes, this is suuuuuch a good idea.

And because I'm me, I don't even have to worry about being too drunk to write something coherent. I've been toying around with the idea for a few days now and so in true Emily style, I have crafted a query letter based on advice from many different online articles and tinkered with this book until I've felt like it's maybe not complete junk. So you know what? Armed with liquid courage, now seems like the perfect time to send it off. If my siblings are going after their dreams, I can too.

I've researched hundreds of literary agents and narrowed down my list to the ten that I felt would most like my story. One at the very top of my list: Barbara Morgan. She isn't the biggest agent in the business, but the books she's sold so far are incredible, and I like how in her bio she says she loves stories and getting lost in them but loves the humans behind them more and enjoys getting to bring their dreams to life. My gut says we'd be a good fit.

The Internet told me to write one query letter and to just change the name for each agent before sending, but that feels lazy and half-assed to me. So I've written ten unique emails spelling out why I am reaching out to each individual and the exact reasons I think my book would be a good fit for them.

I open the first one now—*get ready, Barbara*—and attach the query letter. The Internet says not to include the full manuscript unless asked to do so, but this just feels like a silly oversight to me, so I include it anyway. Save Barbara a step. *What a good decision.*

Before I have time to second-guess, I click the little white arrow and listen to my email whoosh through the interwebs. I bask in the glow of a monumental moment and turn my eyes to Ducky. "Well, I hope you're happy. You missed my potentially life-changing event." She squints her eyes tighter trying to block me out. "Fine. I'll leave you alone."

Just for kicks and giggles, I open the email I just sent and reread it. It all looks great. Flawless, even if my slightly drunk brain does say so itself. Yep, everything is in order. Except . . . *wait.* Something feels off. I keep reading it over and over again trying to figure out what the prodding sensation is in the back of my head. Like I'm seeing something wrong but can't register it. I get closer to the screen and mumble as I read. "Hello, Barbara, I am seeking representation for . . . blah blah blah . . . from Emily Walker . . . to . . ." I gasp. "*No.*"

No, no, no.

This can't be right. It has to be a trick of the alcohol in my system. (Although even I don't think I'm that drunk.)

Oh. My. God.

It seems I've mixed up the emails and somehow just sent my

very explicit romance novel that no one in the world knows I've written directly to the inbox of my school's very, very conservative principal, Bart Killick. This simply can't be true.

But it *is* true. It's there on the screen staring back at me as proof.

I have to fix this! I have to get it back. But how? I can't even think straight through my tipsy brain. Is there a way to grab something from the Internet after it's already shot through time and space? How does the Internet work and why don't I know more about it?

I can barely breathe. What if I get fired for this? How could I have gone from triumphant to my life might be over in a matter of sixty seconds?

The only thought that crosses my mind is: *Help*. And there's only one person that I really trust to fix it. For our feuds and faults through the years, there's one thing I know without a doubt about Jackson—he is the most competent person I've ever met. That's why he's my greatest rival. If anyone can find a way to get my email back into my computer, it's him.

Desperate times call for desperate measures.

I slap my laptop shut and shoot up from the floor. The hollow wine bottle clanks against the hardwood, scaring Ducky in an unforgivable way. But there's no time. I shove my feet down into my red cowboy boots and then hightail it outside. While sprinting across the lawn, I trip on a lump of dirt, and drop to my knees for one embarrassing moment. Every second counts, though, so I haul myself back to my feet and jog to Jack's front door, ignoring my stinging knees.

"Jack! Open up!" I yell while pounding on the door.

Almost immediately I hear Jack's thundering footsteps approach. The door swings open and there's Jackson in his athletic shorts, tugging a navy T-shirt into place. "What the he—" His eyes drop over me and he frowns, taking a hasty step closer to touch my elbow. "*Emily*. What's wrong? What happened?" He's lifting my arm to assess the mud clump I didn't know was sticking to my elbow.

I pull my arm from his grasp and can only swim through the alcohol's haze fast enough to blurt, "At my house! I need your help."

He's little more than a streak as he dashes from his porch, plowing across the yard. I follow after him, barely able to keep up.

Jack barrels into my house so aggressively I'm surprised the door is still on its hinges.

"Where is he?" Jack growls, looking around like a man possessed.

"*What?* Who?"

When he doesn't immediately see anyone, he turns back to me. The room sways a little. "The intruder."

"There's no intruder. Why do you think there's an *intruder*?" That word was difficult to get out the second time. I hold my wobbly head.

"Because you said . . ." Now he looks confounded. "Emily. You ran over to my house in whatever you call what you're wearing—"

"PJs."

"—frantic, with your knees and elbows caked in mud."

"Because I tripped on the way over."

"You said *help*. I thought for sure someone was in your house."

"I'm a little bit drunk." I say this, and it sounds too close to tears for my taste.

Jack's voice softens. "Which only adds to my panic. So tell me now—are you okay? Are you hurt in any way?"

I'm staring at him. Trying to get my hazy brain to make sense of his expression. The fear in his eyes and his racing breath. "You're worried about me?"

A heavy breath drops from his mouth. "Yes! Of course. I mean, *shit,* what kind of monster do you think I am that I wouldn't see you like this and immediately worry?" He gets closer to me. Tentatively. "Tell me you're okay. I need to hear you say it." His eyes run over me one more time but it's more like the look a triage nurse would give you to see if you need to be admitted to the hospital or if you're overreacting.

I cover my face with my hands. The shame of running across the yard, drunk and caked in dirt, has had a delayed response. It's here now and brought all its baggage to stay a while. How could I be so irresponsible? How could I have made so many mistakes in one day? I want to crawl in a hole. I want to hide and never come out.

"Emily?"

"No one hurt me. I'm okay. But I'm just . . . tipsy." I point to the empty wine bottle as evidence. "And I need you to hack into the Internet and bring my email back."

He's frozen, wide-eyed. "Other than the part about you being drunk, nothing you just said makes sense."

"I sent an email! To Bart! And I need it back. Immediately. *Please, Jack.*"

He looks toward my empty, turned-over wine bottle on the floor next to my laptop, and then back to me. "So this is not an emergency?"

"*It is,*" I slur, and get close to him so I can press the heels of my fists against his chest. "Why don't you understand me?" I've never been so frustrated to be drunk in all my life. I need my brain to work right now, and it won't. I need to be Emily Walker, oldest sister who can handle any problem, but I can't find her tonight. All I see is this sad, pathetic woman who hurts and hurts and hurts.

Jack softly wraps his hands around my wrists, cradling them. "I'm listening, Emily. What do you need?"

"I need you to fix it."

"Name it. I'll do it for you." He sounds like he means it.

"Roll back time," I say, and I can't tell anymore if I'm talking about this or about the man holding my wrists.

His eyes drop to my wobbling lips. He stares—his chest expanding with a deep breath while he holds me with the lightest touch. This alcohol has turned me transparent. He sees all the truth swimming in my veins. *Regret. Pain. Loneliness. Helplessness.* "Whatever it is, you're going to be okay. I promise. I'll make sure of it."

Tears I haven't let myself shed in years stream down my cheeks. They burn.

"Which way is your closet?" he asks softly, almost like he's scared to startle me. What I must look like to him to warrant this coddling. I'm broken glass in his hands, and it's going to be unbearable to remember tomorrow.

I point down the hall. "I don't think we're the same size."

He lets go of me with a five-star smile. I watch his retreating back slip down the hallway and into my room. A second later he emerges, my light pink silk robe clutched in his hand.

"Here, will you put this on? I don't care what you say, these are not pajamas and I can see your nipples perfectly through your camisole."

I snort against rock bottom. There's a nice little pity party down here. "Who cares if you can see my nipples?" *No one.* My body isn't that interesting anyway. It certainly hasn't been enough to make anyone fall in love with me yet. Or to make up for the jagged edges of my personality that men seem to hate.

"I care." He drapes the silk robe around my shoulders, and I punch my arms through the sleeves, aggravated we're wasting valuable time because of modesty that I don't even need.

"You've seen a woman's body. Mine is no different."

He pauses, a thick crease forming between his brows. "Emily, you are *the* difference. I'm realizing that." What does that even mean? I'm not sober enough for riddles.

Reading my mind, Jack adds, "And you're drunk. If Sober Emily wants to wear this in front of me, great. But she's not in the room right now, so I'm looking out for her." He steers me into the kitchen. "You're also covered in dirt. And a little blood. Let's get you cleaned up and then we'll tackle the problem."

"It doesn't matter." The wine I drank pours itself out of my eyes. "My life is over. O.E.V.E.R."

"I'm glad you also know the super-secret way to spell 'over,'" he says, but no attempts at humor will pull me out of my misery.

"I *fucked up,* Jack. And now it's only a matter of time until everyone knows."

He spins me around and leans my hips back against the counter to anchor me before wetting a dishrag. He raises the loose silk sleeve of my robe and, with the warm rag, begins cleaning the dirt from my elbow. "Good. It's about time you messed up," he says, before moving to the other side and cleaning me off there too. "It's been excruciating trying to keep pace with you all these years."

His touch is tender and attentive and for a second, I forget all about my manuscript and my impending doom. All I can think about is Jackson, in my kitchen, wetting the rag once again with warm water and lowering himself in front of me. His hand wraps around my calf and gently tugs it forward so my leg emerges from the opening of my robe. So much of my skin is on display right now, but he doesn't look anywhere besides my knee and shin where he's gently, gently cleaning the dirt and blood away.

Chills cover my body. Does Jack see them? Does he know what the sight of him like this is doing to me? Can he feel me reaching back in time to cover my own damn mouth before I lash out at him over the coffee spill? What would life have been like if I had never initiated our war that day? Would we have become friends? Or was fighting always meant to be our destiny?

He moves to the other leg and it's all I can do not to slip my hand into his thick brownish-blondish hair. Such nice hair. Such nonconfrontational hair. Jack is so kind that he doesn't even have a true hair color lest he disappoint anyone's preferences.

Does he ever think about me? Probably not unless it's to imagine I'm roadkill. And besides he was with Zoe, and she was beyond beautiful. And soft too. She was like Annie and Maddie. I am nothing like any of them.

I'm crying again, unable to find the surface of my emotions and taking on water.

Jack sees me and stands, cups my face to wipe my tears from my cheeks, and then pulls me in tightly to his chest. "Say it out loud, Emily. Let me inside that brain of yours."

I'm afraid to. He'll see how messy it is. How dark in some corners. Sometimes it even scares me in here. When I'm not moving, when I'm not busy, when I'm not needed, it's so, so lonely.

"Do you know part of the reason I didn't want you to be my neighbor?" My thoughts and emotions are all tie-dyed—bleeding together into one big shape. "Because everyone loves you as soon as they meet you, but most people only tolerate me. This town, though . . . they *love* me and my spikes. It's my sanctuary. My safe place. Maybe it's because they loved my parents, and they love my siblings—" My voice breaks. "I don't know, and I don't always feel like I deserve it. But they do—and I was afraid that if you moved into my town that I love so, so much, I'd have to watch them fall in love with you over me. Because there's never been room enough for both of us. We are two sides of the same coin—but everyone always chooses you." Sadly, I don't even think I'm that drunk right now. I'm just hysterical. Jack's chest is absorbing all of my salty tears. "And I wouldn't even blame them because you're so damn likable. Even when I've hated you, I've always liked you."

He holds me closer, my cheek smashing against his chest. "People may like me, but they don't know me. I don't think anyone has ever known me quite like you have. And that's part of why I wanted to move back to Rome. Because of *you*. Because through our strange, twisted relationship, you've made me feel less alone. I wanted to be part of this town because I know that for you to love it, it has to be pretty spectacular. And I swear to you, I would never try to steal their love away from you. Couldn't even if I wanted to. They love you more than you know. Believe me, I've seen firsthand how much this town worships you and your spikes."

A broken sob tears me in half as Jack shields me from a little bit of the darkness. We stand here like this for a while—Jack holding me. His body is warm like sheets fresh out of the dryer. This is the first time anyone has ever held me like this . . . or that I've allowed myself to be held. Of course it would be with Jack.

"What else?" says Jack softly. "I want to know."

I sniff and savor the feel of him holding me tight. "I'm intense sometimes . . . but . . . at least I have good nipples, right, Jack? Tell me I do."

I could swear I feel him smile against the top of my head where his chin is resting. "The best I've ever seen, Emily."

CHAPTER ELEVEN

Jack

After a while, when it seems the worst of Emily's panic has died down, I guide her to the couch. She folds over and buries her face in her forearms. I know these emotions are amplified from the alcohol, but I have *never* seen her like this. Wouldn't believe it if I hadn't seen it with my own eyes. Emily—the woman who seems to single-handedly carry the world on her shoulders better than Superman ever could dream—is an emotional (and physical) wreck. And for all my joking that she's a humanoid, I guess maybe there was a part of me that believed she *was* too perfect for raw feelings like this. Too tough for puffy eyes. Too organized for a snotty cry. But here she is, breaking down in front of me. Or maybe the better way to phrase that is *in spite of me*.

"It's over, Jack. My life is over," she mumbles for the tenth time tonight.

"You're a very dramatic drunk, did you know that?"

The sleeves of her robe are stained with wet mascara as she looks up at me. But her gaze snags on the stains and they make her sad all over again. She pushes the fabric up to her bicep and my stomach knots at the sight of the little cuts on her elbows—and knees too—from falling on her way to get me.

"Okay, let me see if I understand this," I say, sitting on the floor in front of the couch with my back to Emily, whose face is now over my shoulder as I open her laptop. "You tried to email something to someone else, and you accidentally sent it to Bart instead? And now you want me to get it back before he opens it?"

"Yes." She sniffs and pushes her golden bangs behind her ear. Her eyes are going to ache like crazy tomorrow from how swollen they are tonight. It's killing me slowly to see her like this.

"Password?" I ask, looking down at the screen resting on my legs.

Her hand extends over my shoulder, her forearm brushing my neck from her sloppy motor skills as she plucks six numbers on her keyboard. Her hand loses life and drops onto my chest.

"You shouldn't set your password as your birthday." I look down at her limp hand. Red polish a little chipped on her thumbnail.

When she doesn't say anything, I angle my face to her, only to find her heavy eyes watching me. "You know my birthday?"

"I've known you since college. Of course I know your birthday. I also know it's your tradition to bring in two slices of pie for your birthday lunch and eat them both yourself."

A little frown pinches between her brows. "I'm too tipsy to understand subtlety right now. Was that a dig at how much I eat?"

"Not at all," I say with a genuine smile.

She shrugs but doesn't move her arm. "I like pie."

"I like that you like pie." I click around her laptop. "I've still never had one from the Pie Shop thanks to your ban."

I imagine bringing her a whole pie to school on her birthday this year so she can eat the entire thing. And on that thought, realizing I'll be here this year and the next—that I won't be in Nebraska, living a life away from Emily—it soothes a part of me I didn't know was aching.

"February tenth," Emily says, pulling me from my thoughts. "Yours is February tenth. Your last birthday I thought about making your favorite coffee beans in the break room in honor of it."

I'm smiling. "Why didn't you?"

"Because it would have been a breach in our unspoken rules."

I nod and suddenly rethink every choice I've made with Emily over the last decade. The source of that initial tug that brought me back to Rome is growing into a new awareness. Maybe I've always picked fights with her because I enjoy it. Because I enjoy *her*. Because we're friends. Maybe we've always been friends in a weird unconventional sort of way. But maybe I'm ready for it to evolve into something . . . conventional.

"I missed my chance to make you birthday coffee," she begins in a sad, resigned tone that turns downright pouty. "Since I'll probably be fired after Bart opens my email anyway."

I can't sit back and watch her shrink into despair anymore. "It's time to tell me what was in the email, Goldie."

She buries her face in the crook of her pink silken arm again. "I can't tell you."

"It's a nude, isn't it?"

"No, it's not a nude!" She groans.

"Fine. A partial nude?"

I can see the corner of her mouth curl up from behind her arm. It does something to me. "There's definitely nudity in it, but it's not mine." *The hell?*

I open my mouth, but no words come out. There was not a single part of me expecting that answer.

"I wrote . . ." She pauses, looks at me, presses her lips together, and then I see the moment she decides to trust me. "I wrote a romance novel. A sexually explicit one that no one in the entire world knows I was writing. And after a terrible day and feeling sorry for myself that Madison didn't come home when I really wanted her to, I had some wine and then thought it would be a great idea to send the book to an agent. But I accidentally sent it to Bart instead."

I am floored. Speechless. Emily Walker . . . is a writer too? How is this possible? How are we always living parallel lives to each other?

She blinks at me expectantly and then shoots up from the couch. "See! I shouldn't have told you! I feel so stupid." She grips her hair, pacing a few steps back and forth, talking loudly and slurring a few words together. "How could I have done this? *How?* I never should have written that damn thing. And now Bart is going to open the email, read the title *The Depraved Highlander and His Lady,* and fire me on the spot."

The Depraved Hi—

I can't process this all quickly enough.

But when the shock wears off, I stand. "You wrote a book titled *The Depraved Highlander and His Lady?*"

Emily levels a finger at me. "Don't you dare make fun of me, Jackson."

"I'm not." I raise my hands in surrender. "I wouldn't do that. I asked a question because I'm processing. I'm an auditory processor." And this is an *onslaught* of information. "Wait . . . did you attach your full manuscript to a query email?"

"Yes."

"You know you're not supposed to—"

"*YES!* I know! But I did it because I'm apparently a mistakes factory tonight." She presses the heels of her hands into her eyes. "You think I'm an idiot now."

"Stop putting words in my mouth, I would never think that about you," I say firmly, pulling Emily's attention back to my face. "And stop pacing. Sit back down. You're swaying like you could fall over any second."

She sits but doesn't look happy about it. "Once Bart opens it, the whole town will know by sunrise and then my life will really and truly be over. It was one thing for my sisters to know I like to read romance, but . . . I'm not ready for the whole town to be in my business about writing it. Not to mention the bigger consequences it could have. Do you think I could get fired over this?"

"I honestly don't know. I guess it comes down to how Bart feels about it and if he decides to tell anyone else on the school board."

Bart is a great guy, but . . . let's just say he's not the kind of guy you'd want stumbling over anything explicit. I once heard him telling the other teachers how disappointed he was in the Hallmark Channel for how inappropriate their kissing scenes have become. He also fired a substitute teacher last year for accidentally cursing in front of the class when she slammed her toe into the desk.

However, this is Emily we're talking about. And she is undoubtedly the best teacher at the school. I've never seen anyone go above and beyond like her. She's always studying new teaching techniques and adapting so that her lessons are more inclusive for different learning types. And yes, she's definitely known as the no-nonsense teacher who gives more homework than the rest and does not tolerate rowdiness in her classroom, but she also goes to every kid's birthday party she's invited to and brings a gift. She organized our school's annual talent show to take place at a nursing home so that the kids could learn the importance of community outreach while also having fun. And last year, when one of her students lost his granddad who he was very close to, Emily saw how he was struggling, and she put together an impromptu class project. She asked each of the kids to bring in a square of fabric, and using liquid stitches, she let all the kids help iron the pieces together to form a little grieving blanket that Frankie could take home and snuggle when he felt sad. She wanted him to know he had a class of kids who cared about him.

Parents don't always like her because she tends to call them out with very little sugarcoating when she sees they're not aiding their children like they should—like when they repeatedly bring their child to school late. And the other teachers think she's a know-it-all who does too much. And I think she's annoying because it's so damn hard trying to keep up with how incredible she is.

Because the fact is, it takes so much emotional energy to be a teacher. And an outrageous amount to be a *good* one. I know it takes a toll on her, and still, somehow, she comes in every year sacrificing so much of herself that most parents and kids will never even know about or appreciate.

No, I'm not all that worried about her getting fired. I'll start a town riot before I let that happen. I'm more interested in recovering her manuscript out of creative sympathy. I know how vulnerable it is to share your writing. Her news shouldn't have to come out like this—where it could become a potential punch line with the town she loves so much.

She groans. "Do you think you can you get it back?"

I've been playing around with her email while we've been talking, and I have my answer. "Do you want the good news or the bad news first?"

"The bad."

"You can't retrieve the email. Some providers allow it, but not this one, it seems."

She is one step away from complete devastation. "What's the good news?"

"Bart—according to the automatic email response you got from him—is out of office for the next week on vacation and will not be checking his email."

"How is that good news?"

"It's good, because it gives me time to help you break into Bart's laptop and delete the email, assuming he didn't take it with him on vacation."

Emily is frozen. "Jack . . . are you the drunk one?"

"I don't drink alcohol," I say, and when she gives me a look like she's about to unleash a million questions, I keep going. "But I am offering to help you."

She stares at me a minute and then sniffs, wiping her face with her sleeve and says the most Emily thing I've ever heard. "I don't need your help breaking into his laptop."

"Ah—there she is." I don't bother to hide my smile. "And yes you do. Because in order to get to Bart's office, we're going to have to get past . . ."

She flinches. "Don't say it."

"Marissa." Our school's crotchety vice principal. She makes Scrooge look like Winnie-the-Pooh.

"And Marissa hates everyone . . . besides you."

I nod. She really does love me for some reason. She's approaching her sixties and has zero tolerance for anyone and everything. But when she sees me, *instant smile*. "I have full confidence that I can distract her long enough for you to get into Bart's office and delete the email."

"Why?" Emily's green eyes narrow. "Why would you help me?"

"Because . . ." *I know it would feel terrible to have my writing exposed before I was ready. Because I think we're friends. Because I'd like to spend time with you.* But I don't say any of this because, like me, Emily does not like to accept free help. It makes her uncomfortable. I need a solid reason that will withstand her pride.

"Because I need your help too." Her eyebrow lifts. "I am going to break and enter with you, and in return I need you to call your ole friend Darrell and get him to renovate my damn house."

"I thought you said you were doing a great job?"

"I've been lying through my teeth. I've done a *shit* job on that house. Can't believe it hasn't caved in on me yet. I'm scared to sleep in it."

She barks a laugh, and then like a superhero rising from the rubble after an excruciating fight scene, Emily sits up. I watch her confidence refill her body starting in her wiggling toes and moving upward. She stands, grabs the ties of her robe, and cinches them tight. Her tears are a thing of the past. "Okay. I'll do it. But I have a few conditions."

"Conditions?" I say to her retreating back. "You can't throw conditions on a favor I'm offering you."

Emily does an excellent impression of a sober woman as she walks to the kitchen—her only tell is the way her body sways a little too much to the right as she goes. Her little cat stirs from the back of the couch as Emily passes, stretches, and follows on the heels of that billowing robe. I go too and watch as Emily pulls a saucepan out of a cabinet. "I don't just give out favors willy-nilly without a cost, Jackson Bennett."

"That's not how this works. I'm the one giving out the favor. In case you forgot, you're in distress. Therefore I'm offering to help you—*if* you go through with your end of the deal."

She leans her silk-clad hip against the counter as she fills the pot with water. "I only asked for technological aid while I'm impaired. What you're proposing"—she really struggled over that word—"is a whole different scope of project. And that requires greater payment." The water sloshes over the edge of the pan, reminding Tipsy Emily that she was in the middle of filling it with water. I lean over and turn the faucet off as she dumps out some of the excess liquid.

"What are you even doing right now?"

"Making buttered noodles. It's my drunk food. Well—our drunk food. Normally I don't drink alone, and Madison is always the one to whip up the noodles. But . . ." Her eyes go distant and sad again. And now I know that *this* is the root of all the drinking and crying tonight. Madison canceled on her, and it was killing her.

She shakes off her thoughts and carries the pot of water to the stove. Her cat jumps up on the counter just before she sets the pot down. Emily scoops her up in one arm, sets the pot on an electric burner with the other. She turns to me and hands the cat off. Emily turns the heat to high.

I go behind her and cut it down to medium. "You shouldn't use the stove while drunk."

She splits the difference and turns the knob to medium-high. "I do what I want."

I look down helplessly at the kitten for backup and then set her at my feet. "Fine. Name your terms for the favor."

"I want all rights to the corner table on Saturday mornings, plus the good parking spot at school for a month when we go back."

"Fifty-fifty on both."

"Seventy-thirty."

I shake my head. Even drunk and cornered by life, she's a firecracker. "Okay. It's a deal."

The cat jumps on the counter once more as Emily cracks open a box of pasta and dumps it into the water. The cat gets passed off to me for the second time, but before she fully turns away, Emily kisses Ducky on the head. It's a swift peek into a side of Emily that most people don't get to see.

"Listen, little fur ball, you're not supposed to be on the counter. It's not hygienic." I carry Ducky into the living room and deposit her on the couch. "Stay," I say with a firm finger in front of her little pink nose. Most cats would swat my hand away; Ducky rubs her face against it.

With Emily distracted in the kitchen, I squat down to Ducky's level. My new spy. "Tell me a secret, what's it like to be adored by Emily Walker?" She nuzzles under my chin this time and curls her tail around my face. "Thought so."

I turn to avoid the slash of her tail in my eyes, and that's when I notice Emily's bookshelf again.

I went on my first roller coaster when I was eleven, and it had a massive drop followed by a corkscrew that took me upside down. Until the moment I saw her bookshelf the other day, I had never felt my stomach bottom out as sharply as it did during that drop. But when my eyes connected with the two sets of books side by side on her shelf, that roller coaster had nothing in comparison. Emily not only has my dad's bestselling series, but she has *mine* . . . and they're sharing the same shelf space.

I don't even realize I've moved to stand in front of it until Emily says, "You're very interested in that shelf." She's right behind me.

I tuck my hands in my pants pockets and attempt a casual tone of voice. "I'm just curious how you ended up with these two mystery series when your other shelves are all full of romance." Which honestly delights me. I love knowing Emily is not only a romance reader but a romance writer.

Her shoulder brushes mine as she comes to stand directly beside me. I wonder if she's leaning on me because she's struggling to stand perfectly straight. "My brother gave them to me. He usually reads nonfiction but after he met his wife, she pulled him into the wonderful world of fiction. My sisters and I all started sharing our romance books last year and Noah felt left out. He lent me these and I really liked them, so I kept them. Don't tell him I still have them." She looks sidelong at me. "Have you read them? You can borrow them if you want."

I nod, smiling privately. "I've read them. Which series is your favorite out of these two?"

Emily grins and I brace for the impact of an answer I might not want to hear. "I enjoy Fredrick's twists, but I like Ranger's storytelling the best. I think he's the better writer."

There is nothing that could have prepared me to hear those words come from her mouth. Maybe it wasn't fair of me to ask her since she doesn't know I'm one of these writers, but also, knowing that Emily always tells me the one hundred percent honest blatant truth no matter what, it makes this compliment somehow sweeter. I know she means it. *Emily Walker thinks I'm a good writer.*

Does she even know I'm Fredrick Bennett's son? I don't try to hide the fact; I just don't advertise it either. But eventually a fellow bookworm puts our last names together and figures it out. A few teachers at the elementary school have.

"Which one do you think is the better writer?" she asks.

"Fredrick," I say without a hint of hesitation, also giving her the unfiltered truth. My dad *is* the better writer. He has twice as many accolades as me to prove it. And yet again, I am so glad I'll never have to publicly sit in his shadow as "Fredrick's son." At least in this moment I'm having a debate with Emily over two writers who are sharing the same shelf. Not a father and son. "His pacing is unmatched. Ranger rushes his endings." Something I've been try-ing to fix.

Emily steps up beside me now, fire lighting her eyes. "There is nothing wrong with Ranger's endings. If anything, he knows when to cut off a book on the best cliffhanger, whereas Fredrick lets it go on and on. Like we get it—the unexpected widow was the mur-derer, and here's a full recap of all the ways you misdirected me into suspecting someone else. It's the same tired old story again and again. But Ranger is different."

"How so?"

She looks right in my eyes and smiles. "He writes with heart. You know . . . that organ you don't have?"

That organ in question is pounding mercilessly against my ribs. It's taking everything in me not to tell her that I'm the man she's defending right now. I'm the writer she thinks is good. *Me.* But I don't because at the end of the day, whatever this new truce is between us, it might be tentative. We've never been able to stay civil for too long. As much as I want it to stick, it's too new to risk with something this important to me.

But I can share at least part of the truth. "Emily . . . Fredrick is my dad."

She doesn't so much as flinch. "Oh, I know." A soft smile. "I've known since college. I overheard you being asked about it by that English professor with the bad breath who always carried the Mary Poppins carpetbag and liked you better than me."

"Yeah—I hated him. Why have you never brought it up?"

She shrugs, and I like the way her silk robe feels against my arm. "Because you haven't. I saw you shut down that day after he asked, so I just got the impression that you didn't like talking about it. It didn't seem like something that should be included in our warfare." She grins. "I don't like taking cheap shots."

Emily is the only person to ever perceive that I don't like discussing my dad. I've always gone through great lengths to make sure no one ever does. But of course she sees it.

"So just now . . . when I was asking you about him?"

"I knew. And I told you the truth. I always tell you the truth."

I absorb this news like water in dry sand. *I like it.* This entire night has been a revelation—a sudden, sharp turn in what's always been a straight road.

"Emily . . . are we . . . friends now?"

"Maybe. We'll see." She pauses and a huge smile overtakes her face. "But don't worry, I still hate you."

Turns out, I've found another situation to rival that roller coaster drop. "I still hate you too."

JACK (11:00 AM): Umm . . . there seem to be about ten different whole pies on my porch . . . is there a pie fairy in this town I don't know about?

EMILY (11:15 AM): Yes—but this time it was me. They're "I'm sorry for snotting on your shirt" pies.

JACK (11:16 AM): That's a very specific pie name. You didn't have to buy me the entire display case, though.

EMILY (11:17 AM): Well, as an official member of Rome, Kentucky, now, it's important you know your favorite type of pie from the Pie Shop. Think of this as your inauguration into the community.

JACK (11:18 AM): Hey, so . . . I don't think I ever said this last night, but . . . I think it's incredible you wrote a book. I hope you're proud. You should be.

EMILY (11:20 AM): You haven't read it. You might be taking that back if you found out how terrible it is.

JACK (11:21 AM): Nah. You did the hardest part. Putting words on the paper. Well done. What made you start writing?

EMILY (11:25 AM): The simple reason: I've always wanted to try it. The complicated reason: Because real life started hurting too much.

JACK (11:27 AM): I'm sorry life has hurt.

JACK (11:28 AM): I never thought my leaving would cause you so much pain 😕

EMILY (11:29 AM): 😑 Go eat your pie.

CHAPTER TWELVE

Emily

"Where are your boobs?" asks Amelia.

"How rude! They're right here!" Annie states, pointing to her chest, hiding somewhere behind the cotton-candy-pink, A-line dress. It has a delicate fabric belt in the same color as the dress, with a cute little bow on the front and white lace trimming on the bottom hem. It's one from my grandma's old wardrobe that we found while going through her closet after she died. It was in a little box in the bottom. A treasure trove of vintage dresses from what looks like the '50s.

My heart squeezes that I never knew these existed. That she never pulled them out for us to play dress-up in where she could see us laughing and enjoying each other's company. My grandma was a very private lady. Kind and sweet—but reserved. The only person who likely knew all her secrets was Mabel—her best friend. Maybe she was open with her husband, but he had died before I was born, so I don't know what sort of relationship they had.

I guess she and I were alike in the fact that we prefer to keep our business to ourselves.

"How did she walk in these things?" Annie asks, stumbling through the living room in the matching pink pumps.

Amelia is losing it laughing. "Annie—I mean this in the best way, you look like a ten-year-old playing dress-up in that outfit."

It's true. The chest is like three sizes too big, and the lower hem sits closer to Annie's ankles than her knees. "Okay, well let's see how well you pull these off!"

She throws a lime-green version of a similar-style dress to Amelia. "Yes, please! Now I truly can live out my fantasy of being Audrey Hepburn." Amelia is well and truly obsessed with the iconic actress. Well, we all are now, but Amelia is the one who introduced us to her through the movie *Roman Holiday*. We watched it together during our very first girls' night before she and Noah were officially together and she was still just a pop star hiding out in our small town for a breather.

Amelia stands with a sassy smile, slips out of her jeans and tee, and steps into the dress. She turns to me and lifts her dark brown hair out of the way so I can zip it for her.

Annie immediately dies laughing. Amelia frowns. "Good god. How did I manage to lose all my shape?"

"Your skin looks like a cadaver!" Annie howls.

Amelia frowns at her. "You've changed. I miss my sweet Anna-banana."

Annie tries to subdue her smile. "I'm sorry. A very, very *beautiful* cadaver. Your turn, Em."

I'm hit in the face with a wad of red fabric. I roll my eyes and follow Amelia's lead, stripping down in the living room.

Amelia points in the general vicinity of my ass. "That's not fair. You can't wear sexy panties on a random Tuesday night."

Annie laughs. "You still don't know Emily very well, then. She's all about luxury lingerie whether it's Monday or Sunday."

Amelia frowns. "You're really not planning on meeting a date later tonight? You just wear stuff like that on the regular?" No one would believe the world-famous pop star Rae Rose was asking *me* that question. Everyone would expect her to be the glamorous, high-maintenance one. But I've found she's the most down-to-earth normal gal on the planet.

"Okay, first of all, stop gawking at me, the both of you. You're making me feel like a stripper. And second, I wear pretty lingerie for me. Not men." I huff a laugh. "It's wasted on men, in fact. They take two seconds at best to say . . . *Sexy,* and then that's it. It's on the floor. I swear that cotton Fruit of the Loom would produce the same outcome." I pull the dress up and slide my arms into the cap sleeves.

"She's an icon, people," Amelia states with a smile.

The zipper is on the side of this dress, so I'm able to fasten it myself. Of course my boobs are spilling over the top a little, but I'm surprised to see that it fits me to near perfection. The bodice is tight with a sweetheart neckline, delicate little cap sleeves, and a full flounced skirt that stops just below my knees. Next I slide into the velvet red heels, and they're a little snugger than I'd prefer but they work.

"Okay, this experiment did not work in my favor," says Amelia.

"Not fair, Emily. The dress even matches your lipstick and nail polish. I should have given you the lime green."

"Ladies, jealousy is not becoming in a woman," I say with a soft smile. "Now who's in the mood for pot roast?" I say in my best 1950s impression of a housewife. "Jim, darling, will be home soon and I made a coconut cream pie that's to die for!" I pick up a pen and pretend to take a sophisticated drag off it and blow out imaginary smoke. "Of course, he gets a little handsy so you won't want to stand too close to him, but who can blame the appetites of men?" We all three titter a slightly hysteric laugh.

"Boys will be boys!" Amelia croons.

"True—but nothing a little poison in his cocktail won't fix!" Annie says with a bright smile. Amelia and I stare at her with wide eyes and slack jaws. "What? Too much?" Her face flushes. "I was just—"

We erupt in laughter. "Never too much, Anna-banana! I love this side of you. I'm just sad Maddie wasn't here to witness it too. She would have peed herself laughing," I say to my normally cherub-hearted sister.

Apparently I shouldn't have made that comment. Annie's eyes take on a serious look. "Are you doing okay without her here?" It's not that Annie doesn't miss Madison too, but she's never been as close to her as I am.

Amelia piggybacks off Annie's question. "I'm sorry she couldn't come back like y'all planned. I'm sure you were really disappointed."

Their probing questions have me taking such deep breaths that my cleavage swells over the neckline of my dress. I would rather be waterboarded than have someone ask me if I'm okay. *Especially when my answer is no.*

Memories of last night slip like a hazy fever dream through my mind. Feeling so sad and lonely that I drank myself into an emotional wreck. Jack holding me in the kitchen. Cleaning the dirt from my elbows and knees. Me sobbing at the table, and him assuring me that my life would go on. My grief and loneliness ebbed a little after those tears. After his touch.

I put my pen-cigarette to my mouth, drag it in, and then tilt my chin up to blow out a long puff. When I look at them again, I am the Emily they know and love. The one who isn't spiraling internally. The one who would do anything, sacrifice everything for them. The one who has an entire secret schedule planned out for this night, that I never told them about but I'm sure everyone knows I made anyway. I like to make sure things keep moving so there are no lulls, even on girls' night.

"Of course I'm okay. Without having to host, it just gives me more time to hide Jim's body before the cops find out."

We spend the next half hour talking about life (right on schedule). Amelia's mom has to have minor surgery, and she's going home to help take care of her for a few days. Annie is providing flowers for another celebrity wedding that's happening in Nashville next weekend. (Her business has really taken off after word got out that her shop did the flowers for Rae Rose's wedding.) And when it's my turn to share, I bypass it by getting them a fresh glass of wine and refilling my water. (Because just the sight of alcohol today is making me feel like vomiting.)

"What's next on the itinerary, Em?" Annie asks, with a grin.

"I don't know what you're talking about," I say in a coy tone. "But hypothetically, if I did have a spectacular schedule for the night, it would be time for a movie."

"Which one tonight?"

"*Sweet Home Alabama*?"

"*What?* Not an Audrey movie? It's girls' night!"

We accidentally stumbled on this tradition of watching an Audrey Hepburn movie for girls' night when Amelia first came to town. She's the president of our little club because she's been obsessed with Audrey since she was a girl and taught us to fall in love with the queen of classic movies as well.

"No—we can't," I say firmly. "It would be wrong to watch it without Maddie."

"She'd understand, though." Annie sips her wine. "She doesn't expect us to stop our lives just because she's—"

"No, Annie. Not without Maddie." My voice comes out harsher than I intend, and when I see Annie shrink into herself, I immediately feel like the horrible villain in a cartoon that some-how grows double in size and absorbs all the light in the room with her darkness. I soften my tone. "I'm sorry. How about a Doris Day film instead if y'all are craving a classic?"

They murmur their agreement, but I can tell they're not happy about it.

However, just as we're starting *Pillow Talk,* a familiar hammer-ing begins next door.

Amelia pauses the movie and looks at me. "He's still over there? I thought you were getting rid of him."

I stand up from the couch and smooth out the skirt of my dress. "I'll . . . be right back."

I don't bother knocking this time as I go to Jack's front door, know-ing he won't hear me even if I do. Instead, I walk inside and find him with his back to me, hammering a nail into a very off-center two-by-four. He's wearing faded blue Levi's, a light gray T-shirt, brown work boots, and a bright-blue-and-white trucker hat—blondish-brownish hair flipping out at his nape in a way that abso-lutely has me drooling. The best part is, he has a tool belt around his waist. Jack looks like a '70s dad that some lucky woman would have absolutely railed after a cookout. He'd get her so pregnant.

I know better than to sneak up on a person with a hammer, so instead, I find a discarded rag, ball it up, and throw it at his head. He jolts a little and spins around. I'm not sure if he was more sur-prised by the rag or the sight of me. I smile, finally seeing that his hat says *Country Roads Take Me Home—John Denver.* Together we look like an ode to the decades. Seventies dad, meet fifties mom.

His gaze travels from my eyes down to the red heels and back up to my eyes before he says a word. "What . . . are you wearing?"

"My nightgown," I say deadpan.

His eyes glitter. "You're forgetting that I've seen what you wear to bed."

I think embarrassment should be creeping over my skin right about now. Instead, something entirely different is. Because he's not looking at me like I should be at all embarrassed for how I showed up at his house last night. Or that I asked him if I had good nipples. Or that he said they were the best he'd ever seen.

I clear my throat. "Hi. So. Since we're friends now, can you refrain from hammering tonight?"

Look how polite I'm being. I even phrased it like a question even though it's absolutely a statement.

"Are we friends?" Jack asks with an amused lilt.

"Aren't we?" Last night certainly felt friendly.

Jack looks me up and down one more time, lightly shakes his head like he's having his own private thought I'll never be privy to, and then grins. "No. Have a good night, Emily." He turns and continues hammering.

The clop of my heels competes with his construction as I close the distance between us, coming up beside him to look over his arm. His muscular, veiny arm. "We're not friends?"

He was doing yard work earlier. I know because I watched him a little too long out the window while sipping my iced tea. And also because his skin is so golden tan now. It looks warm like freshly buttered biscuits.

"We're friends. The no was to your request for me to stop hammering."

I cross my arms. "Friends stop doing construction when another friend asks."

"Not this friend." He reaches behind him with his free hand and pulls out another nail from his tool belt.

"Nice fanny pack."

"Thank you. Nice June Cleaver impression."

"Tell me," I say, tilting my head closer to the wall, more into his line of sight. "How hard was it not to accidentally say June *Cleavage* just then?" I know my breasts look amazing in this dress. I clocked the exact moment his gaze snagged on them after he turned around. After last night, the jig is up that we truly only hate each other. There's more here between us—even if neither of us knows what it is or if we should do anything about it. I tend to lean toward not doing anything about it, since we tried friendship once before and it didn't end well. In fact, it didn't last long at all. No telling how long we'll be able to keep things civil this time.

But the lingering buzz of our encounter last night has me itching to see what it takes to throw this man off his game. To get him to intentionally flirt with me. Without the helmet on.

Call it a scientific experiment.

He centers the nail, his lazy smile tilting. "Go home to your supper club, Elizabeth Taylor."

"Only if you stop hammering for tonight," I say, a little annoyed that he wouldn't take my bait.

"No."

"Why are you being obstreperous?"

"Because I live to hear what colorful vocabulary you'll use when I piss you off."

I turn away with a huff, my skirts dragging against the side of his legs as I do. My eyes wander over his space, taking in the truly terrible construction he's done so far. There's so much drywall dust everywhere. I called Darrell earlier this morning about taking on this project after all, but I haven't heard back yet. I take five high-heeled steps away from Jack, noting the half-empty jar of peanut butter on the counter next to a loaf of bread.

I pivot again and can see straight through the open door of his bedroom. Last I looked in there I saw a corkboard filled with

Post-it notes before Jack pulled me away from it. There's no cork-board today, but there is a book open on the bed. The last book in the series by AJ Ranger that we were discussing last night actually. He has several highlighters and a sheet of little tabs lying on the bed next to the book. Like he's been studying it. Next to it, there's an open notebook filled to the brim with handwritten notes. *Notes about the book?*

I am nothing if not blunt, which is why I look back at Jackson and ask, "Why are you studying *The Hallway*?"

He's in the middle of hammering a nail when I ask the question that apparently startles him so much he accidentally pounds his hammer onto his thumb instead of the nail. "Dammit!" he yells, hammer clanging to the ground as he clutches his hand.

"Oh my god, Jack! Let me see it."

He's hissing in through his teeth, squinting his eyes and holding his hand in a vise grip. "No. I'm fine. Go back home."

"Let me see it, Jack!"

"It's fine, it's just—"

There's red oozing out from his grip.

"—Leaking blood." I roll my eyes and grab his bicep with my hand. "Come on."

"I don't need your help, Bette Davis."

"Impressive classic actress knowledge. But you're coming with me because you need a Band-Aid at the very least and you don't have Band-Aids here."

"How do you know I don't have Band-Aids?" he asks as we take the stairs down the porch, my hand still firmly holding his arm.

I pause only long enough to look at him while I ask, "*Do* you have Band-Aids?"

"No."

"Then keep it moving."

"Your heels are somehow making you faster. And bossier. Have you ever considered the Olympics? Maybe they have a race just for overbearing blondes who—" At this moment we walk into my house, and he spots Amelia and Annie sitting on the couch. "My god, did we enter a time portal, and I didn't realize it?"

"Yes, welcome to *Happy Days*. Sit down at the kitchen table and I'll get the first-aid kit."

I pass through the living room, avoiding the searching expressions of my sisters, and back to my bathroom where I grab what I need. When I come back through, Amelia and Annie are still gaping at Jack, who is clutching a paper towel around his thumb now.

"Ladies, this is Jack, CEO of hell and also my neighbor and nemesis. Jack, my sister, Annie, and sister-in-law, Amelia."

"By 'nemesis' she means 'best friend.'" His eyes catch mine as I sit in front of him. He dips forward and lowers his voice. "I forgot Rae Rose lives in this town. That's Rae Rose, though, isn't it?"

"Stop saying 'Rae Rose' so much. But yes—that's her."

He turns his charming smile to Amelia, and I oddly want to cover it with my palm. "Hi," he says, looking a bit starstruck.

"Hi," she says, looking similarly.

Annie doesn't make a peep. She's sitting like a little pink statue, eyes wide.

I block out my siblings, who clearly have no idea what to do with the fact that I've just paraded my neighbor/nemesis into my house.

"Let me have your hand," I tell Jack, earning his glare again.

"I'm a grown man, I can handle my own wound care. Give me the Band-Aid and I'll be on my way."

"No—you'll have no peer pressure to clean it with alcohol if you take this back to your place, and then it'll get infected. But if I do it, you'll be forced to grin and bear the sting to prove you have a penis. So hand it over."

"My penis?"

I give him a flat look to which he extends his hand with a sigh. "Fine, but I can't promise I won't look at your chest because it's perfectly framed right there in front of my face, and to answer your question from earlier it *was* difficult not to say 'cleavage.'"

Holding back the full force of my grin is nearly painful. "Do what you must, you have my permission," I say as I begin working on his finger. He hisses when the alcohol pad touches his skin. And even though he talked a big game, Jack doesn't stare at my boobs. He's too respectful for that. I almost wish he would because it's twice as unnerving knowing he's watching my face instead. Especially while I hold his hand like this. His big hand. I remember writing a scene about the Highlander's hand and how big and erotic it was. I rolled my eyes while writing it because I'd never been particularly attracted to hands like this in the past, but I know of other women who like them.

Right now, I look at Jack's knuckles and I want to sink my teeth into them.

When my sisters start talking between themselves—or pretending to—Jack leans in close and drops his voice. So close I feel his breath. "Do they know about your secret?"

"No." I place antibiotic cream on his finger.

"Not about the accidental email either?"

"Absolutely not. And we are keeping it that way." Maybe I *am* just like my grandmother. One day my grandkids will open my closet after I've left this earth and find a box of mediocre manuscripts. They'll read them all in the living room and laugh.

He sits back in his seat eyeing me. "I think you're the only person on this earth who keeps more secrets than me."

"What secrets are you keeping, Jackson?" I ask as I wrap the Band-Aid around his thumb. It has a flower print on it. I selected the one with blue petals to match his hat and somehow I know he'll appreciate that attention to detail.

"Enough to make some waves." He pauses and doesn't move his hand after I've finished doctoring his thumb. "Do the secrets ever weigh on you?"

I stare at him across the table. "Do they ever weigh on you?"

He smirks. "I think our answer is the same."

"In that case, you need a smoke as much as I do." I hand him my pen and without looking away from my eyes, he takes it, sucks in a long drag, angles his face away from mine, and blows it out. *Ever the gentleman*.

"Will you let me read it?"

I glance nervously to my sisters but relax when I see they're busy talking with their heads ducked together. "No. You may not read it."

He grins. "Come on. Don't be chicken."

"I'm not chicken. I just don't want to corrupt your innocent mind with all my dirty scenes."

This delights him more. "I love romance books, you know? I've read plenty. I could be a good sounding board too since I know a lot about the writing and publishing process." And again, his eyes do this thing where he looks like he accidentally said too much.

"Because of your dad?"

He stares at me, swallows, and then nods. "Yes. Because of my dad." A pause where he presses his lips together. "I've seen him work through countless stories. I know how to plot, how to find plot holes, and how to edit. I also know that it's important to have someone read your work before you send it off to an agent, and that you might be lucky your email went to Bart instead of the agent because they hate when you send them a full manuscript without being asked. So . . . anyway . . . if you need a beta reader and you want that beta reader to be me—I'm offering myself up as tribute."

Probably so he can laugh at me. Yeah, no way.

"Well, thank you. But after I sobered up, I decided it's probably best I don't do anything with the book anyway . . ." I check once again to make sure no one is listening besides Jack. "It was just a silly hobby that probably isn't even very good. And sending it to Bart made me see how much I don't want anyone to ever read it. It wouldn't look good for a second-grade teacher also to be an explicit romance author, you know?"

Jack is looking at me like he can see right through my lie. He knows I'm just scared shitless. He doesn't challenge me this time, though. "Thank you for the Band-Aid and antiseptic."

"You're welcome. Stop hammering tonight."

He stands, hands me back my pen from between his two fingers, and walks toward the door. "Not without the magic word."

"Over my dead body."

"Good night, Emily. Good night, ladies. Enjoy your supper club."

And with that, he leaves my house, closing the door behind him.

I breathe out and don't realize I have a sappy smile on my face until I look toward my sisters and find them absolutely gawking in my direction.

"What the *actual hell* was that?" Surprisingly, Annie was the one to ask it, and I have to spend the rest of the night explaining to them without really explaining to them just how Jack Bennett and I became friends.

June 11

JACK (9:16 AM): Go inside.

EMILY (9:16 AM): No—this is too fun. I like hearing Darrell
tell you how bad you are at construction.

JACK (9:18 AM): You must not have eavesdropped on the part
where he said I did an incredible job on the inside framing.

EMILY (9:19 AM): Did he?

JACK (9:19 AM): No. Go inside.

CHAPTER THIRTEEN

Emily

The day has finally arrived to save my future—and my ass. It's Wednesday, so we know that Marissa is at the school (Shirley and most of the other staff are thankfully out of town before summer school starts). Jack is prepared to play decoy so that I can sneak into Bart's office, locate the laptop, and hopefully get into it without a password so I can delete the email. *Yeah, not a long shot at all.*

And in return, I've held up my end of the bargain. Darrell finally called me back, said he'd be happy to squeeze Jack's project in, then came out to Jack's place yesterday morning where the two met for over an hour. They walked at least eighteen circles around the house. I could hear Darrell belly laugh all the way from my front porch where I was reading (eavesdropping) when he saw what a horrible job Jack had already done to the inside. Apparently, it would all need to be demolished and redone. I can't describe just how fun it is to have finally found something Jack isn't good at.

Now it's time to get this show on the road and I'm pacing the sidewalk outside the school where I've been waiting for Jack to show up for the last ten minutes.

I look up when I hear a familiar loud engine and immediately spot Jack riding in on his motorcycle. It didn't bother me that he was riding it when he was just some stranger on a bike. But now that I know Jack is the one who owns it, I hate that thing. I hate it so much that I really should look away and properly shun the contraption.

Instead, I watch with unrelenting attention as the man approaches. I catalog each moment like I'm studying for a test on it later. Jack is wearing dark jeans today with his riding jacket and brown boots. It looks less protective than the outfit he was in the other day, which worries me.

The visor on his helmet is pulled down and it's so dark I can't see through it to know if he's seen me yet as he cruises in. Unfortunately, I experience the Helmet Effect all over again because something hot and electric zips through my stomach. *How dare you be so basic, body.* But then I know he's seen me because he does the most boy thing I've ever witnessed. In the empty parking lot, he opens it up and rips through it. Just before he passes me, his helmet tilts ever so slightly in my direction. I can't see his eyes behind that visor, but I know our gazes have just met. *I feel it.*

He passes me, but then in a move that has me sucking in a nervous breath because I'm nearly positive he's about to dump his bike and end up bloody on the pavement, Jack whips the back end around and effortlessly holds control of the bike as he slows down and cruises back my way, taking the empty spot right in front of me.

As he parks, the sun glints off the motor of his bike, which I know nothing about, but see it has *R1* written in matte black on the side. Next, his brown boot hits the pavement. He cuts the engine, and his head fully turns in my direction, hesitating on me long enough that I can see my own fish-bowled reflection mirrored back at me. My green eyes look wilder than I realized. I blink and adjust from my starstruck stance to my usual confident posture. Jack lowers the kickstand and throws his leg over the seat to stand.

"Do you feel better now that you've alerted everyone that there's a penis on the premises?"

"Good morning to you too, Emily," he says, his voice muffled through the visor of his helmet, and God help me even that is sexy somehow. I need him to take off this damn helmet.

"You're late," I say hastily. "Did you not get my text that said to meet me at school early?"

He breathes a laugh and shucks off his gloves. "Apologies. I didn't realize *early* meant *with the sunrise.* But then I saw your truck leave and figured I better hustle. Hence the bike."

I grumble, wishing he wouldn't hustle on that thing.

"You know," he begins while fiddling with the buckle under his chin before lifting off the helmet. *Dammit. It's not better without the helmet.* "If you wanted to make sure we arrived at the same time, you could have come and gotten me to ride with you." His nice golden-brownish-blondish hair is lightly matted with sweat and is flipping up at the nape. He gives his head a little shake and quickly shoves his hand through his locks to de-stick them from his scalp. It looks darker like this. He's a brunette when he's sweaty.

His comment curls up and settles like a purring cat in the back of my mind. We could have ridden together. Because we're friends. I never even considered that option because this is all so new still.

"Or you could have ridden with me on the bike," he says when I don't answer.

"No way. This thing isn't safe," I say, tapping the toe of my shoe against the tire. "You shouldn't even ride it."

"Is anything in life actually safe?"

"Seatbelts have a pretty good track record."

He grins while setting his helmet on the seat and then joins me on the sidewalk.

"Hey . . ." I glance sideways at his face as we walk toward the school. "You're not wearing your glasses." I sound like a child who was promised a sucker and didn't get one.

"Because I wear contacts when I ride."

"Another mark for the cons column," I mumble.

"*Huh.* Emily Walker likes my glasses. Interesting." I shoot big eyes at him and he just grins, pointing lazily at his ear. "I have bad eyesight, but excellent hearing."

Before I can think better of it, I playfully bump my shoulder into his, knocking him off balance for a step. He looks just as stunned by my easy interaction as I feel. I'm that scene in *Willy Wonka* where the people are floating up to the ceiling. I'm light as a breeze in his presence and it's astounding. Over the last few days, our dynamic has completely changed. We are no longer the two people who only see the other as competition. There's more to us now. Layers. Context.

And I'm terrified to like it—because history suggests our rivalry always prevails and we will loop right back where we started. I don't think I want it to this time.

Especially as I catch a subtle whiff of his cologne and a sharp tug of attraction hits me. I wish I could say that the attraction is just biological and aimed at the fantastic body I know lives under his clothes, because that would imply that I can turn this feeling off when he opens his mouth. But it's not like that anymore. The more I get to know Jack . . . the more I . . . God help me—like him.

"You should enter a power-walking competition," Jack says, breaking through my inner monologue and alerting me to the fact that I've been storming down the sidewalk. "Normally I'm happy to keep up, but this leather isn't as breathable as you might think and if we keep it up, there will be armpit chafing."

I press my lips together. "You wouldn't have to worry about chafing if you just drove a normal vehicle like us intelligent individuals."

"You really think it's a good time to piss off the man who's currently helping you get your dirty novel back before anyone reads it? In fact, I think I've changed my mind. You can handle it on your own, Goldie." He pivots and starts strolling back toward his bike.

I shouldn't be so desperate. Shouldn't lay my hand of cards flat on the table for him to blatantly see, but as I watch him retreat with the echo of that cute nickname floating on the wind, I don't even have time to stop myself from reacting. I lurch forward and grab his bicep. "Jack. Don't you dare leave me alone with Marissa today."

He's still walking and I'm holding on to his arm as he drags me with him. The rubber soles on the bottoms of my sneakers are melting from the friction. I'm basically land skiing. "I don't know. It doesn't seem like you want me here all that much."

It's sarcasm dripping off his voice. Mischief painted on his smile, thick as honey. He wants me to play. But I rarely play. Don't even really know how. "Jack, stop. Tell me what to say. I'll say it."

He stops and turns his body sharply into mine, looking down into my face. I don't let go of his arm, so I can only imagine what sort of image we're portraying at the moment. And I can't bring myself to care as his smiling eyes look at my mouth. "I want to hear you say you want me here." My stomach drops. "If I'm going to help you, I don't want to do it under false pretenses. We're both too blunt for that anyway. If I'm going to help you—the most capable woman I know—I want to hear you say it's because you want me here with you."

"Why?"

He shrugs and I feel the muscles in his arm move. "Because I'm selfish. Because I'm a prick. Because I delight in throwing you off balance. Pick any reason you want, the why is not important. If you want me here, you're gonna have to say it."

I hate him. I hate him for putting me under a microscope like this when all I want is to hide. I hate him for seeing that I do want him here. That I need a friend right now and don't want to have to do this alone, and that I don't just want any friend, I want *his* friendship.

His smiling amber eyes are my target. "Jack . . . Don't go. I want you here."

I expect to see his smug smile, but something else wars in his expression instead. Maybe he didn't anticipate me actually saying it. Or it being true.

I only get to internally revel in knocking him off kilter for all of four heartbeats before he's recovering with a devastating smile. He steps forward and angles his mouth at my ear—instinctively, my hand tightens around his arm. He drops his voice and whispers, "Good, now say *please*."

He's already laughing as I shove him away. "Jack, will you *please* go step out in front of a moving bus? That would be so nice of you."

I barely get my own laugh out before we're interrupted.

"Jack. What are you doing here?" Our laughter immediately dies off and we both turn and find Marissa standing in the parking lot, her purse slung over the shoulder of her leopard print T-shirt and a lunch box in hand.

"Marissa!" Jack says, turning on the charm. "Just the woman I'm here to see."

"Me?" Her blue eyes are huge.

"Yep. I think I left my favorite jacket in Bart's office. I was hoping you could unlock the door for me so I can look."

She looks hopeful and far too eager to do Jack's bidding until she swings her gaze to me. "Then why is *she* here?"

Marissa said *she* like I'm the devil spawn from hell right at her front door. I'd like to be. Some nights I dream of horrendous things I could say to this woman. From my first day of working here when I organized the supply closet on my lunch break, she's made it her mission to remind me that *I'm not as special as I think I am,* and that

I better not try to overstep her. Maybe if her attitude was only aimed at me, I'd shrug it off. But she's like this with all of the teachers (except Jack). So naturally, I overstep her every chance I can get.

Bart keeps her around as his muscle because he doesn't have a backbone. He delegates each of his confrontational tasks to Marissa—which means after he reads my spicy novel, she'll be the one to fire me.

I'm just about to open my mouth and tell Marissa just how sick of her attitude I really am, but Jack cuts in first. "I found her walking along the side of the road with her thumb up and a sad sign about losing all her money gambling in Vegas so I decided to give her a lift."

I glare at him and he winks. And to his credit, the hostile energy in the air dissipates. This is why Jack is so easily loved by everyone. He has this uncanny ability to say exactly the right thing when it needs to be said. I usually go for saying the wrong thing and watching the room explode.

Marissa begins walking toward the front door. "You sure she's not here to corner me about some brilliant idea she has?"

Jack falls in step beside me as we follow Marissa. I narrow my eyes at her back, hoping lasers might shoot out. Jack taps the back of my hand with his and like a miracle elixir my anger fades. A new sensation grows in its place.

I force a smile. "I promise, no brilliant ideas here."

Marissa grunts. *Like a cavewoman.* "'Bout time you realize that."

Oh, that's it. I'm going to—

Jack's hand fully slips into mine this time. The air jumps from my lungs. His hand feels so good I actually have to look down at it. I have to see for myself what all the fuss is about. He squeezes once and when I look at him, he mouths, *She's not worth it today.*

And then he pulls his hand away and I want to throw a fit. *Put it back!*

Marissa unlocks the front door of the school and Jack leans in so he can hold it open for her (and me) to walk through. She beams up at him as she and her apex predator shirt glide through the open door. "Always such a gentleman, Jack."

I flutter my lashes up at him as I walk through next. "*Yes,*" I say in a quiet tittering voice only he can hear as I walk through. "*Such a gentleman.*"

"Kiss my ass," that gentlemanly mouth whispers back at me.

I toss him the bird behind my back. He pokes my finger. And I couldn't accurately explain the sensations I'm experiencing right now if I tried. It's . . . so new for me. It's what I imagine the fizzy bubbles in a freshly poured soda feel like.

Once we're inside the school, Jack takes the lead and I drop back to give him some space to work his magic. And work his magic he does. It takes him less than two minutes of engaging with Marissa about her recent trip to Florida to visit her friend and laughing at her unoriginal jokes about catching crabs before he gets her to unlock Bart's door. In fact, she's so pleased to get to do something that he asks that she's practically tripping all over herself to get to the door. Amazing. I always knew he was good at charming people, but I knew it in a resentful kind of way. It's nice to be on the receiving end of it.

"Thank you so much," Jack says, stepping into Bart's office. "I could have sworn I left it in here somewhere." The official plan was to look around the office under the pretense of having left his favorite jacket, and then once we spot the laptop and confirm it's in there, he'll act as a decoy and distract her outside the office long enough for me to open it, pray to the password gods that he doesn't have one set, and then find the email and delete it.

Only problem is . . . Bart's laptop is not in here.

"Dammit," Jack mumbles, realizing the same thing I have. But then he remembers Marissa is watching. "I really hoped I'd find that jacket."

"What color is it?" she asks. "Maybe it's in lost and found."

Jack looks at me and for some reason I think he's silently asking me to respond. That's how we both end up speaking at the same time with different answers.

"Black."

"Blue."

Marissa frowns.

"It's blackish, blueish. Emily and I can never agree on which one it actually is."

"But it's black," I say even though the jacket doesn't exist because in this fake upside-down world I still must win. Jack just grins at me.

Marissa is walking us back out. "Well, I'll keep an eye out for your blue jacket, Jack." *She would.*

"Thanks so much. We'll get out of your hair now." And then as if an afterthought hit him and it wasn't our entire goal by being here, he turns back to Marissa. "Oh, by the way—do you happen to know if Bart is going to do any work on vacation? I sent him an email about a potential curriculum idea and I'm wondering if I should expect an answer soon or wait awhile."

What a smooth little liar.

"I wouldn't hold your breath," says Marissa while unlocking her own office door. "Bart takes his vacation week very seriously. There's no way he's doing a lick of work while he's in the mountains."

"Ah—I guess I'll just have to be patient, then."

I wait until we're back at my truck to show my worry. "It wasn't in there! He must have taken it with him."

"Or, since he isn't planning to do any work, he left it at home," he says, refusing to let me only look on the negative side. But still, anxiety twists in my stomach. When my eyes drop, he ducks his head to catch my gaze again. "Hey. Even if he reads it, it doesn't mean you're automatically fired. There's still a very good chance that he won't care at all. You might have to endure a little moralizing from him, but if anyone can, it's you."

Suddenly, my mom's voice rings in my ears out of nowhere: *Find someone who helps you look on the bright side.*

But jeez, ghost of my mother, that someone cannot be Jack.

"So what's the plan now?" I say, opening my truck and climbing inside. Jack leans one arm on top of it and bends down to see me.

"The good news is, we've got plenty of time now that we know Bart isn't going to be opening his emails until next week. The other good news is I've got some ideas to consider. The very, very bad news is, a few of the backup plans end with me having the bromance Bart has always hoped for."

Before I can chicken out, I blurt exactly what I'm thinking. "Thank you, Jack."

He's too stunned to speak.

"Thank you for what you did back there. You went above and beyond. You are terrifyingly good at maneuvering people. You're like the James Bond of social situations. So charming no one would actually know what a monster you are in private." I say it as a spicy little cocktail of a compliment and old-school barb. The kind we've become comfortable in shooting at each other lately.

I expect him to smirk at me and toss one right back, but instead, I watch the light in Jack's eyes dim.

"Yeah. No problem." He lets go of my door and takes a step back toward his bike. "I've gotta get going." He quickly zips up his jacket, pulls on his helmet, and throws his leg over the bike.

Umm . . . I definitely said the wrong thing somehow. Jack has completely shut down and is ready to get away from me as quickly as possible.

"I'll see you back in our neck of the woods," he says, and then gives me a brief two-finger wave before he backs his bike out of the spot and cruises toward the parking lot exit.

I watch him go, wondering what in the hell I said wrong, before turning my key in the ignition and only earning a little whine from the engine before it quits altogether. I try again, but the second time I turn the key all I get are clicks.

"*Dammit,*" I say, hitting my steering wheel.

I really don't want to have to go back inside and endure Marissa while I ask to use her landline because my phone never gets service at the school, but Jack is already gone and—

I hear the sound of his bike getting louder again. Out my window, I see he's turned around and is heading back in my direction. Had he been waiting to make sure I got out of here okay?

Gentleman, indeed.

"Is it dead?" he yells over his engine after pulling his bike up beside me again.

"I think it's just napping." I try one more time but again nothing happens.

I look up when movement beside my window catches my eye. It's Jack, holding out a motorcycle helmet to me. "I've got a spare just in case."

"No, no, no. I'm not getting on that bike with you."

He shrugs. "Your call. Either you get on here with me and let me drive you home to call a mechanic, or you go back in there and beg your favorite person to let you use the phone."

He extends the helmet farther in my direction. I look toward the school, and then again at Jack perched on the bike, looking tempting as sin.

"Damn you, Jackson." I get out of my truck and slam the door behind me.

CHAPTER FOURTEEN

Emily

"You okay?" Jack asks, getting off his bike to help me.

I have the helmet on my head and am trying to latch the hook under my chin, but my hands are shaking too bad.

I swat his hand away when he tries to help. "Of course, I'm okay. I'm fine! Great. Perfect."

He holds his hands up. "You just seem a little jittery."

"I'm not jittery. I just can't see these damn fasteners under my chin! And it's so hot in here. And . . . Agh!" I drop my hands and stomp once against the ground.

Jack's helmet visor is flipped up so I can see his infuriating smirk. "That was a cute tantrum."

"I don't throw tantrums."

He has the audacity to laugh. "Yes, you do. I've witnessed four so far in this year of our Lord and Savior. And that was definitely one."

"I'm going to smack you."

He points to his head. "Can you do it while my helmet is still on?"

I drop my eyes from his face to the sleek, black death trap beside us. My heart rate ratchets up and suddenly hanging out with

Marissa all day doesn't seem so bad. Maybe she likes to puzzle. Puzzling sounds nice right about now.

"Tell me what's going on in that head. I can see your thoughts running a mile a minute. Are you scared?"

"Stop doing that." I ball my hands into fists.

His eyes drop to my fists and next thing I know, his gloved hands are wrapping around them, gently unfolding my fingers one by one. "Stop doing what?"

"Perceiving me so much!" I look up at him and we're helmet to helmet. "Believe it or not, there are some thoughts and feelings I like to keep to myself." But most of the time I feel liquid in front of him. Like he can see straight through me. He's probably reading these thoughts as I have them.

I'm thinking of a number, Jack . . .

He smiles. "I can't help it. I see you and I want to figure you out. Why don't you ever wear your red cowboy boots to school? And why do your hands ball up so tightly when you realize I've seen something about you? Because you want to hit me or because you're trying to hold back any more feelings from showing? Why did you immediately hate me in college—it had to be more than me spilling coffee on you? And how the hell did you sense there was more to the story of my glasses without me ever hinting at it?"

We're both silent for a few moments in the wake of his flood of questions. And then Jack blinks and steps away, looking almost embarrassed. "Sorry. I didn't mean to say all that. Forget it." He laughs softly and flips his visor back down. "Listen, if you're not comfortable riding with me, you can stay here, and I'll go back to the house to get the Land Rover and then come pick you up." He's walking toward his bike. *Problem solved.* "That way you don't have to see Marissa or ride on the bike."

"Jack . . ." He stops and turns his head back to me. "Why did you have a spare helmet?"

All I can see is my own reflection in his visor. He waits so long to respond that I know he's looking for a lie but can't find one. "I hoped you would ride with me some day and I wanted to be prepared."

My body softens. I take the two steps to put us helmet to helmet again. I lift my visor and lift his next. "And what did I say earlier that upset you?"

He looks away, sighs, and meets my eyes again. "My dad is a narcissist. I don't mean it in a hyperbolic way either. I'm pretty certain that he is an actual narcissist. My life growing up . . . it was painful a lot. And I quickly learned that saying what I truly thought or felt could get turned on me in an instant. Honesty, vulnerability . . . those things were what I got rid of first. And then I learned the art of reading him. Reading his moods and his energy and becoming what I needed to be to get through the day and to protect my mom from his shit. That mechanism bled into the rest of my life too . . . mostly by accident. I read people and adapt before I even realize I'm doing it. It's usually not until later when I'm sitting alone, and I feel hollow and used and upset that I realize I betrayed myself in some way. And so often . . . I'm scared that all this reading and maneuvering people—even if it's with the right intent—is somehow going to turn me into him. So when you made that comment—"

I shut my eyes. "The 'monster in private' one . . ."

He nods slowly. "It terrified me."

I wrap my hand around his forearm and squeeze. "I'm so sorry. It was a thoughtless comment—and one I never would have made if I knew about your dad. And for what it's worth, I don't think you're a narcissist."

The side of his mouth hitches. "Well . . . you would be the best judge."

"Why is that?"

"Because you're the only person I'm nothing but honest with."

His words snip the last vines of loneliness from my heart and replace them with balloon strings.

I lift my chin. "Help me with the buckle."

His chest expands with a breath, and he smiles before closing his visor. "You truly hate the word 'please,' don't you?"

"It's a *terrible* word."

He pinches the front of my shirt and gently tugs me even closer. My stomach muscles clench as his hands move under my chin to secure the loops of the fastener.

I wish his visor were open so I could see his eyes. I like looking into them this closely.

But maybe it's a good thing I can't see his eyes for what I'm about to say next. "I hated you immediately in college because you were the first man to smile at me after my ex broke my heart. I wasn't in a good place to be flirted with." His fingers pause for only a second and then finish up, pulling the strap taut but comfortable under my chin. "The red cowboy boots are my summer treat. I look forward to them every year. If I wore them during the school year, they wouldn't be special anymore." I take a breath. "You're the most intentional man I know. You don't do anything without a reason. And that's how I knew there was a story behind your glasses and why you never wore them. And lastly, my hands ball up because it helps me not cry. I don't cry in front of anyone. Ever." One more pause. "Except you apparently."

His head tilts. "For the record . . . I'll still think you're strong as hell even though you cried around me. And I like that I've gotten to see your summer treat boots." He pauses. "Thank you for telling me all of that." He snaps my visor down. "But if you scream like a little baby on the back of this bike, I'll make fun of you for eternity."

I laugh and smack the side of his helmet. But then he grabs my wrist and tugs me up so close to him our helmets bump. My heart punches against my sternum, especially as Jack's gloved thumb runs up and down the tender inside of my wrist. "I'll be so careful with you, Emily," he says, but I don't have the heart to ask him if he means on the motorcycle or not.

I nod.

He lets me go and situates himself on the bike, twisting to look at me. *God help me, he looks so good.* "Okay, this is your seat," he says, patting a tiny little sliver of cushion behind him that's slightly higher than his seat. "Put your foot on that and then kick over." He lifts his visor once again and looks at me expectantly when I don't move.

"You sure there's not like an extra pop-out seat or something? This looks . . . small."

"It'll be okay. I promise." He extends his hand to help me on. And I still can't quite get used to the sight of him doing that—offering to help me. To touch me. It does dangerous things to my insides. And my outsides. And every side I own.

It's not my prettiest choreography, but a minute later, I'm on the back of the bike with hands primly on Jack's shoulders. I am a two-by-four sitting straight up behind him. "Oh god, oh god, oh god," I say as he adjusts our weight, and the bike leans a little. "I'm going to fall off! There's no way this is safe. Why would you get one of these? This is the stupidest decision you've ever made. And my stupidest decision for getting on here with you!"

"Are you done hollering at me? Put your arms around me and lean in."

"Excuse me? I will not be leaning anywhere."

He laughs. "You think I'm going to drive on the road with your ass dangling off the back like that? Scoot in, hug the bike with your thighs, and wrap your arms around my torso here," he says, taking my hands and pulling them around his body and tugging them together until I lean my chest against his back. *And was it strictly necessary to say* thighs *so erotically like that?* "Better, right?"

I can only make a *mm-hm*-type sound because yes, this is definitely much better. Oh yes, being pressed against Jack's body is worlds better.

"Good," he continues. "Now if you can't tell already, I have helmet coms that let us talk easily to each other. I can turn on music too when you get more comfortable. Only rules are to brace your core when we get ready to stop so you don't slam your helmet into the back of mine, and don't fight me around turns. I know you'll want to lead, but I need you to follow me on this one, okay? Where I lean, you go with me. Don't try to counterbalance the bike yourself or it'll throw my weight off. I lean, you lean, got it, Goldie?"

"Why do you say it like I can't follow directions?"

"Because you don't follow directions. You invent them—but never follow them."

I tickle him and he flinches with a laugh. It stops me dead in my tracks. Are Jack and I playing? Yes. We are . . . and I *love* it. I'm scared of it—this joyous, reckless feeling—but I love it.

"All right, you ready?"

"Quit babying me. I'm fine. If I weren't fine, I wouldn't be on this bike. I'm not scared in the—*eep!*" I scream, squeeze the life out of his abdomen, and tuck my head against his back when he gives it gas and we start rolling.

He's laughing his head off. "You were saying?"

"Shut up and pay attention to the road!"

"Are you scared?"

"No."

"Liar. Open your eyes," he says in that taunting voice of his.

"My eyes are open!"

"Emily . . . open your eyes."

Son of a mind-reading bitch. I crack my eyes open and miraculously, we're not dead.

"Did you see that?" he says. "A snail just passed us."

"And he was going way too fast."

Eventually we roll to a stop at the front of the parking lot (we haven't even left yet?) and Jack looks both ways before telling me to hold on tight again and to lean with him as we take the turn. I think my soul is going to leave my body at these directions, but somehow, we make it. Jack keeps us off the pavement and before I know it, we're cruising down the road, emerald-green fields on both sides of us, sun bright and happy overseeing the entire adventure. Jack keeps the bike at a nice cruising pace that doesn't feel quite as scary as I imagined it would. He does not attempt anything lawbreaking with me on board.

"How ya doing back there?" he asks, and the joyful tone in his voice has my cheeks aching.

"Happy not to be dead."

"Admit it," he says through the helmet coms. "You're having fun as my backpack."

"I'm uncomfortable," I say snootily.

"You're in love with this thrill."

"I hate adrenaline."

"You're a junkie now," he replies.

"I'm impressed, I'll admit it. But I'm not impressed enough to want to do this again."

I'll die before admitting to him how good it feels to have my arms around him. That the competency with which he drives this bike is turning me on maybe the slightest bit. Just a small amount. Tiny. Minuscule. It's manageable.

A few minutes later when we pull up to the stop sign, he taps on his phone screen that's mounted between his handlebars and then music is coming through my helmet. But not just any music. The familiar bars of "Pony" by Ginuwine blare in my ears as we take off.

"What are you doing?" I yell over the music.

"Impressing you enough to make you want to ride with me

again." His helmet angles a little in my direction. And then I gasp when his gloved hand grabs my fist that has been locked against his sternum. He spreads my fingers out flat against his body and then tugs my hands up to the top of his chest. Just as I hear the lyrics to something about a pony and getting on it his hand squeezes mine, pressing it into his hard chest as he slides it sensually down his abdomen. He's singing along to the music and rolling his body like he moonlights in a dark club with a spotlight on the stage and a cowboy hat. *Magic Mike on a bike.*

He's carrying my hand down down down and even though I'm mostly sure he'll stop before my hand reaches the land of no return, I rip it away and smack him in the shoulder. "Pay attention to the road, menace!"

I can hear his low laugh when he cuts the music and takes the handlebars again, leaning forward. "I'm very good at multitasking."

As we cruise for the next twenty minutes through our town's gorgeous back roads, I realize I'm actually having fun. Maybe the most fun I've ever had in my life. And I'm having it with Jackson Bennett. And the fear and anxiety that always guides me, it's nowhere in sight. I'm not thinking about anyone else on this bike besides me, and it's the greatest relief I've had in years.

When we reach our road, Jack asks if I want him to turn in or keep going. It feels like a loaded question—with more than one interpretation. "Keep going," I tell him.

Jack's hand reaches back, wraps around my calf, and squeezes.

That night, with shaking hands and a sober mind, I open my laptop and purposely attach my manuscript to an email and hit send. I flop back on my bed, wondering how long it will take for a message to send one house over.

FROM: Emily Walker ‹E.Walker@MRPS.com›
TO: Jack Bennett ‹J.Bennett@MRPS.com›
DATE: Wed, June 12 9:02 PM
SUBJECT: My book . . .

Have you ever been horny for a Highlander before?
Now's your chance . . .
   1 Attachment: *DepravedHighlander.docx*

CHAPTER FIFTEEN

Emily

It's six-forty-five A.M., a breeze is blowing through my kitchen window and James Taylor is singing "How Sweet It Is" on my record player as I lift my cup of steaming hot coffee to my mouth. That's when Jack opens my front door. No warning knocks. Just steps right in like this is his house too. I squeak a noise at the intrusion and barely manage to scoot away from the slosh of coffee over the edge of my mug.

He's holding a big stack of papers in his hands, and there's another pile under his arm.

"Jack!" I press myself back into my kitchen counter, feeling incredibly skimpy in my nightgown. It's the exact color of champagne and of course made of silk because that's the only fabric I will let touch my skin at night. It's a short little number with a slit up to my hip. Oh, and it has these cute little lace straps with bows at the juncture of each seam. Fine, let's be real, it's lingerie. And I'm not wearing a bra because this is my home, and I will not endure that torture device first thing in the morning. It's my favorite gown but definitely inappropriate for standard visitors.

"Oh good, you're up." He hasn't looked up from his engrossing papers yet. And I'm worried that when he does, he's going to see a lot more of me than he's expecting.

"What are you doing in my house before seven in the morning? And ever heard of knocking?"

"We're past knocking. It's a waste of time."

"I beg to differ." I set down my coffee mug to cross my arms over my chest. He looks up finally as he steps into my little galley kitchen, full of light with window sheers being tossed by the breeze. And when he sees me, it turns out I had nothing to worry about. Jack doesn't look fazed by the sight of me in the least. *Good?*

I, however, can't help but swoon a little over the sight of him. He's a mess. His hair is disheveled, his jaw is lined with stubble, there are dark circles under his eyes, and his T-shirt is not only inside out but backward. And he's wearing dark gray jogger sweatpants. *Sweatpants.* Jackson owns sweatpants. I imagined he slept in chinos.

"Emily Walker," he says in a firmer tone than I have ever heard from him. "This"—he raises one of the stacks of papers in the air, wiggling it a bit—"is incredible."

I'm lost. I'm lost in a dream—that's what this is. It has to be. I'm in sexy, flimsy clothes, birds are chirping, James is singing, and Jack is in my kitchen babbling on about something that I don't care at all about because it's not actually important to the plot. The plot is that we are going to have sex in my dream and that's the whole purpose of it. That must be what is happening.

Why am I so attracted to the sight of him disheveled? Why do I want to bite his elbow? I'm ninety percent sure that's a weird thing to think.

"What's incredible?" I say, giving in to the dream's silly little side plot.

He frowns lightly at my sensual tone of voice. "Your book."

My dreamland bubble pops, and I yank myself upright when I confirm that this is reality. "My . . ." I blink a few times. "My book? That's my book."

"This is your book."

"You're reading my book."

"I *read* your book. Twice," he says. "Saw it come through my email when I got into bed and meant to read only a chapter and instead, ended up staying up the entire night to read it."

"Twice."

He grins. "Twice."

"And you printed it out? You own a printer."

He looks confused. "Doesn't everyone?"

I need to sit down. I need to . . . there's nowhere to sit. There's nowhere to escape. The dreamy sunlight from a minute ago is suddenly a piercing spotlight. I'm now searching through our entire interaction of the last minute to remember what it was he first said. *It's incredible.*

"You liked it?"

His eyes are bright and a little wild. "I loved it. And it's not that I didn't think you would be a good writer, it's just that when I read stuff from friends or novice writers I try to go in with pretty low expectations because I never really know what I'm going to get, but I should have known better." He cracks another smile. "I should have known you would approach writing with the same precision and expertise you approach everything else in life, Emily." He steps forward, a little breathless. "It was exceptional. You have to do something with it. It would be a shame for this story"—the pages wobble in his hand as he shakes it firmly again—"to live in a drawer."

I'm light-headed. Jackson Bennett thinks I'm a good writer. Thinks I could do something with this work. I turn away from his intense gaze and retrieve my coffee again; I drink it too fast and burn my tongue. "Shit." The mug goes on the counter again and I whirl around. "You're not lying to me, are you? Just saying what I want to hear?"

"I always tell you the truth. That's our thing, right? For good or bad, it's nothing but the truth."

Jack read my book.

I breathe in, resisting the burn of my eyes. This book . . . it was so deeply personal. I wrote my feelings on those pages. I wrote my struggle with grief. With anxiety after childhood trauma. I wrote about how I feel like the walls close in on me when I'm alone. And although Jack doesn't know that any of that is personal, it is, very deeply personal. And he liked it.

"I . . ." My eyes bounce everywhere, and I decide I need something to do with my hands so I turn and pour Jack a cup of coffee too. I add two splashes of flavored vanilla creamer too because I know he doesn't like his coffee black. "I don't know if I want to do anything with it yet. It's . . . terrifying."

"Unfortunately, I can promise you that feeling never goes away, no matter how many books you publish."

I hand him the coffee mug and watch his face closely. "That's how it's been for your dad?"

He takes the hot cup from my hand and stares at me a beat longer before answering. "No, actually . . . My dad has never lacked confidence. Even when he should." He sips his coffee. "But others I've known have definitely felt the terror."

I nod, unable to shake the feeling that there's more he hasn't told me.

"So what now?" I manage to ask despite my wobbling legs. "I mean, hypothetically . . . if I wanted to do something with this, what is my next step?"

That light floods his eyes again. "The next step I would suggest is to edit what you have. I went ahead and made some notes for you if you want them. And then after you've done another edit or two, you can either decide to get additional reads or take it on submission to find an agent. Unless you want to self-publish it, though I'll admit I don't know much about that. But I can find out if you want me to." He pauses with the most uncertain expression I've ever seen from him. "I mean if you want help, I want to . . . be the one to help you. I have resources and I'm happy to use them for you." I've seen a lot of sides to Jack. But this one is brand-new. He's excited. He's happy. He's in his element and feeling silly about showing too much joy. Jack, as it turns out, *loves* talking about writing.

Maybe it's because of his upbringing and watching his dad walk through all of it, or maybe it's because he secretly wants to be a writer himself. All I know is it feels good being on the receiving end of his attention like this. His excitement is contagious, and the fact that he's feeling it toward something I wrote—it's giving me that same confidence I felt after riding with him on his motorcycle. It's got me considering my future in a new way.

Over the last two years, I've become conscious of how I used to hold my siblings back from their dreams because I was afraid of them leaving me behind or them getting hurt. Afraid of that ever-creeping loneliness taking root in my heart and leaving a permanent ache. But that awareness has led to me championing my siblings toward their dreams even if I secretly—and like a terrible, horrible monster—hoped they'd fall through. Misery and fear will do that to a person, though.

I'm in possession of enough self-awareness at least to know that I was in the wrong. To bury those feelings and pretend they didn't exist so I could outwardly cheer them on. I've made helping them achieve their dreams my whole personality. My main objective. And I never realized until this moment how much I needed someone to do that for me. How good it feels to be on the receiving end of a person believing in you.

"What kind of notes?" I ask with equal parts anticipation and dread.

He smiles. "Well, that depends on what you want from me. If you need a cheerleader who only focuses on the good parts of your story and lavishes you with compliments and praise until you find your footing and confidence to dig into the meatier stuff—then you'll want this one." He holds up one stack of papers.

"And the other one?"

His smirk turns into my favorite smile. The one that reminds me of a jungle cat stretching out in a patch of sunlight. "The other one is not for the weak of spirit. It's brutally honest and doesn't pull any punches."

"That one," I say without hesitation. "I'm no wimp." My smile is just for him.

And something about it seems to snap Jackson into an awareness he hasn't had until this very moment. His eyes now drop to my body with a leisurely perusal that has chills blooming across my skin. His jaw flexes and I watch his Adam's apple bob as he swallows. "God, woman. How many of these outfits do you own?"

About time you noticed. Except, no. I don't want him to notice. Do I? Ugh, I'm all conflicted and inside out. He's my nemesis—but also . . . my closest friend? Neither of those titles, however, lends itself to a casual quickie to relieve tension. The struggle, I realize, is that he is wildly attractive. Even when I hated his guts, I knew he would look incredible naked. And now that there's an emotional vulnerability to this dynamic—which does not come easily for me, I might add—it's throwing gasoline on the fire.

I resist the urge to cover myself like I've done something wrong. "This is my house, I'll remind you. And you didn't knock. Seeing more of my skin than you'd like is the consequence of your actions."

His mouth tilts. "Who said anything about me not wanting to see your skin?"

And now I'm nervous. Why am I nervous?

Jack and I have always been equally matched in all ways, but secretly deep down, I've known there's one area where he would easily outpace me. Jack exudes sensuality. And I've never felt overly confident in that department. I mean, I'm not terrible by any stretch of the imagination, but I've never considered myself as overachieving in it either.

I clear my throat and pull the manuscript from his hands. "Let's see what kind of remarkable insight you've given me," I say sarcastically, because I can't actually let him see how eager I am to read his thoughts. It'll go straight to his pretty head.

I pad to my breakfast nook, coffee in one hand, manuscript in the other, and set them both on the table. I feel Jack following behind me. I pull the chair out, sit, and begin flipping through. There's a lot of ink on this page from his pen. And though I should probably be nervous, I can't help but smile at his handwriting. It's meticulous. It's clear he's used a ruler when underlining certain parts. There are also tabs marking the sections with his notes, and at first glance they appear to be color coded.

The first few notes, I agree with immediately.

Pacing issues.

This passage could be moved up.

Dig deeper here? What is she really feeling in this scene?

This line doesn't make sense.

He wasn't lying—these notes are brutally honest. And I'm grateful for it because it makes the sections where he's highlighted and added *I love this* feel all the more honest and important. Like little hugs.

I pause when I get to the only chapter with no notes.

"Why didn't you critique the intimacy scene?" *Intimacy scene* feels like the mature and professional way to refer to the chapter in question. Like when you go to the gynecologist, and you talk about your *breasts* even though you never say that word in your life because why would you when *boobs* is sitting right there.

I slowly turn in my chair to find Jack leaning his shoulder against the kitchen entryway, arms folded, ankles crossed. He's got a little frown behind his glasses. How is it possible for him to look so damn attractive with his shirt on backward? "I didn't know if you'd want me to. Didn't seem right without permission."

I'm used to confrontation from him. These other C-words, though—consideration and consent—turn my heart into an over-ripe avocado. So mushy my thumb would go right through the skin. What a terrible thing.

"You have my permission now. Tell me what's bad about my intimacy scene."

CHAPTER SIXTEEN

Emily

For possibly the first time in the history of knowing Jack, he looks unsure. Nervous. "I don't think so."

"Why? You critiqued every other chapter just fine."

His gaze is so connected to mine you could zip-line on it. "This is different."

"How is it different? I write romance—the sex is an important part of it. I want to make sure it's up to par too." I shouldn't push this. I feel the edge of something at the tip of my toes and I shouldn't take another step. But I do. "Unless you don't think your skills are good enough in that arena to be of any real help to me."

He pushes off the wall, smiling quietly. "I've never been baited so much in my life." He pulls a chair out and takes it. "Fine. You really want me to say what I think? Here we go. First, it lacks emotional depth. The rest of your book is packed full of feelings, but when we get to your sex scene, it's basically just graphic words for what's happening. It gives the impression that your main character, Kate, is moving through the motions but not actually feeling anything."

Oh god. What have I done?

He continues, back in work mode—completely oblivious to the fact that my breathing is shallow. "Next, she does all the work. For instance, this part . . ." He's pointing to specific sentences like he's pointing out solar systems on a map of the galaxy. *And here is where the heroine straddles him. And if you look over here, you'll find his bonus hand job.* "The entire scene just feels one-sided to me. Like he's on the receiving end of all the pleasure and Kate's working her ass off to make it great for him. But then . . ." He pauses and shakes his head in near disbelief. "It's just over."

I swallow, feeling sick. Turns out I was unprepared for those sorts of insightful comments. "What do you mean it's just over? Is there supposed to be a song and dance to conclude it?" My voice has never been so high-pitched.

"She leaves his house in a rush after. Why not have them lounge around a bit and snuggle? Give them some emotional intimacy in that moment at least."

I want to gag on that word *snuggle*. "Because . . . she's busy. She has places to be. People to see, Jack. She doesn't have all day to lie around in his arms and swoon over him. She's an independent woman who wanted sex, got it, and needed to get going."

"But that's not strictly true, is it? She loves him all through this story, even if she doesn't realize it at first. She wants him for more than just sex, obviously. So why not give your readers more here?"

"Maybe she doesn't know how, okay?"

I think it's the sudden clip to my words that finally clues Jack in to my mood. Understanding touches his face. Softens it. He looks at me from behind those glasses as he sits back in his seat, angling his body in my direction as he drapes his arm over the back of his chair. "I see now."

"You see nothing," I reply, snapping the manuscript pages over so they're in a nice, neat pile again. Show's over. Case closed.

He grins. "Why don't you snuggle after sex, Emily?"

He could at least have had the decency to ask me if I do or not. But of course he just acts like he already knows. Like I am some obvious, garish painting whose meaning he immediately understands.

"It's a waste of time. I've never seen the purpose of it."

"The purpose of it is comfort. Pleasure. Connection."

"I don't need any of those things."

"Have you *ever* snuggled after sex?" Why are we saying the word *snuggle* so much? It's a silly-sounding word. It should be stripped from the English language.

"No."

"Not even in a long-term relationship?"

I tap my finger on the table. "These questions are pointless, and they have nothing to do with my story."

"They're not pointless. It's important to interrogate where our words are coming from. When we write, we are putting our own thoughts and feelings down, yes, but also wearing someone else's skin for a time." *Jack definitely just said* we, *didn't he? Does this mean he writes too?* I don't get a chance to dwell on it because he continues on quickly. "You might not like snuggling, but Kate, your main character, does. That's why the scene felt so strange to me. She's so full of feeling and then suddenly, we get to arguably one of the most important scenes in the book and suddenly she's one and done. It's important to question whether you're putting too much of your own experience in, or if it's organic to Kate's character."

I meet his gaze even though my skin burns with embarrassment. I force myself to nod toward the manuscript. "I guess you could say that, yes, in a nutshell, this is what I'm used to. I've never had a partner who . . ." I grit my teeth to get through saying this out loud. "Well, the only real relationship I've ever had was in high school, so I don't think that counts. And as an adult, if I've wanted a good time, I've had to make it happen. And then after . . . I've never seen any point in hanging around with any of them. I have a fantastic mattress. Incredible sheets. I like things how I like them, and I don't see the need to lie around playing pretend that I'm a romantic leading lady when I constantly feel like a side character. So yes, when I hook up, it's for a specific purpose. Hopefully he has a good enough time that he'll call me again even though I don't like to cuddle, I'm not flexible with my schedule, and I insist on cracking the eggs in the morning because I can't stand shells in the scramble. Are you happy now?"

There. I said it. My humiliating words fall like smoke bombs in the room, replacing our oxygen with something unbreathable.

Jack's gaze sharpens on my face, his jaw flexing. "I'm the farthest from happy I could ever be," he says quietly. "I hate everything about what you just said. Especially the part where these assholes are out there taking from you and making you feel like there's parts of you that you should be ashamed of."

I stand, my chair scraping the floor, and walk back into the kitchen, pulling a carton of strawberries out of the fridge and carrying them to the sink to wash them. "Don't pity me, Jack. I have a good life. So what if my sex life is lackluster? I'll learn to write better scenes that are less stilted regardless. But unless you truly have some constructive criticism on how to improve the scene, this topic is closed."

I flick on the faucet and dump the strawberries into a colander to run under the water. It was a bad idea asking for his input. I didn't even consider that he would take a magnifying glass to my real life. And this lingering feeling is why I don't want a relationship. I'm fine with one and done. I am fine with never liking anyone enough to even slightly consider snuggling. Coming back home alone is so much more preferable to always stressing and wondering if I'm going to be enough for someone or if I'm going to say too much, show too much of myself, and scare them away when I'm just getting comfortable.

I'm lost in thought, washing the strawberries so thoroughly they are practically reborn. And that's why I don't hear Jack walk in behind me.

"Okay." His voice carries gently over my shoulder. "If you want constructive criticism, then let me show you what I mean."

My breath catches as his hands enter my field of vision and bracket me on either side of the sink. "There's not a damn thing wrong with you, Emily, or the way you have sex. Not a *single thing*. And when I say I'm upset, I mean that I'm upset you haven't had the kind of attention you deserve. You don't owe any man anything—and if he doesn't know from the first second of talking to you that he's the luckiest son of a bitch in the world for getting any attention from you at all, he deserves to be run over with a truck." He reaches forward and cuts the water. Touches my hip with his hand and gently turns me to face him. "I have practical ideas for your scene. If you want them."

Oh.

He steps back and gives me space to consider. "Yes, tell me your ideas."

He shakes his head. "I want to *show you* the difference between your scene as it stands now, and what I think could be more meaningful . . . to the readers."

"Show me?" I say, wishing my voice sounded more confident than it does. "Are you offering to . . . have sex with me right now?"

"Not quite. I'm not sure our . . . friendship . . . could withstand something like that. But I think we could stage-block it out. I'll walk you through the overview. Maybe it'll help you focus on the emotional side I'm trying to evoke and potentially give you a different perspective to write with. One you've maybe not experienced firsthand before."

The transcript of his words would read as harmless and matter-of-fact. A Method acting of sorts, since I've only had lousy sex thus far and as a romance writer would benefit from the hands-on learning experience. But I read the subtext in his eyes.

Jack's ulterior motives are as stark as a plane shooting across a clear sky, and I'm walking toward them with my eyes wide open.

I suck in my last normal breath before what I'm certain will change the way I categorize time. From now on there will only be BSB (before scene blocking) and ASB.

"Okay. Let's do it."

One quick breath is all he needs before pushing off the counter and taking my hand.

"Where are we going?" I ask.

"Your scene starts inside the front door of Kate's cottage. So we're going to the front door."

We round the corner, and he drops my hand when we're standing at the door. I hate how much I miss the contact immediately. Jack has held my hand a few times now and each one is better than the last.

"All right, what next?" I ask, mustering more bravado than I feel.

"Now show me what happens in your scene."

"You're kidding. I thought you were the one blocking the scene. I didn't sign up to act out my own words."

He smirks. "Intimidated by me?"

Always. But I can also appreciate a good challenge.

I put my hand directly on the center of his chest and shove. He stumbles back until he's flush with the door. Just like in my scene. I step closer and rise up on my toes, nearly level with his blazing eyes. "Insert hot passionate kiss here that has them dropping clothes, sinking to the floor, and her straddling him as they both climax together." I notice his pupils flare and I smile. "Careful, Jack. So far, it doesn't look like you're too bored with my scene."

His answering smile terrifies me. He leans close, pushes my hair back from my ear and over the back of my shoulder, exposing my collarbone, and whispers low, "But that's the problem. It's not about me. It's about you. And so far, all you've been worried about is how I am responding." He runs his hand from my shoulder down to my fingers, takes them gently, and then guides me with him to turn our bodies and reverse our positions. "Now . . ." he says. "What if your scene was all about her instead? What if the primary focus was her pleasure?"

"That seems selfish," I breathe out.

The curve of his mouth is a potent drug. "I love when a woman is selfish."

His index finger touches the place just below my navel and pushes ever so gently. I go back against the door as easy as a feather tipped over in the wind. He doesn't follow me immediately, though, like I did with him. He stands there and his eyes take a slow caress over every damn inch of my body. Suddenly, I'm aware of how thin this fabric is. Sheer. I think of telling my sisters that I wear this type of lingerie for me. Because a man would never appreciate it the same. But Jack is appreciating it. He's even nice enough to voice it. "This gown is beautiful on you."

His gaze skips down me like rocks across a pond. Each stop is punctuated with special attention. A devouring, hungry look on his face that has *want* flooding my body and chills pricking my skin. His eyes are invisible hands—I feel them everywhere they linger.

Finally he steps forward and runs his finger along the thin strap, following it down toward my chest but stopping at the little bow. "Do you know these outfits torture me? Every single one of them."

Oh god, oh god, oh god. Is this part of the scene?

He dips his face and breathes his way down my temple to my ear. "I like them on you a lot." He pauses.

"Is this you starting the scene?" I ask.

"Sure." He smiles. "And next I'd probably ask what you like." He pauses, lips hovering over my skin, and I imagine that a kiss on my shoulder would normally happen in that moment. "Do you orgasm easily, or does it take more time?"

"Umm. Is this an example of potential dialogue or are you really asking me?" I sound scandalized. How dare he say the O-word so casually to me. *Jack*. The man who didn't even say goodbye to me before he left town is using my own desire to pin me to the door.

"It's up to you . . . choose your own adventure, scene-blocking edition. Feel free to skip or . . . engage at any point."

This should be illegal.

"Um . . ." I clear my throat. "It's rare if it happens with someone else."

"I see," he says tenderly. "Do you feel like you can tell your partners this ahead of time?"

"God no. It would put too much pressure on them." His body heat curls around me like steam.

"Maybe on someone who's too immature or selfish to be having sex. I like to know." His thumb touches the inside of my wrist and draws the smallest circle. My eyes flutter closed, and I feel like I could pass out. Jack's body is heat, just out of reach. He's close but he's not pressing himself against me. Not giving what my body is craving.

I like to know.

What do you like?

I love when a woman is selfish.

I have never encountered a man like this in the wild. The men I've been with have never even slowed down enough to process the need for these questions. Sex for me has always been A + B = C.

Meanwhile it seems Jack has been out there performing advanced algebra.

He hooks his finger under my straps, tauntingly slow. I open my eyes and look down at where he could easily flick the thin fabric from my body. I wait in anticipation. Will he do it?

"In your scene, you have them naked in seconds. But if it were up to me . . . and if I knew the woman in question needed a little more attention to reach climax"—his finger slips away, his knuckle grazing my shoulder as he does—"I'd peel these flimsy clothes from you so slowly you'd want to die. I'd memorize every inch of skin I was given the privilege to see." He pauses and squints one eye like he's working on the details of a drawing. "After releasing your straps, I'd let the gown dangle around your waist for a bit rather than taking it all the way off. I think small moments of savoring like that go a long way."

His finger skates down the side of my torso, barely touching me all the way until he reaches the lace trim at the side of my thigh. "I'd bunch this up so I could touch all the places it's hiding." His eyes watch my face and I feel like I'm in the most sensual haze of my life. And then, Jack sinks down in front of me to his knees. The same position he was in back in the kitchen that night, but so, so different now. His eyes trace the cut of fabric that exposes the smallest sliver of skin from my thigh to my hip. "Assuming there's another scrap of fabric under here . . ." He taps my hip bone. I nearly vibrate like a rung bell. "I'd probably . . . or rather I'd have your hero hook the side of it with his finger like this and pull it all the way down." My imagination is on fire. "Step out of them please, love."

It's all pretend. It's all pretend. It's all pretend.

I raise my feet, miming the action of removing my panties. Oh boy, even thinking the word *panties* with Jack right here kneeling like that seems so wrong. In the very best way. Jack's gaze devours me like this—as if I'm actually standing here completely naked in front of him. He can see right through my clothes. His hands wrap the back of my legs, the most reverent touch in the world. His gaze lifts to me as he runs his hands up my calves and stops, holding on to me just above the bend in my knee. "Then I'd tell you to take one of these pretty legs and, if you're comfortable, hook it over my shoulder so I could taste you until I wrung every bit of pleasure from you at least once."

I have to brace my palms flat against the door just at the thought. His eyes trail back up my legs, his hands gliding with him as he stands. "Only then, once I knew you were good and ready, I'd scoop you up . . ." And he actually does, bending to take my legs out from under me and carry me to the couch. "And I'd put you here." He sets me onto the couch. "I'd take off my clothes for you, and then climb over you." His clothes stay put (regrettably), but he does gently climb over me. Except he doesn't press into me like I need. He uses all of his muscle to keep most of his body off me. But I'm dying for it. Dying for him. So far, this is the best sex I've ever had, and we haven't even really touched.

His inked forearms are on either side of my face, and it's an effort not to turn and kiss his arm. His skin would be blazing against my lips, I just know it.

"Now, if you really wanted to be on top, I'd consider it at this point. But see, you'd have to convince me that it's exactly what you wanted, and still . . ." In a deft move, he wraps his arm around my lower back until he flips us and somehow I'm on top of him, straddling him with his hands holding firmly around my hip bones. "I wouldn't let you do all the work." His grin up at me is absolutely devastating. His eyes drink me in. This isn't real, and yet it is painfully realistic. "I'd tell you how beautiful you are. How I think you're the strongest woman I know, but I also really admire the soft places you hide away. That you're scared of. I'd tell you I want you to let go and let me take care of you like this. That you're safe with me." He traces my collarbone with his finger, and I can't help it, but my eyes are stinging and misty. What would this be like? What would it feel like to have someone saying these words to me and meaning them? (Even as I think it, something in me whispers that Jack does mean them.)

Some of the emotion sharpens when the corner of his mouth tilts. "And then I'd work with you until you were sweating and crying my name. Until I wiped everyone else from your mind."

Ah—and there's the cocky man I know.

His body is firm and taut beneath me, and I have to try very hard to breathe normally. Not to move exactly how my body is begging me to against him. He's right. I've never made love like this. Nothing even close to it. And this was only an overview. Everything in comparison has been lifeless and gray. I never thought of *efficient* as a bad word until now. I never want efficient again. I want lazy. I want intense. I want blazing eyes and sweet hands and desperate words all over my body. *This man,* I think with frightening honesty, *I would want to snuggle.*

And he knows it.

He squeezes my hips like he can sense how badly I'm resisting giving in to what my body wants right now. "So what's your verdict on my scene?"

The verdict is that I'm in trouble.

I lean over, putting my hands on the couch cushion beneath his head. I bring my lips to his but don't kiss him. "I'll consider it."

Now he's struggling to breathe. I can tell. His eyes shut for a beat like he's in pain. It would be so easy for both of us to give in right now and end this torture. I'm so ready I could cry.

Maybe we could just . . .

I cover his hand on my hip and slide it back over the curve of my ass. He groans and the sound weaves between my ribs. "Jack . . . what if—"

My phone rings.

It rings loudly from the wall, and I roll off Jack and thump to the floor. Jack is catapulting upright. The ringing seems louder than normal. Feels like a siren. A warning.

We hold eye contact for long enough to exchange the same thought: *That really almost happened.*

I go answer my phone and now I'm Method acting a zombie. It's Madison—finally calling to catch up. And normally I'd be ecstatic to hear from her. I'd drop everything with joy. But right now, all I can do is watch Jack offer me an awkward wave and then walk out the door.

A little thought flashes quickly like a lightning bug: *I wish he were staying.*

June 13

JACK (7:45 AM): How dare you allow me to act out a sexy scene with you while my shirt is not only inside out but also on backward? I just got back and looked in the mirror . . . this is appalling.

EMILY (7:46 AM): It was surprisingly endearing.

JACK (7:48 AM): That's worse.

JACK (7:50 AM): Also . . . you said the only relationship you ever had was in high school. Was that the ex that broke your heart before we met?

EMILY (7:55 AM): Yes. His name was Liam. And the drama around it would have made an excellent Netflix series.

JACK (7:56 AM): What happened?

EMILY (8:01 AM): Oh, you know . . . girl and boy are in love from freshman year all the way to senior year. But as it turns out, girl loved boy a lot more than he loved her. Boy is a liar. Girl is brokenhearted and jaded and would like to wipe the male species from the face of the earth . . . and then girl goes to college and meets a new boy who spills coffee on her and then tries to smooth it over with flirting, but she's scared and hates boys now, so she bites his head off and begins a decade-long feud with that boy. It's basically your classic tale.

JACK (8:03 AM): What happens when girl and boy #2 mature and get older?

EMILY (8:04 AM): They still fight a lot. But they're starting to grow on each other.

JACK (8:15 AM): PS. You could never be a side character.

CHAPTER SEVENTEEN

Jack

'm midshower when it goes ice cold.

"Shit," I say cranking the knob all the way to hot. "*Shit, shit, shit.*" It's somehow getting colder with every second. Construction officially starts tomorrow—Monday—and it can't get here fast enough. I am sick of living in this place. I'm sick of not having a kitchen. Of sleeping in a small-ass bed. Blame it on my upbringing, but I am not good at roughing it. I unapologetically enjoy comfort and nice things. Which is one reason it's been great spending a fair amount of time over the last few days at Emily's house.

It's happened by accident. She was gone all day Friday with her sister Annie, delivering a flower order for an event a few hours out of town. A little thunderstorm rolled through, so she texted me asking that I go check on Ducky—who apparently doesn't like storms. Ducky seemed fine to me, but I didn't want Emily to worry, so I stayed and worked on my book at her house from the comfort of her couch. Emily came home that evening and found me there, lying flat on her couch, with my laptop propped up by pillows on my lap, and Ducky curled up on my chest, her little orange face tucked under my chin. Turns out, I'm a cat person.

Emily stared at me for three beats and then asked if I wanted to stay for dinner. She put a frozen pizza in the oven, and we watched a movie together while we ate. I thought it would be awkward and tense after our scene blocking that almost turned into so much more the other day, but no. Emily was Emily and seemed determined to (A) not mention it and (B) act as unruffled as ever. And I sure as hell didn't bring it up because this . . . whatever this is feels fragile and I won't dare break it.

The next morning, she popped into my house without knocking (retaliation) and asked if I'd go with her to an estate sale to pick up a massive new rug she bought dirt cheap (after an impressive round of haggling) for her classroom next year. On our way home, we passed a used bookstore and stopped in. She found a pirate romance from the '80s that's definitely seen better days, but she swore Annie would want it. And as if the universe was laughing at me, on a stand by the register was a signed hardback edition of my first book. My heart raced as Emily eyed it, picked it up, and inspected the signature for so long I thought she was memorizing the curve of each loop. And then she bought it—claiming it was a sin to pass up a signed edition.

I felt as tall as an ant in that moment for not telling her the truth. The deeper into this friendship we get, I know Emily would keep my secret if I told her. That's not what worries me anymore. Now it's that we are finally . . . friends. In the past, competition has always gotten in the way of that. What happens if I tell her I'm a published author after learning she's going after the same dream? Will it throw us right back into the center of the arena? I'm not ready to find out.

With ice-cold water, I scrub down my body as quickly as

possible, submerging only when it's absolutely necessary. But when my landline—yes, landline—starts ringing from my kitchen, I decide to end the torture and get out.

"Just a second!" I yell as if whoever is on the call can hear me. I towel off at warp speed, pull on my black boxer briefs, and then snag my glasses off my bedside table on the way to the kitchen. I whip around the corner and lift the phone from the receiver.

"Hello?"

"Were you just on a run? Why are you so out of breath?"

"Who is this?" I ask, scrubbing the towel against the back of my head.

"It's me. Jonathan."

"Who?"

"Johnny!"

Water drips off my body and pools at my feet. "Bonnie? I don't know any Bonnies."

"Johnnyyyy," he says, dragging out the name to overenunciate each letter. Not kidding, I've played this joke on him no less than three times and he falls for it every time. "Your agent!"

"My agent isn't named Bonnie."

"No—it's Johnny with a *J* as in *jam*."

If I were warmer right now, I swear to God I would tell him *Jam* is a strange name. Instead, I laugh. "Ohhhhh, Johnny. Why didn't you say so?"

"Son of a bitch, you knew the whole time, didn't you?"

"Yep."

"You're lucky you're my biggest client."

"I remind myself of this every day. What can I do for you, Johnny?"

"I got an email from Denis yesterday." Denis is my publicist. "I'll give you three guesses for why he was emailing me and the first two don't count."

"He wants to know what shampoo I use since my hair is so luscious. He wanted to tell us he's quitting publishing so he can pursue his lifelong dream as a zoologist. And, oh, let me see . . . he wants me to reveal my identity along with book four's title on *Good Morning America*?"

"Damn. He emailed you too?"

"Yep."

"Crazy he's going to become a zoologist, huh?"

"To be honest, I saw it coming." I'm not sure most agents could put up with my shit, but Jonathan—he's great. A little gullible at times, but the best person I could ask for to manage my career. He was brand-new to agenting when he answered my query, and some might have found partnering with someone so inexperienced a very scary gamble. But I liked that he needed me as much as I needed him.

He was also the only agent who not only said they loved it but admitted that my manuscript was raw and needed a lot of work. All the other agents blew smoke up my ass and said it was perfect and ready to go on sub—and if there's one thing I hate, it's being lied to. I crave brutal honesty.

The guy was approachable, and we shared the same vision for my books. Best of all, he respected my decision to remain anonymous after I opened up to him about who my dad was. He was the only agent I felt comfortable telling. I doubt many others would have supported my choice not to ride my dad's coattails all the way into the bookstore like Jonathan did. And he's been true to his word that he would protect my privacy ever since. He never pushes me to tour or have a social media presence. I mean, I have accounts on all of the major platforms, but they're mainly full of graphics and a few vague lifestyle photos that don't show my face.

And actually, I think people like the mystery of it. Pun intended.

The more I think of Jonathan, though, the more I wonder if

he'd be a good fit for Emily as an agent too. I want to ask him, but something tells me I need to ask Emily if she'd want that first. Maybe this is something she wants to do on her own.

"I'm sure I already know the answer, but I'm still obligated to ask. Will this be the year that AJ Ranger finally unveils himself as Jackson Bennett?"

"No," I say firmly. "Books are selling just fine without my face being on them." *Just fine* would be an understatement. My books all debut as number one *New York Times* bestsellers . . . and usually hang pretty close to number one for a few months. Right there next to my dad's.

"Don't worry about it. I'll email Denis and tell him it's not happening and to drop it once and for all. If you ever decide you want to step into the limelight, we'll let him know, but I'll make it clear it's unacceptable for him to continue to bug you about it."

I sigh a little with relief. "Thanks, Bonnie."

Our conversation ends abruptly when my front door flies open and in strolls Emily. "Jack, I just heard that—"

She freezes, eyes melting over my body.

"Jonathan, I gotta go." I hang up the phone, and Emily makes no move to turn away. She doesn't blush. She doesn't stagger. She stares boldly at my body, and lust is written all over her face. It's a delight to see.

"Well, well, well. You've finally caught me in my pajamas," I say, enjoying the way her eyes finally lift to mine and smirk.

"I should have known you'd be a Calvin Klein man." The space between us pulses. Begs us to get closer. If we hadn't been interrupted on the couch the other morning, we absolutely would have had sex. And I can't decide yet if that would have been the best or worst decision in the world.

"What's wrong with Calvin Klein?"

Her eyes rest on the corner of my body where my hip bone

meets with the waistband of my boxers. She looks like she's imagining hooking her finger inside. "So high-class. Snooty." She grins. "You can never just buy the Target brand of anything."

"Says the woman who sleeps in silk lingerie. Face it, Emily. We're the same."

"No, because I have a few nice things that I had to save way too long to afford or used a coupon to buy. You have no shortage of nice things. How do you afford it, Jack?" I don't think this is about her thinking I'm snooty anymore. This is Emily's nose catching a scent again. This is her trying to work out the answer to a question that she's not even sure she's asking yet.

"Maybe I used a coupon too."

"On your brand-new Land Rover?"

"Dealerships are doing incredible things these days to move inventory."

"Jack . . ."

"Emily. Don't worry about me. I have excellent money management skills."

"But terrible taste in jewelry," she says with a quiet smirk, her gaze dropping to my plastic candy necklace.

I smile and touch the colorful string around my neck. "You know why I wear these necklaces, right?"

"Because you want everyone to know you're whimsical and fun?"

I laugh. "Yes. But also because they're gifts from my students over the years. It started at my old school. One of my first students gave me a friendship necklace. The one you've probably seen me wear a few times. The next year another kid noticed I liked to wear my friendship necklace, so during teacher appreciation week, he gave me one too. Over the years the kids noticed, and it's become a thing. I get at least one new one every year. I think I have like twenty at this point and I rotate them out."

"I see," she says, eyes blazing like this answer couldn't have been better. And my skin is melting under her attention. I can't think straight in these conditions. I want her, and standing here in my underwear in front of her, there's certainly no hiding it. But I'll be honest, I have no idea how to move forward. We are teachers at the same school. We are neighbors. I'm attracted to her (and maybe even have feelings for her?). And now we're also friends, to top it all off.

Almost as if Emily and I are having these thoughts in tandem, she clears her throat and turns toward the door. "I wanted to tell you that I heard Bart is coming home tomorrow. I've decided to break into his house tonight, and I was sort of wondering if—"

"I'll be there. This idea is much more preferable to the one I was considering."

She turns back. "What was yours?"

"I was going to surprise him when he got back with a coffee and basically invite myself inside to chat. I would have gotten an urgent email on my phone I needed to look at, but it wouldn't load so I'd need to use his computer. I'd delete the email while I was logged in."

"I mean . . . not the worst idea actually."

"A good plan B. I'd rather give your option a shot first, where I don't have to pretend to pal around with Bart if possible." Bart is . . . well, *judgy* would be the best word for it. He's not a terrible guy or anything, but he is a people pleaser's worst nightmare to interact with. He looks like he's waiting for you to slip up. I'm always exhausted after talking to him.

"Well, thanks for being willing to risk an afternoon with him for me."

"Hey, actually . . ." I pause, wondering if I should really bring this up while I'm still standing here in my underwear. "Hang on a second." I go throw on some athletic shorts and then meet her at the front door again. "So I don't overstep, I wanted to ask you before I did anything. But I was wondering if you'd like for me to talk to my—" *Damn,* I almost did it again. I quickly reword. "Friend. One of those resources I told you I had in publishing. He's an agent and might be interested in reading your book for representation. Or at the very least, connect you with an agent who might find it a good fit?" When she doesn't respond right away, I feel compelled to defend my case. "This actually happens more than you'd think in the industry. It never hurts to pull strings with people you know to get a foot in the door."

I would have asked my dad to do it for me too if we had a different relationship. If I knew he wouldn't use those strings against me or to further his own agenda.

Emily's eyes are wide. She's stopped breathing. I'm not sure if this is a good sign or a bad one. "I see. And you want to pull strings for me?"

"Yes. If you'll let me."

Emily nods once—looking stoic. But I see her balled-up fists at her sides. She's trying not to cry. Happy tears? Or frustrated?

Finally, she rubs her lips together and blink blink blinks. "Thank you," she says quietly. "I would definitely appreciate you reaching out to your connection."

I let out a relieved sigh. *Happy tears.* "You're welcome."

A beat passes where we just stare at each other. I don't know what Emily is thinking, but for my part, I'm trying to absorb the realization that the tug I was experiencing in Nebraska—the constant thoughts of Emily and what she's doing—was right. I thought I would come back and be reminded of all the reasons she and I could never work. Instead, all I'm realizing is just how freaking much I like Emily Walker.

A soft, tentative smile pulls Emily's lips. "Okay . . . I'm going to go. But . . . I'll see you tonight?"

"See you tonight."

June 16

JACK (12:13 PM): I talked to my friend, and he said he doesn't acquire romance (his loss) but he has an agent friend who does. I told him your premise and he pitched it quickly to her . . . and . . . she said yes. She wants you to send the first eight chapters.

EMILY (12:16 PM): WHAT! Who is the agent?

JACK (12:16 PM): Colette Menton

EMILY (12:17 PM): Colette Menton!!!!! *Faints*

JACK (12:18 PM): :) I take it you've heard of her

EMILY (12:20 PM): She is the top agent for selling romance!! I didn't even have her on my list of agents to query because I was sure that would be reaching too high.

JACK (12:22 PM): No way. She'd be lucky to snag you. Can you have them edited by tomorrow morning to send to her?

EMILY (12:26 PM): Actually . . . I don't know. I'm not sure that the story is ready. And I just looked at her bio . . . it seems sort of intense. Maybe I should wait and work on this some more before I send it?

JACK (12:29 PM): My friend said she's open to queries now, but that her window closes very quickly. If you think you want her as your agent, you gotta submit soon. The story is incredible, Emily. Bet on yourself.

EMILY (12:35 PM): Okay. I'll do it! I can definitely have them edited by tomorrow morning.

CHAPTER EIGHTEEN

Emily

"Oh my gosh, this is such a horrible idea," I say, crouched behind the little stone wall of Bart's house. We parked down the road and walked what felt like eighteen miles to get here, which was rough on my body that has been doing nothing but sitting all day. The second after I read Jack's text about sending my chapters to Colette, I edited the shit out of those first eight chapters. Tomorrow morning I'll be sending my book through the ether to land in Colette Menton's inbox, and it could change my life forever. Colette is worlds bigger than Barbara, and although I'm a little hesitant to sign with an agent with so many clients and whose bio said *she prides herself in selling books of higher-than-average caliber,* it feels good to inch a little closer to turning a dream I've kept stuffed away into something tangible. I can't fully process it yet.

"Yeah, it's a bad idea for sure."

I whip my head in Jack's direction. "You were supposed to make me feel better by saying we're not doing anything wrong because we're not actually going to steal anything."

"No, we'd still go to jail if we get caught."

"Maybe you'll go to jail, but I will remind Sheriff Tony that I bought fifteen boxes of his daughter's Girl Scout cookies this year and get off with a warning."

"You're not even going to attempt to get me out with you?"

I shrug. "Why should I?"

"Because I'm pretty," he says with the sincerest expression. "And you'd miss my company."

I squint. "Debatable."

"Let's test it." Jack stands and dusts his hands off against his navy pants. It's actually the most somber I've ever seen him dress. Between the pants, brown boots, and gray Henley, there's not a pop of color on him. It makes me think I should have worn something sneakier too. Instead, I'm in a pair of high-waisted jeans and a red-and-white floral top with cute little pearl buttons lining the front. Very impractical for a heist. But very cute. I regret nothing.

When Jack takes a step, the main floodlights of the backyard flare to life. My heart pounds as he brazenly walks right up to the back door.

"Jack!" I whisper loudly, but he just waves for me to follow.

I scurry up behind him, checking over my shoulder like a SWAT team is going to suddenly pounce from the woods and arrest us. So far so good, though.

"How are we going to get in there? Oh—are you picking the lock?" I ask as he drops to his haunches.

"I'm sincerely flattered that you think I could pick a lock." He reaches under the little frog gnome by the door and withdraws a shiny key.

I gasp in delighted shock. "How did you know that was under there, Sherlock?"

"My senses were tingling. Also last year when Bart was out of town he asked me to come put a package inside his house. Key is in the same place it was then."

Jack inserts the key inside the lock and turns it. It opens easily and my stomach swoops with anticipation. A wave of cool air-conditioning billows out to welcome us. The grin Jack tosses me over his shoulder, however, is far more welcoming. I don't know what to do about the fact that I seem to have a full-blown crush on Jack.

Or no. Not a crush. Something bigger and scarier. I think about him constantly. If anything funny happens, I want to email him or text him or run next door and demand he hear about it. If I can't sleep, I find myself tiptoeing toward the front door, my greedy little feet set on scuttling across our lawns like a hermit crab until I end up in his bed.

I don't like change. And I'm terrified of relationships. But I find myself contemplating both of those things with him. Which is why I must resist. *You need more time,* I chant to myself like a witch over a cauldron. *Let the feelings cook before you act on them.* There's no rush. And if they're still there in a month or two, maybe I can consider it. Safety is key here.

"After you, Emily Stalker," says Jack, extending a hand for me to pass through before him.

"Quit calling me that. I am not a stalker, and someone might get the wrong idea."

His fingertips brush mine as I walk by. "Says the woman currently breaking into a house in the dead of night." Once we're inside, he softly closes the door behind us, and we're plunged into darkness.

"It's nine P.M., hardly the dead of night."

Jack and I click on the flashlights we brought and shine them around the kitchen. "I've actually never been here before."

"Really?" He illuminates a giant rooster print above the little breakfast table. There's an apple print border wrapping the room, with blue-and-white-striped wallpaper covering the lower half of the wall. "I've been here twice."

I shine the flashlight at Jack's face, and he grimaces. "When was the second time?"

"To have breakfast with him."

"You had breakfast with Bart?"

"Why does that shock you?" I like how his voice sounds a little like sandpaper when he's quiet.

"Because other teachers have invited you to do at least a hundred things with them and you always declined and gave a bogus reason like your dog was sick and needed to be taken to the vet."

"Taking a sick dog to the vet is a valid reason."

"Sure. If you owned a dog."

His quiet laugh is delicious. "Busted."

After verifying that there's no laptop anywhere on the counter, we meander into the next room. A formal dining room. Equally dated as the kitchen. Wallpapered in burgundy. Large china hutch on one wall, full of dishes.

"I always wondered why you never did hang out with any of the teachers outside of school. I know you were invited to Hank's several times. And Rachel's murder mystery party. I thought for sure you'd go to that."

He shines his light in my direction but not quite in my eyes because he's nicer than me. "What's your guess? I know you have one."

We're on opposite sides of the formal dining table and slowly meeting around the far side. "Zoe was jealous? Didn't want you spending after-hours with other people?"

We stop right in front of each other. Close enough that I can hear his hint of a laugh. "You really didn't like Zoe, did you?"

"She made you feel bad about your glasses." I reach up to touch my index finger to the side of the frame like I'm petting my favorite animal. "I hate her."

He smiles. "I know you're not gonna like hearing this, but she wasn't an evil person. She had her good moments."

"Did she cheat on you?"

He squints. "Yes. But I don't believe the fault was all hers. I contributed to the problems of our relationship as much as she did."

"Was her cheating a onetime mistake? Or was it an affair?"

He sighs. "You're a relentless pain in the ass when your nose catches a scent."

"Thank you. Answer the question."

"An affair." He looks away and then back. "She was cheating for a year. It's part of why she wanted us to move to Nebraska. He had moved there first."

My stomach bottoms out. "*Jack.*"

"No. Don't do that. You don't know the ins and outs of our relationship. I was just as much at fault as she was."

"Why? Did you cheat too?"

He looks appalled by this concept. "No."

I groan and turn away. "See. You're too nice."

He's trailing behind me. "Something I never thought I'd hear you say."

"What do you think you could have possibly done that would have warranted her cheating for an entire year and moving you guys to Nebraska to be closer to the man she was cheating with?"

"I was distant. I never really opened up to her. I never loved her like I should have because . . . well . . . I didn't love her."

We're in the living room now. "You . . . didn't love her? Why did you stay with her for so long?"

In his silence, I count four ticks of the grandfather clock down the hall. And then . . . "When I was a kid, we moved away from the house I was raised in and into a big fancy one in a gated community.

I hated it there. It didn't have my favorite worn-in carpet or cool secret hiding place under the stairs. And I made the mistake of telling my parents. I told them I hated it there and I wanted to go home." At some point during this speech, I've gravitated closer to Jack. "My mom started crying immediately because she felt so bad I was unhappy, and my dad couldn't stand when my mom showed emotion. He told me to look at what my being a spoiled brat had done to my mom. He said he was only trying to make our lives better, that I was being ungrateful, and that he didn't even want to talk to me if I was going to act so spoiled. He slammed the door to his office, and then my mom went in her room and bawled because she couldn't make anyone happy."

"Oh, Jack . . ."

"I think that's the first time I remember feeling like I'd rather bury my own feelings than be the cause of so much pain again." He shrugs. "It got worse over the years, and every step along the way has been a snowball of that moment. Little by little I shut myself down. Avoided confrontation because facing it felt like I was being chased by an imaginary bear rather than just an argument."

"Do you feel like that when we argue?" I hold my breath waiting for his response. If he says yes, I'll never forgive myself. And I wonder when exactly this happened. When did Jack go from someone I hoped would step on a nail to a man who has warm flesh and blood and a golden heart beating under his cozy knit shirt. A heart I very much care about.

His smile is so soft it's made from the same silk as my favorite PJs. "I never feel that way when we argue. It's always been different with you."

"Why?" I need to know.

"I think because when we would fight, I'd show you my absolute worst again and again, and you kept coming back for more. You never shut the door on me. My thoughts and opinions have always been safe with you. And God, Emily, I can't tell you how good it is to always know exactly what you're thinking with no mind games in the way."

I know what he means. I feel the same way. I have freedom from perfection with him, and that's the best gift I've ever received from anyone.

"But to answer your earlier question, no, Zoe didn't keep me from socializing with the teachers. I did that all on my own because I don't . . . I don't like to get too close to people. I always have this feeling like something will go wrong if I do—so it's been easier to keep to myself. Even with Zoe. So that's what I mean when I say it wasn't all her fault. She probably felt lonely in our relationship too. That's why I can't hate her."

I have to turn away so I don't wrap my arms around him and squeeze. He's just so . . . he's so good. His heart is kind and empathetic. And I really, *really* like him. It's a big problem to have when I'm trying to convince myself not to do anything about my feelings. "Listen to me, Jack. No matter what you say, you did not deserve to be cheated on. If she was lonely, she should have ended it before moving on to someone else or communicated with you to fix it. Don't take on the responsibility of her mistake." I pause. "But if you don't want to hate her, fine. I'll hate her enough for the both of us."

"Thank you," he says with a soft grin, then shifts uncomfortably on his feet, clearly ready to be finished talking about Zoe. "All right, let's find this damn laptop."

We both leave the living room and walk down the hallway. I shine the flashlight against the wall of photos and find a slew of images of Bart as a young man with a woman I don't recognize.

"Strange to think of Bart with a wife, right?" Jack says, coming to stand beside me.

"I've never seen a picture of her before." All I know is that she died at some point in the '90s.

"Yeah. And he doesn't talk about her much. But that morning I came over for breakfast, he did tell me he hasn't changed a thing since she passed. That's why the house looks frozen in time."

My heart squeezes with recognition. *I know that kind of pain.* The grief that makes you terrified to let go of the time you were once happy. Suddenly I wonder if this will be me one day: living in a home that I'm afraid to change, afraid to grow in because I'm so scared of leaning into the pain of change.

It feels lonely in here. And maybe it's just because the lights are off, but there's an eeriness to it. I don't want to live in a house like this one day.

But I'm not quite as stagnant as I used to be, am I? I wrote a book. And I'm taking a chance on myself and sending it to the best agent out there. And I'm breaking and entering with my ex-nemesis who is now my friend. There's hope for me yet.

"Emily," Jack calls from down the hall. I was so lost in thought I didn't even realize he had walked away. "I found his laptop."

The relief that floods my body could rival a tsunami. I hurry in the direction of his voice and hang a left into the home office where Jack is seated behind Bart's desk. The screen lights up, illuminating Jack's face when he opens the lid. He looks like a cartoon character who's just discovered a treasure chest.

"Is it password protected?" I ask, coming around the side of the desk.

Jack's slow smile is all the confirmation I need. "Nope."

"God bless Bart and his trusting heart. Do you see the email?"

Jack doesn't get to answer me. In the next moment our gazes snap to each other as the sound of a key rattling in a door lock trickles through the room. "Is that . . . ?"

CHAPTER NINETEEN

Emily

"Someone's coming in the back door," Jack says, snapping the lid of the laptop shut and standing. "I thought you said he was coming tomorrow?"

"That's what Shirley said! What are we going to do now? I was bluffing earlier. I only bought eight boxes of Girl Scout cookies! That's not nearly enough to keep me out of jail."

As I'm frantically whining, Jack has placed his hand on my lower back and is pushing me toward a closet we passed in the hallway. He opens it and nudges me inside with the coats and cleaning supplies. He follows right behind me.

The closet is so small, we barely fit in here together.

My heart is racing but quiets a little when I shine the flashlight up and see Jack's lazy smile. I'm not here alone. I'm with Jack.

We listen silently as the back door opens and there's the sound of someone humming that we both recognize. Bart hums eighty percent of every day.

"It *is* him!" I whisper, and Jack presses his finger to my mouth.

He leans in, his breath sliding against my jaw as he whispers in my ear, "Don't panic. We're not caught yet."

Oh, but I'm fully committed to panic by now. I've only been in here thirty seconds and I'm already cramped in a suffocating way. A hanger is pressing into my shoulder blade and my hip is jutting out at a strange angle. It's so dark, and if Jack weren't in here with me, I'd be hyperventilating.

"We're going to have to wait until he goes to bed and then we can sneak out," he says once again into my ear, and the only positive part of this experience is that we're so close. I can feel his words as they rumble through his chest.

We're both marble statues in the cramped closet as we listen to Bart hum around his kitchen, opening and closing cabinet doors. I think he's making something to eat. My stomach growls in response and Jack looks down at it, making a hush expression. When we hear Bart's footsteps getting closer, Jack clicks off the flashlight and we hold our breaths. *What if he opens this closet?* I might not have gotten fired for the email, but I sure as hell will get fired for breaking and entering his home. I'll make sure Jack doesn't, though. I'll bargain and beg and plead. Anything to make sure he doesn't lose his job.

Bart's footsteps continue to approach and it's now I realize that Jack is holding the laptop under his arm. *Shit.* If Bart goes in his office, he's going to see that it's missing. Why didn't Jack stop us from doing this? This was a terrible decision. It was thoughtless, it was—

Jack's hand presses into my lower back, pulling my hips flush with his. "*Breathe,*" he tells me as quietly as the breeze. "I can feel your heart racing. It's going to be okay."

My lungs release a breath. Tension flows out of my muscles. *It's going to be okay.* I'm always the one promising that sentiment. I happily take on the responsibility of everyone's burdens because I only ever feel good when I'm being useful to someone. But hearing those words whispered softly to me . . . it's heaven.

And the best part is, he's right. Bart doesn't go into his office. His footsteps fade in the direction of his living room and then we hear the sound of his TV clicking on. I sigh and Jack's hold around my waist loosens. Safe for now.

Knowing he's out of visual range, Jack clicks the flashlight back on and shines it around the minuscule space and then sets it up against the wall. He looks around like he's hoping a second bedroom will spring out of nowhere, and when he verifies it's really just this little closet, he lowers himself to the floor, legs extending out and sandwiching my feet. His shoes touch the opposite wall.

He looks up at me and wordlessly pats his thighs.

I frown. He smiles and pats again. He lifts his right eyebrow and tilts his head in an "It's going to be a long night" expression. I'm almost one hundred percent sure that sitting on his lap would be a very bad idea given the current state of my feelings toward him. But I also know that standing in this position for any length of time is going to destroy my back.

I tentatively shuffle around and lower myself to his lap, pretty much squatting so I don't put my full weight on him. Jack huffs a chuckle at my nervous energy, takes my hips, and pulls me down firmly into his lap. His arm wraps around my abdomen like a seatbelt. There. Problem solved. Just my body sitting on Jack's body. No big deal.

Except it's a very big deal. His thighs are firm beneath my ass and the weight of his forearm is downright erotic. We're so close and personal. I'll never be able to erase the feel of him from my mind.

With his arm still around me, he leans over to grab the laptop, places it in my lap, and opens it.

Outside the closet, sounds of a game show blast. It really can't be good for Bart to listen to the volume that high. But inside the closet, Jack fulfills my wish from that drunken night in my living room. *I need you to fix it.* His finger moves across the track pad as he opens Bart's email account and scrolls down the list of unopened emails until he finds mine. *There it is.*

He selects it, then sends it to the trash. And because Jack is competent and doesn't leave ends undone, he then goes to the trash bin, selects my email once again, and permanently deletes it.

I take in a deep breath, then let it out in one final rush.

It's done.

"Your book is once again your own," he whispers, silently closing the laptop and setting it aside.

"Thank you." I twist a little to look at him over my shoulder.

"You're welcome. But you could have done it on your own."

"I know."

"But you wanted me here?"

I swallow and grin. "And you wanted to help me."

"I did."

"Why?" I ask, hopeful to be granted the answer my heart is secretly looking for.

His eyes drop to my mouth, and my skin warms. "That day when I flirted with you on my motorcycle, and you thought I was someone else . . . it gave me a taste." His eyes lift. "And then that night when you needed someone, I realized it could give me a real shot at becoming more than just your nemesis, and I wanted to take it. I wanted to be your friend."

"My *friend.*"

We are both well aware that friends don't sizzle with this kind of tension. Friends don't look into each other's eyes like this while one friend is on the other friend's lap.

He smiles. "Give or take."

The back of his knuckles finds my jaw to brush the softest touch across it. Longing coils around my spine and tenses my thighs. His palm settles on the juncture of my jaw and neck, right over my hammering, traitorous pulse. It speaks to him loud and clear.

"Why didn't you say goodbye to me?" I didn't realize that question was still hovering so close to the surface until I ask it.

His brows pull together behind his glasses. "When?"

"When you left Rome, to move with Zoe to Nebraska."

"Did you want me to?"

I'm not quite ready to answer that honestly. "You said goodbye to everyone in the school but me. Everyone. I even came outside to see you off. Just in case. But you didn't even look in your rearview mirror at me."

I hate how vulnerable that makes me sound. It conjures a memory of me standing in the parking lot with my chin held high, completely unnoticed by Jack as he drives away.

He looks devastated. "I didn't know you were out there. I would have stopped."

"But you didn't even come find me for one last fight."

He nods. "That's because I purposely avoided you."

"Oh." I want to scramble off his lap and find distance now, but Jack's seatbelt arm won't let me yet.

"Because that's the exact moment I started to realize I was a shit human who had gotten myself into a big mess."

"What—"

"Emily . . . I didn't want to say goodbye to you because the prospect of my last encounter with you being one where you looked apathetic to my leaving—I couldn't bring myself to do it. And that startled me more than anything." He shakes his head. "I was marrying someone else and avoiding saying goodbye to *you* because it was going to hurt. The morality of that alone was bad. And I thought—I *hoped* that if I just moved to Nebraska and went about my life it would be okay. I'd forget about you."

"But you didn't?" I ask with two scoops of hope in my voice.

"No. It felt wrong being so far from you." I know what he means. It's a sensation I felt but wasn't able to explain. A wrongness. The feeling of he was there, and I was here, and it wasn't supposed to be that way, even if we were enemies. We were always supposed to be near each other.

Jack stares at me and I stare at him, and we're lost in this vortex of *what do we do now?*

"Emily . . ." he whispers.

"Jack . . ." I respond, and twist around a little more to face him.

We hang like professional acrobats in this torture. There's no escaping it tonight. I'm hiding in a closet with my (ex-)nemesis, and it's time to face the facts: I want him, and he wants me.

His eyes are on my mouth, our pheromones are clogging up the air, and we only have seconds to hammer out the details. "I . . . I feel like we should think this through, but . . ."

I inch closer. "But it's hard to think when you have a mouth and I have a mouth."

"Exactly," he breathes out, his thumb sweeping across the tender skin just outside the corner of my lips.

"Let's think tomorrow."

He shakes his head lightly, fingers sinking into my hairline. Quicksand is pulling us under. "You won't avoid me?"

"I'm a grown woman, Jack. I know how to let whatever happens in a closet stay in a closet."

His eyes wander all over my face and neck like he's deciding where he wants to start. With his hand still on my jaw, he dips forward and presses his mouth to mine. It's an immediate hit of heat. A head-to-toe sweep of pleasure. I suck in a breath through my nose and hook my arm around Jack's neck.

He pulls away and then presses in again. It's even better the second time. The kiss is deeper, our mouths open a little. It's cute. Like saying into a mic, *test, one, two, three.* I really like his mouth. His lips are soft and full without being too much. At the first touch of our tongues, I feel his smile—his teeth against my lip—and it turns the Christmas lights on in my heart. Jack just tasted me, and . . . it made him happy. *I* make him happy.

But then Jack's mouth slants over mine in a kiss that erases the word *cute* from the slate. It goes from soft and sweet to hungry and spicy. It comes with a challenging sweep of his tongue that I immediately match and then lob my own back with a nip of his lip. Jack groans and I put my hand flat to his solid chest to feel it. I'm chasing sensations and collecting them all in my pocket for later.

I can't get close enough now, for me or for Jack. His hands go to my torso, where he's nudging me to turn and face him. I shuffle around as quietly as possible and straddle his lap, knees on the ground. No sooner than I'm seated, he pulls me in tightly against him, wrapping his arms fully around me. I run my hands down the expanded muscles of his back as our mouths explore and claim and tease. *Of course,* I think like a lightbulb illuminating in my head. *Of course it would be this way with him.*

When Jack rolls his hips into me, and I feel just how much he wants me, a blowtorch singes a line down my spine. I am hot and needy in a way I've never experienced before.

His mouth leaves mine to graze his teeth down the column on my throat, and I let my head fall back to expose every inch for him—arching as his fingers take over where his mouth can't reach. And as he traces over the subtle curve of my cleavage, any last kernels of my good judgment turn into crushed coals, sparking embers through my veins.

I want his mouth on me again, so I tip forward and take it, sliding my fingers into his hair as his hand savors and learns me. Need builds in the base of my spine and my body snaps into autopilot. It demands that our clothes be off. It insists on taking as much contact and friction as possible.

"How do you feel this good?" he says, words scraping over my jaw.

"Vitamins."

His chuckle is decadent, and I swallow it up.

Jack smells like green body wash, is morning-cup-of-coffee-warm, and touches like a mythological god that can heal. Our kisses are too frantic to belong in this quiet closet. They're punctuated with jagged breaths and it's becoming increasingly difficult to keep our movements to a minimum. I slide my hands under his shirt, over his chest, and brushing against the necklace lying against it. It's a thin gold chain today with a little heart on the end. I want to take a sledgehammer to the walls of this confining space to spread his long body out on the floor so I can appreciate all of it with complete focus.

Jack's gaze lingers on my hair for two beats before his hand is releasing my clip and letting my hair fall down my back. His private smile whispers triumph. And then his fingers move to toy with the little white buttons of my shirt that begin right between my cleavage, undoing them with swift magic all the way down to my belly button while he kisses me. "I love this shirt. I've been dreaming of popping these buttons open since I first saw you in it tonight." His rough palm glides over my shoulder as he pushes the fabric aside. "I love that it matches your red nails. They drive me insane." At his thorough exploration of the terrain under my shirt, I have to bite my lips together to keep from making sounds that would get us caught. Conscious thought is a struggle, though.

I have never felt so wonderfully outside myself while doing this kind of thing before. Usually I'm always thinking through the logistics, overly worried about the next step. But I couldn't form a strategic thought right now if I tried. The only word pulsing through my mind is *Jack*.

His name winds down through my ribs and narrows my focus on the place where our bodies meet. Where we're moving against each other and nearly lost to the world entirely. And that's when the TV turns off. The sudden drench of silence is as loud as an alarm. The floor creaks beneath us ever so silently and Jack and I go still as death. We're both taking in shallow, frequent breaths, listening as Bart snaps his recliner shut and then tracking his heavy footfalls out of the living room, down the hall, and then finally, up the stairs.

With every thud against the floor, the need holding my body hostage recedes a little. Finally, when all is silent again, I meet Jack's gaze. His hand is still holding my breast and at this point, it just feels comical. He gives me a lopsided, apologetic smile that dips into my stomach before he's sweetly tugging my shirt back onto my shoulder. One by one, I watch as he buttons me back up.

We share a look and one final soft kiss before I peel myself from him. With hands on my hips, he helps me stand. Wobbly legs are my factual evidence that what just happened was real.

Water starts rushing through the pipes in the walls and we both decide Bart must be getting a shower. Now is our moment to escape. I open the closet and step out into the dark hallway, waiting as Jack replaces the laptop on the desk. We silently pad through the house and out the back door once again, locking it behind us. And when we're back in Jack's SUV, all I can think is that it should have been more difficult. All of it: the sneaking, the breaking and entering, the closet hiding, and then of course . . . the making out. I am convinced that with anyone else, it wouldn't have worked.

But with Jack, I'm starting to realize, everything just feels right.

It's a short drive home, and we're both quiet during it—busy contemplating our next steps. Whatever that was back in the closet, it was *good*. And it's not finished.

Jack pulls into his driveway, puts his SUV in park, and then turns to look at me, lit only by the moon and stars. "So . . ." he says.

"So . . ." I respond.

We're incredible with words.

And again, my heart picks up. In the silence, we're saying so much. I'm not ready for this night to be over, and neither is Jack. Which is why he leans in to kiss me again. I promised I could compartmentalize anything that happens in the closet, but this is very much outside the closet.

I don't get the chance to worry any further, though, because Jack's phone starts ringing on the console between us. The screen lights up with the caller ID: *MOM*. Jack looks at the time, frowns, then says, "I'm sorry—I need to take this. She never calls at night."

"Of course," I say, meaning it, because if anyone will be sympathetic to familial responsibility, it's me.

"Hey, Mom," Jack says after answering the call, and I can't help but melt a little at how soft his voice is now. "Everything oka—"

He frowns again, deeper this time. "What did he say before he left?" Jack opens his door and gets out, closing it behind him like he wants privacy.

And I sit in the SUV for two more minutes before I remember that I have my own house next door. I climb out, register Jack's concerned expression, and then give him a gesture that says *I'm going home. I'll see you later.*

He surfaces from the evidently heavy conversation with his mom to look disappointed by this turn of events. We both know there's no recovering the mood after this, though. And maybe it's for the best.

But then he gives me a quiet smile and presses his phone to his chest to muffle his words as he says, "Good night, Goldie."

FROM: Jack Bennett <Bennett.Jack@Greenfield.edu>
TO: Emily Walker <Walker.Emily@Greenfield.edu>
DATE: Tue, Dec 9 11:00 PM (10 years ago)
SUBJECT: Library

Did you make it home? (Asking because if not, I won't
have to work so hard to beat your grade in history.)

FROM: Emily Walker <Walker.Emily@Greenfield.edu>
TO: Jack Bennett <Bennett.Jack@Greenfield.edu>
DATE: Tue, Dec 9 11:10 PM (10 years ago)
SUBJECT: Library

I'm home. (Study up.)

CHAPTER TWENTY

Jack

"So anyway . . . he did come back around two A.M., but I'm worried about him. He's doing this more and more," my mom says, lifting her coffee to her mouth for another drink.

We're sitting at the Hot Bean (which is either the very worst or very best coffee shop name—I haven't decided yet) because after the night she had, I thought she might need some decompressing. I invited her to Rome for the first time to see my house (from the outside because Darrell and his guys are inside working today) and tour the town. Also because I'm worried about her. I'm always worried about her actually, but especially after she calls me in tears like she did last night.

There are dark smudges under her eyes from sitting up most of the night waiting on my asshole father to come back home. Apparently when he hadn't surfaced from his office in a while, and she wanted to make sure he was okay, she went into his office even though his door was closed (a cardinal sin to Fredrick). He blew up at her, saying she'd interrupted his flow and he wouldn't be able to get it back now because of her. She apologized (which I hate) and said she'd leave him alone from then on, but he's a petulant child and said it was too late, the muse was gone. He got up, grabbed his keys, and went right to his car. Wouldn't tell her where he was going either. *Classic Fredrick.*

That was when she called me. Worried that he hadn't come home yet and afraid he'd gone to a bar. After a painful moment having to watch Emily go into her house, I spent awhile talking my mom down. She texted me around two A.M. that my dad had come home safely—and thankfully, not drunk.

I study the dark circles under her eyes now, then have to avert my gaze to the coffee shop windows when a rage builds inside me. "You don't deserve to be treated like that by him. Or anyone. You were just checking on him and he was a jerk to you. That's not okay."

My mom shrugs off my comment like she always does. She's endured Fredrick's gaslighting for so long now that she can never see when he's manipulating her. "I shouldn't have interrupted him, though. I know better than that—but he had missed lunch and dinner. And his stress has been so high with this book that I honestly worried something had happened to him in there."

"Mom, those are good reasons to interrupt someone. Dad is just an entitled asshole who thinks he's the god of creative writing and should be treated like it. It's bullshit. There's a difference between feeling grumpy from deadline stress and what he does. The way Dad acts is not normal or healthy."

I've pushed too hard. I can see her shutting down. It's what always happens anytime I try to bring up the truth about him. I know what she's feeling now because I've felt it too: like you're doing something wrong by calling out his toxic tendencies. Like you're betraying him in some way even though *he* was the one who hurt you. I'm by no means fully healed of the wounds my dad left— I likely will be trying to cauterize them for the rest of my life—but

I have spent enough time now recognizing where the wounds come from that I can talk myself through the logical truth of it all.

But my mom—I worry she'll never get away from him long enough to find healing at all.

"Mom," I begin gently, and adjust my glasses. "Have you ever thought of leaving him? I remember you saying once you didn't sign a prenup—so I know you'd get money in the settlement. Probably a lot of money to keep you comfortable. You don't have to keep enduring—"

"He has his issues"—she cuts me off—"but he's a good man too. And he's always taken care of me. I just need to get better at waiting until he's out of these stressful deadlines to approach him. I'm sorry I panicked and called you last night. I hope I didn't ruin your evening."

I don't have the heart to tell her that she *absolutely* ruined my evening. Ruined what was sure to be the best night of my life, in fact. What happened with Emily in that closet—it felt like it was always meant to happen somehow. Like the pieces of my life slotted into place the moment my mouth touched hers. All I wanted was more. Still want more.

I can't get her off my mind. I want to spend every second of the day with her. I want to make up for every day of every year I spent fighting with her instead of loving her. Lately, it's been seeming like she feels the same way too. I can feel it in her touch. I can see it in her smile. Hear it in the way she says my name.

Which means it's time to tell her about my writing career. And I'm dreading it. Everything seems so hopeful between us right now, and I don't want to mess it up. But keeping it from her and pursuing a relationship only to tell her the truth later down the line—that *would* mess it up. I'm not willing to hurt her like that. And this unfortunately means that until I can find a time to tell her, I can't kiss her again.

"But listen, I'm confident your dad will come out of this mood and then be his normal self again," Mom says, like this isn't his normal self. Like this isn't part of the patterns that make up who he is as a person. She's right, though, he'll finish his book and then lavish her with affection and attention and fun things and it'll last for just long enough for her to believe that he truly loves her, and then he'll rip his tenderness away as quickly as he gave it—and make her feel like his retreat is her fault. He used to do it to me too before I learned how to outsmart him.

Now I never give him pieces of myself. I have zero hope for us. It's a weird thing to let yourself grieve your parent who is still living, but I've done it—do it regularly, actually. The only reason I go around their house now is because I love my mom and can't let her weather him alone. I'm afraid he's slowly crushing her spirit more and more each day. Which is part of why I don't plan to ever come out from behind my pen name. If I do, I know for a fact my dad won't welcome me in their house anymore.

Mom finishes off her coffee and sets it aside just as the bell above the door chimes. I look up, hoping to find Emily. When I realize it's not her, my face falls before I can catch it. And of course, my mom notices and a puzzled look pulls her brows together. I don't get much time to consider what she might think, because the two women I've come to understand as the matrons of the town barrel through the doorway.

"Move your ass, Harriet!" barks Mabel, coming in second. "I want to get a juice before next year."

"I am not, and no part of me belongs to, a donkey, Mabel, so don't refer to me as that."

Mabel comes up beside her. "Well, I have another name in mind for you, but I don't think you'd like that one much better."

Harriet looks unimpressed. "I think you'd be a lot happier person if you'd use that Bible I gave you last Christmas."

"I use it," says Mabel indignantly. "It stabilizes my wobbly chair in the dining room."

Harriet's eyes widen in horror. "Don't you tell me that you have the Lord's holy words wedged under your rickety old chair!"

"Nothing rickety about it. My papaw made those back in the day and it's an honor for that book to be used in such a way!" She frowns when Harriet takes one big step away. "What are you doing now, you old kook?"

"Getting far enough away from you so the lightning won't touch me when it strikes you down!"

"Now listen—"

"Nice to see you two in good spirits today," I say, interjecting before things escalate further. My mom looks like she's thoroughly enjoying the show, but I'd rather nip it in the bud before an old-lady brawl takes place in front of us.

"Jack," says Harriet. "Always nice to see—wait, who's this sitting with you?" She and Mabel approach the table.

"Mabel, Harriet, this is my mom, Diana."

My mom usually has anxiety meeting new people, but Mabel doesn't give her a chance to retreat into herself. "Diana," says Mabel, reverently. "Now that is a beautiful name you don't hear much anymore. And look at your eyes, Lord, you and Jack are matching. They're exactly the same color as my favorite bottle of Jack Daniel's."

My mom laughs and then shocks the hell out of me when she says, "Do you know I love to add a splash of it now and then to my hot tea at night. I sleep like a baby."

Mom keeps alcohol at home? She must keep it hidden if she does. Probably keeps a lot of herself hidden just like I do.

Mabel pats my mom on the shoulder. "A woman after my own heart. Welcome to Rome, Kentucky, Diana. We love your son. Now, come visit me anytime you've got a hankering for some Jack

Daniel's and a splash of hot tea." Mabel winks and a minute later, they're over at the counter ordering their Hot Bean juice to go.

"They seem nice," my mom says, then casts a yearning look out the window at the town. "Before I had you, I wanted to live in a small town."

"Why didn't you?"

"Oh . . . well. You know. Your dad really liked Evansville, so I thought it would be a nice place to live too." She turns a fake smile back to me. "I'm glad you get to live here. I never thought you seemed happy in Evansville with Zoe."

"I *wasn't* happy there. Or with her."

The bell above the door chimes again, and this time when I look up I find Emily walking in wearing a crisp white T-shirt tucked into faded high-waisted jeans with a brown braided belt. Her hair is in that damn clip and the memory of removing it from her hair slams into my stomach. Emily immediately approaches our table and I stand so quickly my thighs bump into it, making it wobble.

"Hi," I say with this massive humiliating smile.

Luckily, she mirrors it back to me as she eyes my checkered white-and-green crochet knit polo. I have it open over a white tank top with gray twill trousers. There's a necklace with sunflower beads around my neck. "Hi."

After a beat, my mom leans forward. "Hi."

"Oh, sorry, Emily, this is my mom, Diana. Mom, this is my . . . Emily."

My mom stands so they can shake hands, and then my mom grins at me. "I didn't know you had an Emily. It's nice to meet you."

Super, Mom.

Emily laughs. Actually laughs. "It's nice to meet you too. What he was going to say but quickly changed his mind was, 'This is my *nemesis,* Emily.'" Amusement marks her face. "Your son and I have a bit of history."

There wasn't even a small part of me that was going to say *nemesis*.

"Well, you've got to sit down with us and tell me all about it, then," my mom says, her eyes lighting up in a way I never saw from her when I introduced her to Zoe. Then again, she was standing next to my dad when the introductions happened—and when he's around, she tends to hang back and let him do all the talking. It's so good to see her like this.

Emily looks at me with an unsure expression—her golden brows pinched together. "I don't want to intrude."

And even though we're not alone, I still tell her the truth. "You can intrude on me anytime you want."

June 21

EMILY (5:15 PM): So Friday night at Hank's is sort of a big deal around here. You haven't experienced one yet, and I think it's definitely time. Me and my siblings get there around 7:00 if you want to join.

CHAPTER TWENTY-ONE

Emily

lied to Jack.

I said I knew how to let what happened between us in the closet stay in the closet. At the time, I thought what I was saying was true, but it turns out, I have never been more wrong. Because what happened in the closet changed me. I am a different woman after having Jack's hands on my body.

I am a woman who wakes up and her first thought is *I wonder if Jack is awake yet.* A woman who has endlessly dirty dreams where we're back in that closet but never get interrupted. A woman who has typed the words Do you want to come scene-block snuggling with me? five different times into her text box and then deleted it before sending each time. (So maybe I'm not completely different.)

And Jack? He doesn't seem to be as tortured as me. We've hung out a few times since The Closet—mainly so he can listen to me panic that Colette won't like my manuscript—but each time he never once tried to kiss me again.

Not. Once.

What the hell is wrong with him? I've given him ample opportunities too. Two days ago at The Diner, we were sitting at the bar, and I looked over my shoulder at him with a grin that said *oh hello would you please put your lips on mine?* He just picked up his coffee and took a long drink. And because I know that Jack has never once in his life been clueless, I have to assume he's resisting me on purpose. Maybe he doesn't want to kiss me again. Or maybe he thinks a fling would be a bad idea between us. (It would.) (But maybe I just don't care and want it to happen anyway?)

I can't take the uncertainty anymore, though. I have to find out the answer soon, and I'm hoping that it will be tonight. It's my favorite time of the week: Friday night at Hank's. I pull into the gravel lot, dust kicking up behind me, and park next to Noah's orange-and-white truck—just under the neon sign illuminating *Hank's*.

As I'm getting out, Annie pulls in on the other side of me. All that's missing is Maddie's truck for it to look like a true Friday night.

"Emily!" says Annie, practically jumping from her truck in her floral dress and boots the moment it's in park. "Wait!"

"I'm literally waiting. You don't have to jog."

She breathes out like she just sprinted a mile when she gets close. "Whew. I hate running. I don't know how Will does it every morning. Anyway, I'm glad I caught you before you went in. I need advice about something . . ."

"Who do I need to beat up? Did someone hurt your feelings? Is it Will?"

"What!" She laughs like she can't tell if I'm serious or not. I'm actually not sure if I'm serious or not either. "No one hurt me. Definitely not Will."

"Okay . . . usually you ask me for advice when someone's said something offensive and you don't know how to respond. So this is me saying, I'll happily respond for you."

"Stop that. Everything is good. Better than good, actually. And that's why . . ." She bites her bottom lip and crinkles her nose like a bad case of butterflies has swept through her. "I think I want to accept Will's proposal . . . by proposing to him myself."

My stomach clenches.

"*Wow, Annie!*" I say, trying to sound in awe and not gutted. "You feel ready now?"

"I've felt ready for a long time now if I'm being honest."

I take her by the shoulders and tug her in for a huge hug. Partly because this news deserves one, and partly because I need a second to fix my face. "This is incredible news."

And it really is. I am so happy for Annie because she and Will are perfect for each other. But I also can't shake the urge to cry either.

"Why do you need my advice, then?" I ask when we pull away.

"Oh! I was wondering what you think about the way I'm planning to do it . . ."

———

Annie and I walk in together like nothing of incredible life importance just took place in the parking lot and go to our usual table. Noah, Amelia, James, and Will are already here.

"Hiya!" I say, grabbing a seat and slinging my purse over the back of the chair as Annie makes a beeline for the seat next to Will.

All eyes turn toward me, and no one says anything.

Noah folds his arms.

Amelia leans forward, resting her elbows on the table.

Will grins.

Annie lifts a taunting brow like we didn't already interact in the parking lot and all the way inside the building.

James taps his finger on the table.

It only takes me a second to realize what's going on. I groan and tilt my face up to the ceiling. "Who told you about the coffee?"

"James," they all say in unison. The man in question doesn't even have the decency to look guilty.

He shrugs. "I heard it from Mabel."

Bringing my gaze back to my smug siblings (and friend), I sigh. "Fine. Yes. I had coffee with Jack and his mom the other day. It's not a big deal."

"It's a very big deal considering he's a man you've claimed to hate, and now, over the course of a month, are meeting his mom. Is there something we should know about?" says Noah.

"No. There's not."

Annie tilts her face and narrows her eyes. "Maybe we should call Madison and see if she can get it out of you."

"She can't tonight. I already texted her earlier to see if she wanted to be on FaceTime for this, but she's out on a date tonight. She said she'll be busy . . . *all night*."

James suddenly stands up from the table. "I'm going to go get another beer. Want me to grab you one, Emily?"

Odd. I mean—it wouldn't be odd if this were the only time James has removed himself from a conversation when we started talking about Maddie and her life in New York—but it's not.

"Yeah, thanks."

Once he leaves, my siblings get right back to business. "Okay," says Amelia, "catch me up. We're talking about your neighbor who you patched up during our girls' night, right? And we are only freaking out that Emily met his mom because they used to be enemies?"

"*We're not freaking out*," I say quickly and firmly hoping my siblings will get it through their heads once and for all that my life is not open for debate. "This is a non-issue. I walked in while he and his mom were having coffee and they invited me to sit. There's nothing deeper here." *Lie*. That coffee felt significant. It was Jack letting me into his life a little further—something I know isn't easy for him.

"We're just . . . sort of . . . friends," I say, hoping this pacifies them.

Will tries to trick me. "But how are his abs?"

"I wouldn't know," I say firmly. Except I do know. And he has a fantastic torso. It's the stuff of dreams. My dreams every night this week, in fact. But I am not ready for my siblings to know that I have feelings for Jack. Because I don't even know what to do with them yet, and getting these nosy Nellies involved would only further complicate the situation.

"When you find out, tell us," says Amelia with a wide smile. "Don't leave any detail out. Take a picture if he'll let you."

Noah glares at Amelia, but there's a playful twinkle in his eye that I don't miss. "We've only been married a year and you're already drooling over other men?"

Amelia lays her head on his shoulder. "I just like to see you get jealous. You get frowny and . . ."

I tune out.

It's becoming increasingly difficult to hang out with my siblings and their significant others. Because while Noah and Amelia are doing some sort of weird public conversational foreplay, Will and Annie are kissing. I'm not kidding. This happens more than you'd imagine. They look at each other, fall into their own little world, and then *bam* they're making out in public. If you had told me a year ago before they started dating that my sweet baby sister Annie— the wholesome, sugar-cookie sister—would be making out in public with her tattooed retired bodyguard boyfriend, I'd have laughed in your face and assumed you were drunk.

James has the right idea, so I get up and leave my overly

affectionate siblings alone to make out like weird teenagers at the table and join him at the bar.

"Should we just start making out to be included?" he says when I lean on the bar beside him.

I laugh—knowing he's not serious and still halfway wishing we both did find each other attractive. It would solve a lot of issues. James is safe. He's rooted here. I wouldn't have to worry about anything unpredictable from his corner. Too bad I've never been able to think of him like that.

"Sure, I'm game if you are."

He stares at me a minute with that gorgeous, tanned, trademark James Huxley smile, and then it fades, and an entirely different story unfolds in his eyes that I can't read. I don't think I'm supposed to read it either. "If we just give them another minute they'll get it out of their systems."

With a nod, I take a swig of my beer and look up at the Christmas lights that are strung year-round like a net over the ceiling of the bar. The energy at Hank's is like putting layers of icing on a cake. At the beginning of the night when it's just me and my siblings and a few other randoms around the bar, the atmosphere is pretty thin. It's just an old place with beat-up, creaky floors and vinyl-covered barstools that are never not a little sticky. And then the later the night gets, the more layers get swiped on. Suddenly the jukebox starts, cowboy boots scuff to the rhythm of a line dance, laughter echoes from all directions, and that's when the vibes turn truly thick with honky-tonk decadence. It's my place. My home. My people. I love it here.

I want Jackson here too.

The thought strikes me like lightning. I look to the door and watch a few more people filter in—a group who have to put their cigarettes out outside the door before entering. None of them are Jackson.

James and I sit here and sip our drinks in silence as the bar hums to life. I can tell it's going to be a wild night. Every now and then there's a full moon and people seem to come out of the woodwork. Hank's is very much a local hot spot, but it's grown in popularity for the surrounding towns too. Everyone comes here. Everyone except one new town citizen, it seems . . .

Why is he not here? I invited him.

I glance at the door every time it opens. The fifth time this happens, James calls me out on it.

"Who are you looking for?"

"Hm?"

"You heard me just fine."

I roll my eyes. "I'm not looking for anyone."

"I invited him too."

I give away my eagerness when my head whips in his direction. "You did? When?"

He grins. "Funny how you know exactly who I'm talking about." He swigs his beer. "This morning. I ran into him in town while I was dropping off an order at the market. That okay?"

I fiddle with my beer and look over my shoulder annoyed when someone jostles me as they pass by. "Yeah. It's fine." Better than fine. I'm glad he did. I'm sure I made Jackson happy. "So . . . do you know if he's coming, then?"

James leans on the counter, dipping his head to catch my eye. "Quit it."

"Quit what?"

"Quit hiding. Quit protecting yourself so damn much."

"*Excuse me?*" I say, making sure he hears the agitation in my voice.

"Just go text him and ask why he's not here if you want him to be. There's no shame in laying out your feelings for people to see." He picks up his beer. "Trust me—if you hold out too long, you might miss your opportunity."

"When the hell did you become a walking fortune cookie? And what opportunity did you—"

"Come on, let's go back to the table. They're done swapping slobber," he says, cutting me off and leaving me to wonder if that statement was about Maddie. Surely not. Those two have been like siblings. They bicker and make fun of each other and . . .

That's exactly what I've been doing with Jackson all these years.

Beer in hand, I return to the table with my back to the door intentionally. I don't need to keep track of who enters. It's a useless waste of energy and I won't allow myself to do it. I force myself to focus on talking with my siblings—but even that gets more difficult as the bar reaches an all-time-high noise grade. It's not my imagination that it's getting more packed in here by nonregulars either, because Amelia casually reaches into her purse and pulls out one of Noah's baseball hats. She slouches into Noah's side, and he puts an arm around her. *Incognito mode initiated.*

Normally we would all be a few beers in by now, but the place is severely understaffed tonight. There's only one waitress and . . . "Dammit. Hank is bartending tonight," I say, but no one hears me. I hate when everyone calls out of work the same night and makes Hank bartend. The man needs a double knee replacement but refuses to get it. Nights like this on his feet for too long put him in a lot of pain.

Noah draws our attention, raising his voice over the music and noise. "Uh—so listen, guys. While we're all pretty much here, Amelia and I have some news."

Rocks drop into the pit of my stomach because I don't think I can take any more news tonight. I'm in a bad mood now from the overly crowded atmosphere and because Jack hasn't shown up or bothered to text to say he's not going to make it. And more importantly, I think I know what this news is about.

Smile, mouth, smile.

I hold my breath as Amelia picks up where he left off. "Well . . . as y'all know, my label wants me to tour for my upcoming album after taking the last one off. And . . . I've decided that I want to as well."

Don't drop the smile.

I see Noah squeeze her shoulder as he looks down at her with a smile. "And I'm going to go with her. For the entire duration of it this time. I don't want to miss out on it, and now that Grandma isn't . . ." He trails off and there's a moment of gut-wrenching emotion that hits us all. "Well, anyway. It's a good time for it."

I force myself to smile even wider—it's bordering on clownish. My lungs are broken, however. I can't breathe.

My grandma is gone. My sister has moved away. My baby sister is getting married and who knows what changes that's going to bring. Now my brother is leaving too.

The busy bar moves at half speed around me. Annie leans over and hugs Amelia, telling her how happy she is for her that she gets to tour again and assuring her they will come visit a lot on tour. Will says something about how weird it will be not acting as her body-guard for this tour. And James and Noah are having a side conversation that looks positive. And me. I'm smiling. So big that sweat is starting to collect on the base of my spine.

In the past, I would have chosen this moment to voice my panic. To tell Noah not to go and that we need him here. That I need him here—though I'd never admit it like that. I'd blame it on Grandma. On the pie shop. On anything that I could possibly sink my fearful claws into to get him to stay. But not anymore.

Now I just stuff my fear and my hurt and my sadness in my Trea-sure Chest of Doom and hope that'll be enough to pretend it doesn't exist.

"So exciting!" *I feel like I'm going to throw up.* "I'll look after the Pie Shop for you while you're gone and keep things running smoothly." At least that aspect of my life is always the same. The Pie Shop has been in our family for generations, and it's a comfort to know that I can always count on it. The same floorboard will always squeak. My name is scribbled under the countertop. In the walk-in pantry there's a section of the wall dedicated to tracking our heights. And my favorite of all, there's a curse word written in Sharpie in the bottom, darkest corner of the pantry where no one can see it but I know it's there because I remember watching Maddie write it when she was twelve. I tried to clean it off after she left so Grandma wouldn't see it and get her in trouble. But Grandma caught me furiously scrubbing it and assumed I was the one who wrote it. I took the fall for Maddie and got grounded from TV for a week.

Noah's smile has a touch of pity to it when he looks at me. "Actually, Em, I won't need you to do that. Jeanine needed a change. She's going to quit at The Diner and work for me at the Pie Shop full time instead. Since it's a manager position she'll get paid more than she did at The Diner and you won't have to work yourself to the bone between school and the shop. It's a win-win." He pauses to assess my expression. I don't know what he sees but whatever it is, it brings him to add, "I thought this would be easier on you."

"Oh." I blink and pick up my beer, needing something to do with my hands. "You're right. That's perfect! Yes. A win-win for sure."

Keep smiling, Emily.

He doesn't need me.

Keep smiling.

No one needs me anymore.

Don't cry.

Madison is gone for good and I'm going to lose everyone else too.

Keep smiling, dammit. Keep yourself together so they don't see how raw you feel. So you don't mess up and say something you'll regret.

Before I can talk myself out of it, I go to the bathroom, stand on the toilet in the middle stall, and hold my phone toward the ceiling, grabbing the one bar of service we've learned exists in this exact spot. And then I send a text I'll probably regret tomorrow.

June 21

EMILY (8:32 PM): It's rude to turn down an invitation to
Hank's.

CHAPTER TWENTY-TWO

Jack

'm outside Hank's debating whether I want to go in or not. I look at the text from Emily for the hundredth time, once again trying to read between the lines. I know her well enough now to sense there's something deeper happening here.

It's rude to turn down an invitation to Hank's. Which in Emily language means *I hate that you're not here.*

I was at home attempting to outline a chapter when I got this text, and I dropped everything.

Things between us have definitely changed. I like Emily. I'm attracted to Emily. And I . . . no, God, why am I lying even to myself? I more than like Emily. I'm quickly becoming obsessed with her. Part of me is wondering if I've been fighting with her all these years, resisting her, because some part of me knew . . . I knew she could do some real damage to my heart if I let her.

But the more I get to know Emily, the more I'm inclined to think she'd do everything she could to protect my heart before destroying it.

It's rude to turn down an invitation to Hank's.

I stare down at my phone and then at the doors. Bars are not attached to good memories for me—and I haven't stepped foot inside one in a very long time. I've sworn to myself that alcohol will *never* be a part of my identity. But Emily is in there . . . and something happened tonight that made her want to text me.

I pocket my phone and go through the doors. The first thing I notice is how busy it is. It's around eight-forty-five and I swear the whole damn county is pressed in here. It's hot, it's loud, and it's sweaty. But I smile because there's something about it that's infectious. Everywhere you look, someone is throwing their head back laughing, cheering for a friend to chug their beer, couples who clearly got a babysitter for the night making out on the dance floor, in their booth, over at the bar. Apparently there are a lot more young people in this area than I originally thought. They've come out of the woodwork to gather under the neon light of Hank's.

The wildest part of this place, though, is the bar itself. There are at least twenty people gathered around waiting for drinks. A large group of men too—college-aged and midtwenties—packed together and all but drooling over the gorgeous blonde serving drinks. I do a double-take.

Holy shit, that's Emily.

Surely that can't be right? Emily doesn't bartend. Does she? But while pressing my way through the crowd and closer to the bar, I hear her laugh, see her smile, and know that it's absolutely her. And also that every single person at this bar is eating out of her hand—which surprises me none. She's bossy, sharp-witted, and beautiful, a dangerous combination in a bartender.

"Jake! Quit pushing your way to the front. Rudeness isn't going to get you a drink any faster! Chester, whatcha drinking tonight?" she asks, yelling over the head of a sullen-looking college kid.

"Emily darlin', my usual, please!" an older gentleman with a long Santa beard yells back.

She grins. "So a pitcher and a ride home from Jerold?"

"That'll do!"

Everyone at the bar laughs. Emily goes on like this with a few others, teasing and making drinks like it's her sole purpose in life to work behind this bar. She looks effortless. A natural. And sexy as hell.

Sweat is coating her neck and chest where her white tank top is scooping down—showing just the slightest, most torturous amount of cleavage I've ever seen in my life. The fabric clings tight to her perspiration and her long golden-blond hair sticks to the side of her arm as she spins around the bar, making drinks at the speed of light.

I realize I've been standing here staring when a firm hand claps on my back.

"Jack. Glad you decided to join us. You staying for a bit?" It's James. He's smiling in a good-natured way, but I'm still so thrown off guard by the sight of Emily behind the bar that instead of answering, a question flies out of my mouth.

"Why is she working back there?"

James smiles fully and looks to Emily. Something about his smile toward her makes me irrationally angry. Possessive. *Don't smile at my Emily like that.* "She was a bartender here through college, and usually jumps back there when Hank is too covered up to handle it all. She can't stand seeing him in pain with his knees and gets mad when his employees call out on a Friday night knowing he's going to have to take over for them." We both stare at Emily. "And just look at all those poor idiots hanging onto the bar hoping to get a smile from her." He chuckles like this doesn't make me want to rip each one of them off their ass and take their seat and then put a TAKEN sign on each empty stool.

"What about you?" I ask, turning my eyes directly to him. I'm smiling, but by the way his eyebrow lifts when he takes in my expression, he knows it's not all that friendly. It's just me, a man in trousers and linen button-up, staring down a farmer in Wranglers and a white T-shirt who could undoubtedly beat me to a pulp if he wanted. But I find myself standing here willing to risk it all for the woman behind the bar.

"I'd be a lucky bastard to snag a woman like Emily. But you'll be happy to know, she's never looked twice at me, and I find myself stupidly attracted to brown-eyed brunettes. To my absolute detriment."

I'm so relieved I can't even bring myself to deny the "you'll be happy to know" part. Because I don't know what Emily is to me, but I know that the idea of her with him makes me want to die.

He suddenly chuckles, shakes his head, and claps me on the shoulder. "You can relax these. I won't fight you over her today." His smile fades. "But I swear to God, I will if you hurt her."

"Always encroaching on my territory, James," says Emily's brother Noah, walking up to us. "Aren't I supposed to be the one saying scary shit like that?"

"Gladly, but your sorry ass is too scared to do it, so I fill in when I can."

Noah crosses his arms. "Not scared of him, just to be clear." He jerks his chin in my direction. "Scared of her when she finds out I've been meddling behind her back. You must have a death wish, Huxley."

James frowns in the direction of Emily, who seems to be losing ground with the crowd. The college boys are getting too rowdy. And although she's doing a good job of reminding them to back up and wait their turn, I can see by the way she keeps stretching her neck to the right that she's stressed. Her fists ball up now and again too. I look around for some kind of backup to call for her, but all I see is one waitress walking around looking equally frazzled.

I watch for another minute until Emily turns away from the bar and her shoulders slump. She looks down at the line of empty glasses and takes a deep breath. The sweat on her back is seeping through her tank top.

"Can y'all finish giving me this shakedown later? I promise to piss myself with fear next time."

James frowns. Noah looks amused and extends his hand toward the bar in a "go right ahead" motion.

An instinct I've never felt before grabs me by the scruff of my neck and drags me heart-first to the bar. I have to elbow a few guys out of the way, but then I slip casually behind the bar, stopping directly behind Emily. She whirls around when she senses the presence of someone behind her, and then I don't know if it's in my head or not, but she seems to sigh with relief.

"*Jack.*"

"I heard it's rude to turn down an invitation to Hank's, so here I am."

She smiles. "Took you long enough to get here."

"I didn't mean to keep you waiting."

We stare at each other, processing the shift in atmosphere between us, until some dick throws a balled-up napkin at my head. "Quit distracting her! Either help or get out."

Emily's cold glare shifts slowly to the guy with a death wish. But I put my hand on her hip and squeeze once before taking the bar towel from her hand and throwing it over my shoulder. "First, drink some water and then finish what you were doing. I'll crowd control."

"You don't have to, Jack. I didn't mean to call you down here to help out."

"So you admit it, that text was to get me down here."

"You wanted to be part of this town. This is the way to become one of us."

I lean toward her ear. "So it had nothing to do with wanting to see me?"

"Not at all."

"Hm. Too bad. I kind of wanted to see you."

"You did?"

I hold up my thumb and forefinger, showing an inch of space between them. "Only a little."

Another balled-up napkin hits my head.

"All right," I say, turning to the bar. "Which one of you meat-balls threw that one? You get your drink last. And you." I point toward another guy. "I heard that lewd comment you made about her. Get out of here. You don't get a drink. Everyone else, back the hell up and pretend you have manners."

CHAPTER TWENTY-THREE

Emily

It was a hell of a night. And Jackson stayed with me the whole time until the last tab was closed out. Even Hank himself didn't stay that long. He just told us thanks in his gruff way, said we'd get to keep all the tips, and an extra envelope of cash would show up in our mailboxes soon. I would have turned him down, but . . . I'm living on a teacher's salary, so I think I'll take that money with a grateful heart.

Now it's just me and Jack closing the place up.

"You really don't have to stay and help anymore," I tell him, as I run a wet soapy rag across the bar top. "You don't work here, so cleanup is not expected."

He's across the room flipping chairs onto tables looking incredibly out of place in his mint short-sleeve button-up, playful tattoos, and navy corduroy trousers—surrounded by a neon glow and dirty floors.

He gives me that smirk. "You don't work here either."

"Yeah, but I used to, so I know the routine. You'd never stepped foot in here before tonight."

"I don't mind." His forearms flex as he lifts another chair, flips it upside down, and rests the seat on the table.

"But there's no construction at your house right now. You sure you don't want to be home enjoying the quiet instead of here wiping down an old bar?"

He gives a turned-down smile and makes his way over. "Now, Emily, you wouldn't be trying to get rid of me, would you?"

"I've been trying to get rid of you since the day I met you," I say, a return to an old jab that now feels like a caress. But maybe I am trying to get rid of him, because I feel *nervous* around him right now, and I don't know how to navigate that. If he stays, I have to ask him the question that's going to put my feelings in front of him on a silver platter.

He rounds the bar. "I could have sworn that we are now . . ." He stops close to me and dips his head to whisper in my ear, "*Friends.*" He pulls back, eyes widening like he just said the dirtiest word known to humankind.

It *is* dirty. Because friendship implies a certain vulnerability I don't give many people. Jack has become someone I like to be around. Look forward to seeing. Can't get enough of. And tonight when he looked out at the crowd that was overrunning me and told them to shape up, god help me, it swept me off my feet to where I could barely function. *Jack would never crack shells into his eggs.* It's only gotten worse as the night has gone on. He hasn't once asked me what he should do while closing tonight.

Most men jumping into a situation like this would be floundering. Especially when they see me in charge and running the show. They'd be full of "What can I do? Where should I put this? What needs to be done?" Not Jack. Jack immediately got to work busing tables and carrying dishes into the kitchen. He wiped down surfaces. Swept the floor. He saw what needed to be done and did it.

"Friends, huh? Weird—I don't think friends try to get into other friends' pants while trapped in a closet."

"That's where you're wrong." He playfully tugs my belt loop. "I've gotten into plenty of my friends' pants. But only while trapped in closets."

"Ahh—so that's why you haven't tried it again. Because we haven't been in a closet?"

His expression shifts from playful to searching. "Have you been hoping I would try it again? I'm sure there's a closet in here somewhere."

My heart races. Now is my chance to say yes. To confirm it and launch us into a new realm. But I get cold feet.

"You wish," I say, walking past him and into the kitchen, where I flick off the lights. He follows. "But that was a good line. Maybe I'll add it into my next book . . . for the villain to say."

This answer delights him even more somehow. "The villain is always the true hero in a romance."

I open the men's bathroom and cut the light next. Jack is still right behind me, following step for step. "And just how many romances have you read other than mine, Jack?"

"I've actually read a lot of romance. Was that not evident in the notes I left on your manuscript?"

I pause at the sink after wiping away the water splotches from the faucet and meet his eye in the mirror. "Do you really?"

"Why does that shock you? I'm a write—" He stops quickly and then continues. "I'm a writer's son. I grew up in a home that was very pro literacy. My dad was of course primarily a mystery writer, but my mom was an avid romance reader. I started picking her books up in high school and got hooked."

"Because of all the sex?"

His smile is delicious. "I definitely enjoyed those parts. But . . .

it was more than that too. There was an emotional connection in them that I didn't see a lot of in other genres. Found family. Strong friendships." He shrugs easily like his words are no big deal. "I've always struggled with connection. So it was nice to get it in books if not anywhere else."

There's so much I want to ask him. He's talked about his upbringing in little bits and pieces, but I want to know it all. Every small detail. "Have you ever thought about writing?"

His face is unreadable now. Frozen and blank and whispering secrets all at the same time. "*Yes,*" he says slowly as if he has to choose that word very carefully. "My dad wouldn't like it, though."

"I'm sorry he's like that. Having your child share your passion should be a joy."

His smile turns bitter. "I think it's supposed to work that way. But when your parent is a narcissist, nothing goes as planned."

I've met a few dads in my time as a teacher who showed narcissistic tendencies, and each and every one of their kids comes into class carrying the weight of everyone else's moods on their shoulders. The only time they get in trouble is when they're caught helping their friends cheat on a spelling test because they don't want to see them fail. Most of them have straight As on all their report cards and bottle up every feeling they've ever had. These are the kids that I catch staring at my *All feelings are important* poster with longing in their eyes. In their homes, their feelings are never important. Instead, they're used against them.

"What are you thinking about?" he asks quietly, reading me like always.

I give him part of the truth. "The kids at school with parents like your dad."

He nods. "The kids I became a teacher for."

I should have considered that Jack's heart is full of empathy. I find that teachers are often the most compassionate people on the planet. Yes, we may enjoy leading or organizing or imparting knowledge, but at the heart of it, many teachers get into the career because of our own brokenness. We become the kind of teachers we needed.

"Who have you been teaching for?" he asks, and pushes a strand of hair back from my temple.

I reach back into my own memories. "I'm there for the kids who have their worlds ripped out from under them. Who are hurting so bad they feel like they might not survive another day, but still walk their younger siblings to class to make sure they get there safely." Emotions clog my throat, so I snatch a roll of toilet paper and carry it with me into the women's bathroom, remembering that the last stall was empty earlier. Jack follows me in but stays behind at the sink while I go into the stall.

His voice carries to me. "I should have known from the start that we were both traumatized. It checks out."

I can't help it—a laugh jumps out of me. It was such a wonderfully unexpected thing to say. To cut pain with humor is my bread and butter. *Jack would love my "dead parents" quip.*

Before I get the chance to respond, there's a sudden clap of thunder, so loud it shakes the bar. One second later, the lights go out. I freeze, my hand on the toilet paper roll I just finished placing into the dispenser, and blink into the dark.

No, no, no.

I don't like this. I don't like storms—none of us Walkers do— and I definitely don't like being in a pitch-black bathroom stall all by myself during one.

"Jack?" I say, trying to keep my panic from my tone.

"I'm here." His voice is getting closer, and I hear his footsteps. "Lightning must have hit a power line. Which stall are you in?"

"This one. Do you have your phone on you for a flashlight?"

"No, it's out on the bar. You?"

"On the bar too." I run my hand against the plastic wall until I find the opening. And then I extend my hand out in front of me and come in contact with Jack's abs.

"Whoa, Ms. Walker. Buy me dinner first," he says, torso flexing against my hand.

I pull my hand back immediately. "Sorry! I can't see anything."

"I'm kidding," he says with the tremor of amusement in his voice. "Touch me anytime you want."

Oh.

There's a beat of nothing until suddenly I feel his hand on the outside of my shoulder and his fingers slide down my arm to my fingers, folding ours together like it's the most natural thing in the world. But it doesn't feel at all natural. It feels electric. New and thrilling. Like something I don't have the vocabulary for—and it's just his damn hand.

"Why . . . are we holding hands?" I ask him, and I could swear I hear his smile curl his lips.

"Buddy system. If we're holding hands while we walk through this dark creepy bar, the bogeyman can't get us."

"This feels like an excuse to make a pass at me."

We're on the move now. He's leading us cautiously through the bathroom. The door squeaks and he shifts to hold it open with his back while I walk through, hands still linked together like we are two people who need each other.

"Emily, you should know by now that if I was making a pass at you, you wouldn't have to ask to confirm that's what I'm doing."

"Charming asshole."

"Oh—I've been upgraded to *charming*."

He walks beside me for a beat until he's taking the lead again. And for some reason, I easily let him. In fact, I enjoy being able to focus all my attention on where our hands are joined. And I could probably blame this heightened attraction on the fact that it's been awhile since I've slept with anyone. But I'm almost certain it has more to do with the fact that I'm falling head over heels for Jack Bennett.

"All right, we're at the bar," he says into the dark. "I'm going to let go of your hand to feel for our phones."

"I don't need the play-by-play. I'm not scared," I say in a snippy tone because if there's anything I dislike more than needing someone, it's someone *thinking* I need them.

"I forgot you're never scared. Just like you never throw tantrums."

I would pinch him if I could see him.

We're side by side blindly feeling around the counter for anything that feels like a phone. "I can't find mine. You?"

"Nothing." Another crack of thunder hits the room, followed by an empty silence I don't like. Maybe that's what leads me to say, "I'm not scared of storms . . . but my brother is."

"Noah?"

"Yeah."

"I'm having trouble picturing it for some reason. Did he have a bad experience in a storm or something?"

"You could say that. Our parents were killed by a storm when we were kids."

I feel his body go still. It's easier to say it in the dark—when I don't have to see the pity on his face. It's the look every single person gets when I say those words. And I understand why; it's only natural. It's a painful, difficult thing to imagine happening to anyone, let alone a child. But I still don't like to see it. Because every damn time, it rips open the wound. The wound that won't heal. The wound that sits dormant under my skin until I twist uncomfortably from time to time and it's raw again.

"I'm sorry. I didn't know that happened."

"And here I thought you read minds all this time." *Jokes, jokes, jokes.* They're what keep my Treasure Chest of Doom locked.

"How old were you?" Jack says, facing me now.

"Eight—second grade." I've memorized the script. I recite it now with a monotone delivery, zero pauses and emotionless accuracy. "They were adventurous, my parents. They went hiking and camping in Colorado like they'd done countless times before, but a storm came that time, and they didn't have enough warning to get off the mountain. Doctors suspect it was lightning that struck their tent."

"Shit, Emily. I'm so sorry."

I shrug like he can see it. "Me too."

"But you're not scared of storms?"

I laugh once. "I'm the oldest daughter, I'm not scared of anything." I pause as memories hit me wave after wave. And for the first time in my life, I say them out loud. "Someone has to hold it together. Someone had to lift the blanket on her bed and let her sisters climb in when the thunder would shake the house. Someone had to assure them that her bed was the safest place in the world." *Even when my own hands were trembling.* "I was always promising them that I would never go anywhere, and my door would always be open for them."

Jack's hand finds mine again. He squeezes lightly, and I squeeze it back.

"And even though Noah is three years older than me, he'd always find his way into my room too, nervous, shaking and pacing the room, unsure of what to do when the panic would grip him. So I would give him tasks to keep his mind busy. *Get the flashlight in case we lose power. Wake Grandma up and ask her to check the Weather Channel.*" I can still picture his efficient nod before he'd dart out of the room. "Maddie . . . she needed hugs. Big, tight ones. She needed me to stroke her hair and whisper over and over that everything was going to be fine. And Annie . . ." I squint in the dark. "It was always a bit of a mystery to me as to what she needed. She would go silent and still. When I'd hug her, she'd just say she was okay, and I could help Noah and Maddie."

"And what did you need?" he asks.

How have I never asked myself that question? No one else has either.

Tears sting my eyes. "To go back to a time when my biggest worry was which cereal I'd eat for breakfast. To the Christmas when my mom and dad bought us a four-wheeler and we all spent the entire day in the freezing cold riding around the Huxleys' farm." I press my lips together as a wave of emotions washes over me. "I needed stability and reassurance that everything was going to be okay—but both of those things died with my parents, and I've never gotten them back."

"And what about now?" he asks softly.

"Now . . . I need to be okay with being alone. Because everyone moves on eventually. But not me . . . I'll always be right here where they left me."

He's quiet for so long. I could be standing completely naked on a stage under a spotlight, and I'd feel less vulnerable than I do now. The worst part is, I didn't even realize until just now that I've been chasing and protecting a safety that I outgrew a long time ago.

But then he steps so close I can feel his body heat. "I haven't been in a bar since I was nineteen. My dad used to be a functioning alcoholic most days and then occasionally he'd disappear for days at a time and drink himself into oblivion."

"Oh, Jack. I've never heard that about him."

I could swear he's sneering in the dark. "No one has. It was his best-kept secret that the man who could charm millions during his television interviews would get blackout drunk at night. And that when he was drunk, he would yell at his wife and rage at his son and somehow manage to twist it every time to where it was our fault for not understanding what he was going through." *This time, I squeeze his hand.* "And one day, my mom was a wreck and asked me to go get my dad from a bar near our house for her. I did. And when I got there, I tried to get him to get up from the bar, but he wouldn't budge. There were a few people watching and I was so pissed and humiliated and hurt that this was who I had for a father . . . so I told him for the first time that I hated him. I told him he was worthless and the biggest fucking fraud I'd ever seen in my life. And then he finally stood up, only to smack me in the face while everyone was watching. I brought it up to him once, several years later, and he just denied it and told me I was being dramatic and making stuff up to embellish the story. He didn't give me an apology and I quit hoping for one."

"Jack . . ." I grip his shirt and he rests his hands gently over my white knuckles.

"I'm telling you this because I haven't stepped foot in a bar since that day. I've tried to go with friends before and failed because I could never fully face that memory. Didn't want to. But knowing you were inside tonight and needed me, it got me through the doors." He pauses. "You are not alone, Emily. I would walk through my worst memories to get to you every single time."

My heart is pounding so hard it hurts. "Jack. Can I . . . Can you . . . Can we . . ."

He slips his hand around my lower back and pulls me up close. "Can we what, Goldie?"

"I don't know exactly because it's complicated being neighbors and colleagues and now a friend that I really don't want to lose . . . but . . . I can't ignore this anymore either. I want more with you. I need to go slow, but . . . I can't just be friends anymore."

His response is a kiss that nearly knocks me over. We collide in a desperate tangle. He cradles the back of my neck as his mouth slants over mine again and again. I grip his back and sides and shoulders until I ultimately settle my hands into the back of his hair. His perfect color-changing hair. It's brown tonight.

Jack's hands glide down my body, grip my hips, and lift me onto the counter. We never stop kissing, though. It's the kind of desperation I assumed only existed in the movies. In books. Now it lives under my skin. Rushing through my veins.

But then all too abruptly, Jackson pulls away. Not just pulls away, he takes a full two steps backward. Opening up a cavern between us. "Shit. I didn't mean for that to happen."

The lights turn on like the universe is forcing us to take a good long look at what we just did.

"I'm sorry," I say, embarrassment swallowing me up. I press my palms to my overheated face. "I thought we were on the same page, but . . . this is why you haven't kissed me again? You didn't want to? God—I'm sorry—"

"No! That's . . . so far from the truth." He huffs a laugh, and his smile is so fragile and uncertain. I've never seen him look like this. "Believe me, I have wanted to kiss you again, Emily. Every second of every damn day. But I promised myself I wouldn't until I was ready to be honest with you about something. And I haven't been able to find the right time because . . ." He rubs the back of his neck and meets my eye with resignation. "I'm scared to death it's going to change everything."

I swallow thickly. "You have a secret family, don't you?"

CHAPTER TWENTY-FOUR

Jack

"No! I do not have a secret family," I say to Emily, who looks like she's sitting on pins and needles instead of a bar top.

All week I've been searching for the perfect moment to tell her the truth, but I'm realizing that the perfect moment is never going to come. And the longer I wait, the more difficult it's going to be to tell her.

I walk back to Emily and stop just in front of her, not touching. My heart is thundering in my chest, and breathing has never been so difficult. Other than my agent, Zoe is the only other person I've told about Ranger. It was easier to tell her. I knew she wouldn't care. But Emily . . . our long history of competition rolls out in my mind and threatens everything.

"You're scaring me, Jack. Just tell me."

I breathe out and rub the back of my neck. "Umm . . . shit. Okay. First, let me say, this isn't something I tell anyone. So I didn't keep it from you out of malicious reasoning. It's just a secret I've always kept, and I plan to keep from now on too."

Emily looks like she might be sick. The feeling is mutual.

"But I want you to know now, because . . . well, shit, no, I'll tell you that after."

Emily shakes her hands out like they're wet. "Oh my god, Jack! Spit it out!"

"I'm AJ Ranger."

For a man who's supposedly good with words, I dropped those like I was holding a hot cast-iron skillet. Emily is nearly frozen if not for her blinking eyes. I don't dare move closer to her. The hazy silence is choking me, but I've got to push through. Because I refuse to lose Emily.

"It started as a secret because of my dad. I didn't want him to know I was a writer and turn it into something about him. Writing—it brings me so much comfort and happiness. I didn't want him to take that from me. And then when I submitted my first manuscript and got an agent, I made sure it all happened under a pen name. Zoe knew, but I asked her to sign an NDA first. I didn't want any traces to come back to me, because then I'd be connected to my dad professionally. People wouldn't be discussing my book as a debut author; it would all be about how Fredrick Bennett's son wrote a novel and how it compared to his." I shut my eyes tight and breathe out the words "I didn't want that."

When I open them again, Emily's face is still unreadable. She looks braced, though. Looks like a woman who has taken a lot of unexpected punches from life and is waiting to see if this one is going to be as painful as the others.

"I didn't tell you originally, because . . . well, our friendship was so new after years of fighting. I didn't know if I could trust you yet. But then when we got closer, I didn't tell you because I was scared that this would seem like one more arena we could compete in." I venture a half step closer. She doesn't move an inch.

"My writing has always been everything to me, Emily. The most precious thing in my life. But lately . . ." My voice shakes. "That title is shifting to another area of my life. I want something—whatever you'll give me—with you. But I didn't want to ask for it on false pretenses. I want you to know me, all of me. And I want a shot at us. But if this changes things for you, I understand. And you have to know . . . I would never let this become a competition between us. I will continue to support your writing. To pull for you. To root for you and do everything I can to help make your dreams come true." My chest expands on a full breath, and I let it out in a rush. "That's it. That's everything."

After several moments of dead silence, Emily—the woman turned marble statue—says softly, "You're AJ Ranger."

I nod.

"You've been a published writer for . . ."

"Since I was twenty-five." I wish I were in her head. I hate that this is the first time I can't read her.

"Seven years," she says like she's running back in time to see exactly where she was when I published my first novel.

Again I nod.

"So all the times you gave me advice based off your dad's experience . . . it was really yours?"

"Yes." I swallow. "It killed me not to tell you. So many times I almost did."

She's quiet for a few more beats, and then she lightly gasps with some kind of understanding. "This is how you're rich. The Land Rover. The motorcycle. The clothes. Paying cash for the house!" *No one in this town can keep a secret.* "You're not constantly going into debt?"

I let out a short laugh—of course she would have been worrying about that. "No—I'm not going into debt. I . . . have made quite a bit of money off my book deals and sales."

She bites her lip, nodding before her head angles away and her eyes study the floor. Her brows twitch together the slightest bit. "I think I need . . ." She lets that statement dangle a torturous amount of time. "I think I need some time." Her eyes lift to me. "To process all of this."

Those words are a horse kick to my stomach. "Of course. Take all the time you need. You know where to find me."

She stares back at me and nods.

It's understandable that she'd want time to digest this. I've essentially been lying to her for years. Emily is someone who values absolute honesty—which is what I like about her most. But I'm sick to my stomach thinking that revealing this secret is what could end any chance of me and Emily before we really started.

I turn away, take my keys from the counter, and walk toward the door.

"Jack." Her voice stops me. When I turn around, her smiling poison-ivy-green eyes rip my heart out and steal it away. "Turns out I didn't need long to process." She drops down from the counter and faces me. "I want you."

I drop my keys and we both launch ourselves across the room. We collide in the middle and it's beautiful chaos. She kisses me recklessly. I kiss her like the dehydrated man in the desert chasing a mirage for years that turns out to be real.

She puts her hands on my jaw and pulls away enough to look at me. "I have so many more questions, but for now, I want you to know I'm done meeting you in the arena. I'm proud of you, Jack. You're an incredible writer. I'm lucky to know your secret. Thank you." She punctuates it with a kiss as I'm struggling to hold the mist inside my eyes. "And I'm happy to sign an NDA if you want. I'll keep your secret."

This time I dip down and kiss her slowly. Lips pressing and pulling so sweetly. "I trust you more than anyone in this world. I don't want an NDA. Just you. I want to take you home. To your bed."

"I never take guys back to my house or my bed."

I cradle her face and run my thumb below her lip. "I don't want to be one of the guys. I want to be yours." I kiss her softly. "You don't have to be mine if you don't want, and I won't expect too much too soon. We don't have to label it yet, and we can take things slow. But tonight, I want to spend time with you in your favorite place."

She grins up to me, eyes sparkling with emotion. "You're gonna have to beg a little."

I laugh and drop my face into her neck, placing one hot open-mouthed kiss against the skin just below her ear. "*Please,* Goldie—oh god, *please*—let me come home with you."

She hums deep in her throat. "All right. Let's go."

CHAPTER TWENTY-FIVE

Emily

I've been here before—standing just inside my house with Jack—but this time is different. This time, it's real. Or maybe it was real then too . . . but this time, it means something.

When Jack told me at the bar who he is, my first emotion was not anger or hurt. Not even betrayal or fear. It was awe. I'm in awe of Jack, and not at all surprised to learn he is one of the most incredible mystery writers of our generation. My immediate thought was: *Of course he is.* But not in a negative way. I've seen how he lights up when he talks about writing, and it feels like a gift-wrapped present to understand where that light comes from now. The only part of all this that makes me sad is that no one else will ever know it's him who has written all of those incredible novels. All because of his asshat father.

But he told *me.* He trusted *me.* I'll never take that for granted.

Now I close my front door and lock it behind me as we step inside. It's always a little weird to feel full steam ahead in one location and then get in separate vehicles and try to reignite that flame in a different one. It's given my nerves too much time to set in.

What if I can't get back into it? What if this ends up like every other encounter I've had?

"Nice place," Jack says, pretending to look around like he's never been here. He spots Ducky asleep on her mushroom bed and points. "Cute cat."

I laugh, anticipation swirling in my stomach. If this were anyone else, I would attempt to crush my anxiety by faking confidence. I'd make the first move. I'd rush it and get it over with. But this is Jack . . . and I'm learning nothing is the same with him. Including my approach to sex.

When he notices I haven't moved from the door, he eyes me and tilts his head—a calculating smile slanting his mouth. I've never been so thankful to be read in all my life. I don't have to voice my worries. He's tracking them line by line.

He walks over to me, so close I have to angle my face up. I get a kiss on my forehead and then he bends and scoops me up in his arms. "Excuse me, but . . . I need you to come with me," he says, carrying me back to my room while I'm quietly laughing into his shoulder.

Inside the bedroom, he kicks the door shut with his foot and then swiftly sets me on my feet. When I'm standing, he lifts the bottom hem of my tank top and peels it off my body. I'm wearing a fantastic bra that accentuates my cleavage perfectly, and no sooner than Jack looks, his head tips back on a groan like I am the most fantastic thing he's ever seen.

"God, you're gorgeous." His eyes scan me again and then his body melts toward me. "I know I said I'd peel these clothes off you slowly, but it was a necessity for that piece of fabric to be gone immediately."

"Good. I feel like you've been peeling clothing off me slowly for weeks," I say, to which he grins proudly.

His hands slide softly onto my waist. My body flames at the first touch of his skin against mine. "I have wanted this for so long," he says, walking us to my bed, where he sits down on the edge and then hooks an arm around my abdomen and pulls me down into his lap. My back to his chest.

His warm mouth explores the side of my neck, and before we get too far, I feel compelled to remind him of one thing. "Jack . . . remember it might . . . it might take me awhile."

I feel his smile as his hands slide around my rib cage and up to circle both of my breasts. He hums softly next to my ear. "That'll be fun."

And with those words, the anxiety that always grips me in the bedroom recedes enough to let me focus on the feel of his body against mine. Of the soft scratch of fabric against my back. Of his breath and mouth working over the skin of my neck and shoulders as his hands pay reverent tribute to my chest.

Slowly, his right hand extends out over my knee and then gently, torturously, glides up the inside of my thigh. My shorts are still on, but his hand dips into the leg and inches to my hip bone until he encounters the hem of my underwear. His hand flips palm up so he can hook his fingers under the fabric. But then he pauses.

"This would be a good time for me to clarify that you want this and it's okay?"

I nod almost frantically, making him chuckle. "Yes. I want this. Keep going."

"Hm," he says as his knuckles move down my skin at a creeping pace. Only a half inch. "I might . . ." He kisses the side of my jaw. Licks my earlobe. "But earlier tonight a woman reminded me of a very persuasive word."

His hand, still on my left breast, travels across my sternum and right down into the opposite cup of my bra. I gasp and my head drops back against his shoulder. Jack knows how to multitask because his knuckles under my shorts are still moving down, down,

down, but so damn slowly. I'm dizzy with sensation. And all I can think is that Jack Bennett's hands are all over me right now. An electric thrill chases that thought up my spine.

"I hate saying that word," I say, breathless and hazy but still willing to put up a fight.

"I might be able to convince you to like it," he whispers against my ear, and then does something with the hand inside my bra that has me realizing he might be right.

His knuckles are torturously close to where my body is singing with need, but he is still adamant on not moving until he hears what he wants. I happily cave. "*Please, Jack. I need you to touch me.*"

And he does.

His fingers finally meet me where I'm aching. He kisses up and down my neck as his hands create magic against my body, and maybe it's because I feel so safe with him, but for the first time, I tip over the edge easily. My eyes close out the world around me as my body chases the sensations of ecstasy winding and pulsing under my skin. And Jack doesn't gloat that he was able to do what no other man has for me. Instead, he whispers how wonderful I am against the top of my shoulder, sprinkling kisses and compliments everywhere his mouth can reach.

A minute later, I'm spinning around and working the buttons on his shirt, releasing them as quickly as I can until my favorite torso in the world is revealed. I push him back onto the bed, climb onto him until I'm straddling his hips, and then part the fabric of his shirt so I can lay my hands flat against his flexing abdomen. I brush my fingers against the ridges of his stomach, marveling at the intricacies of *Jack*.

What a sight he is, lying on my bed, shirt flung open, pants low on his waist showing the dark band of his underwear, black tattoos dotting his arms and a beaded necklace at his throat. And of course, the cherry on top: his glasses. He looks edible.

I tip forward, and he leans up to meet my mouth in a toe-curling kiss when my phone rings.

His head drops back defeatedly against the mattress. "Not again."

I wince, bending to grab my shirt and tug it on quickly. "I'll be right back. It's Noah. I usually call him after a big storm to make sure he's okay, and because I didn't tonight, he's probably worried. Let me answer really fast and I'll be back."

I make the mistake of looking over my shoulder before leaving. And the sight of Jack sprawled out on my bed with his shirt open is not an easy one to leave. "Right back! So fast!" I say, rushing from the room and into the kitchen.

After answering the phone and in the hastiest way possible telling Noah *I'm fine, love you, bye,* I hang up and get ready to dart back into my room where I'm going to shuck the pants off of Jack quicker than a—

My laptop is open on the kitchen table. And I have one new email.

Something inside me warns not to click the alert, but I've never been very good at listening to warnings. I glide my finger over the track pad and click the email icon. It opens and my eyes collide with a message from Colette Menton.

CHAPTER TWENTY-SIX

Jack

It's been five minutes since I heard her hang up with Noah. At first, I thought maybe she had to go to the bathroom or something, so I've been lying in her bed staring at the ceiling wondering how I'm so lucky to be here. Tonight has been a dream. And at the same time, it feels like a fulfilled prophecy. All I've been able to think this entire night while holding her and touching her is that *I love her*. I am so in love with Emily Walker. She knows who I am now—no more secrets—and she still chose me.

I scrape my hands over my face, smiling behind my palms because I am so terrifyingly happy. Finally, I go meet her in the kitchen to see what's holding her up.

"Everything okay with—" I stop short at the sight of her.

She's staring down at her laptop with a devastated expression. Absolutely gutted at whatever she's looking at. Instinctively, I know that whatever this is, it's about to change the course of our night.

"You okay?" I ask, cautiously walking toward her.

She doesn't move. Doesn't seem to be breathing as much as she should be. When I get to her side, I lay my hand across her lower back and glance over her shoulder to what she's reading. It's an email. It's . . .

Oh shit. It's an email from Colette Menton. And from the looks of it, it's not a good one.

I scan the email quickly, reading it and then rereading it because I almost can't believe what she's saying. In one short email she has completely dashed Emily's hopes for this book. I've read a lot of blunt and honest feedback about my stories, but this . . . this is *tough.* She doesn't pull any punches and finds things with the story that, in my opinion, are too critical.

I disagree with her on nearly all fronts.

The email starts nice enough, saying she has to pass on the project because, sadly, it didn't speak to her like she hoped. I wish she'd stopped there. She goes on to say that because Emily is a good friend of such a successful writer as AJ Ranger, she will give her some feedback that might help her in future submissions. (*Super. So glad she brought me into this.*) Colette matter-of-factly lists each potential issue with the story. She states that the characters lack any depth. The romance, she claims, is flat and dry as burned toast. The sentence structures are amateurish. The concept, apparently, is a winner, but the overall story needs more work than Colette is ready to sign on for at this time. She wishes Emily luck, but suggests she pause and learn more about character development before proceeding with more submissions. *Asshole.*

This is bad.

Colette is a top-of-the-industry agent—and maybe this is my fault, but I really wish this weren't Emily's first experience with a rejection. There is no reason for an email this blunt, and it leads me to believe that it's good Emily isn't going to sign with her. Emily is tough, but she takes criticism very personally. I'll never forget the year she called out a mom for pulling her daughter out of school too many days for seemingly no reason, and the mom lashed back by attacking Emily's teaching style and overall personality. Emily took it on the chin, but I walked by her classroom after school and heard her crying, alone at her desk. I couldn't go and comfort her. Not only was I with Zoe, but Emily wouldn't have wanted me to see her like that. So I found Madison in the parking lot about to go home and told her I thought Emily needed help carrying something out. I don't know if Madison comforted her that day, but I like to hope so.

But tonight, I'm here.

"Emily, I know this probably hurts, but just because Colette says it doesn't make it true." I put my arm around her to pull her into my chest, but she immediately shrugs me off and steps out of reach. My muscles tense with alarm.

She doesn't meet my eye as she says, "Colette thinks my book is"—her voice cracks—"*garbage.*"

"And she's wrong. Colette never should have said all—"

"*No, Jack,*" Emily snaps, finally meeting my eyes. "I never should have sent it in the first place." She's in her head, not listening to a word I'm saying. It's clear Emily has grabbed on to these words from Colette like they're the next ten commandments beamed down from God himself. It's bullshit. I hate it. I hate Colette for sending this to Emily. And I hate that I was the one to encourage her to do it—especially when she had apprehension. I thought I was doing the right thing, but I should have let her listen to her gut.

And now I feel like she's slipping from me while standing right there.

I take a step forward. "Hey. Please hear me. I don't know what the hell that woman's problem is, but I've read your book. And it's incredible. Don't lose hope because of this one rejection."

Her eyes dart away and back to me, fury blazing hot. "It's clearly not incredible. It's junk. And maybe you were just horny enough

for me that you overlooked serious issues and had me submit a terrible book to the best agent out there."

I flinch against her words. "Don't do that. Don't diminish my
opinion just because I also have feelings for you. That's not fair."

"What's not fair is that you rushed me to send it out before it
was ready!"

"I thought it *was* ready, Emily. I really thought it was great. I
still do! And this . . . this feedback, as shitty as it is, is a part of the
job. Sometimes they're right. And sometimes they're just people
having bad days and taking it out on your work. Just like you're
doing to me right now. Take some space from this and tomorrow,
decide what you actually agree with and what—"

"How many rejections did you get when you submitted to
agents?" Her hands are balled up at her sides and I hate it.

"You said you were done meeting me in the arena."

Her hands are curled so tight I can see the whites of her knuckles. "This isn't me competing with you. It's me not wanting to
receive comfort and advice from a successful author when he might
not have ever experienced this in the first place."

I sigh, knowing my answer isn't going to help. "None."

"And how many editors turned you down after you and your
agent pitched?"

I sink my teeth into my lip until it hurts and look away. "None.
The book went to auction."

Emily blinks back fast and furious tears. "Exactly. You don't
know what this feels like—so don't pretend you do."

I want to argue, but she's right. I don't know what it's like. My
experience was rare. I had agents clawing to win me as their client,
and that's an entirely different situation than this. "Okay, you're
right. Then tell me how it feels. Don't push me away. Let me help."

"No," she says, voice shaking, eyes drifting away from me again.
She's erecting a wall directly between us. "You have helped enough.

I am done with it. I'm not submitting this again to anyone. It was stupid to do it to begin with. Clearly, I'm not made to be a writer."

"Emily . . ."

She's going for her laptop.

With a tense voice, I ask, "What are you doing?"

"Deleting it. Sending it to the garbage where it belongs."

Before she can click a single button, I shut her laptop. Her eyes rise to mine, flaming.

"Take it out on me. All your anger. All your humiliation. Take it out on me because I can stand it. But I'll be damned before I let you wreck something that you've worked so hard for. Something that you deserve. Something you love."

"Maybe I don't love it! Maybe it was just a nice distraction for a while but now I'm at the end of the road with it!" I refuse to read into that as a double meaning, even though I feel like she meant it to be one.

"That is absolute bullshit, and you know it. This was making you happy. Going for a dream of your own ignited a spark in you that you liked. And writing . . . you found a home in it. I know you did. I saw it in you."

"Jack . . ." she says in a clipped tone, tears building in her eyes. "Just . . . can you go? I don't . . . I don't *want* to take it out on you. And I don't want to be around anyone right now. Certainly not AJ Ranger."

I grimace. "I can't leave until you promise you're not going to delete your book."

She's staring a hole through the laptop. "It's none of your business. My decisions are my own."

"Dammit, Emily, they don't have to be, though! Just talk to me. Tell me exactly what hurts. Let me be here for you," I say, my voice pleading now.

She's fed up. Her thighs are flexed like she's trying to grind the pain away under her heels. "I want to be alone, Jack. I want to deal with this in my own way like I always do."

I bend to catch her gaze. Something inside is warning me to stop—but I don't because now I know what it's like to have Emily in my arms, to be on the receiving end of her glowing smiles, to be someone she wants to talk to, and I can't lose her. I won't. "Do you actually want to be alone? Or are you just uncomfortable with someone seeing you in a moment of vulnerability?"

Her eyes narrow. "What does that mean?"

"Don't hide yourself away because this is hard and new and hurts."

She scoffs. "I don't think a man in your position gets to offer that kind of advice."

My head kicks back. "And what position is that?"

Emily's voice lowers. "Jack. For years you have hidden your entire incredible writing career because you're afraid of what's going to happen if you step into the spotlight. You only told me tonight, years after knowing me, because you were finally comfortable and ready, but you're demanding vulnerability from me when it best suits you. *That's. Not. Fair.*"

Silence falls for three beats after her words. And dammit, she's right.

"What are we doing right now, Emily?"

She laughs a harsh laugh. "I don't know. I have too many feelings at the moment, and I just want to be alone to process them."

"Is this how it's going to be? Because I thought we were becoming more to each other."

"And I thought you agreed we can take it slow."

The world is spiraling around me. Every word I think comes out. "Maybe we should have stopped to discuss what *slow* meant. Because it seems like what you want is friends with benefits. And I can't do that. I need more." It's true—but I regret saying it immediately. Now is not the time. I know this, and yet I can't bring myself to stop pushing.

She takes in a huge breath, and then it trembles out. I have no idea how the night ended up this way.

"Jack," she says, anger mixed with sensitivity. "I don't think we should discuss it tonight. It's best you leave and that we take time separately to figure out what we want."

I stare at her, feeling the space between us grow and grow and grow. This is what I've always wanted to avoid by getting close to people. It's why I never opened up to Zoe. Because then there was potential to feel this same ugly feeling that would attach itself to me as a kid when I'd watch my dad shut the door on me.

I feel sick watching Emily walk to the door and put her hand on the knob. But she doesn't open it yet. When I walk to her, expecting her to let us leave this without another word, she looks up at me. The fire in her eyes is gone, and my chest loosens a little. "I'm angry right now—but not at you. I'm hurting, and . . . I don't know how to deal with it yet. If you stay, I will say more hurtful things I'll regret later, and I refuse to do that to you." She reaches out, takes my hand, and squeezes it. "We need to take a breather because it's a new situation for us both. It's not goodbye. It's reevaluating. *Agreed?*"

Some of my tension subsides. "Thank you for that." I squeeze her hand in return. "But if you decide you need me later, I'll be here in seconds."

I open the door to leave, but standing on the other side, key in hand and bags beside her, is Madison. Her tearstained face smiles weakly at us.

"*Honey, I'm home,*" she says in a singsong tone that doesn't match her tears.

Emily doesn't even wait to ask questions. She nearly barrels through me to get to her sister, where, despite the fact that her own world is falling apart, she wraps Madison in a hug.

CHAPTER TWENTY-SEVEN

Emily

I watch Jack walk away, and in an alternate universe, I go after him. It feels wrong to see him leave.

Five minutes ago I just wanted him gone. I didn't want to deal with this . . . this . . . heartbreak while he was looking on. I didn't want to have to process the fact that I poured my heart into something, and Colette stomped all over it while a wildly successful author was looking on. I wanted to wallow in my anger and use it to build myself back up, brick by furious brick.

But if Jack stayed . . . I would have broken into a million little pieces, and what if what he saw was too much for him? Likely, he thought the last time I broke down in front of him was because of alcohol. I don't know how to tell him that this pain is always hovering just below the surface these days. It's not alcohol induced. It's raw and it's lurking and I'm not nearly as capable of handling my shit as I seem.

I love Jack. I realized it back at the bar. I love him, and I think I have been in love with him for a while. But the last person I let myself love like this was Liam. I swore I'd never put myself in the situation to be left open to so much hurt again.

So maybe Jack was right. Maybe all I want is friends with benefits. Someone I can have without him having *me*. If he's not okay
with that . . . I don't know that I can move forward with him.

I can't consider any of this now, though, because Madison is
here, sobbing in my arms on the front porch as I watch Jack disappear into his house without looking back.

"I hate it there," says Maddie, head buried in my shoulder. "I
hate New York."

————————

After getting Madison inside, I told her I'd put on some hot chocolate. It's a habit left over from my grandma. When we were upset,
she'd sit us down with a cup of hot chocolate, even in the summer,
and by the time we were at the bottom of the mug, we'd have completely poured our hearts out to her. Even me. Mentally, she's been
gone from us for a long time, but physically, she's really and truly
gone now. It's my job to uphold the hot chocolate ritual.

Pretty much as soon as she walked through the door, Maddie
dumped her bags and made a tearful beeline for the bathroom. She
said she wanted to take a shower and then we'd talk. I put some
water in the kettle on the stove and took her bags back to her room
and unpacked them into her drawers.

I think she knew I'd do this, because she doesn't even come
back out for her bags once she's out of the shower; she goes to her
room and then comes out in baggy cotton sweatpants and a bright
pink T-shirt. She took out her contacts and is wearing her turquoise-
frame glasses. Seeing her here like this is a sight for sore eyes.

Maybe she'll decide to stay and not go back.

There's a steaming mug of hot chocolate with marshmallows
waiting for her at the table, but before she sits down, she wraps me
up in one more big hug. "Thank you, Em."

"You don't have to thank me. I'm always happy to make you hot chocolate." I offer her a smile, but I realize as I do that it's an effort to form it. Normally, when I'm sad and Maddie or Annie or Noah comes home needing me, it heals me in a strange way. But tonight, the ache left from a rejected dream and watching Jack walk out the door is pulsing with pain.

She smiles as she sits, drawing her feet up in the chair, wearing the look of a woman at peace for the first time in a long time. "It's so good to be home. You have no idea."

"Maddie . . . what's going on? I thought you were happy in New York."

She looks down at her hot chocolate, tapping the outside of the mug with her thumb. "I wanted you to think that, because I wanted it to be true."

"But why?"

"Because I . . ." Her voice cracks and she rolls her eyes away to stave off tears. "I feel like such an idiot, Emily. Like such a little baby that misses home. I thought I was going to go to the big city and achieve my dreams and be that woman who thrives in a good trouser-and-sneakers combo. I convinced everyone here that I wasn't made for the small-town life and I needed to go to the city where I belonged."

"And that didn't happen?" I ask, trying not to sound too hopeful.

"No. Not at all. You know who I am in New York? I'm the woman who cries on the subway because I miss my truck. I cry on the sidewalk because I'm so tired of hustling everywhere I walk or else I'll get run over. I cry alone in my bed at night because I miss my family so damn much. Everyone in New York seems so sure and full of purpose and confidence and I just feel like an impostor. A country bumpkin who will never belong."

The image she's painted wrenches my heart. "What about classes at least? How are those going?"

She shrugs a shoulder. "I do like the classes—I'm . . . I'm learning a lot and my instructors are all incredible. I still love cooking, and trying out new recipes in my apartment over the weekends has been the only thing keeping me going."

"That's good. And what about all the guys?"

She wrinkles her nose. "They've been a needed distraction from my loneliness, but that's it. I haven't found a single guy out there that I've wanted to see twice. I've wanted to tell you so badly, but I didn't want you to worry."

"Madison!" I lean forward onto the table. "Why wouldn't you let me worry? It's what I do best!"

She huffs a sad laugh. "Because then you'd tell me to come home for a visit, and I would, and it would hurt so bad to leave again. It's why I never come home to visit. It's too hard to go back to New York and get into a routine." She pauses. "But now . . ."

I try not to look too hopeful. "Now?"

"I'm ready to face the truth—I'm not cut out for New York. And I want to come home. Even if everyone here thinks I'm a failure or a pathetic little baby."

I nudge her knee under the table with my foot. "We would never think that. And you didn't fail. You just realized it wasn't what you thought it would be—and that's okay. You can always come home, Maddie. New York doesn't have to be for you. But hey, at least you tried it, you know?"

"Really?" There's hesitation in her face. Like she's scared to let herself feel joy over this.

"Yes. Come home, Madison."

She smiles fully, sighing a year's worth of sighs. "Okay. I will then. I'm coming home."

God, it feels so great to be the pieces-picker-upper again. I needed this. And besides that, my heart is glowing thinking of having my sister back home once again. We'll have our regular Hearts tournaments again before Noah and Amelia leave, and even when they're gone, we'll still get to have sister nights with Annie. Maybe she'll even want to come back to work at the school.

But then there's a flicker of something inside me that suddenly doesn't quite feel right. Even as Madison is looking relieved and finishing her hot chocolate while talking about how she's going to have to email her instructors and that she'll have to arrange a good time to go out to New York and get her stuff, I'm only half listening. The other part of my brain is holding a flashlight and trying to chase down the sensation of discomfort.

Madison is still talking a mile a minute as I pick up her mug and carry it to the sink and rinse it out. But then, all of a sudden, her voice goes silent. After I load our mugs in the dishwasher, Maddie's voice carries again. "Emily . . . I was going to search for a new movie we could rent, but . . . what is this?"

"What is wha—" I freeze once I turn the corner and see what Madison is looking at. She has my laptop open on the other end of the table, and thanks to her knowing my password, I'm willing to bet she's looking at the email I never closed.

"Did you . . . did you write and submit a romance book to an agent?"

I blank, trying to think of a good lie. Something that will cover my tracks and throw Madison off my scent. But when her dark brown eyes lift to mine, an unexpected dam of emotions breaks. Everything I've kept bottled up since first finding that email from Colette rushes to the surface, and before I know it, I'm sinking to the floor—sobbing.

Maddie drops to her knees and grabs me around the shoulders in the fiercest, most protective hug in the world. She pulls me into her arms, and I let her even when my pride is demanding that I get up.

Instead, I sit here for a while, crying and crying and crying while Maddie rocks me in her arms. She pushes my hair from my temples while I continue on as a disgusting conveyor belt of snot and tears. I'm going to be so embarrassed about this tomorrow but for tonight, I cry.

"Emily, tell me what happened."

So I do. It's a muffled mess but I somehow get it out even between the hiccups. I tell her absolutely everything except for the part where I love Jack and that he's AJ Ranger. And all while I'm talking and relaying the story of writing and editing and how much hope I felt for the whole process until Colette dumped it into a trash compactor, I realize that every damn thing Jack said was right. I love it. I love writing more than I've loved doing anything in a long time. And to give that up would hurt more than I care to think about. Possibly more than hearing Colette tell me my characters were as bland as burned toast.

It was just so unexpected. Maybe I was naïve, but . . . I thought it was good. I thought the book was good and I loved my story.

Madison's face is livid. "I am going to fly back to New York, because I assume that's where Miss Colette lives, and I'm going to chew fifteen pieces of Dubble Bubble and then I'm going to stick them all in her hair while she's sleeping. And then after she wakes up and sees the horror show in her hair, I'm going to pop out of the closet and cut it all off in the most jagged terrible cut she's ever had!"

I laugh and wipe my nose. "Stop it."

"No." She squeezes me like I'm a giant lemon. "No one is mean to my big sister and gets away with it."

This of course brings fresh tears to my eyes. My heart whispers to me how deeply it needed this.

"I'm sorry for crying so much," I say, pressing the heels of my hands into my eyes. "I seem to be doing this a lot lately."

"That's okay. I always cry a lot. It feels good."

I know this about her. I've witnessed it. I've held her through it.

And I've always been jealous of the way Maddie is reckless with her emotions. She throws her arms out wide and sends tears from her eyes that could rival Niagara Falls. And then ten minutes later, she's dancing and singing along to her favorite pop song while making brownies on a random Tuesday at three-thirty. Her capacity to feel everything all the time is astounding. And I've missed the wild energy she brings to every space she enters.

"I hate to cry." Just saying the word seems to have the same effect as mentioning a yawn. I'm sobbing again. "I don't know how to stop once I get going."

Maddie laughs gently at me. "That's probably because you're always holding it in for too long. The trick is to have little breakdowns all along the way."

I look up at her, trying to determine if that was a joke, but it wasn't. She's serious as she pets my hair out of my face. "I'm no therapist by any stretch of the imagination, but I do have quite a bit of experience with tears—and in my thirty years on this earth, I've found that crying starts to feel like exercise. The more you do it, the more comfortable you become with it. And then it isn't so overwhelming anymore." She shakes me gently on my shoulder. "Cry more, Emily!"

"But that sounds atrocious."

She lets go now and crosses her legs. "You would think that."

I use the back of my hand to absorb the wetness from my face. "I'm sorry I'm dumping all of my problems on you, though. I feel terrible about it since you were having such a bad night too."

"I'm not sorry at all. I'm thankful for it, in fact. It was nice to know for once when you need some emotional support."

"That's not your job, though."

"And it's never been your job either," says Maddie, her voice shockingly firm. In fact, it's a tone I didn't even know she was capable of using. I watch silently as she tips forward and sandwiches my hands in hers. "Emily . . . you take on too much—and you hold your-self to this impossible standard of living that no one can survive on. And to be quite honest, it's nice to see that you struggle just like the rest of us. That you need me occasionally just like I need you. So stop letting your pride and your perfectionism get in the way, and let me make you brownies, and tuck you into your favorite blanket, and coddle you while you feel like shit . . . okay?"

I nod, knowing she's right. "Okay."

"Good. And then . . . tomorrow, you're going to let me read your book so that I can lavish you with compliments and tell you what an incredible writer you are so that you'll send the damn thing out to more agents."

"Maddie . . . I don't know if . . ."

She puts her finger to my lips to silence me. "No excuses, Emily. You're the toughest woman I know—and you deserve everything your heart desires. Not only that, but if Jackson Bennett thought your book was good, I know it is because that man has the best taste in the world." She says this not even knowing that he is a world-famous author. "You can do hard things, Emily. I've seen it. This is just a new kind of scary for you. It's something you're doing on your own, not for anyone else, but for you. And that can make a person feel extra exposed sometimes. But that doesn't mean it isn't worth it to push through—because the reward in the end will be that much sweeter."

And there it is. That flicker I couldn't pinpoint earlier grows to life, bold and bright.

I stare at her, my heart sinking from what I need to do. "Dam-mit, Madison."

"What?"

I shut my eyes. "I wish you hadn't said all of that."

"Why?" She chuckles. "Because it was so inspirational it hurt a little?"

"Yes. And because now I have to tell you that you can't come home."

Her smile falls. "*What?*"

I lean forward and cup her face. "I love you. More than anything. And I love having you here, but New York is your hard, scary thing. And if you quit now just to come back home where you're comfortable and safe, you're going to regret it. I can't let you do that. Go back. Get your culinary degree and *then* come home. Or . . ." I can't believe I'm going to say this. "Or maybe try out another state. One that fits your vibes more. See where your career can take you. Maybe it'll end up being the best thing that's ever happened to you."

I kiss her forehead and drop my hands.

Her chin wobbles. "Thank you, Em."

"And thank you. I . . . I really needed this tonight." I've needed it for a long time, and it feels good to stop fighting it.

"Call me more often when you're struggling, okay? Don't keep it all to yourself anymore. We need each other and that's good."

"And tell me when you're missing home. If it's during the summer, I'll come ride the subway with you until you feel better. And if it's during the school year, I'll send you a big care package."

"Deal. But for now, how about I make us some brownies from scratch while you tell me everything about Jack that you left out the first time." Her eyes twinkle. "Like why his shirt was wide open when he left."

"Ugh. I need a break from thinking about Jack tonight. Tomorrow?"

"Fine." She pouts.

Except we don't get up immediately because Ducky wanders over and distracts Maddie with her supreme cuteness. My sister smooshes her face violently into the side of Ducky's stomach and promises to buy her an entire cat kingdom if she will love her more than the rest of us Walker sisters. And knowing I don't have to be alone tonight with my sadness, but I have my sister to help me shoulder some of it—it has me feeling like a Bob Ross painting when he adds some happy little clouds to the sky.

Would it feel this way with Jack too?

My gut says yes.

My fear, however, isn't ready to let go quite yet where he's concerned.

UNSENT DRAFT (1 YEAR AGO)

FROM: Emily Walker ‹E.Walker@MRPS.com›
TO: Jack Bennett ‹J.Bennett@MRPS.com›
DATE: Sat, Sept 2 11:45 PM
SUBJECT: Congratulations?

I just heard the news about you and Zoe. I think I'm supposed to offer you congratulations on your new engagement—but I can't. I know we've never really been friends so I have no right to be speaking in your life like this, but . . . I don't think you should marry her. Something feels off about it.

   And also . . . sometimes I think maybe we should be friends. Put our feud behind us for good?

   I don't know . . . I've had some wine. I probably won't send this. But in case I accidentally do—you should know, I don't think I really hate you at all.

CHAPTER TWENTY-EIGHT

Jack

"I appreciate you letting me check in so early, Mabel," I say after she hands me my room key over the counter. When I got back to my tarped-up, sawdust-covered house last night, I quickly realized an accident of some kind must have happened that day while they were working, because my AC was out. It was hot and oppressive in there. So if my night wasn't bad enough, I added sleeping in 1,000% humidity to the situation.

I didn't actually sleep, though. I tossed and turned all night, restless with memories of my conversation with Emily. And after the sun was up, and at the first appropriate hour, I went straight to Mabel's inn and asked for a room for the weekend. A technician will be coming out to my house later today to work on the unit, but I figured why not go ahead and book a room for a few days just in case.

"It would have been rough trying to get through this hot weekend without AC," I tell her, as I follow her up the stairs.

"Don't blame you a bit. It's gonna be hot as hell the next couple of days." The stairs creak under her loafers. Once we're on the second floor, she turns left down the hallway and stops in front of a door labeled THE PINK ROOM. She opens it for me and waves for me to step inside.

Good God, it is a palace of ruffles. It's not just a tribute to the color pink, it is the full embodiment of it. The space is somehow louder than my anxious mind. Which—is maybe a good thing.

"I love giving this room to men," she says with a chuckle. "It never stops being funny to see the look on y'all's faces when you step inside. Most men look like they might catch feminism if they're in here too long."

"Thankfully I already caught that 'affliction' years ago. Now I'm just worried I'll lose touch with space and time when you shut the door behind me."

Mabel cackles and I've never felt so proud of a joke. "Go on and get settled, and then maybe once you've had some time to cool down in the AC you can tell me the real reason you're at my inn instead of that shitty one you fed me downstairs." She lifts her eyebrows.

"I—" I pause. "It was a real answer."

Her eyebrows somehow lift even farther. "Jack, you can't fool me. I'm a hundred-and-one-year-old woman, I invented lying."

"Are you really a hundred and one?"

"No. Now tell me what's going on. You and Emily have a fight?"

I laugh harshly. "There isn't a me and Emily."

"I told you to quit with the bullshit. If you don't want to talk about it, just say so, otherwise quit lying to me." Her hands are on her ample hips now, yellow dress as bright as the morning.

"All right—I guess you could say we had a fight and it's going to be awkward to live next door until we sort it out."

"What was the fight about?"

I don't know how to explain it. If I even want to explain it. What was discussed between me and Emily last night was personal. And the more time I think over what I said, the more I feel like I was in the wrong. If I tell Mabel, she might not like me half as much from here on out.

"Nope," she says with a country bite. "Quit trying to find the perfect thing to say and spit it out. I don't tolerate pretty words. They make me feel queasy."

Fine, then. "I think I was a dick to Emily."

"There we go! I can work with this." Mabel shuffles over to the bed and sits on the bottom edge, patting the spot beside her. "Don't worry," she says with a sly grin. "I'm no cougar, you can sit by me."

"I appreciate that clarification."

She winks as I sit down, and then her expression sobers. "Now what did you say to our town's Queen Bee?"

"I can't tell you all of it because that would involve divulging a secret of hers that I need to keep. But in a nutshell, she had a hard day yesterday—and I wanted her to let me be there for her—but she was dead set on weathering it alone." I dread saying the next part. "So then I essentially gave her an ultimatum. Either she opens up to me, so we have a meaningful, real relationship, or we go back to nothing."

Mabel nods. "So essentially you said, *Love me how I want to love or else*—every woman's favorite thing to hear."

I groan and drop my face into my hands. "I know! It was rough."

And on top of it, I tried to tell her exactly how to feel about her email with Colette. It was my chance to prove I could be someone safe in her life and I steamrolled right over her. I know that Emily doesn't like to be cornered. And I know how hard criticism is for her, and yet, like Mabel said, I essentially demanded she love me in that moment rather than asking myself what she needed.

You only told me tonight, years after knowing me, because you were finally comfortable and ready, but you're demanding vulnerability from me when it best suits you.

She was right. I didn't realize it until now, but I've been trying to rush this between us. I don't think I've ever really felt loved until her, so last night, I tried to capture it before it was gone.

Mabel pats my back affectionately. "Now listen, it's not as bad as all that. But I want to tell you something about Emily. Something I've never told anyone, and I'll deny it until the day I die as well as call you a liar if you ever tell a single soul . . ."

I look at her, but she seems to be waiting for some kind of reassurance. "I promise I won't repeat it."

She nods firmly. "I love those Walker kids. But I like Emily the most." Her smile glows with tenderness. "She's tenacious, strong-willed, protective, and has a well of empathy inside her heart that I'm yet to find the bottom of. When I look at her, sometimes I see myself. And because of that, I know that Emily is probably scared to death of you."

"Of me?" I ask, having a hard time picturing the Emily who has fought with me for more than a decade the least bit scared of me.

"When I met my late husband, oh lordy, I was terrified of him. I'd lost a lot of people I loved in my day, and I couldn't stand the thought of losing him. I tried and tried to push him away so I could lose him on my own terms. Thought that would be easier. But that sorry fool." Her smile turns nostalgic and private. "He kept coming back for more, because for some reason, he thought I was worth it.

"It took some time and lots of small moments of building trust between us, but eventually, I learned to rest in my love for him instead of fear it." She stares out at the memories floating through her mind for another moment, and I don't dare interrupt. A few moments later, her smile changes to something lighter and she looks at me. "I have a feeling you're a sorry fool just like my sweet husband. And I'm willing to bet all my hidden money that you got possessive of Emily yesterday because you love her, but you have your own wounds you're bringing to the table."

"I think you're right. But what do I do now? . . . Also, why do you have hidden money?"

She ignores my last question. "*Now* you decide if she's worth it to you to go slow or not. To give her strong, fierce soul space when she needs it, and to trust she'll invite you in when she's ready. To let her heart love you softly until it's ready for something bigger." She stands and smooths out the wrinkles of her dress. "Now, of course, if what you need is opposite of what she needs—then maybe this love is one that was only meant to sweep through like a breeze. We encounter those in life from time to time. Doesn't make them less wonderful to experience just because they come and go quickly."

When she's stopped smoothing her dress, I reach out and take her hand. "Thank you, Mabel. I didn't grow up around people I could be honest with." I have to swallow back the lump in my throat. "I appreciate you letting me be open with you today. I think I want to be someone who does this kind of thing more."

"Good. Life can be a little shit sometimes. But shit also makes great fertilizer." She pats the back of my hand that's holding hers. "Grow from your experiences, don't let them smother the light out of you."

Mabel leaves a few minutes later after telling me to ring downstairs if I need any extra towels, and all I can do is lie back on the bed and stare at the ruffled canopy above me.

UNSENT DRAFT (FOUR MONTHS AGO)

FROM: Jack Bennett ‹J.Bennett@MRPS.com›
TO: Emily Walker ‹E.Walker@MRPS.com›
DATE: Wed, Feb 21 1:34 PM
SUBJECT: I think I miss you.

I'm sure you're still rejoicing through the hallways that I'm gone—but I thought I'd just tell you that I broke it off with Zoe. It didn't feel right anymore with her. I'm still here in Nebraska, but I don't like it here at all. Would you be upset if I came back? . . . Would you be happy? I don't know why, but I can't stop thinking about you. Everywhere I turn I expect to find you there. I don't know . . . I guess I'm wondering if maybe you're out there thinking of me too?

CHAPTER TWENTY-NINE

Emily

Now that Maddie has officially decided to go back to New York and finish her degree, she's only here for a quick trip. Basically long enough for us both to wallow and pump each other up and then fly back out tomorrow morning.

It's been so good to have her here, though—I've smothered her with hugs every five minutes and given her a manicure because her nails were chipped within an inch of their life. I helped her balance her checking account, which had been grossly unattended for far too long, we squeezed in a Hearts tournament with Noah and the girls last night, and now we're having our sister hangout/Audrey Hepburn movie night. Or technically movie afternoon since we're also doing a family dinner tonight on James's back porch.

We're even watching the movie in James's living room to consolidate time. Also because James has the nicest house out of us all. His gorgeous farmhouse is situated on the Huxley farm and was inherited from his parents when they downsized to something more manageable. The house looks like it was lifted right from a

Nora Ephron movie set. His mom has always had a love of interior design, and it shows in how she helped him refurnish this place after they moved their stuff out.

There are softly striped fabrics, luscious thick drapes, and a big couch so plush you'll give your soul up for a chance to sit on it just one more minute. Warm oak hardwood floors and the kind of lighting that soothes something buzzing inside you. You would never expect a place like this to belong to a man like James. A farmer through and through.

I wonder if I'll still get to help Jack shop for his house when it's finished.

And that's been happening today too. An all-day mental Jack-a-thon (which sounds much dirtier than I'm intending). It's basically just a frustrating nonstop loop of *I love him, I'm scared to love him, but I love him*. Round and round it goes.

"My God, Emily! You had him get down and dirty by the front door?" Madison screeches from the couch, knees up to her chest, oversized T-shirt draping her shorts, making her look pantsless. Her eyes are glued to her phone.

That's the other thing I did today: I told each of my sisters about my book.

I'm glad I did. They've spent a solid chunk of time full-on squealing, which has helped me replace some of my *it's trash because Colette thinks it's trash* feelings into *she can go to hell* feelings instead. Well, not completely, because after looking over her notes, like Jack predicted, I've found two points she made that I do agree with and will change. But overall, I've decided, as my grandma used to say, someone must have peed in her Cheerios that morning.

The time with my sisters has been healing. When I first unloaded the truth to them, there was a lot of feet kicking and screaming, and then several minutes of oohing and ahhing over my plot. And then a moment I'll always remember for the rest of my life when Annie looked me straight in the eyes and said: *Emily, I'm so proud of you*. Annie and I are close, but we've never had quite the connection that Madison and I have had, just simply because of our age proximity. But in that moment, I felt the strongest tether to Annie. She's learned to step into herself over the last year, even when it's been uncomfortable, even when it meant confronting each of us sisters about the way we've treated her with too much fragility in the past. And today, that woman looked me in the eyes and said she was proud of *me*.

I didn't, however, have the heart to tell them about accidentally sending my manuscript to Bart, though. Not because I'm ashamed anymore, but because it's my and Jack's secret. Something that's just ours in this world where nothing makes sense, and our futures are uncertain, but . . . at least we'll always have the manuscript heist.

"I only emailed it to you five minutes ago, Maddie. How are you already to the sex scene?"

She looks at me like my head is a potato. "I searched the document for the word 'nipple' so I could get to the good stuff quickly. Do you guys not do that?"

"No!" Annie says in outrage from where she's curled up on the other side of Maddie on the couch. "That's terrible, Madison. The steam hits so much better if you let the story build around it. Build the connection first."

Madison laughs like this is the most hysterical thing she's ever heard. "Maybe for you three delicate flowers. But for me . . . I don't care when the steam hits, I'm here for it."

Amelia bonks Maddie in the face with a pillow. "Yes, we gathered that when you FaceTimed us from the bathroom because there was a man in your bed."

There's a beat where Madison tosses me the quickest look. *They've been a needed distraction from my loneliness.* I'm so glad she let me into that part of her heart. And I am nothing if not faithfully loyal, which is why I don't call her out when she smirks at Amelia and says, "Don't be jealous just because you're locked down to my snoozy brother and I'm free as a bird."

The microwave beeps in the kitchen, signaling that the popcorn is finished, but I'm too engrossed in this conversation to care yet. I also like to stand by in case I need to play referee.

Amelia puts her foot in Madison's face. "Noah wasn't snoozy this morning."

Madison gags. Annie covers her face with her hands. I, too, am barely holding down my lunch at the thought of my brother not-snoozing anyone. But good for them. Healthy relationships and all that. I just don't want to hear about it.

"Annie," says Madison, swiveling her face to our baby sister. "How is your sex life with our favorite bodyguard? Wait—why am I even asking? I know it's incredible. In fact, don't tell me. I'll be too jealous."

"What happened to Ms. Free as a Bird from a minute ago?" I ask, saving Annie from her pink cheeks and having to respond to Maddie's intrusive question. She's changed a lot over the last year, but she's still Anna-banana in a few ways too.

Madison shrugs. "I implied I was having sex. I never implied it was *good* sex."

And of course, that's the moment that James walks into the living room holding a bowl of popcorn. His eyes—I notice—lock on Madison. He steps up to her from behind the couch and sets the bowl of popcorn directly in her lap. "Here's your popcorn you made that I told you not to make. Thanks to you my kitchen is going to smell like it for a week."

"Aw, Jamesie," Madison says, raising her hand to playfully pat his cheek like an old granny showing affection in church. "Admit it, you miss me around here!"

The look James gives Madison makes my insides constrict. He *does* miss her.

Does Madison know what she's doing to him? I don't think so since she's always playfully antagonizing him. The rest of us know, though, judging by the way we all seem to be wearing matching expressions of discomfort as we observe James's longing look for Maddie as she pops a piece of popcorn into her mouth with seemingly zero awareness.

"You know what I miss, Madison? My T-shirt." His eyes drop to the article of clothing in question. "Have you had it in New York this whole damn time?"

And then something flashes in her eyes for the briefest of seconds that makes me wonder if she's not so clueless after all. Considering how much she's missed home too . . . I can't help but wonder if she's been holding on to his T-shirt because she misses *him*. "I found it at Noah's place before I left. Finders keepers. . . ." Her brown eyes slide up to him. "Losers weepers."

He can't fully hold back his grin. "Annoying little shit." He flicks her nose and then steals a handful of popcorn before walking out his back door. Madison watches him go, swallows, and then turns toward the TV and watches Audrey Hepburn zip through town in her little red car wearing a fantastic monochrome white outfit. Complete with white sunglasses and hat that sort of resembles a bucket but on Audrey is painfully chic.

"We can all agree that Peter O'Toole was one of Audrey's sexiest heroes, right?" says Amelia, deftly changing the subject away from the awkwardness that just unfolded in front of us.

"Definitely . . . he actually reminds me of J—" I stop myself before I finish that thought out loud. All three ladies heard it, however. They heard it and they look like wolves starved for dinner now.

"Ladies," says Madison, sitting up straight. "Notice the goofy smile!"

"Hey!" I say, and lob a pillow across the room that doesn't quite make it to her.

"The bright dopey eyes!" Amelia adds.

"*Again*. Hey!"

"The flushed cheeks!" Annie tacks on while cupping her hands around her mouth to assure everyone heard her.

Madison's expression is greedy. "You were going to say 'Jack,' weren't you! Because you love him! Because he stole your heart right out from under you."

I roll my eyes, even as their words hit like direct missiles. "Please. I wouldn't even care if he packed up all his bags and moved to Australia." It's a blatant lie. I'd be *devastated*. I'd race to the airport without luggage and beg the person behind the ticket counter to send me wherever Jack Bennett went. But for the sake of getting my siblings to drop it, it's off to Australia with him.

It would be so much easier if I didn't care about Jack. Instead, I've been wondering nonstop how he is after our fight. Why his SUV has been missing since yesterday morning. Sometimes I wish I could go back to hating Jack and living my safe little life of solitude. But of course I'd have to go and fall in love with him instead. And I really, really do love him.

The problem is, I don't know if I can give him what he wants. There seems to be a broken, jagged disconnect between what my heart wants and what my body will allow. Each time I mentally walk myself down the path of telling Jack I love him, and that I also want the kind of relationship he described, my body tenses up. Fight or flight kicks in and a thousand memories rush to the surface.

People I love die. Or they hide things from me and leave. Or they simply outgrow me and move on. The one constant in my life has been me, at the end of the day, alone in my bedroom. And if I let myself love Jack fully with arms outstretched wide and he leaves me, it will break me.

"Oh! Not to change the subject," says Annie, popping up from the couch. "But this reminds me of something!" We watch her disappear into the kitchen, and when she comes back, she's holding an old piece of paper. No. Not an old piece of paper—an old photo, I realize as she hands it to me. "I found it taped to the wall in one of James's greenhouses. I asked him if I could have it and of course he said yes."

The picture trembles lightly in my hand as tears flood my eyes.

"I guess their garden did grow," Annie says, leaning down to kiss the top of my head.

In the picture, my mom and dad are standing together, his arm around her shoulder and hers around his waist, smiling hugely to the camera. Behind them is a flourishing garden full of sunflowers and dahlias.

My heart jumps into my throat. It feels as if my mom and dad are reaching through time and hugging me when I need them most. Reassuring me that even in unfavorable circumstances, even when it feels like all odds are against me, with hope and care, good things find a way to thrive.

"Thank you for finding this, Annie. I needed it more than you know."

———

"The pancakes will be out in a minute!" Amelia yells from James's kitchen to where the rest of us are already gathered on the porch.

We all groan.

"I heard that!" she yells again. "But this batch is going to be good, I can feel it."

We—meaning me, James, Annie, and Will—all look to Noah. He shakes his head *no* with a quiet frown. We groan again. Amelia has been trying to perfect these pancakes since she and Noah met and they somehow have gotten . . . maybe not worse (because I'm not sure that's possible), but different. Noah offered to finally give her his recipe and sadly for all of us, she declined. Her desire to make the perfect pancake is personal now. She doesn't want his sorry old recipe; she wants to create her own.

Which means we've had to try every chewy, burned, crispy, and oddly gooey pancake under the sun. I'm convinced she'll never accomplish it. And that's not just pessimism, it's history proving my point. The universe simply dumped too much talent into the singer/songwriter/performer part of her brain and had none left over for baking. This keeps life fair.

"Don't worry," James says, kicked back in his seat at the end of the large porch table. "I made scrambled eggs, biscuits, and bacon too."

"And I"—Maddie jumps in, leveling James with a saucy look—"made grown-up food. A salmon and spinach quiche."

"Yeah, and you destroyed my kitchen in the process. You better clean up before you leave." Any of their earlier tension seems to be gone. They've sunk back into their normal routine of bickering over nothing.

She lifts an eyebrow at him. "Make me." She then shoves his booted feet to the floor. "No feet on the table, Jamesie. Why can't you be more civilized like Tommy." Tommy is James's younger, more selfish brother.

His boots hit the floor with a thud, and he sits forward so his face is a few inches from Madison's. "Civilized, meaning an asshole who's obsessed with his own reflection in the mirror? No, thanks."

"He's not an asshole," Madison says, and we all roll our eyes because even I can admit that he's a little bit of an asshole. But he's a gorgeous asshole, and for that reason, Maddie has had the biggest crush on him since she was little. Thankfully, Tommy rarely ever comes around Rome because he's too busy doing whatever it is he does. (Mainly women, according to James.)

My brain immediately vaults itself back to another gorgeous man that I can't get off my mind. Ugh. But every time I close my eyes, we're back in my room and he's looking at me like I'm the first sunrise after winter.

"Now, children," says Will, putting his butterfly hand on James's jaw and turning his scowling face away from Maddie. "Let's not bicker at the table. It's impolite. Whose turn is it to try Amelia's pancakes, anyway?"

We all immediately hold up our thumbs and slam them down. James is the last one to get his thumb on the table. We point and laugh at him like the mature adults we are.

"Dammit!" He groans, hanging his head. It pops back up just as quickly. "Emily—you owe me ten bucks for the beer Friday night. I'll call it even if you're taste tester tonight."

"No way." I would pay him a hundred dollars right now just to ensure I didn't have to take a single bite of that pancake.

He's hunting for more prey around the table. "Annie . . . you know that flower discount I give you?"

"Don't you dare try to take that from her!" I say, laying my palms flat on the table and leaning toward him. "You lost fair and square!"

Everyone continues to banter and bicker and poke fun at each other around the table and for a minute, all I can do is sit back and watch with a smile on my face. Sometimes I wonder what my parents would think if they could see us all grown like this, sitting on

James's porch overlooking the vast farmland that's been in his family for decades. The same farm my parents worked on when they first married and where my mom planted her flower crop.

I look at each of my siblings' laughing faces (James included in that statement) as the string lights around the porch sparkle in each of their eyes—the sound of summertime crickets and some old country music playing in the background with Amelia cooking up something atrocious inside in the kitchen.

I live for nights like this with these people. They create the illusion that I'm within reaching distance of those comforting childhood days. But I can't let myself dwell on that feeling too long anymore. I need to see this moment for what it is. Beautiful. Ever changing. We're not kids, and Mom and Dad are not somewhere off in the distance. Annie is a woman with a thriving career and a man she loves. Noah is married with a wife (a world-famous one at that) and is soon going to support her on tour for a year. Maddie is out there getting her dreams and conquering the culinary world. And for the first time, while not trying to keep them hooked to a fishing line, I can think of the changes in their lives with some joy.

It's okay that time is moving and changing. Maybe it's okay if I move and change too.

"Aha!" James shouts, suddenly pointing at the porch door at my back, making us all startle. "He's the last to arrive, so he has to be the pancake guinea pig."

He?

Everyone turns and looks over my shoulder, and for some strange reason, I feel a change in the air. A chill runs down my spine like the warning of impending danger. *Impending delight.*

"You made it!" Maddie says happily, standing up from the table and going to greet—

Jack. My Jack.

And I watch as my traitor sister is giving *my Jack* a hug.

"Everyone, I assume you've met Jack by now? Jack, everyone! Grab a seat. There's one over there by Emily." My gaze connects with Madison's, and she winks at me and mouths *You're welcome*.

How dare she! How dare my family meddle in my life like this. How dare they love me this much. And how dare my face betray me with a smile at a time like this when I should be upset to find him here. I don't have my answer for him yet! I haven't had enough time to perfectly craft the words to convey: *I'm afraid of how much I love you*.

But as my eyes connect with Jack and his retro orange-and-white-striped crew-neck shirt, I'm so relieved he's not in Australia.

He walks closer to the only available seat at the table, which I'm just now realizing has been added purposely! They all knew? I will kill them all after I finish hugging them furiously, because Jack is here and even though nothing is settled, my heart feels at home.

"Hello, Emily." *God, just the sound of his deep, smooth voice melts me.*

I can't help my grin. "Hello, Jack."

"Is it okay that I'm here?" he asks quietly.

We have a lot to talk through and figure out after how we left things the other night, but oddly, I'm glad this is how we're seeing each other again for the first time. Hidden emotions inside my Treasure Chest of Doom scream that he belongs here with me and my family. That whatever conversation we have on the horizon, it'll be okay. Because I can trust Jackson Bennett. Maybe I can even trust what we have together.

"I'm happy you're here," I say with gut-wrenching truthfulness.

Suddenly aware of eyes on me, I turn to see my entire family watching. But when my head aims in their direction, they each do some version of whistling and looking around into outer space.

"Okay, guys, they're—Oh, hi!" says Amelia, the screen door snapping shut behind her. "Jack, right?"

"That's me," says Jack. "And you're . . ." There's a moment where he looks unsure of which name he should call her by. And I have to admit, I love seeing him flustered. Who knew Jackson Bennett could get starstruck?

"Amelia," she supplies, carrying her tray of death-cakes to the table. "All my friends and family can call me by that name."

"I'm honored for the privilege, then." *God . . . I love when he talks like Fitzwilliam Darcy.*

Amelia approves too. She widens her eyes at me before she goes to the table. And now Jack is lowering himself into the chair beside me and I'm momentarily drugged off his scent. He smells fresh from the shower. Like a white bar of soap has recently glided over his taut, tan skin.

Amelia sets the tray of pancakes in the center of the table.

Noah grins. "James, I believe you get the honor of the first—"

"Jack should get the first pancake!" I fire out, making everyone jump from how loudly I blurt it. "He's the guest, after all." And yes, maybe it's unfair, but suddenly I feel like putting him under a little test. A final quiz before I officially make up my mind about us.

Jack looks at me—calculating. He knows something is going on here, but still he says, "Sure, thank you."

"Great!" Amelia beams. "Tell me how they are. I tried adding a little more sugar to this batch."

Oh no, that's never good.

The plate of pancakes gets passed around the table, and Jack seems to study everyone's faces as it passes through their hands without anyone taking a pancake for themselves. But when the plate makes it to me, I don't hand it to him. Instead, I serve him myself—forking pancakes onto his plate one by one.

After three pancakes, and when I'm loading up a fourth, he stops me. "That's plenty, thank you."

I blink innocently at him. "Oh. Sorry. Is that too many?" I slap a fourth on because no matter how close Jack and I are, I will always needle him. It's our love language. "Syrup?"

"*Please*," he says in a way that intentionally brings the memory of the last time that word was used between us to the front of my mind. His own brand of needling.

Once he notices everyone watching closely, and because Jack is Jack and has to try to charm the pants of everyone in attendance, he ventures into polite conversation while cutting into his pancakes. "James, your farm is incredible. Did you always want to take it over?"

James adjusts his dirt-stained Carhartt hat and sits forward, like he's just turned on a big game and can't miss a second of it. "We're not in summer school, Mr. Bennett. We don't do ice-breakers at this table. Let's see you eat the damn pancakes."

I stifle my laugh behind a napkin and Jackson just cuts his eyes to me.

With hesitation, and everyone staring a hole through his face, Jack cautiously lifts the fork and takes a bite. Only because I know him, I can read the minuscule hesitation, the spark of disgust in his eye that, to me, reads as plainly as words on a page: *Oh god. What is this shit?* But Jackson is a master, so in a blink, he's chewing his way through that pancake like it's the finest filet mignon. Judging by how much he's having to chew, I'm betting that was one wild bite.

"So?" Amelia looks hopeful as she watches, and of course he can't bring himself to let her down with honesty.

"Mmm." He swallows, and Jackson should be a damn Emmy-nominated actor for the part he just sold us. "It's . . . *wow*."

I'm going to perish from restraining my laughter so hard. Noah and James look like they're in similar boats. They know there's no way this shit is good.

"What's your favorite thing about the pancake?" Amelia asks, endearingly hopeful.

Noah clears his throat and with a deadpan expression says, "I'm honestly dying to hear as well."

Jack nods and effortlessly gives everyone else at the table a heads-up about what to expect. "Definitely the Tabasco sauce . . . that's a unique touch."

"Ah! You could taste it? I was trying to go for one of those sweet and spicy flavors like Madison is always doing with her recipes." She then turns and slaps Noah's bicep. "See. He likes them. Will you try it now?"

Noah grins at Amelia and wraps his arm around her shoulder to pull her into his side and kiss her temple. "I'm devoted to you in every way. But do I really have to eat that pancake?"

"Yes."

He smiles tensely and makes a casual *gimme* gesture with his fingers in my direction. I send the plate back his way happily.

"Anyone else want one?" Amelia asks.

There's a quick and furious mutter of *no*s and *not me*s. "Oh, come on! He liked them."

Madison cackles. "And the poor man was clearly lying through his teeth judging by the way Emily was about to combust from laughing at him! No, thank you. We'll wait and see on the next batch."

Amelia looks like a puppy kicked out in the rain on a cold winter's night, which is no doubt why Jackson raises his hand to get her attention. "Actually . . . I do like them. They're different. I'll take another if no one is going to have one."

I have to grip my thighs, because something about the look on his face has my stomach clenching and swooping at the same time. Jack is giving everyone a dad look. He's quietly reprimanding my siblings for not supporting Amelia—a job that is normally mine. And it's going to make me cry.

Madison scrunches her nose. "No—actually. I do want one."

"Me too," says Will with a valiant attempt at a smile. "I'm not scared of Tobasco sauce."

James narrows his eyes at Jack, disliking this new show of dominance in our family circle but seemingly respecting it all the same. "All right, dammit. I'll take a pancake too."

Amelia is beaming now even though she knows everyone was heavily influenced by Jack. And it's hard not to let my voice betray my emotion as I finally ask for the plate to be sent my way too.

The conversation flows back to normal as plates of eggs and bacon and Madison's breakfast quiche get passed around family style. But Jack's eyes float in my direction, where I've been sitting here trying to choke back tears because . . . he fits perfectly here.

He nudges the side of my thigh with his knuckle. "Emily . . . I need you to know . . . I'm so sorry for pushing you the other night. I was . . ." He pauses. "I was worried about you, and I didn't know what else to do because I could see you shutting me out and it terrified me. But I was wrong for not giving you space when you asked for it. For going back on my word of being okay with going slow . . ." He breathes out and shakes his head, turning more fully in my direction, seemingly unworried by the fact that anyone could be watching or listening. "You make me feel wild, Emily. I've never cared about anyone like I care for you. But I'm so sorry. I'm sorry for all of it, including trying to fix how you felt about that email." He pauses. "If you'll let me, I'll figure out the right balance of taking care of you and pissing you off when you want me to." His smile is promise. "I'm a quick learner. Whatever you want out of the relationship, I'm happy with that."

Emotions clog my throat. "So you really do still . . ." I glance around the table to make sure no one is listening. "You still want me? Even after I pushed you away and then made you eat shitty pancakes?"

He looks at me like he's genuinely confused. "Emily . . . when I told you I care for you, I mean it. It's not that I care for some aspects of you, not that I care for you when you're in a good mood . . . I care for you always. I want you, *always*. The good, the bad, and the in-between. *I. Want. You.* Sharp edges, hot tempered, fiercely protective, gooey heart . . . all of it. All of you. But I'm not going to rush you again or push you into anything you're not ready for either. In the end, if all you want is friendship, I'll take it."

"I . . ." My breath is an earthquake. "I need to . . ." I don't finish my sentence. I can't because these tears that always seem to be hovering on the edges of my skin lately are about to break through.

I push back from the table and run to the kitchen.

CHAPTER THIRTY

Emily

I'm hiding in the kitchen like a coward.

More specifically I'm hiding in James's walk-in pantry with the door shut like a coward. I've never hidden from anything. I'm the one who would jump in front of a moving car for a friend. I would climb to the top of the tallest tree in the town to get your cat down. If there's a tornado, I'll cover your body with mine. If someone is chewing out a waitress in a restaurant, step aside because they now have to deal with me. But when Jack said *I want all of you,* I'm suddenly runaway bride and hyperventilating in a pantry as a bag of potato chips pokes me in the shoulder.

The pantry door flies open. "What the hell are you doing in here?" asks Maddie.

I grab her wrist and tug her inside, shutting the door behind us. "Can you *shhhhhh!* Obviously I'm hiding."

The pantry door opens again. "From who?" asks Annie.

Madison grabs the hem of Annie's shirt and reels her inside. We close the door.

"From *him!* Jack."

"Why would you be hiding from Jack?" Madison asks at full volume. "He's so gone for you it's almost painful to watch."

"Can you keep your voice down?" I frantically whisper. "Jeez."

The door opens again.

"Why are we keeping our voices down?" Amelia steps inside the pantry voluntarily and now me and all of my sisters are squished in here like sardines. A cereal box is pressing into my hip and someone's bacon breath is wafting into the air like a poorly scented candle.

I wiggle for a little space but it's no good. We're all shoulder to shoulder. "I'm hiding from Jack," I repeat for the hundredth time.

"I'm sorry," Maddie says with regret in her tone. "This is my fault. I thought it was the right move to invite him."

"Maybe you two should date instead. Clearly you're two peas in a pod trying to force my hand on stuff." Maddie has the audacity to look like she's actually considering it. I level a finger to her chest. "Don't you dare."

"Why?" She grins and widens her eyes like a know-it-all. "I thought you said he didn't steal your heart?"

"Yeah, well . . ." I toe a loose potato on the floor out of the way. "He might have borrowed it after all."

They all three gasp.

"Do you want a relationship with him?" asks Annie, with enough tenderness it feels like a blanket wrapped around my shoulders. Bless her for not asking me outright if I love him.

"I don't know what I want. I thought I was okay with giving up on having some big romance. I had my routine and my cat, and my career, and those things made me happy . . ." Yes, I was lonely too. But sometimes it's easier to choose the pain you know than the pain you don't. I can't imagine how painful it would be to integrate my life with Jackson's and then lose him. "But of course Jack had to be Jack and flip everything upside down because he delights in nothing more than ruining my perfect plans."

"And now you're thinking you might not want to give up on a big romance for yourself?" asks Amelia.

I scrub my hands over my face. "I'm thinking I wish someone would just tell me how to go back to normal."

She shakes her head with a soft smile. "You know what I think? I think normal isn't going to be enough for you anymore."

"Same," says Annie. "I've been in your shoes, Emily. And I know the look of a person who's recognized that their needs have changed. And it's scary as hell."

My eyes prickle. "I don't want to change."

"It's good to change. It hurts a little at first but then it starts to feel like stretching first thing in the morning. Like you don't realize how badly your body needed the movement."

Madison chimes in, talking in a robotic cadence, "And you know . . . just as iron rusts from disuse, and stagnant water putrefies, or when cold turns to ice, so our . . . intellect"—she pauses and then continues in a rush—"wastes unless it is kept in use."

We all blink at her. She holds up her phone and the Google search engine. "I wanted to add something to the conversation, so I looked up quotes about change, but Leonardo da Vinci really let me down in the second half there."

I pat her back. "It's the thought that counts."

Light floods the pantry again when the door yawns open. For half a second all I see is a male form and I'm terrified it belongs to Jack. I'm not ready to acknowledge his statement yet. And I don't want him to know I'm hiding in a pantry to avoid my problems.

But it's not Jack. It's Noah.

"Okay," he says in his gruff way. "Everyone except Emily, scram."

Madison pouts. "What? Why? I want to hear what you are going to say."

"Tough," he says, crossing his arms in his trademarked Surly Pose as Amelia has always called it. "Out."

Everyone goes, but Amelia is the last one to leave. He gives her a soft smile on her way out and pats her butt. Once they're all gone, he closes the door behind us again. "It's time we talked."

"About the weather? It *is* unseasonably warm at the moment."

He doesn't acknowledge my quip. "Let's talk about what happened with Liam all those years ago."

The floor almost falls out from under me. Noah has never, not once, tried to press the topic of the breakup that changed the entire course of my life—and possibly even rewired my brain, even though he was witness to it. Everyone took my words at face value when I said it was a mutual breakup that hurt, but I'd get through it. Noah is the only one who knows the truth.

"I don't want to talk about him."

"We're going to—because it's important to this moment. Emily, you were always so tough and independent after Mom and Dad died, but never so closed off as you are now. It's like that day froze a layer of ice over your heart so thick it stopped beating normally. And you know why I think it was? Because you've regretted not going with him."

A record screeches in my mind. Because after Liam and I talked in my room, I had opened my bedroom door to find Noah standing there listening. I always assumed he knew exactly what was said. But it turns out he didn't hear it all that well.

"You think. . . ." I laugh like a gust of wind. "You think I regret not going with Liam?"

"Yes. I think you chose to stay home with your family because you would sacrifice every bit of your happiness to make your siblings happy. I think you were worried to leave the girls without someone to take care of them. Because let's face it, Grandma was sweet and tender, but she didn't have that motherly edge that you do."

"Well, you're right about one thing—I was afraid to leave them. And you." I pause and refuse to cry this time. "But the truth is, I would have. I loved him enough that I absolutely would have. But . . . he didn't ask me to go."

Noah is understandably speechless.

"Didn't want me to go, I should say. He needed to experience life without me. Wanted to date other people." And by other people he meant Brittney Daniels from our graduating class who *did* get into the same college with him. She was a lot like Annie. I doubt she's ever sent back an incorrect meal in her life. "He was there to break up with me, Noah. It was never mutual. I was just too embarrassed to tell anyone that. To tell anyone that the boy I loved with all my heart didn't really love me back."

Noah wraps me in a bear hug. One so tight I can barely breathe. And guess what? I cry again, since it's all I do these days. Because I'm a mess. Because all the darkness I've been experiencing on my own the last year is leaking out through my eyes on a continual basis for everyone to witness.

He sighs into my hair. "I'm sorry, Em. I didn't know. I should have asked more questions back then instead of assuming you were okay because you said you were."

Not that it's his fault at all, because I played a very convincing part of *Girl Who Is Just Fine,* but I do wonder: If my family had made more of an effort to talk to me during that time about what happened with Liam instead of accepting my righteous independence, would I have healed faster? More wholly? Would I have been in a better place by the time I started college and not told Jack to piss right off?

Maybe there's no real point in asking these questions, or maybe self-reflection is the key to a lifetime of healing. All I know is that despite everything, I still found my way into Jack's heart. And now he wants me. Or he says he does. But Liam said that at one time too. So how do I trust it's real this time?

"Listen," Noah says, shifting the hug so he can look down at me. "I'm not . . . I'm not very good at all this. Pep talks and feelings aren't really my thing."

"No, really?" I ask sarcastically because it's my sisterly duty.

"But when I was going through a hard time, you told me something that really helped me. So I'm going to say it back to you." He pauses. "*Maybe not everything will end in hurt. But we'll never know if we don't try.*"

I laugh at hearing that bit of wisdom from my few sessions of therapy thrown back at me before I stopped going altogether because it was too damn painful week after week. I decided it was easier to shove it all in my Treasure Chest of Doom instead. "I meant that advice for you, not me."

He smiles. "Let yourself have this one. Be open to seeing what happens. Don't let him be the most wonderful thing that never happened to you because you were scared to give it a try. Besides, the Emily I know can handle just about anything. If it doesn't work out in the end, you'll get through it. It may not feel like it for a time, but it won't break you. And no matter where we are in the world, us Walkers will always be there for you when you need us. You just have to say so."

I swipe my hand across my wet cheeks. Noah's words have swelled me up with so much encouragement and confidence I could hot-air-balloon this whole house to Paris.

"You're better at pep talks than you think," I tell him, patting the outside of his arm.

He smiles. "Amelia is rubbing off on me, I guess."

"I'm glad you took a chance on her, Noah. I . . . I love seeing you happy."

"And I loved seeing you happy Friday night at the bar with Jack."

I nod. "I need to go talk to him."

Noah stops me before I fully make it out of the pantry. "He's not here anymore."

"What?" *Did he leave because of me? Is that it? He's given up this quickly? I know I'm a pain in the ass but—*

Noah gives me side-eye as he can apparently sense the direction of my thoughts and isn't impressed I've regressed so quickly. "He told me to tell you that he'd find you later, but that something important came up with his mom and he needed to go out to Evansville." He shakes his head with a laugh. "Poor guy even took a Tupperware full of Amelia's damn Tabasco pancakes to go. It might have been a strategic move on his part to win me over, and I'll be damned if it didn't work perfectly."

CHAPTER THIRTY-ONE

Jack

I hate this dining room table.

My dad once did a photo shoot in this house when I was fifteen for a magazine article about his life, his family, and following his muse. My mom and I were with him for one of the setups where we were playing a board game right here, on this table. I'd never once played a board game with my dad before that moment. Before the shoot, my mom practically threw it at me when she realized the plastic was still on it so I could run into the kitchen and crack it open with a knife. It was the strangest feeling being photographed as we smiled and laughed playing a game we were pretending to have played hundreds of times before. We didn't know the rules. Or the objectives. So we rolled dice and moved pieces around the board for no reason at all.

The person on set whose job was to make sure none of the lighting equipment scraped the floors looked at me after our segment and said, "Man, I'm jealous! You've got such a cool dad."

I knew he was just saying it to be nice, so I agreed and then went in my room and threw a pillow at my window—wishing it would be enough to shatter it, and terrified at the same time that it would.

"Your mom told me about visiting your new place in Rome, Jack," says my dad from his throne at the head of the table.

"Yeah? I'm really happy there. When it's done it'll—"

"I just think you'd be better off putting teaching behind you and doing something important with your life. Seems like Rome is a dead end too. Just an old rotting town."

My mom texted me somewhere in between me pulling up to James's place and Emily darting into the house. It was the kind of text I've come to understand as an SOS from my mom. *Can you come for a late dinner?* It's innocuous. If he read her text messages he'd see nothing but a mom inviting her son over. But I got the message. What it really means is *He's in a mood. Please help.*

I know my place tonight: peacemaker. But it's a struggle to respond to his comment tactfully. "Oh, I don't know; the town is full of good people, and working with kids is pretty important to me."

"The women can do that job just fine. You should be doing more."

I set down my fork and it clanks loudly against the plate. "I don't believe in gender-specific jobs. It's an honor for me to teach those kids how to read and write—and a damn hard career."

My mom clears her throat, looking panicked. She saw him trending toward a mood that preludes a rage fit, and she hoped I would intervene like always to smooth him over before it got to that point. I usually ask him questions about his books and act impressed with his answers and before long, he's feeling high enough on himself again to act civil. It's a bad pattern we've fallen into.

But tonight, it's feeling too difficult to sit at this table and move pieces around an imaginary board game again. As long as we keep playing, my dad will always win.

Fredrick raises a cut of steak to his mouth, finally looking at me instead of his plate. "I just think your intellect could be used elsewhere. You're my son; I'm sure you could accomplish big things if you wanted to." This isn't the first time he's said this to me. For him, working in education will never be considered "big things."

I clench my teeth. "I'm happy teaching, Dad."

He's chewing and talking at the same time. "But that can't be enough for you. However, if you want to use these summer months wisely instead of playing fixer-upper in a decrepit town, I could help you find a new career path that would better suit you. Maybe you could put that English minor to good use and try your hand at some editorial work. I have connections."

My blood is simmering. "I don't need your connections."

Fredrick scoffs. "Do you think it's easy to get into the publishing world? If you tried to do it yourself, you'd have to start at the bottom. But with my help, you could go places right away. Finally do the Bennett name justice."

He's getting angry—looking to pick a fight. I've been here a few times with him before. Something in his life isn't going the way he wants, so he hyperfixates on me and what I could be doing better according to him. Spoiler: Nothing will ever be good enough.

Now would be a good time to agree and show my gratitude for his help, even if I don't end up needing it, because he will inevitably lose interest in me when his "muse" returns and he goes back to his usual routine of writing and blocking out the rest of the world.

But I can't.

I don't want to anymore.

"Did you get a bad review or something? Your editor give you some rough feedback? Is that what this is about? Because it seems like you're trying to pick a fight with me."

"*Jack* . . ." my mom pleads.

"Excuse me?" my dad asks.

"Do you even realize you do this? You pick fights with everyone around you when you're mad. I have spent my life tiptoeing around your moods just so you'll be a little more bearable. Because you make this entire world revolve around you and your moods and it's exhausting. And heartbreaking. And you *never* apologize."

"I don't know what you're talking about," he says, eyes looking a little wilder. "Excuse me for having a stressful job. And I never once asked you to 'tiptoe around my mood.'" He puts air quotes around those words. "You did that all on your own."

This. This is why I don't try to call him out on his shit. He doesn't hear me—or anyone—ever; he only listens for sound bites that he can use to twist and throw back at me. It's a never-ending battle.

He continues, looking more self-righteous by the moment. "Tonight I was only offering to help you achieve bigger success. Maybe even spend a little more time together in the process. You should be grateful that I even offered since my schedule is tight. I won't make that mistake of extending my help or connections again, though . . . you can be sure of that."

There it is . . . the door shutting in my face again. It's the same damn thing every time, but now, I'm keenly aware of just how much of a toll it takes on me. And that maybe I don't have to participate. Maybe it's not my job to keep this pretend, fragile peace.

I left a home full of people who love each other and who were willing to let me inside their circle tonight, to come here and boost the pride of this pathetic man who is never going to love me back like I deserve. The problem is, I want my mom to be happy and safe, but if she doesn't want those things for herself too, I can only help so much.

With courage I've never experienced in this house before now, I know what it's time to do.

I look toward my dad. "But see, that's part of the problem. I've learned never to accept your help even if I need it, because it always comes with strings."

My dad suddenly stands up from the table to tower over us. "Do you have a problem with me, Jack? Quit pissing around and say it if you do."

My gut instinct is to shrink away. Take back what I said until his temper subsides. But I remind myself that I'm not a kid anymore. He has no power over me. So I stand too. Eye to eye. "Yes. I do have a problem with you, and I wish I'd told you sooner. The only reason I have held back all these years is for Mom. I can live with you not loving me. I can live with you being a self-centered asshole for ninety percent of my life. But I love Mom—and she deserves more than what you give her. And if you get nothing else out of what I say tonight, I hope you at least hear this: Treat her better."

Sadly, I know this won't sink in to my dad's brain because nothing has in the past. He'll reshape the narrative somehow to come out in his favor. To pin him as the victim of tonight's events rather than the reason this is all happening. This speech isn't so much for him as it is so my mom can hear someone fight for her. So she can hear out loud in his presence that she is worthy of more than this. That we both are.

"Get out of my house," Fredrick says, his face turning red. "I won't be treated like this in my own home. Not after I raised you with every comfort you could ever want. Not when I have been nothing but faithful and devoted to my wife. I won't listen to this childish tantrum of yours." The wife in question is currently sunk back into her seat, dabbing the streams of tears falling from her eyes, afraid to speak up on either side. I hate that I'm putting her through this, but I don't see a different way anymore.

I make sure his eyes are connected with mine when I say, "Okay,

I'll leave. But I'm not going to be coming back." And that's it—I don't give him an explanation because he will only twist it or argue with it if I do. I only said it out loud for myself.

"I can't believe how ungrateful you are." He hitches his head to the door. "Go."

I should leave without another word. But high off adrenaline from finally telling him what I've wanted to say for years, I decide to stop hiding. "By the way, you're wrong. I didn't need your connections. I was able to write a bestselling series on my own. And when my fourth book comes out next year and you watch it top the charts—I want you to know that AJ Ranger did it without using your fucking name."

His eyes register shock and I'm sure later I'll regret telling him who I am in this dramatic way, but right now, it feels great.

"Get. The. Hell. Out."

I do. I grab my keys from the table, and I walk out of his house feeling proud and lighter for the first time.

I'm almost to my car when my mom's voice calls out, "Jack! Wait." She rushes up to me and wraps me in a hug. "I'm so proud of you," she whispers through tears and cracked emotions. "I had no idea you were . . . well, it doesn't surprise me actually. You've always been so bright and imaginative. I'm so happy to know you're a writer."

She pulls away and wipes a tear from her face. "And I'm so sorry I've been pulling you back inside that house all these years. I didn't realize . . . I should have realized that it was hurting you, but I've been selfish. I'm so so—"

"Mom," I say, gently holding her shoulders. "It's okay. I love you, and I wish I could keep being here for you, but I just can't. You don't have to stay with him, though. You can leave. My house and my town are always open to you. Go pack a bag right now and you can ride back with me."

I wish I could see her fighting, but there's not even a war

happening behind her eyes—just resignation. It kills me. And this is when I realize that even this relationship hasn't been healthy. I've carried too much of her burdens.

She pats my face. "I can't leave him yet, Jack. He needs me. And maybe . . . maybe after all this he'll see he needs some help and he'll talk to someone."

Maybe . . .

But not likely.

"I just wanted you to know that I'm proud of you, and I understand why you can't come home anymore."

My eyes are burning and my jaw hurts. I lean down and kiss my mom's cheek. "I love you, Mom. Don't forget my door is always open for you. And I'll see you soon."

———————

I can't bring myself to go to the inn yet and risk running into anyone from the town when I feel like this, so I drive to my house with the hope that I'll find that my AC has been fixed and I can sleep there tonight.

When I pull into my driveway, my body is in fight or flight. Most everyone who has grown up with a parent like mine knows that after a situation where you put yourself forward and speak your truth, there is always a reeling discomfort in its wake. Like I want to run as fast as I can but also hide in a dark hole at the same time. I'm at war with wondering if I truly stood up for myself or if I just taunted him. Is it a moment I should be proud of or was I really just throwing a tantrum like he said?

This is what he does. He gets in my head and disrupts my sense of self until I'm all turned around and dizzy.

I get out of my SUV, slamming the door a little too hard behind me. I think I'll get on my bike. I think I'll run it hard all night until I end up somewhere out of gas and far far—

"Long night?" Emily's voice washes over me like a cleansing wave.

I turn and squint in the dark until I see her in her driveway, sitting in the bed of her truck, leaned back against the cab. I should probably go inside right now. Should probably not face her while I'm so unstable. But I can't keep my feet from crunching over the gravel and grass to get to her. My entire body is dragging me to her like it knows she is safety.

"How long have you been out here?" I ask when I get closer and note the laptop, blankets, and support pillow behind her back.

She meets my gaze. "Not long. Since I got back from the farm."

I cock my head. "Which was?"

"About two hours ago."

I couldn't keep the smile off my face even if someone threatened to key my Land Rover. "And why have you been out here?"

"Are you just going to stand there all night gloating that I've been worried, waiting for you, or are you going to join me?"

"Am I invited?"

She holds up a beer bottle for me. I don't give it a second thought before shaking my head. "No, I don't—"

"It's a ginger beer," she amends softly, looking shyer than I think I've ever seen Emily look. "Alcohol free." Or no, maybe not shy . . . tender. *Vulnerable.*

The emotions I've been shoving down my throat since I left my parents' house are now bubbling up. "You didn't have to do that for me. You don't have to drink that when I know you like beer."

"I know I don't," she says with a taunting Emily smile. "And that makes it all the more fun."

I eye her pallet with open longing now, my bones feeling so weary I could fall over. She scoots over and pats the spot beside her. A minute later, we're shoulder to shoulder, backs leaning against the truck window and staring up at winking stars, ginger beers in hand.

"Do you want to talk about it?" she asks.

"Not yet." I shift to look at her. "I want to make sure we're okay. And Maddie. What happened with her?"

Her face angles in my direction and the moon reflects in her sharp green eyes. "It's a long story that I'll fill you in on later. But for now, you can know that she let me cry on her shoulder and I realized I need to do that more often." She pauses, her eyes dropping to my hand, and then she reaches over to take it in hers. "Jack . . . thank you for wanting to be there for me the other night. And for encouraging me not to give up on my dreams. Historically, I have an incredible record of handling things on my own pretty well. But lately . . . since my grandma passed . . ." She presses her tongue into her cheek. "Um, there's just been this . . ." She's pushing through stopped-up emotions. "This sadness and loneliness that I have struggled to climb out of. And I don't like for people to see me in those places, because I'm afraid if I do, I'll be even harder to love."

I push her hair back from her face, just wanting to be close to her. "I can relate."

"Of course you can," she says with a smile. "That's why you scare the hell out of me. I've never . . . I've never met anyone who makes me feel so seen and known as you do, Jack. And to be honest, your friendship lately"—tears race down her cheeks—"has been one of the best things to ever happen to me. And I was scared that you'd think you wanted me, and then you would get close to me and realize that I'm too tough to love. Hell, I'm difficult to even be around some days, and now I can add *sad* to the list too."

She shrugs. "I guess I'm saying I don't actually want to go slow with you. *I love you, Jack.* I don't want to be friends with benefits. I want to hug each other when we're sad and help each other find the bright side of things when all we can see is the dark." Her hand squeezes mine like she's reminding herself I'm still sitting here. "And I realize I don't have a lot to offer you at this moment in my life besides a very messy person who is somehow also a perfectionist and enjoys bickering more than she should. I can be a porcupine sometimes, but I also make really great buttered noodles and have the best movie nights with an incredible selection of snacks, and, oh!" She brightens like she was struck by a revelation. "I can also help you grade papers when you're behind. I'm very good at grading. I have a supercute sticker stash too that you're welcome to use anytime you—"

I kiss her.

I kiss her long and slow for just a minute. Just a heartbeat. My tongue sweeps her mouth in a lazy summertime backstroke. And then I pull away and I hold her face in my hands—forehead to forehead. "I love you too, Emily . . . I don't need anything from you other than for you to unlock the door for me so I can come lie with you when the darkness is too heavy to crawl out of. And if you need to fight, you can fight with me. And if you want to make love, make it with me." I kiss her once more. "You think you're unlovable, but I think I've never known how to love until knowing you."

CHAPTER THIRTY-TWO

Emily

Our kiss is different this time. There is no restraint or a hint of indecision. We are fully giving ourselves to each other with this kiss, with our touches, with our bodies.

I love him, I love him, I love him, I think as I climb over his lap and kiss him deeper.

I love you, I love you, I love you, his hands say as they skirt up my abdomen and chest, sinking into the back of my hair to leverage a firmer pressure of his mouth against mine. I push against his shoulders and Jack sinks back into the bed of the truck.

"Here?" he asks, looking up at me from where his head is laid back against the pillow from the little pallet I had made earlier.

"Here," I repeat back to him as I lean down and kiss my way up his neck. Tasting the salt of his skin and the scruff on his jaw. "Madison is inside, and I don't want to wake her up." I pull back enough to grin down at him. "Plus, there's no phone out here."

I close my eyes against the incredible feel of Jack's rough fingers when he pushes the wall of my hair back from my face and over my shoulder. "As long as you're sure. I can wait if you don't want it to happen out here."

I lean down again, hovering close enough to his mouth that he can feel my smile. Poison-ivy eyes looking into amber whiskey. "I don't want to wait another damn minute. So no teasing tonight. I need you."

His answer is to curve his hand around my ass and squeeze. Jack lifts his head to catch my mouth, coaxing it open as his tongue tastes me again and again. I slide my hands under his shirt and up his heated skin until I can feel his pounding heart. His ribs expand with a deep breath and need melts into my body, consuming me. I want to kiss him forever. I want to live inside it. I think I can find the answers to the beginning and end of time in Jack's mouth if I keep kissing him long enough.

I love him. That thought sweeps through me again as recklessly as a storm. I love him and it feels so natural that I'm wondering if part of me has always loved him. He must feel the way that question extends itself through my body, because his mouth slows and he pulls back enough to look between my eyes. "Everything okay?"

I nod and touch his lower lip with my thumb. Amazed that I can. "I was just thinking. Back in college . . . did you stay as late as me in the library because you were studying?"

He goes completely still for a beat, then takes my hand in his, winding our fingers together between our faces. He looks at my red nails and then kisses them one by one. "No. I stayed because I didn't like the idea of you walking alone to your car after dark. I might've hated you, but I also wanted to keep you safe."

I look in his eyes as a hurricane of emotions tears through me. "Oh god—I was afraid you were going to say that."

"Is that a bad thing?"

"Yes. Because . . . now I regret hating you for so long. Now I really want to go back in time and laugh when you spill coffee on

me and come sit at your table in the library and ask you if you'd like
to be a writer one day. I want to start over."

"Absolutely not," he says, tugging his shirt off his body and then
peeling mine off next. He reaches behind me and unhooks my bra.
He reverently pulls the straps off my shoulders and then tosses my
bra completely out of the truck. The moon softly illuminates his
face enough for me to see him look absolutely destroyed with
desire at the site of my naked chest before seemingly remembering
what he was going say. He pulls me down onto him so we're bliss-
fully skin to skin. "I don't know about you, but I needed those years
of feuding. I don't think I'd feel as close to you as I am now without
them." He pauses and laughs lightly. "Which probably means I
need a ton of therapy but whatever." He lifts his head and kisses me
once—and it's so damn hot the word *dirty* crosses my mind. "Let's
not regret anything. Let's enjoy where we're at."

I smile down at him. "Easy to do when we're both half naked in
the bed of my truck."

"Yes, which reminds me." Jack reaches between us to unbuckle
my shorts and I do the same with his trousers. We both share an
uncoordinated moment of shimmying out of our pants and scoot-
ing up onto the pillows, but it's not awkward. It's wonderful.

He turns us, taking such care to hold the back of my head so I
don't bump the hard floor of the truck as he lays me down. He
adjusts up to his knees, hooking his fingers into the band of my
underwear so he can pull them off me, sliding them gently down
my thighs and over my feet. He tosses them up into the corner of
the truck bed instead of flinging them off the side like he did my
bra. *A gentleman, this one.*

I'm lying completely naked under the stars for Jackson Bennett, and the way he looks at me and touches me and sighs over my
skin like he's finally somewhere he was always meant to be, it feels
like capturing the sun. I'm a kaleidoscope of love and sensation, all

twisting and shifting to create the most wonderful moment I've ever experienced.

And now I tug at the band of his underwear, eager to have all of him like he has all of me. A beat later, he's naked too and I have never witnessed a more perfect man. But then he takes his glasses between his fingers like he's going to take them off. I put my hand on his tattooed forearms. "Don't you dare take those off."

"They get in the way sometimes," he says with a touch of self-consciousness.

"Good," I say. "I like knowing they're there."

Need nearly chokes me as Jack lowers himself between my legs, his necklace brushing my chest as he lets me have his full weight. His mouth takes mine in a kiss so deep and exploring that my legs move with a mind of their own to wind firmly around his hips, spurring the moment into a frenzy of wanting. My nerves are electric, sharpening that delicious pressure building in my core. We're both taking and taking and giving and giving. It's a tangle of limbs and moonlight. It's hot skin and sweat-slicked bodies. It's the crinkle of a foil wrapper and then groans and gasps of pleasure as Jack finally rocks inside me.

"*God,*" he says, head falling to the side of mine, hand gripping the bunched-up blanket beneath us as I raise my hips and meet him movement for movement. He can't decide where to touch me so he's everywhere—savoring me inch by inch. I want to sink my teeth into the curve of his shoulder and then kiss it like the sweet breeze blowing over our bodies. I do both of these things and it sends Jack spiraling closer to his release.

His hand moves between us once again to touch me exactly where I need so that I can fall with him. Jack goes first, and the sound he makes sweeps me away too. We grip each other tightly as our bodies pulse and flex, and the first thought that strikes me when my soul reenters my body is not one I've ever thought before. *I'd really like to snuggle with this man.*

Jack goes up onto his forearms, his candy necklace dangling between us as he looks down at me with that ridiculously sexy, lazy smile of his. He presses his mouth to my throat again. "This is the best night of my life."

June 23

JACK (12:07 AM): Did you get scared and leave your house? I can go back to my own bed if you're uncomfortable with this. I swear it's fine if you need more time to adjust.

EMILY (12:08 AM): Settle down there, Ranger. I'm just getting us waters and a snack.

JACK (12:08 AM): Oh. Thank you.

JACK (12:08 AM): But also . . . you're not actually going to start calling me that, right?

EMILY (12:09 AM): Oh, Ranger, it's like you don't even know me.

JACK (12:09 AM): Fine, but not in bed.

EMILY (12:09 AM): ESPECIALLY in bed.

CHAPTER THIRTY-THREE

Emily

I wake up in my perfect bed next to Jackson's perfect body and I breathe the same perfect air he's breathing and for the first time in a long time, it goes right into my lungs and zips into my bloodstream. It doesn't have to get through the elephant that's usually blocking my airways. I don't know what the future holds, and maybe I'm starting to sort-of-kind-of be okay with that concept. Because I'm okay with the idea that for today, I'm happy.

I open my eyes and breathe him in. That glorious man-skin smell. It's salty like a kettle chip and warm like a dinner roll. *Am I hungry?* I'm hungry for more of Jack.

He must feel me stir because we're facing each other, and his eyes open slowly like mine. I smile at him, and he smiles at me, and we're both obviously contemplating making what happened last night a double feature. That is, until a throat clears at the end of my bed.

I jolt upright, pulling my sheets to my collarbone while I glare at my sister, who is standing at the foot of my bed like an absolute creep. "Madison, what the hell?"

Madison's smile looks like she should be holding a bloody pitchfork. "Are you my new brother?" she says to Jackson, delighting a little too much in being a menace.

I hurl my pillow at her and then rip Jack's out from under him and catapult that one next. Maddie is cackling like a witch brewing something extra special in her cauldron as she scuttles out of the room. "I need you to take me to the airport in thirty minutes, though!" I'm out of bed and slamming the door behind her. Locking it. "Don't dawdle, Emmy! I have a plane to catch and a big city to conquer. Also, nice to see you again, Jack!"

"Nice seeing you too, Madison!" he calls out from the bed, where I turn to find him looking like a sleepy, studious model. He's clothed only in his tattoos and the drape of my sheet across his waist, propped lazily on his elbow, muscular shoulder sagging toward the mattress. He put on his glasses too. Good lord, this man. All loose-limbed with his hooded eyes and scruffy angles. This looks like a man who knows his way around a woman's body—and let me tell you, I can confirm that he does.

Apparently while I've been standing here, he's been having a moment about me too. "Shit, look at you."

"Who, me?" I say with false modesty as I stand here in a sexy pink-and-white gingham-patterned sleep set. Right after we—ahem—finished up in the truck, Jack looked unsure of how things would go. Or more like willing to step back and let me set the pace for our new relationship. I'm so used to Jack fighting with me on who will call the shots that I nearly busted out laughing when I slid off the truck's tailgate and he just sat there with his legs dangling off the back, his crooked, self-deprecating smile stealing my heart.

"Good night?" he asked, the question mark a strong punctuation.

I took his hand and guided him toward the front door. "You know what I think it's time for, Jack?"

"I can think of several great options actually."

"It's time for you to be the first man to try out my incredible mattress."

"I get to take your mattress's virginity? This is an honor."

And it was gratifying that he made so many moaning noises when he finally lay on it that I had to slap my hand over his mouth so Madison wouldn't wake up and get the wrong idea.

But here he is now, lounging in my bed in the full light of morning, looking so attractive I could cry, because as rumor has it, he's mine.

I've floated closer to the bed, and Jack reaches out, pinches the fabric at my navel, and tugs me even closer. "Come back to bed."

"Now?"

"Yes."

"Why? I'm already out."

"Because I'm still in." His hand is skating up the back of my thigh and under the hem of my shorts.

"But . . . but . . ." My bones are melting. "I've gotta take Madison to the airport in thirty minutes. I've got stuff to do." His hand glides completely up under my shorts and over the slope of my ass. I shove my fingers into his hair (blond today) and he looks up at me. Hands tender, eyes blazing.

"Just for a minute . . . come back to bed. I won't let you stay too long."

I can see it now, my future sprawling out in front of me where I have trouble saying no to Jackson ever again. We're not going to be competing over a parking space because we'll ride together. We're going to be disgustingly cute.

I turn and sit on the edge of the mattress. Jack's arms go around my middle, quickly flipping me up and over him until I'm facing the opposite wall. He curls in behind me as the big spoon with one arm under the pillow and curving up and over my chest. The other wraps around my lower abdomen like a lazy python, curling and constricting in the most fantastic way.

When I've thought of snuggling, it's always been something flippant and silly. A complete waste of time. But this. This is different. It's as if Jack knows that my body needs pressure to rest. I'm wearing him like a parachute. And with the feel of his body intentionally holding on to me, mine relaxes. I point and flex my toes. I brush my fingertips up and down his inked forearm.

"Your fingernails drive me insane, have I ever told you that?" he says softly next to my ear.

"No, I don't think you have."

"They do. I don't know what it is about that red, but I want to bite them."

"That's okay. I've decided I want to live inside your skin. Is that creepy?"

"A little, yeah," he admits casually. "Can I offer you one of my sweaters instead?"

A giddy swirl hits my stomach. I have to kiss his arm. "Even better." We lie here a minute before I realize something important. "Wait! You never told me what happened with your parents last night."

Lying this close, I feel his muscles tense. Whatever happened, it was not good.

He hums in my ear like he's contemplating which moment of the night to begin at.

"The beginning," I tell him, assuming I've read his thoughts correctly. "Tell me all of it."

He rests his chin above my head on the pillow and tells me everything. Tells me how the house has always felt like a humongous monster to him. How hard it was having an alcoholic dad but having to pretend to the world like everything was okay. And how his dad only sobered up when he almost lost his career—but it had nothing to do with him or his mom. He mentions how all of this led to him taking on the responsibility of protecting his mom from a young age. And how last night, while sitting at their table, he put a stop to it.

He kisses the side of my face and holds on to me tighter like I'm the one with the parachute now. "I couldn't sit there any longer and allow myself to feel used. So I told him the truth. About all of it. I even told him that I'm Ranger, and I told both of my parents that I wouldn't be coming back. I said goodbye to that house and that way of life for good."

"*Jack,*" I say tearfully, twisting to look at him. I want to find something encouraging to say. Something worthy and important. "I'm so proud of you. That had to be incredibly difficult. And you did it."

His smile is sad. "Thank you. It felt right. I just . . . I hate that my mom won't leave. But I told her that if she ever did need somewhere to go, my door would be open to her."

"And mine," I say, meaning it.

This is what chokes him up. I see tears collecting in his eyes, so he shuts them until he gets a handle on them. I want to tell him it's okay if he cries in front of me, but this has been a big week. We'll get there eventually.

"So how do you feel today? Now that your parents know about Ranger?"

"Surprisingly good," he says after sufficiently pushing his feelings away again. "In fact, I think it's time to come out from behind the name."

"Really?" I say with a huge smile because it honestly delights me. "I am in full support of this decision." I want everyone to know that those incredible books belong to Jack. I want to be able to shout his accolades from the rooftops. But mostly, I don't want him to have to hide himself away ever again.

I nuzzle into his chest. "I can't wait to brag to everyone that I'm dating the best mystery writer on the planet."

He hums and I feel the vibration against my cheek. "I knew you only wanted to date me for my status in the book world."

I shrug. "It's fair since you're only in this relationship for my magical mattress."

"It *is* a great mattress." He breathes in, pulling me in even tighter. "I love it. And I love *you*."

Those words. My first reaction is to take a sledgehammer to them until they're nothing but dust where I can never find a trace of their existence again. Because what if they don't last?

But then I force myself to put the sledgehammer down this time, and instead I run my hand across the slopes and valleys of those beautiful words. Right now—Jackson Bennett—loves me. And that's something to delight in. The fear and trepidation can just take a hike.

We both jump out of our snuggly cocoon when Madison pounds on my door. "HEY! You better not be getting frisky in there— *although I'd actually be proud of you if you were,*" she says almost to herself. "But that's not the point! I'm going to miss my flight if you don't get your ass moving, Emily Walker."

Jack kisses the side of my face. "Come find me when you get home, Goldie."

CHAPTER THIRTY-FOUR

Emily

"You're quiet over there," I say to Madison as we near the air-port, a light rain drizzling down the windows.

"Hm?" She straightens up and looks away from the window, where her forehead has been plastered for the entire ride with zero words leaving her mouth. Which has to be a record for her.

Normally I would have noticed it sooner, but I've been lost in my own thoughts too. Of Jack. Of Us. Of last night.

I turn my attention back to Maddie. "You've been silently star-ing out the window like you're re-creating a sad music video."

"Well, I couldn't waste the rain, could I?" She laughs lightly. "No—I'm good. Just . . . feeling sad to leave."

My chest tightens and I resist the urge to whip the truck around and take her back home. Instead, I reach over and take her hand. "You're the bravest girl I know."

Her laugh is a cross between a chuckle and something stuck in her throat. "That's because you haven't seen me clutching the seat in the back of New York Ubers." As if to prove her small-town point, cars zoom past my old slowpoke truck on the interstate.

"So . . . you and Jack. I'm sorry I had to interrupt you this morning."

"No you're not, you little shit," I say, flashing her a sideways grin.

"Yeah, I'm really not." She grins right back. My sister. My best friend. Even after all the separation and secret-keeping, we still ended up here—teasing in my truck. And I'm starting to think we always will. Maybe we're not growing apart, we're just living in different directions at the moment, happy to meet back in the middle when we can.

"I like him, by the way," says Maddie. "He's good with you."

Now I'm smiling like a fool at the road. "I like him too. I've decided to keep him."

"Good."

"What about you and . . ." I almost say *James*. His name is on the tip of my tongue but I can't bring myself to do it. I'm still not certain that whatever I'm sensing between them isn't something totally made up in my head. Something I'm hoping for because maybe it would mean Madison coming back to town.

"There's no one in particular in my life right now. In fact, I think I've decided to take a hiatus from men for a while."

I blink over at her a few times, frustrated that I have to bring my eyes back to the road instead of analyzing every tiny expression that crosses her face. "A hiatus? What happened? *Did* something happen? Give me his number. If someone hurt you, Maddie . . ."

She's smiling. "Ah—there's my overprotective sister I know and love."

Fine, old habits can't just die overnight, now can they? I'm not sure the urge to nurture and protect my siblings will ever die off, to be honest. I've spent my life essentially raising them. I've loved them more than I've loved myself most days. And I'm coming to terms with the fact that it's okay that I don't operate quite like everyone either. Not everyone has raised their siblings or known tragedy at the tender age of eight. I've gone through a lot, and now that they're grown, maybe I can look at it less like losing them, and more like letting go so I can stretch out lazily in the sun. Where Jack can skate his hands up and down my sun-heated skin. Where my frozen heart can twinkle beautifully in the sunlight. I think letting go might not be so bad.

Madison is staring out the window again like she's looking into another dimension. "I just . . . the future is so unknown. I want to focus on myself and what I want out of life for a while without a guy distracting me."

I squeeze her hand once more before letting it go. "I'm here for you anytime you need me."

"I know."

"Um, but actually. I did have a question for you . . . I was wondering how you'd feel about me switching things up in the house?"

"Switching things up how? Like Jack moving into your bedroom?"

"Ha! No. That's . . . well, that sounds really nice actually, but that's something I'll save for the future rather than right now. I need a little more time to adjust to having a relationship than that."

"I'm really proud of you by the way, Emily. I'm not sure if I've told you that. But . . . it's inspiring watching you face your fears with Jack. You are, as always, my hero." The way she says *hero* . . . with zero irony or humor, but the same way a little kid might say it while staring up at Wonder Woman. Yeah, it has me gurgling tears. And then my tears make her tears simmer until we're both hiccuping.

"Stop. I have to drive!" I wail.

"You stop!" She slaps my arm. "Why are *you* crying?"

"Because you told me to cry more often!"

"Well, wait until I'm out of the truck next time!"

This is how we pull up at the airport. Fizzing emotions out our eyes and noses. Disgusting messes. I pull up to the curb in front of her airline and we both give each other one painful, wordless, puffy-eyed look before climbing out of the truck to meet around at the tailgate. I pull her suitcase to the ground and she takes the handle from me. "You never told me what you wanted to change . . . in the house."

"Oh." It feels silly to say now while waiting outside the truck and staring into my sister's eyes that are holding more and more untold stories by the moment. But I can't do that. I can't stop living anymore while waiting for them to need me. "I want to turn your room into my office to encourage me to keep writing, because it has the best natural light." She looks punched in the stomach. So I hurry to explain, "And then turn Annie's old room into a guest room. That way you'll still have somewhere to stay when you come home, but since you don't do it all that often anymore and you'll probably end up settling somewhere else after you—"

"No—yes. Of course you should do that, Em." She's blink, blink, blinking. I want to scoop her up, take her home, and wrap her in a blanket. "It's . . . that makes so much sense! It'll be the perfect place for you to write. Yes, do it!" She grabs me, wraps her arms tightly around my neck in one of her ferocious hugs that I love so much, and then she pulls away. Smiles way too big. "I'll text you when I land."

"Okay. I love you, Maddie."

"I love you, Em." She's backing away with her luggage, mist in her eyes. This is always the most painful part of saying goodbye. The last moments before she turns away and I go back to missing her. "I'm going to read the rest of your dirty novel on the plane!" she yells so that the entire airport can hear her and then turns away with a laugh that I'll bottle up and hold on to until next time she comes home.

I shuffle my way back inside my truck and drive home. I don't turn on any music, and that clawing sadness tries to take root again. But I push it back a little with small reminders that I have things to look forward to. I get to finish my book. I get to finalize my lesson plan for the upcoming school year. I get to design myself an office. And my favorite of all, I get to see Jack . . .

I have to stop for gas before I hit the back roads that will take me into Rome, and while standing outside my truck waiting for the extra slow pump to push overpriced gasoline into my adorable rust bucket, I get out my phone to see if I have any missed texts from Maddie already. Or Jack.

I do have a long string of texts, but it's not from Jack. It's from a group of teachers, which is odd. I scroll through them quickly.

MONIQUE: OMG did you guys hear the news?

BRITTNEY: About Jack?????

MONIQUE: YES! I couldn't believe it.

TIFFANY: Wait—I haven't heard. What happened?

MONIQUE: Jack's dad went live on Instagram just now, revealing that Jack Bennett is actually AJ Ranger!! He said Jack's been keeping it a secret all this time because he's camera shy so he wanted his dad to be the one to reveal it since he has been such a big help with his books.

TIFFANY: WHAT! Also who is AJ Ranger?

MORGAN: Are you kidding me, Tiffany? It's that mystery writer of the series I lent you over the summer. The one you loved so much.

TIFFANY: Omg! WHAT! I'm even more in love with him now. Now that he's single again maybe I've got a shot.

The hell you do, Tiffany.

I stop reading even though the texts go on and on and on. But I can't breathe. After everything Jack went through to make sure my writing wasn't revealed before I was ready, and then turns around and has his entire career outed without his consent. And to have his scumbag dad phrase it in a way that completely steals Jack's thunder and hard work while also trying to take credit?

It's lucky for Fredrick I don't know where he lives. Lucky for me too, because I'd end up in prison if I gave in to my current rage.

Instead, I drive home as fast as my truck will allow.

CHAPTER THIRTY-FIVE

Jack

It's out.

My . . . identity is out on the Internet without my consent.

Because I apparently love pain, I watch the video another time. My dad's face—misleadingly soft and approachable—fills the little box. Hearts flood the right corner of the screen as he proudly announces that his son, Jack Bennett, wanted him to be the one to finally reveal his identity. I flinch when a picture of my face comes on the screen, followed by all the books I've written. My dad smiles like he's proud. Like he's been in on the ruse the whole time. A king admiring his little prince. He insinuates all through the gruesome video that he's flattered to have been able to mold my creativity and help me get where I am.

In one ninety-second video, Fredrick Bennett kicks the legs out from under my seat.

And it's my fault. I'm the one who told my dad in some righteous act of heroics. I feel sick. I should have known better. He can't tolerate being bested, so I should have considered that he would try to undermine me in some way that leaves him controlling the narrative around my success. Fredrick Bennett would never fight a bloody war; he only fights with pinpoint accuracy. Poison down the throat.

I'm lying on my terrible mattress staring at my ceiling as construction sounds outside my bedroom door, and my phone relentlessly vibrates beside me on the bed. Questions being lobbed at me from all corners of my life. Personal and professional. *Is this true??? How have you kept this a secret?! Can you sign my books when we go back to school???* And then there are the constant phone calls from my agent that I keep leaving unanswered because I feel too heavy to acknowledge them.

What I have always considered to be my safe place in life to escape to is now sitting on full display for everyone to gawk at. Even worse, it's sitting in my dad's display case, being used as one of his trophies.

Maybe if I lie here long enough it'll all go away. One big bad dream.

The power tools stop outside my room and low voices take their place. And then my bedroom door opens and for one absurd second I worry it's my dad with a live camera about to force me to admit he gave me all my ideas. It's not my dad. It's Emily.

"I heard the news" is all she says before she looks around my small, sparsely furnished room and frowns. I peel myself up into a seated position as she approaches because I can't let her see me this miserable on day one of our relationship.

"How are you?" she asks, coming to sit by me.

"I'm okay."

But Emily just looks in my eyes, tilts her head, and asks again, "Jack . . . how are you?"

I shut my eyes. "I'm not okay."

She lays her head against my shoulder and slides her hand into mine. "You deserved to be the one to tell the world. Not him."

Outside the door, the sounds of construction resume. Emily stands up from the bed, tugging my hand so I'll get up with her. "Emily . . ."

"Come with me."

"I'm not feeling very entertaining right now."

"Jackson Bennett," she says, stepping between my legs to cradle my face and tip it up to look at her. "You said you'd sit with me in my darkness; don't you dare keep me out of yours. There's not a single thing you need to say or do, just come with me."

So I do. I get up, and with Emily holding my hand, I follow her through my construction zone, out the front door, and across the yard to her house. She ushers me inside the quiet and then steers me to the couch. I'm gently pushed by the shoulders until I sit, and then I'm pushed even more so that I sink fully back into the comfort. She buzzes around the living room collecting things. A fuzzy blanket that she drapes over my lap. A cushy pillow that she places under my feet on the coffee table. She goes back to her room and emerges with Ducky, placing her right into my arms where she immediately goes back to sleep and purrs like she's the happiest cat in the world.

Emily rushes into the kitchen and comes back with a bowl full of what looks like candy salad. There are seriously five different types of fruity candy in this bowl. She then curls up next to me on the couch, candy bowl clutched to her and TV remote in hand.

"What do you want to watch?" she asks, looking over at me as if everything she just did was completely normal. "What?" she asks when I just continue to stare at her with questions stamped all over my face. "I can't fix what happened to you this morning and I can't make your dad pay like I want either, but I am excellent at comforting the people I love."

I lean over and kiss her, savoring the way she smells and feels. The heaviness in my chest recedes. I may have lost the safe place I needed all these years, but I have found a far more incredible one for the years ahead.

"And to think you consider yourself hard to love." I kiss her temple. "Loving you is the easiest thing I've ever done."

CHAPTER THIRTY-SIX

Emily

The shower water is scalding but it's nothing compared to Jack's palms as they scrape deliciously around my skin. We've done nothing but couch rot all day. He was pretty sullen at first, but after bingeing nearly an entire season of *The Golden Girls* (his choice) with his phone nowhere in sight, his spirits lifted. Lifted enough to have sex on the couch—which admittedly makes almost everyone feel better. And now, he's sudsing me up like his life depends on it. He's already washed my hair and conditioned it, peppered my entire body with kisses so sweet I could die, and now he's washing me. Head, shoulders, knees, and toes. He keeps squinting because he's not wearing his glasses or his contacts. *Scrumptious.* I love him.

I turn and loop my arms around his neck and say it out loud.

He smirks. Kisses me, and then says, "Mm. I love . . . your nipples."

"Romantic."

He laughs. "You already know I love you. It's time I wax poetic about these nipples you once asked me about and I couldn't give proper feedback on. But now that I've really been up close and personal," he says, covering me with his hand, "I just need you to know that I'm a big fan."

"Oh god—you're never going to be able to be mean to me again, are you?"

"I don't think so."

"That's insufferable. You're just going to be nice from now on?"

"I would honestly love to be *very* nice to you every single day."

We eventually—after another delayed interlude where I'm a little nice to Jack—step out of the shower. I move right into a fluffy towel that Jack is holding open for me and then he wraps me tightly like a human burrito. He kisses my head and pats my toweled ass as I shuffle past and sends me on my way. But on my bed, I find a little gift. One of his Mr.-Rogers-wannabe knit sweaters. He must have run home and grabbed it for me before he joined me in the shower.

Five minutes later, clad in his oversized sweater and a pair of comfy shorts, I meet him in the kitchen. I'm dressed for winter and he's only wearing his glasses, boxer briefs, and green beaded necklace. We both have wet hair, and he's . . . making dinner. He does a double take of me in his sweater when he sees me walk in and then his attention is back on his task at hand, but with a quiet grin.

"What are you making?" I ask, watching him chop veggies.

"A little scrambled-eggs-and-veggies hash. Is that good with you?"

"Absolutely." My stomach growls as if to punctate my answer. "I'll crack the eggs."

Jack stops me with an extended forearm and then points away from the kitchen. "No. I'm cooking you dinner."

Here's the thingy-thing, though—I've been here before. And when I can't make a polite face while crunching through the unborn-chicken housing in my food, Jack might get offended. "It's no big deal. I'll just do the eggs."

He sees through my easy-breezy. "Get your ass out of the kitchen, Goldie."

"Jack . . ."

"Emily, I swear to god, if you insult me any further by suggesting I can't crack a damn egg without getting shells in the mix like your other nitwit boyfriends, I will—why are you smiling?"

"Because . . . you're still you. You're not nice to me all the time. It's just . . . it's a relief. I like bickering with you."

He breathes out a smile. "I'm going to make you dinner. Okay? I'm going to make you dinner because I love you and I want to take care of you sometimes. And I will in no way allow any eggshells on your plate because that's just disgusting. All right?"

"Can I . . . can I at least hang out?"

"Do you mean silently judge my process while I work? Yes. You may, but only because you're pretty." He's leaned over now and has picked up Ducky, who looked as if she was about to jump on the counter. He's holding her like a toddler on his sturdy hip bone and cracking eggs one-handed into a mixing bowl. Not a single shell falls into it and Ducky looks like the happiest cat in all the land.

I take in the sight of Jack Bennett standing in my kitchen in nothing but the necessities, holding my cat and cooking me dinner. His hair is a messy damp ode to the sex we just had, and his grin is an ode to the sex we will have again.

When he's finished cooking and we carry our plates to the table, I finally ask him the question that's been burning through me. "Are you okay?"

He stretches out his long legs under the table. "I don't know how I feel yet, to be honest. I mean, in a way I was ready for the world to know. I had already decided that I would announce it. But it sucks that this is how everyone found out. It kills me that he gets some credit for what I busted my ass for all on my own."

"Can I say something?" I ask, taking Jack's hand.

"I love when you say things."

"I want to murder your dad."

Jack barks out a laugh. Oh, it's wonderful. I love when he finds me funny. I love when my sharp, rude humor tickles his fancy in the same way it does mine. How did it take me so long to realize that what I saw in Jack as competitiveness was mostly us deeply relating?

Jack tugs my wrist so that I'm pulled into his lap. "Don't worry about me. Because one person in my life you haven't met yet, and I can't wait to introduce you to, is my agent, Jonathan. He has been in my corner since day one and will absolutely make sure my dad doesn't get away with this. In fact, I'm willing to bet he's already concocted two different PR responses to my dad's video. A message where I'm grateful to finally have the news out and excited to meet readers and booksellers and other authors, brushing over what happened with my dad and not mentioning him at all. Or one where I'm thankful to finally have the news out, and I also publicly renounce my dad and explain that he did not have permission to share the news."

I slide my hand around the side of Jack's hair—*brunette tonight from the shower.* "Which one will you pick?"

He's thoughtful for a minute. Kisses me once and then smiles. "The second one. I'm done absorbing his shit, and I'm ready to be a little authentic."

I'm so proud of this man I could burst.

"Now I have a question for you." He leans back in his chair, hand relaxed across my thigh. "Are you going to move forward with your book?"

I breathe in, hold it, and let it out. "Yes. I am." A look of relief sweeps over Jack's face. "I . . . agree with some of the things Colette said and I'm eager to get to my corner table this weekend and start working on it. But there was a lot I don't agree with as well. My sisters are reading it now and they promised to give me honest feedback—so maybe if their opinions align with Colette's, I'll consider changing those parts; but if not, I'm going to keep it how I want it and hope to find an agent who sees the same vision I have for the story."

"That's an excellent plan. And again—I'm so sorry if I pushed you to submit it before—"

I cover his mouth with my finger. "That was a good experience. I learned from it. And the only thing you're guilty of in that situation is being the most supportive person I could ask for. Onward and upward, right?"

He nods, softly smiling at me. "I think we're going to be okay."

"I think so too."

And the next morning, when I feel the bed dip and watch Jack grab his pants and silently pad toward my door, I don't even panic. I don't even fear that he's changed his mind and is leaving me. It's a monumental moment in Emily Land.

"Where are you going?" I ask, and he pauses and turns to me with a smile. He makes his way back to my side of the bed, pushes my hair back from my face, and leans down to kiss my cheek.

"Someone's coming to look at my bike."

My eyes fully pop open now. "Because it's so pretty?"

"Yes. And because he wants to buy it."

"Jack!" I sit up.

He silences me with his finger like I did for him. "It's been fun to drive but make no mistake, that bike is not important to me. *You* are important to me. And I only had it for so long because . . ." He pauses and swallows, clears his throat, and tries again. "I've never felt important to someone else before. And now that I am— I don't take that lightly. You've endured so much grief already. I won't needlessly be the cause of any more of it in your life. The bike goes."

I smile and then bite his finger. Just a little. Enough to make him grin.

13 YEARS AGO

FROM: Emily Walker ‹Walker.Emily@Greenfield.edu›
TO: Jack Bennett ‹Bennett.Jack@Greenfield.edu›
DATE: Thu, August 18 9:10 AM
SUBJECT: This means war . . .

Hitting on me after spilling coffee all over my shirt was one thing . . . but taking the seat at the front of class that you SAW me going for??? Unforgivable. We will not be friends and I wanted to make sure you know it.

FROM: Jack Bennett ‹Bennett.Jack@Greenfield.edu›
TO: Emily Walker ‹Walker.Emily@Greenfield.edu›
DATE: Thu, August 18 9:45 AM
SUBJECT: This means war . . .

We'll see about that. I'm very good at winning people over. It's all in the long game.

CHAPTER THIRTY-SEVEN

Jack

've spent most of the day on the phone with Jonathan and Denis, coming up with an official announcement and rebuttal to my dad's video. I sent them a brief email yesterday after Emily and I talked everything through and basically said: *I've seen it, and I give you permission to go forth with epic plans to reveal the way it should have been done in the first place.* Denis is like a kid in a candy shop. He's been training his whole life for this moment.

I shouldn't have been surprised when on our call earlier he informed me that I'd be flying out tomorrow for a *GMA* interview, have several other interviews throughout the day, and then finish up at *The Late Show with Stephen Colbert.* Apparently people were more excited to interview me than I imagined. I guess I've been able to compartmentalize my success before with the pseudonym. It was never mine. It was always Ranger's. But now, overnight . . . it's mine.

Emily keeps telling me to absorb it. To let my heart have it. But it's difficult and going to take some getting used to.

"I never asked you . . ." she says from the driver's seat of my SUV as we cruise down Main Street. She'll always love her truck, but she said she wanted to give my snooty Land Rover a try today. I think she likes it, judging by how she keeps running her hand over the leather console. "Are you going to keep teaching? Now that the news is out?" She says it so upbeat and easygoing—but God, do I know this woman. I hear the slight constriction in her vocal cords. The tightness around her eyes as she smiles. She wants me to feel zero pressure from her while making this decision—but clearly she has strong feelings about it.

Lucky for her, I don't have to keep her waiting on the answer. I've already turned this question over in my head a hundred different times and every way I consider it, the answer is the same. "I'm going to keep teaching."

Her lips let out a nearly undetectable sigh. "Are you sure?"

"Some things are going to change for me. Like having to get used to doing interviews and book tours. But not that. I love teaching—and I feel lucky to be at a school that makes it easy to love. I'm not ready to give that up yet. Also without me the teachers would have to drink your shit coffee every day and I can't do that to them." She smacks the back of her hand playfully against my chest. "Besides, I think I'm one of those authors who need a day job. If all I did was focus on my writing, I'm pretty sure my creativity would shrivel up and die."

She laughs. "Me too." And then she seems to stop herself. "I mean . . . I'm in no way comparing myself to you. You're miles ahead of me, and I can barely call myself an author. I just meant—"

I lay my hand on her thigh and squeeze. "Don't backtrack. I love hearing you refer to yourself as an author. Because you are. One book or twenty—it doesn't matter. You put words on paper and created a world that readers are not going to realize they even needed until after they read it and it fills something up in them. Always own that."

"Actually, all of this has had me thinking . . . if I ever get this book deal—"

"Pen name or real name? The age-old question."

The wind tosses her hair because she may have traded her old truck for my SUV today, but she's still got the window down, refusing to use the AC. "I'm leaning toward a pen name since I'm going to be writing explicit content and still teaching second grade. But . . . I don't think I want to be completely hidden like you were."

"Somewhere in the middle? You can absolutely do that. Parents still might recognize you or find you on socials . . . but that wouldn't be the worst."

"Wait," she says, glancing briefly at me. "I've been meaning to ask you how you came up with your pen name. Why Ranger?"

"Oh." I was hoping she wouldn't ask. "Well, the AJ part is just my first and middle name swapped. Jackson Alexander. And Ranger . . ." I grimace, knowing she's going to eat this up. "Ranger was actually the name of the stuffed bear I slept with as a kid. He was the first comforting thing in my life, and so it felt right to give that name to the next comfort too. My books."

She presses her hand dramatically to her heart like she's just been stabbed. "That is so sweet it physically hurts."

"Yeah, yeah," I say, swatting her hand playfully away from her chest. "Back to you. Do you have a pen name in mind yet?"

"No." She grins and looks at me from the side of her eye. "But you know what this means? I might eventually have to tell Bart about my book . . . after all we went through to keep it from him."

"I'd do it again in a heartbeat." I pick up her hand and kiss her knuckles. "It let me sneak into your heart when you weren't expecting it. Plus, I'll never regret buying you more time to reveal your book on your own terms when you want."

Her smile is sad when she looks at me. "Jack . . ."

"No, no. Don't give me that face. I'm good today. I'm feeling confident about my next steps."

"Good." She pulls into the community parking lot and cuts the engine. Taking a little hairbrush out of her purse, she smooths it through her hair, because even though she prefers the window down, she's still Emily and doesn't want a hair out of place. Before we get out, I can't help but lean over and steal a kiss. She steals one right back.

I take her hand once we're out of the SUV, and hand in hand we walk from the parking lot toward the flower shop. It's surreal to look to my left and see a reflection of Emily in her cream linen summer dress and me in my bright-blue-and-green-striped knit tee, holding hands—two people the universe constantly threw together until we realized we were meant to be.

And today I get to go to my first family function with her as her boyfriend. It's Will Griffin's birthday and Annie is throwing him a surprise party in her shop. Except . . .

"Emily, this doesn't look like a normal surprise party," I say as we step inside.

There are warm string lights all over the place, and hundreds of magnolia flowers dotting every surface. It's the most romantic surprise party I've ever seen.

Emily doesn't have time to answer me because Annie pops up in front of us.

"Hi!" she says, giving Emily a kiss on the cheek and a quick hug to me. She's wearing a floral sundress, and her hair is braided in one thick rope over one shoulder.

"You look so beautiful, Annie!" says Emily with misty tears in her eyes. "Do you need anything?"

"Nope. I'm good," says Annie, looking at Emily with an expression so full of underlying meaning it makes my chest ache. Emily feels it too because I can see her throat working to keep her tears back.

Annie lightly pushes Emily's shoulder. "Now get back there with everyone else and be quiet!"

"Okay, we're going! Just let me know if you need—"

"EMILY! GO!"

Laughing, I take Emily's hand and pull her toward the back of the store, where I see Amelia's head peeking out from the storeroom.

And suddenly, it all clicks. "This isn't actually a surprise party, is it?"

Emily smiles with her lips closed and shakes her head side to side. We just barely make it into the back and greet Noah, Amelia, James, and Mabel (and Madison through FaceTime on Amelia's phone) before the front door is jingling open.

Will's voice fills the space. "Anna-banana, are you—" His voice stops. Emily is vibrating with energy beside me. She can't take it anymore and peeks out from behind the curtain separating the main space from the storeroom. Everyone else quickly does the same and I imagine we must look like six floating heads stacked on top of each other this way.

But there he is—Will, with his butterfly tattoo that I'm incredibly jealous of, is standing at the entrance of the shop, surrounded by magnolia flowers and faced with Annie Walker, down on one knee. She begins with "Wilbur, William, Wilton, Griffin . . . I am so deeply in love with you. . . ." And the man is all flexing jaws, misty eyes, and a bobbing throat as the love of his life proposes to him.

"You've asked me a few times already, but my answer was always *not yet*," Annie says, taking his butterfly hand. "But now, I've never been more ready in my life. Will . . . would you pretty please with sugar on top marry me?"

He has her off the floor in less than a second, sweeping her into his arms, tears racing down his cheeks and kissing the daylights out of her. We wait until he pulls away just enough to mutter, "*Yes, Annie. A million times, yes. I would love to marry you.*"

We all shout and whoop and rush out of the storeroom. Amelia and Emily are nearly tackling Annie and Will to the ground with hugs. He doesn't give a shit about them, though. He continues kissing Annie like this is his sole purpose in life.

And later, once we've celebrated at the flower shop for a while, we move to Hank's to keep it going. The bar is much less crowded than it was the last time I was here, so we commandeer a few tables and push them together. Everyone is gathered around, loose-limbed, laughing, and looking so content together. *And I get to be part of it.*

While Noah and James tell me they heard about Ranger and congratulate me on my success (something I'm going to have to get a lot better about receiving), Emily goes up to the bar. I'm trying to focus on the conversation with the guys, but how can I when a woman like Emily exists and is leaning over the bar top? *Impossible.* I want to take her home right now.

She walks back a few minutes later with her red-tipped nails wrapped around two ginger beers, bangs curling up from the humidity, and long legs extending out from her short dress, making me absolutely eat my heart out. She kisses me, and I tell her again that I love her—because I'm not sure I can say it enough—and then she takes the seat beside me. I grab the chair leg and tug her even closer.

With my arm around her shoulder and her hand on my leg, we sit back and savor the night. After a while when her elbows have moved to the table and our stomachs hurt from laughter, Emily glances over her shoulder at me, a smile lingering on her lips from something Noah said. When she catches me watching her, she leans back in her chair, winding her arm around my shoulder and threading her fingers through the back of my hair.

"What's that look for?" she asks.

"Nothing." I kiss her cheek.

Just deciding I'll do whatever is necessary to make sure I get to spend the rest of my life with this woman.

EPILOGUE

ELEVEN MONTHS LATER

May 23

EMILY (10:10 AM): IT'S OUT, IT'S OUT, IT'S OUT!!! MY
DEAL ANNOUNCEMENT IS PUBLISHED!

JACK (10:10 AM): I finally get to know the pen name you
picked?! TELL ME.

EMILY (10:11 AM): ☺☺☺

LITERARY DEAL REPORT

Fiction: General/Other	May 23

Emmy Gold's ***THE DEPRAVED HIGHLANDER AND HIS LADY***, in
which Kate, the youngest daughter to the Duke of Dalton, avoids a
tedious season in London and runs away to her eccentric aunt's home in
the Scottish countryside, but along the way, meets a roguish highlander
with a propensity for stealing hearths, to **Sophia Chen** at **Silver Quill**,
by **Barbara Morgan** at **Bookmark Literary**.

JACK (10:12 AM): I love it, Goldie.

JACK (10:12 AM): Also, I'm off my Zoom call with Johnny, so I'll
meet you at the corner table in thirty minutes.

EMILY (10:13 AM): I've got your seat saved.

ACKNOWLEDGMENTS

Here we are again, at the end of another book that I can't even believe exists. I can't tell you how many times a day I stop and think to myself, "Is this really my job?!" I love being a writer, and I love giving in to the constant imagination taking over my brain. And none of this would even be possible without you, my incredible readers! So first, I want to thank you. I hope that Emily and Jack's story brought you joy. And I hope that if you found yourself relating to Emily and the sadness she tried to keep hidden, you're encouraged to let someone come sit with you in the darkness. No one should face scary feelings alone. You are loved, you are brave, and you are strong—keep going, dear reader.

And now to my team who works so hard to bring my books into existence: To everyone at BookEnds Literary, especially my agent, Kim, I am so grateful for your constant support. I'm so lucky to have you in my corner. You are so fierce yet so kind, and that's an incredible balance to strike—you make it look effortless. And Maggie! The number of things you keep track of for me is honestly incredible. I don't know what I'd do without you! (I'm pretty sure no one would ever get an email response from me without your gentle reminders.)

And to my team at Dell: I am convinced you are the best

publishing family on the face of the earth. First, I want to thank my editor, Shauna. I have grown so much as a writer and a person since working with you—and it's mainly due to how much you've helped me learn to trust my own inner voice. That doesn't come easily for me, but I truly feel like I've gained new wings since working with you. You are gracious, kind, inspiring, honest, and such a safe harbor in this tumultuous world of publishing. Thank you. You mean the world to me. And also to Mae, who does so much behind the scenes work! Thank you for your kindness and support!

And to the gals in marketing, Taylor and Corina, who are responsible for the way my books shine out there in the world, thank you! Not only are you incredible at your jobs, but you're fun and encouraging! I'm grateful for you and humbled that you continue to respond to my emails and texts when ninety percent of them are anxiety-induced monologues.

And to my amazing publicist, Brianna, I am indebted to you. I am quite certain that without you my head would actually fall off. Thank you for everything you do for me! And we share a love of everything bagels—basically the strongest bond in existence.

Now for my family and friends! You guys all keep me going. There one hundred percent would not be any more Sarah Adams books without you. Especially my husband, Chris, who has met me in my darkness more times than I can count. This entire book is a love letter to you and how you are always my safest person in this world. I love you.

Last, I want to say a massive thank-you to teachers everywhere. How you continue to show up day after day without the thanks you deserve is beyond me. You are heroes. THANK YOU. Please take care of yourselves—I know you're worn out.

And if you made it this far, I can't wait to hopefully see you again in the next book . . . our final trip to Rome, Kentucky!

Hugs! Sarah

ABOUT THE AUTHOR

SARAH ADAMS is the author of *The Rule Book, Practice Makes Perfect, When in Rome, The Match, The Enemy, The Off-Limits Rule, The Temporary Roomie,* and *The Cheat Sheet.* Born and raised in Nashville, Tennessee, she loves her family and warm days. Sarah has dreamed of being a writer since she was a girl but finally wrote her first novel when her daughters were napping and she no longer had any excuses to put it off. Sarah is a coffee addict, a British history nerd, a mom of two daughters, married to her best friend, and an indecisive introvert. Her hope is to write stories that make readers laugh, maybe even cry—but always leave them happier than when they started reading.

authorsarahadams.com
Instagram: @authorsarahadams

ABOUT THE TYPE

This book was set in Hoefler Text, a typeface designed in 1991 by Jonathan Hoefler (b. 1970). One of the earlier type-faces created at the beginning of the digital age specifically for use on computers, it was among the first to offer features previously found only in the finest typography, such as dedi-cated old-style figures and small caps. Thus it offers modern style based on the classic tradition.